MANGAMAN

by **BARRY LYGA**   illustrated by **COLLEEN DORAN**

MANGA
MAN

HOUGHTON MIFFLIN
HOUGHTON MIFFLIN HARCOURT
Boston   New York
2011

All rights reserved. For information about permission
to reproduce selections from this book, write to Permissions,
Houghton Mifflin Harcourt Publishing Company,
215 Park Avenue South, New York, New York 10003.

Houghton Mifflin is an imprint of Houghton Mifflin Harcourt Publishing Company.

www.hmhbooks.com

Lettered by Lois Buhalis and Tom Orzechowski
The illustrations on this book were done in pen-and-ink on Bristol board,
with hand-applied tone sheets, as well as digital drawing in Photoshop.

Library of Congress Cataloging-in-Publication Control Number 2011403000

ISBN 978-0-547-42315-9

Manufactured in China
LEO 10 9 8 7 6 5 4 3 2 1
4500292025

To Kuo-Yu Liang, who inspired it without knowing.
—*B.L.*

To Takayuki Matsutani and the staff of Tezuka Productions
for the original awesome East Meets West experience.
And to J. Michael Straczynksi for the hardware and hugs.
—*C.D.*

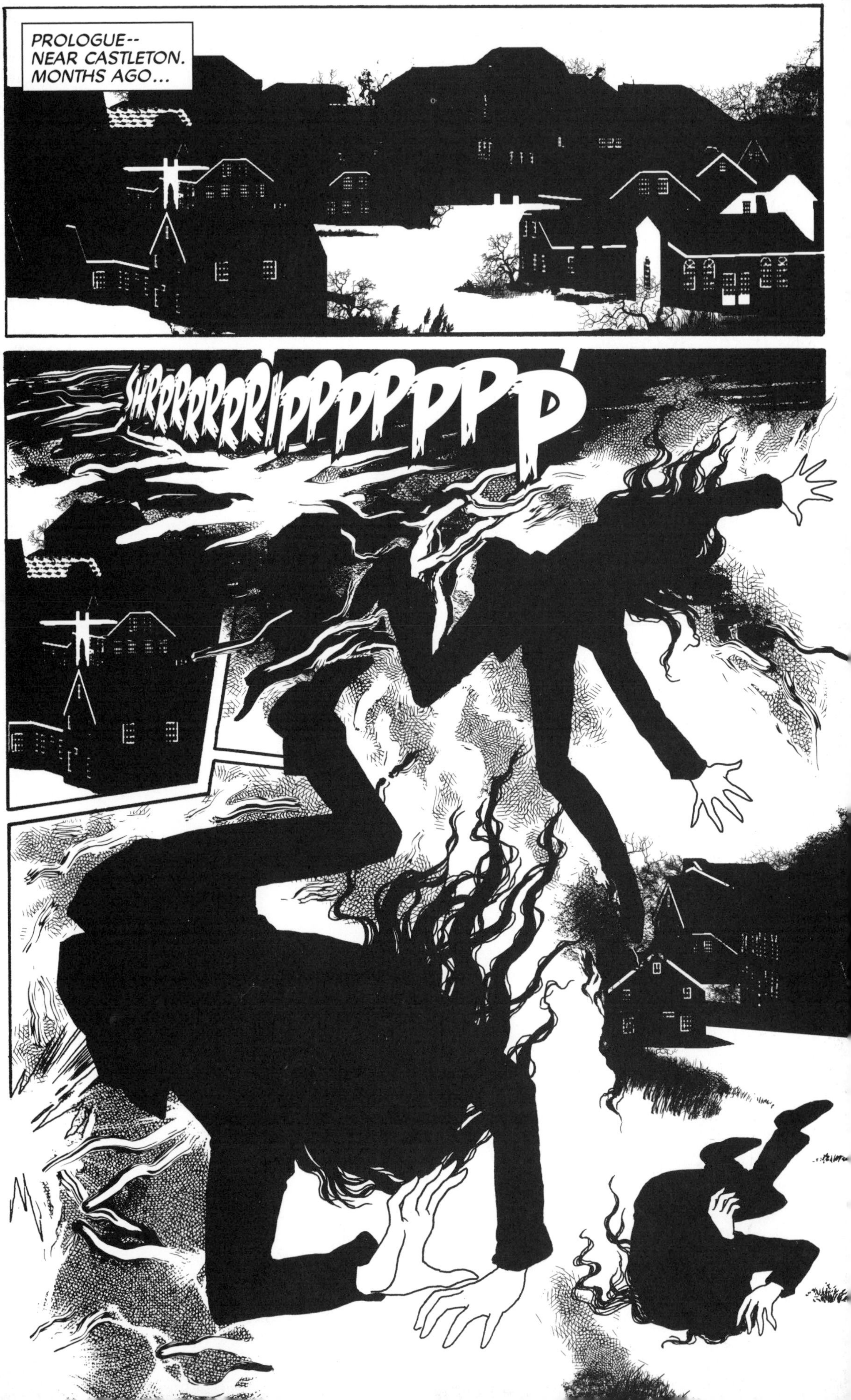
PROLOGUE--
NEAR CASTLETON.
MONTHS AGO...
SHRRRRRRIPPPPPPP

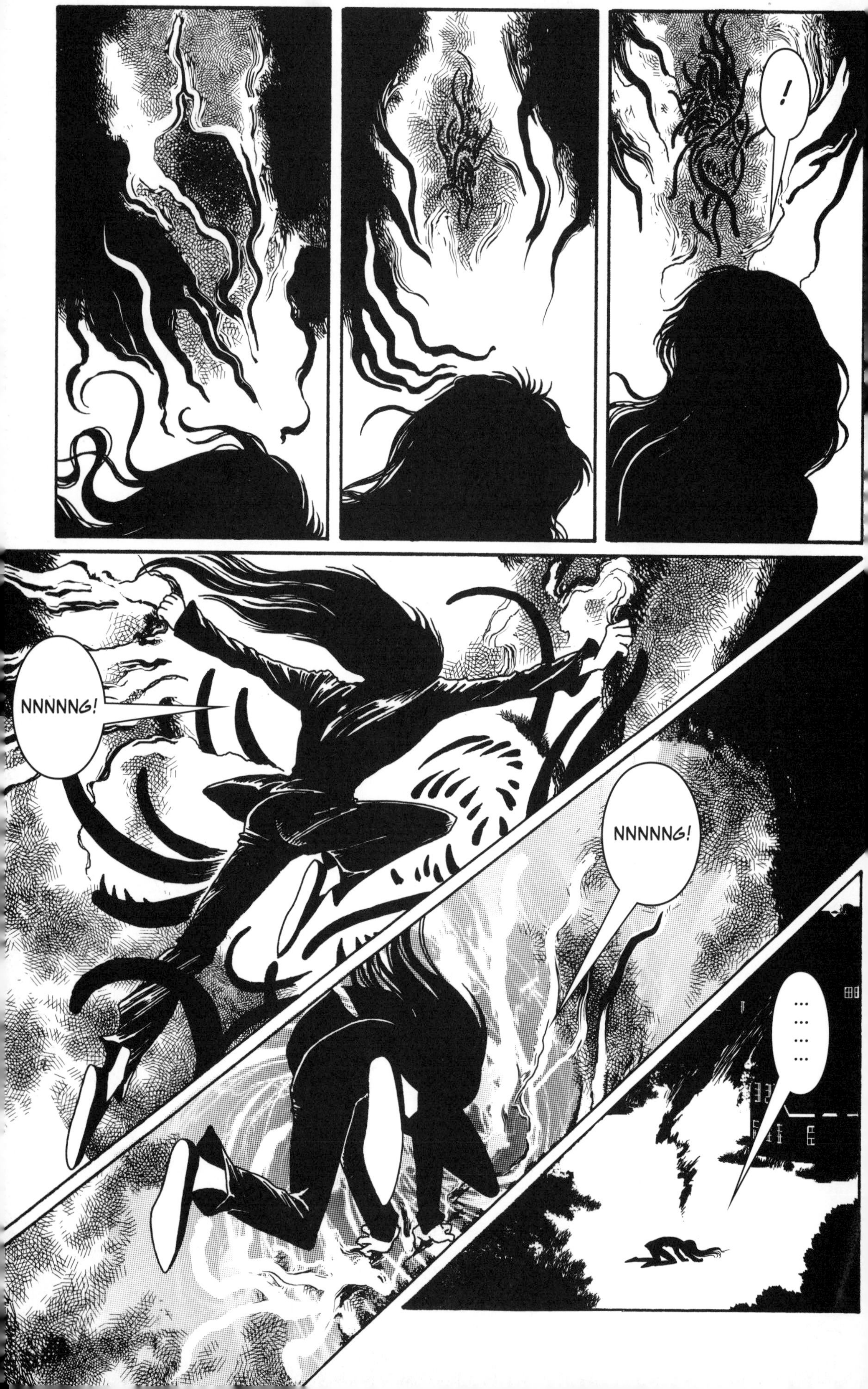
!
NNNNNG!
NNNNNG!
....

CHAPTER 1

LEXA: *He's real! He's real!*

MARISSA: *What are you TALKING about?*

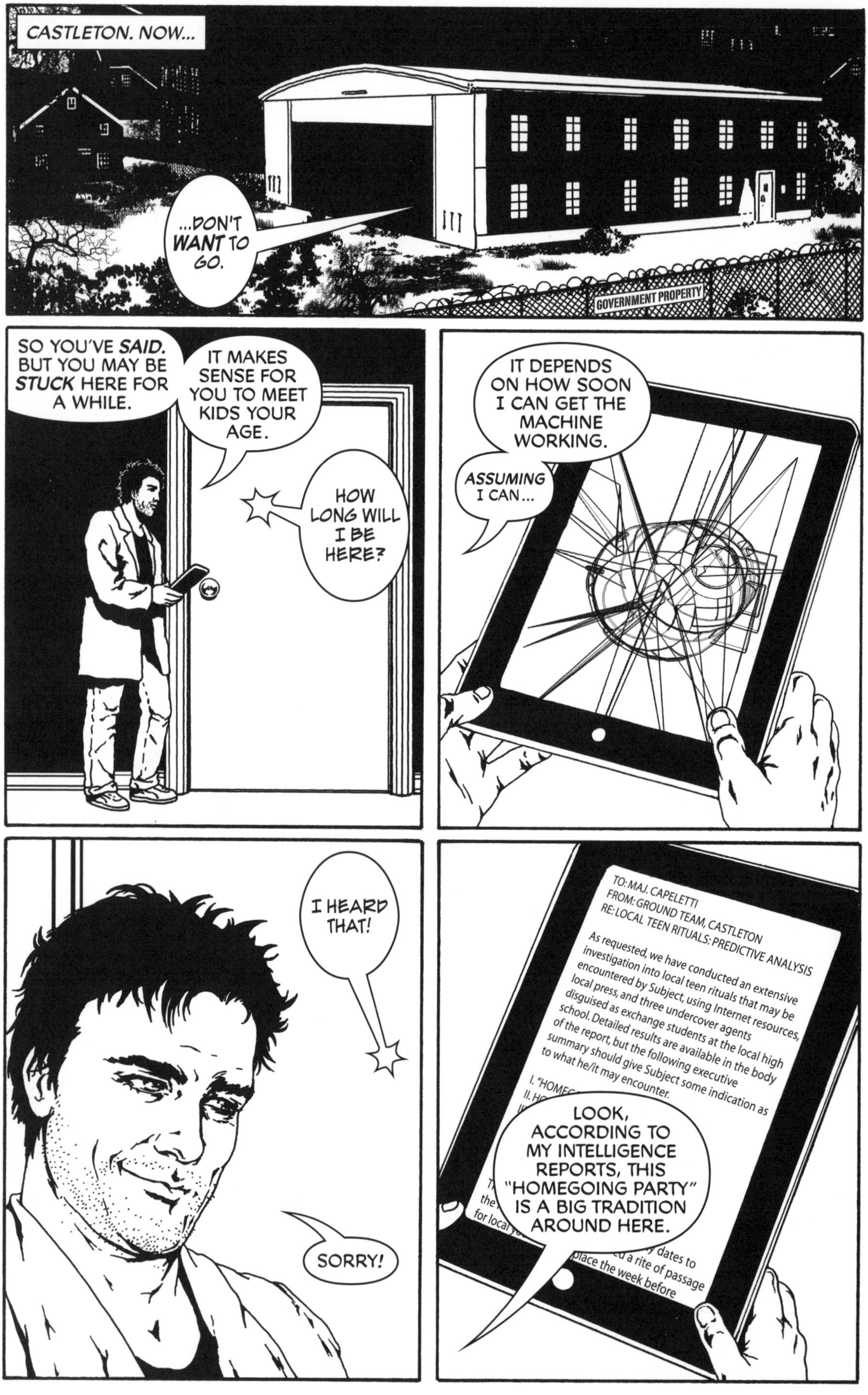
CASTLETON. NOW...
...DON'T *WANT* TO GO.
GOVERNMENT PROPERTY
SO YOU'VE *SAID.* BUT YOU MAY BE *STUCK* HERE FOR A WHILE.
IT MAKES SENSE FOR YOU TO MEET KIDS YOUR AGE.
HOW LONG WILL I BE HERE?
IT DEPENDS ON HOW SOON I CAN GET THE MACHINE WORKING.
ASSUMING I CAN...
I HEARD THAT!
SORRY!
TO: MAJ. CAPELETTI
FROM: GROUND TEAM, CASTLETON
RE: LOCAL TEEN RITUALS: PREDICTIVE ANALYSIS
As requested, we have conducted an extensive investigation into local teen rituals that may be encountered by Subject, using Internet resources, local press, and three undercover agents disguised as exchange students at the local high school. Detailed results are available in the body of the report, but the following executive summary should give Subject some indication as to what he/it may encounter.
LOOK, ACCORDING TO MY INTELLIGENCE REPORTS, THIS "HOMEGOING PARTY" IS A BIG TRADITION AROUND HERE.

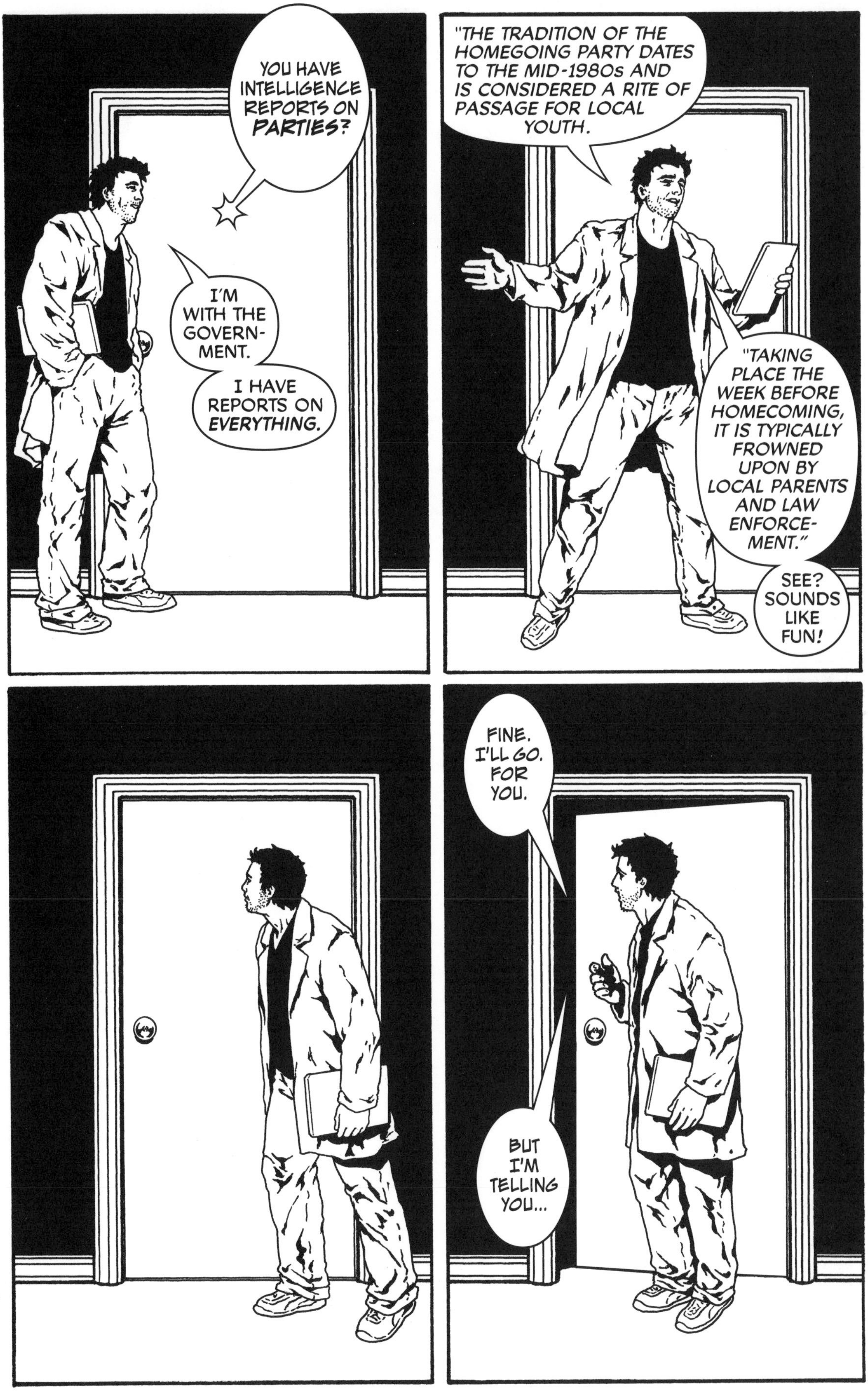
YOU HAVE INTELLIGENCE REPORTS ON PARTIES?
I'M WITH THE GOVERN-MENT.
I HAVE REPORTS ON EVERYTHING.
"THE TRADITION OF THE HOMEGOING PARTY DATES TO THE MID-1980s AND IS CONSIDERED A RITE OF PASSAGE FOR LOCAL YOUTH.
"TAKING PLACE THE WEEK BEFORE HOMECOMING, IT IS TYPICALLY FROWNED UPON BY LOCAL PARENTS AND LAW ENFORCE-MENT."
SEE? SOUNDS LIKE FUN!
FINE. I'LL GO. FOR YOU.
BUT I'M TELLING YOU...

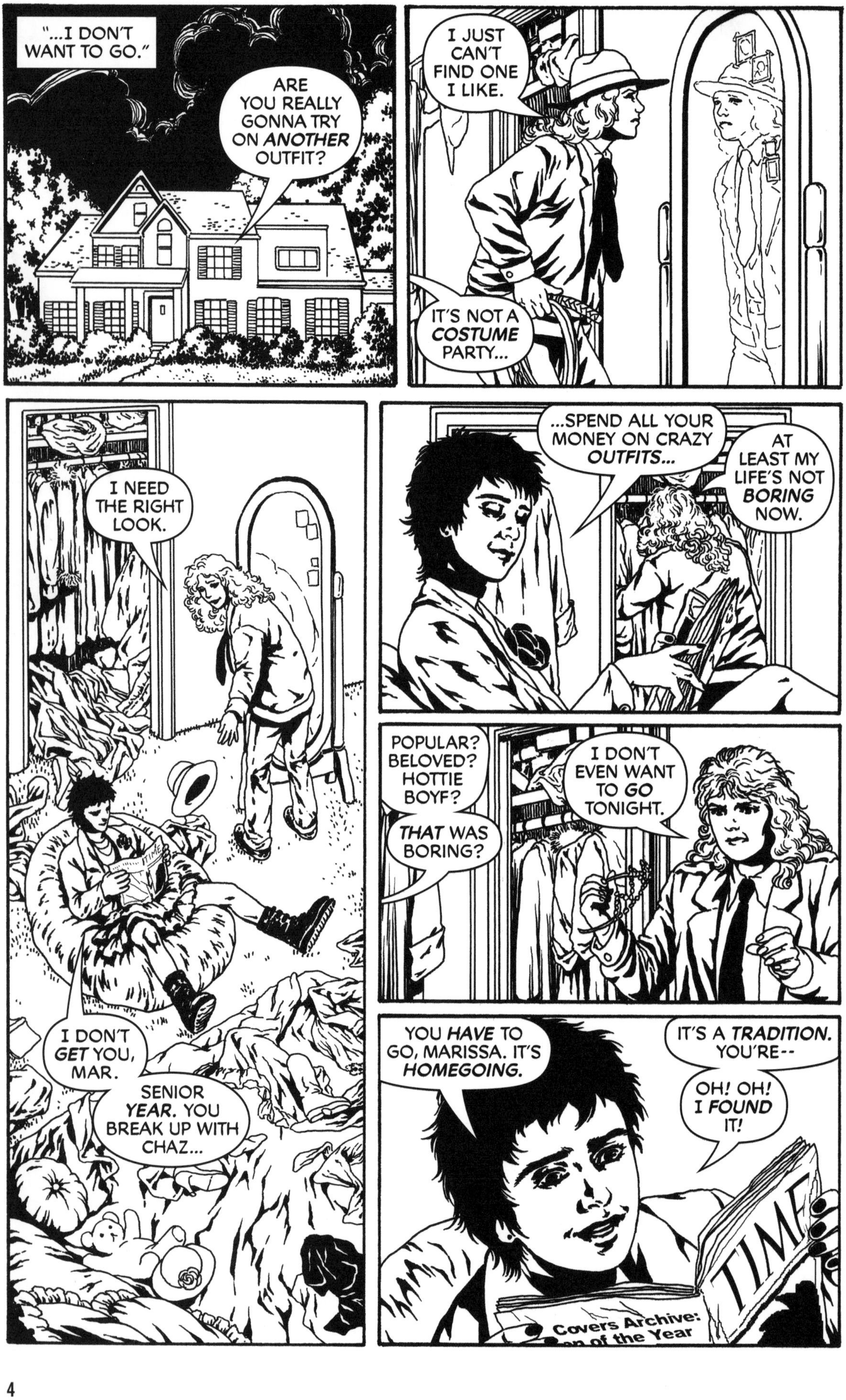
"...I DON'T WANT TO GO."
ARE YOU REALLY GONNA TRY ON *ANOTHER* OUTFIT?
I JUST CAN'T FIND ONE I LIKE.
IT'S NOT A *COSTUME* PARTY...
I NEED THE RIGHT LOOK.
I DON'T *GET* YOU, MAR.
SENIOR *YEAR.* YOU BREAK UP WITH CHAZ...
...SPEND ALL YOUR MONEY ON CRAZY *OUTFITS...*
AT LEAST MY LIFE'S NOT *BORING* NOW.
POPULAR? BELOVED? HOTTIE BOYF?
THAT WAS BORING?
I DON'T EVEN WANT TO *GO* TONIGHT.
YOU *HAVE* TO GO, MARISSA. IT'S *HOMEGOING.*
IT'S A *TRADITION.* YOU'RE--
OH*!* OH*!* I *FOUND* IT*!*
TIME
Covers Archive:

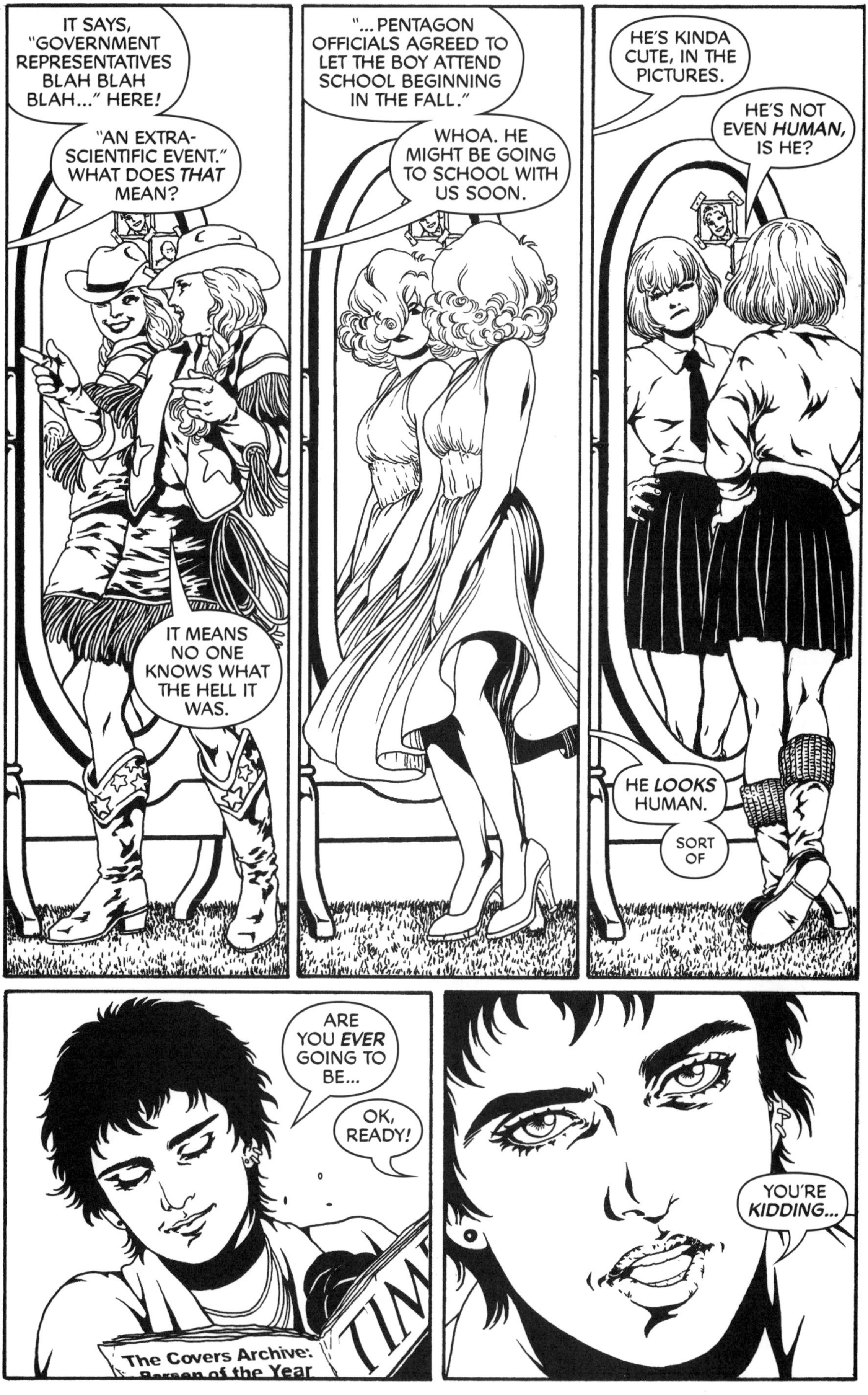

IT SAYS, "GOVERNMENT REPRESENTATIVES BLAH BLAH BLAH..." HERE!
"AN EXTRA-SCIENTIFIC EVENT." WHAT DOES *THAT* MEAN?
IT MEANS NO ONE KNOWS WHAT THE HELL IT WAS.
"... PENTAGON OFFICIALS AGREED TO LET THE BOY ATTEND SCHOOL BEGINNING IN THE FALL."
WHOA. HE MIGHT BE GOING TO SCHOOL WITH US SOON.
HE'S KINDA CUTE, IN THE PICTURES.
HE'S NOT EVEN *HUMAN,* IS HE?
HE *LOOKS* HUMAN.
SORT OF
ARE YOU *EVER* GOING TO BE...
OK, READY!
The Covers Archive: Person of the Year
TIME
YOU'RE *KIDDING...*

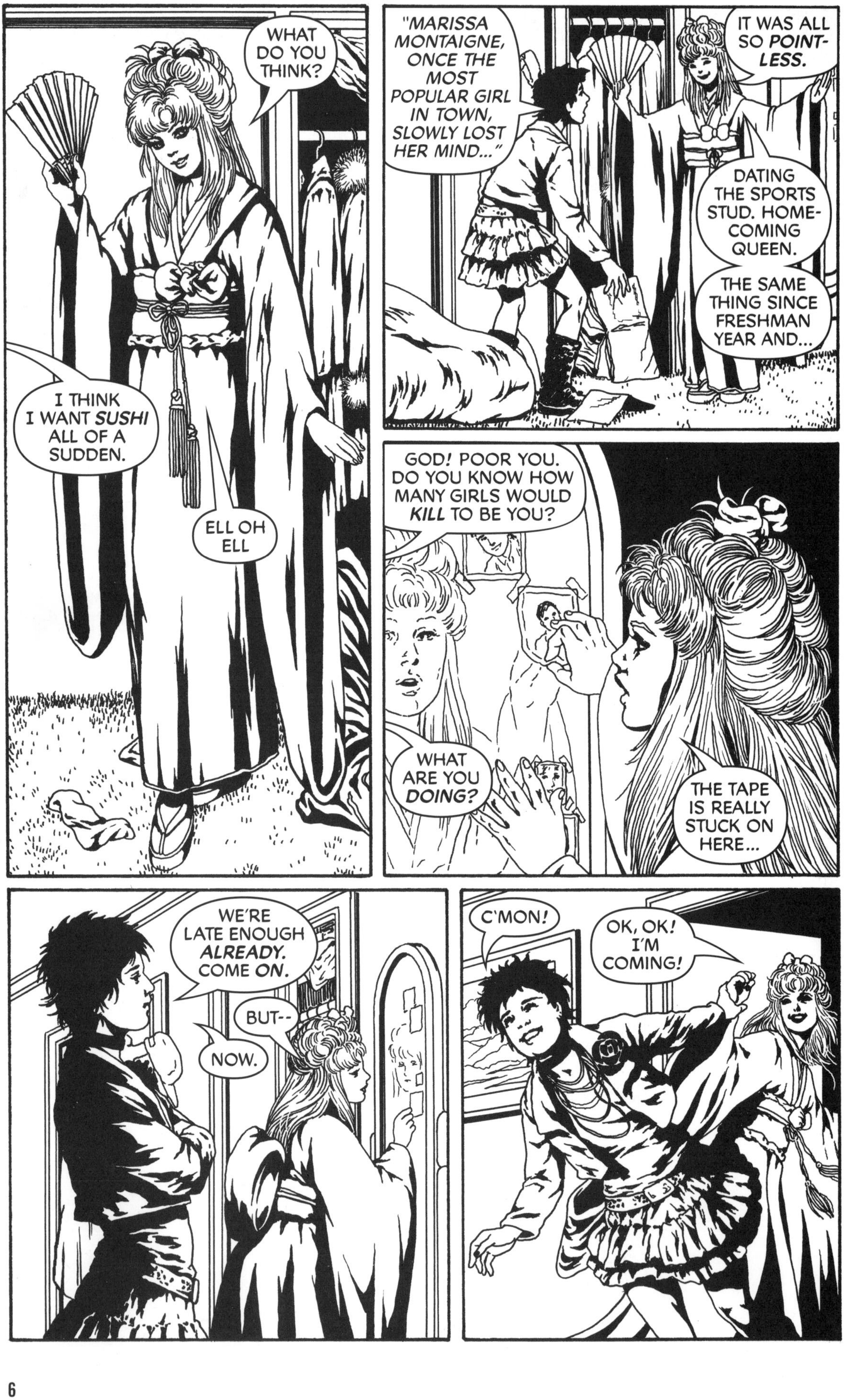
WHAT DO YOU THINK?
I THINK I WANT *SUSHI* ALL OF A SUDDEN.
ELL OH ELL
"*MARISSA MONTAIGNE, ONCE THE MOST POPULAR GIRL IN TOWN, SLOWLY LOST HER MIND...*"
IT WAS ALL SO ***POINTLESS.***
DATING THE SPORTS STUD. HOMECOMING QUEEN.
THE SAME THING SINCE FRESHMAN YEAR AND...
GOD*!* POOR YOU. DO YOU KNOW HOW MANY GIRLS WOULD ***KILL*** TO BE YOU?
WHAT ARE YOU ***DOING?***
THE TAPE IS REALLY STUCK ON HERE...
WE'RE LATE ENOUGH ***ALREADY.*** COME ***ON.***
BUT--
NOW.
C'MON*!*
OK, OK*!* I'M COMING*!*

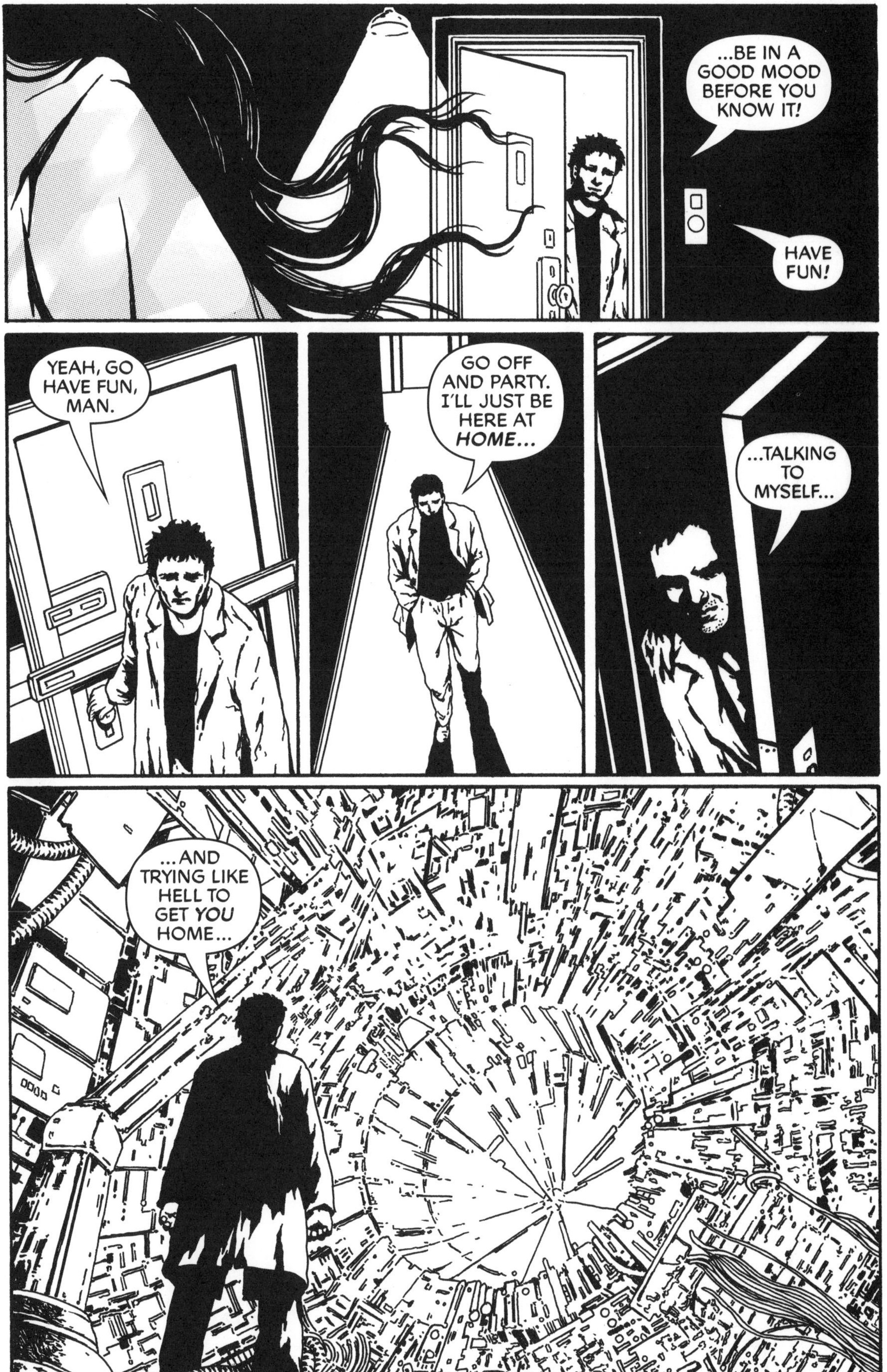
...BE IN A GOOD MOOD BEFORE YOU KNOW IT!
HAVE FUN!
YEAH, GO HAVE FUN, MAN.
GO OFF AND PARTY. I'LL JUST BE HERE AT *HOME*...
...TALKING TO MYSELF...
...AND TRYING LIKE HELL TO GET *YOU* HOME...

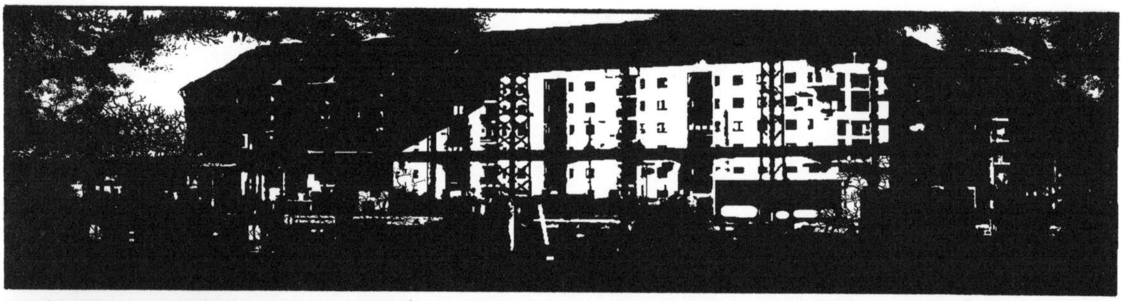

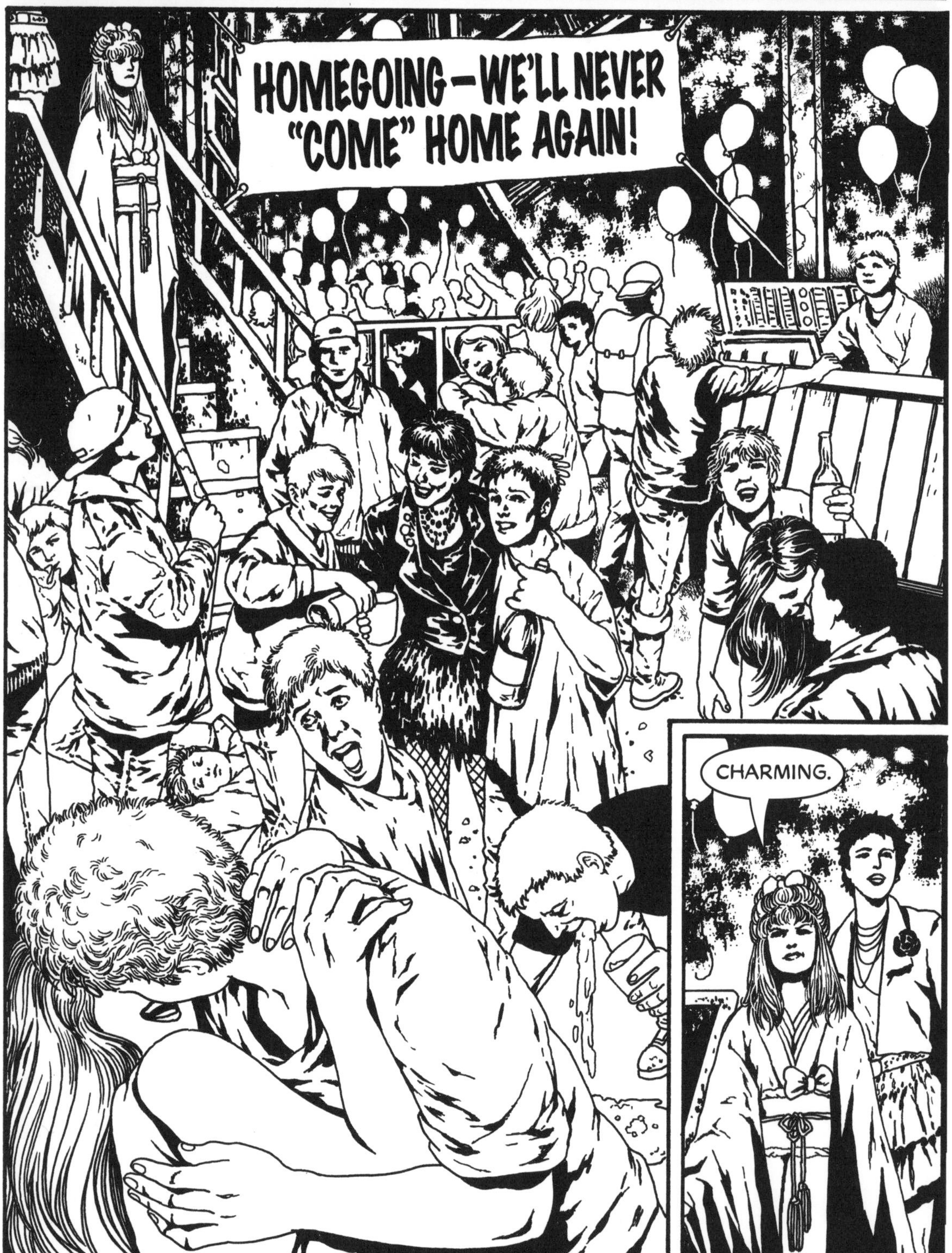
HOMEGOING—WE'LL NEVER "COME" HOME AGAIN!
CHARMING.

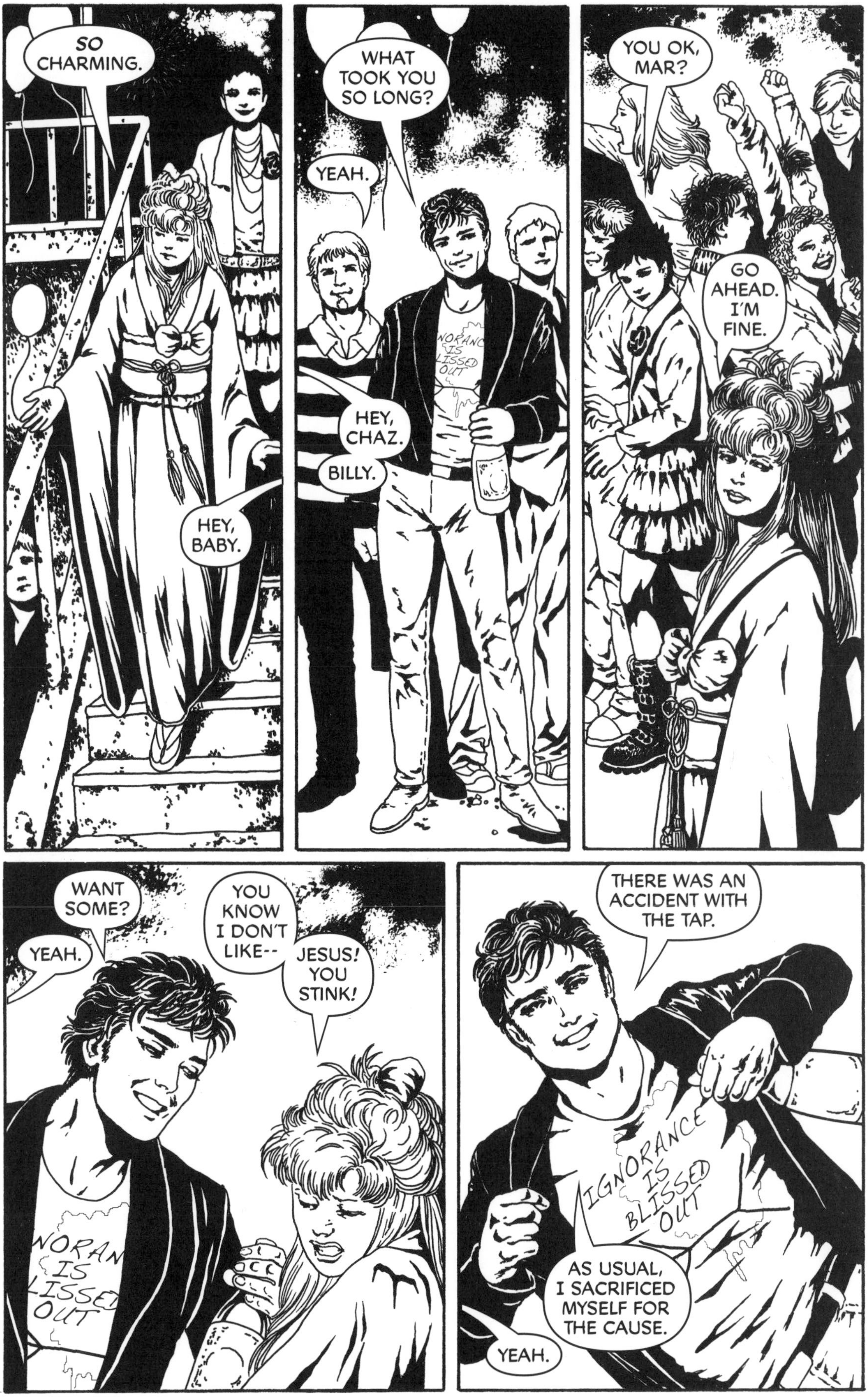
SO CHARMING.
HEY, BABY.
WHAT TOOK YOU SO LONG?
YEAH.
HEY, CHAZ.
BILLY.
YOU OK, MAR?
GO AHEAD. I'M FINE.
WANT SOME?
YEAH.
YOU KNOW I DON'T LIKE--
JESUS! YOU STINK!
THERE WAS AN ACCIDENT WITH THE TAP.
IGNORANCE IS BLISSED OUT
AS USUAL, I SACRIFICED MYSELF FOR THE CAUSE.
YEAH.

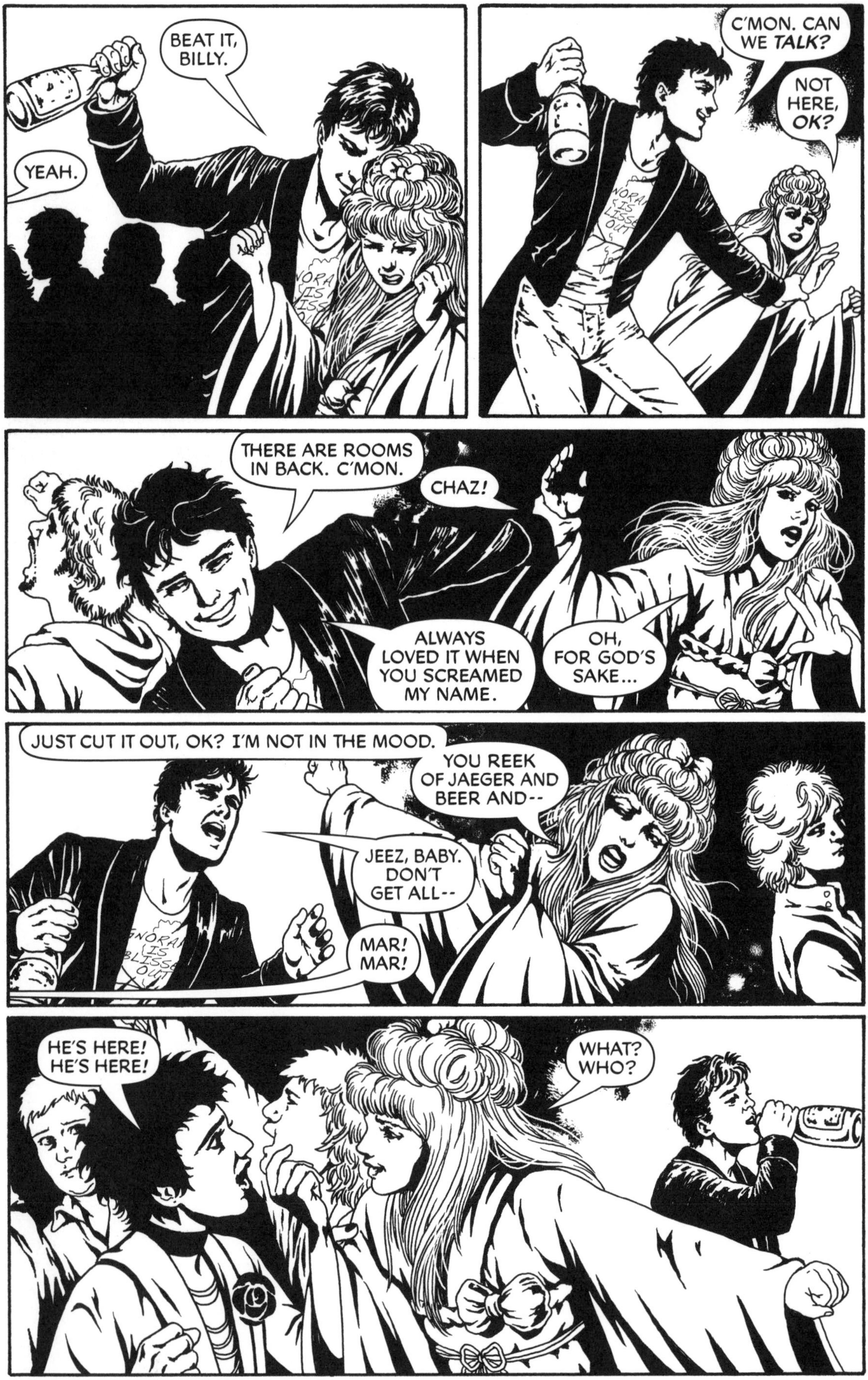

BEAT IT, BILLY.
YEAH.
C'MON. CAN WE *TALK?*
NOT HERE, *OK?*
THERE ARE ROOMS IN BACK. C'MON.
CHAZ!
ALWAYS LOVED IT WHEN YOU SCREAMED MY NAME.
OH, FOR GOD'S SAKE...
JUST CUT IT OUT, OK? I'M NOT IN THE MOOD.
YOU REEK OF JAEGER AND BEER AND--
JEEZ, BABY. DON'T GET ALL--
MAR! MAR!
HE'S HERE! HE'S HERE!
WHAT? WHO?

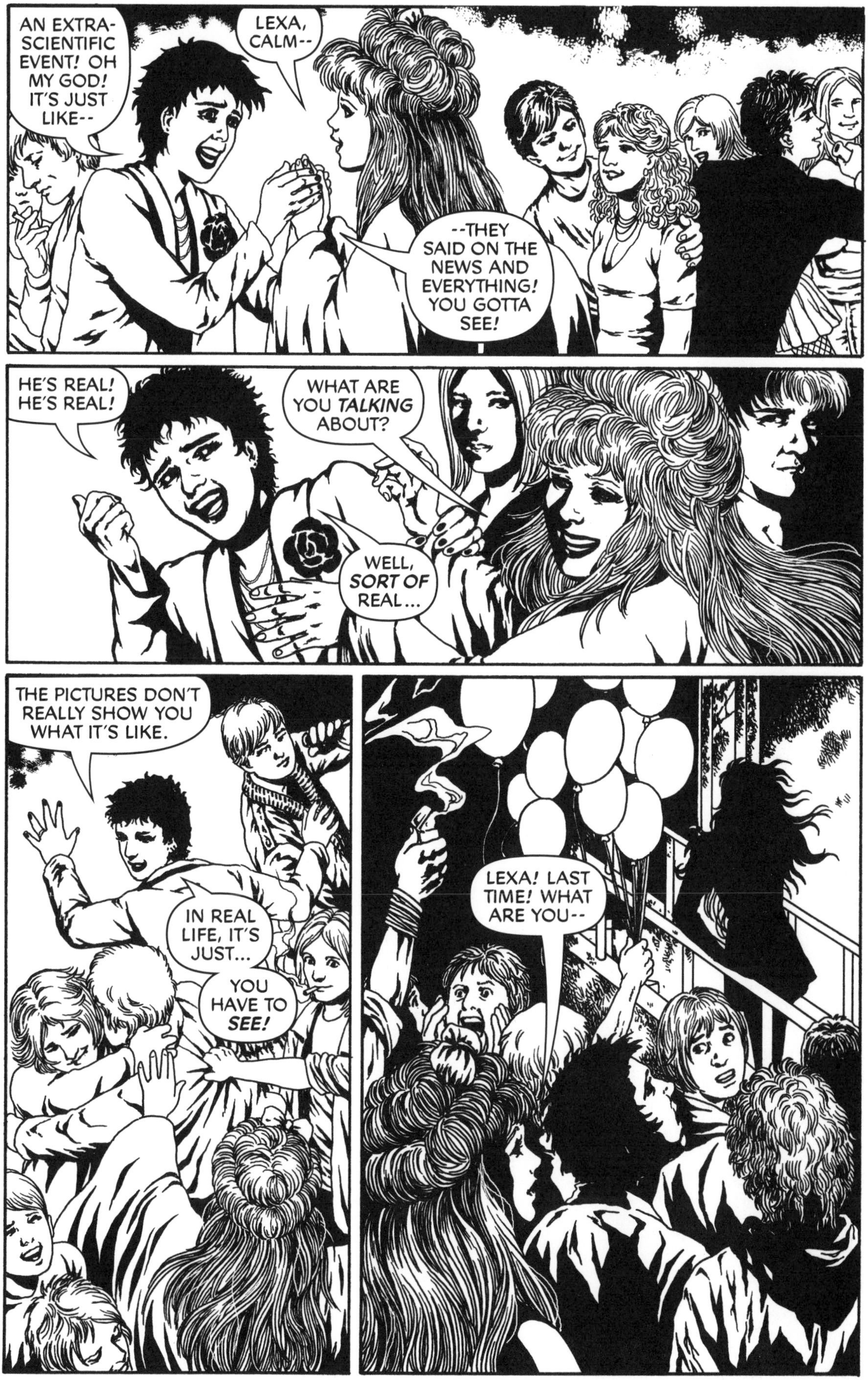
AN EXTRA-SCIENTIFIC EVENT! OH MY GOD! IT'S JUST LIKE--
LEXA, CALM--
--THEY SAID ON THE NEWS AND EVERYTHING! YOU GOTTA SEE!
HE'S REAL! HE'S REAL!
WHAT ARE YOU *TALKING* ABOUT?
WELL, *SORT OF* REAL...
THE PICTURES DON'T REALLY SHOW YOU WHAT IT'S LIKE.
IN REAL LIFE, IT'S JUST...
YOU HAVE TO *SEE!*
LEXA! LAST TIME! WHAT ARE YOU--

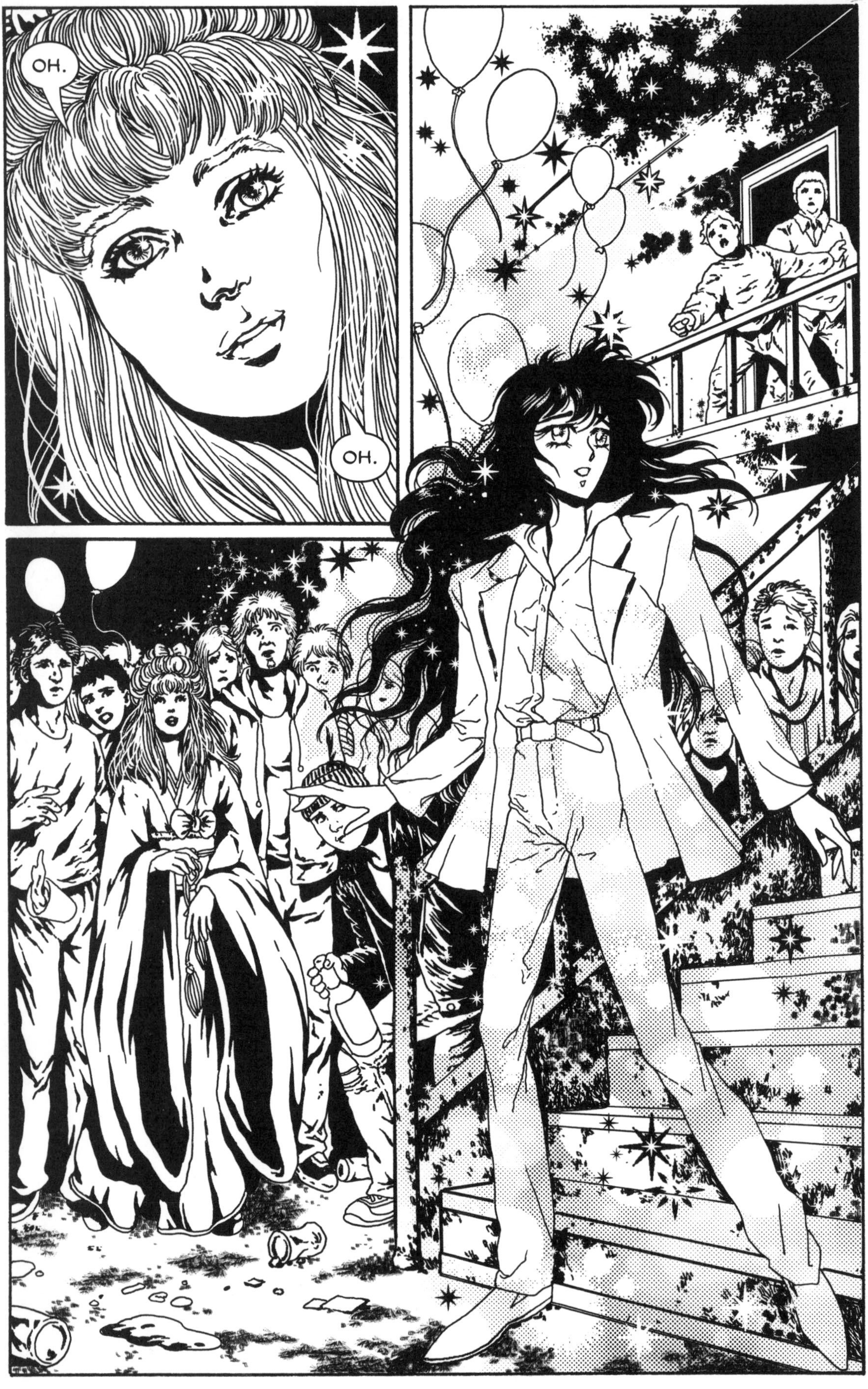
OH.
OH.

CHAPTER 2

RYOKO: *Big-time high school challenge!*

Awesome karate fight!

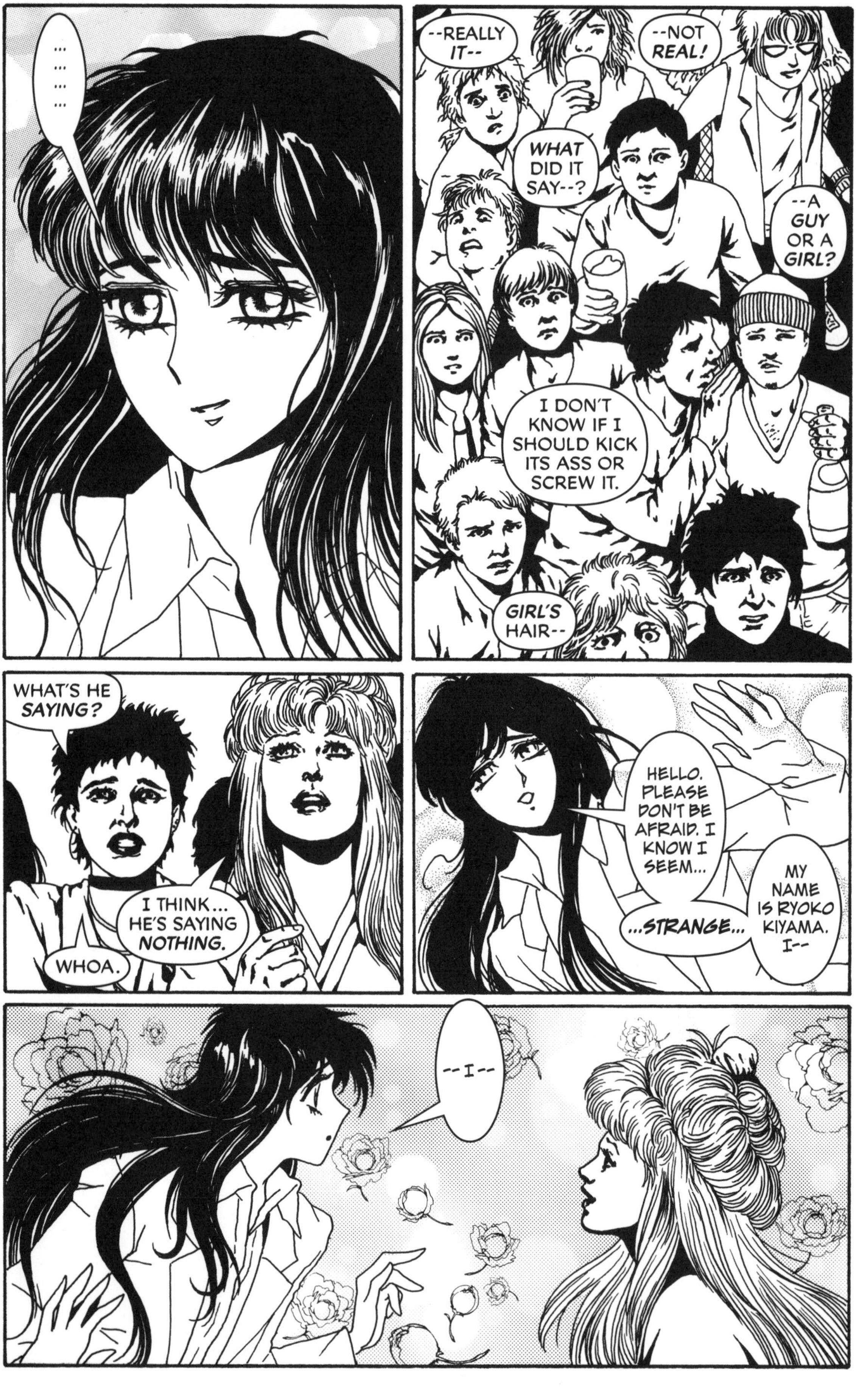

... ...
--REALLY IT--
--NOT REAL!
WHAT DID IT SAY--?
--A GUY OR A GIRL?
I DON'T KNOW IF I SHOULD KICK ITS ASS OR SCREW IT.
GIRL'S HAIR--
WHAT'S HE SAYING?
I THINK... HE'S SAYING NOTHING.
WHOA.
HELLO. PLEASE DON'T BE AFRAID. I KNOW I SEEM...
...STRANGE...
MY NAME IS RYOKO KIYAMA. I--
--I--

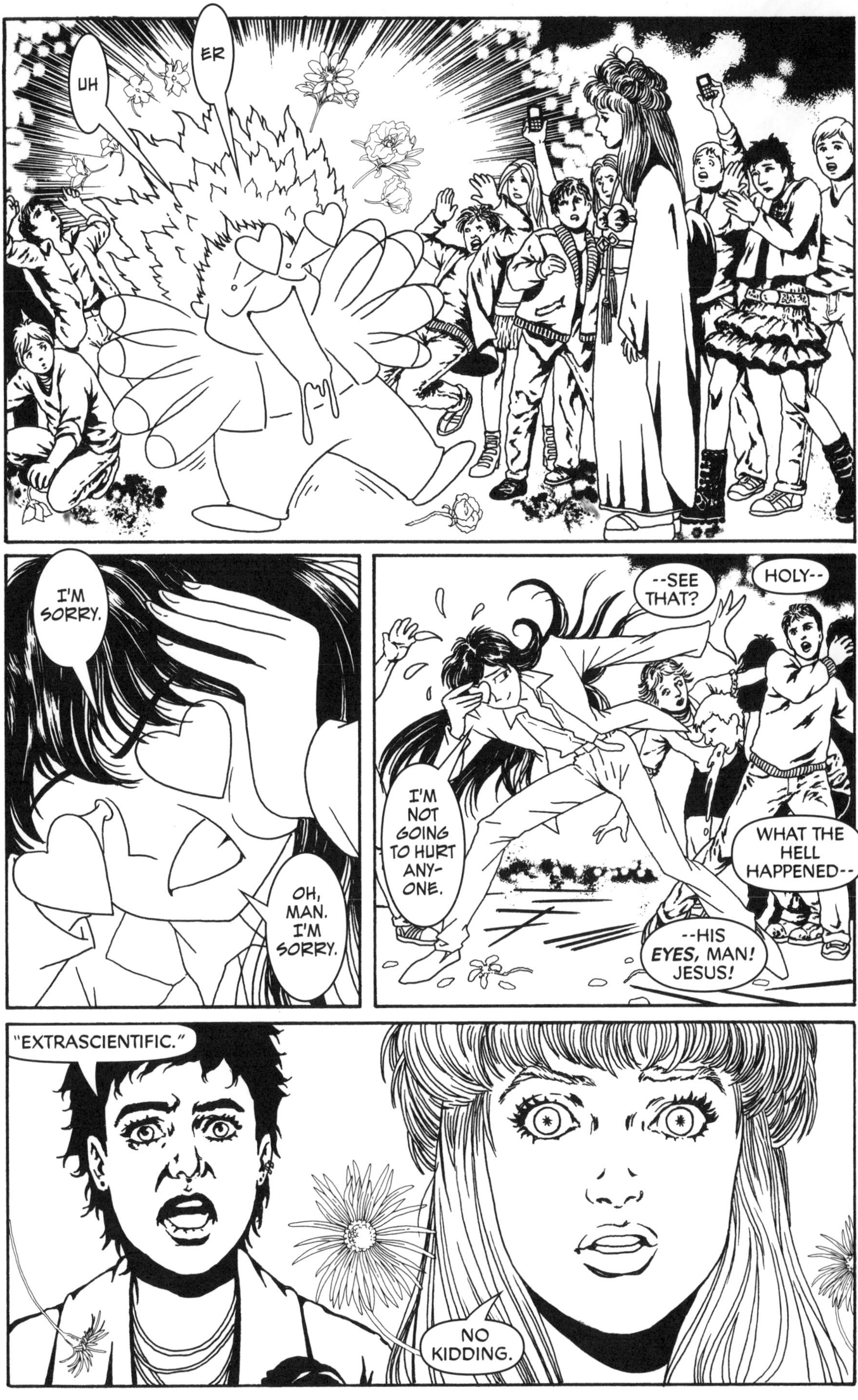
UH
ER
I'M SORRY.
OH, MAN. I'M SORRY.
--SEE THAT?
HOLY--
I'M NOT GOING TO HURT ANY-ONE.
WHAT THE HELL HAPPENED--
--HIS *EYES*, MAN! JESUS!
"EXTRASCIENTIFIC."
NO KIDDING.

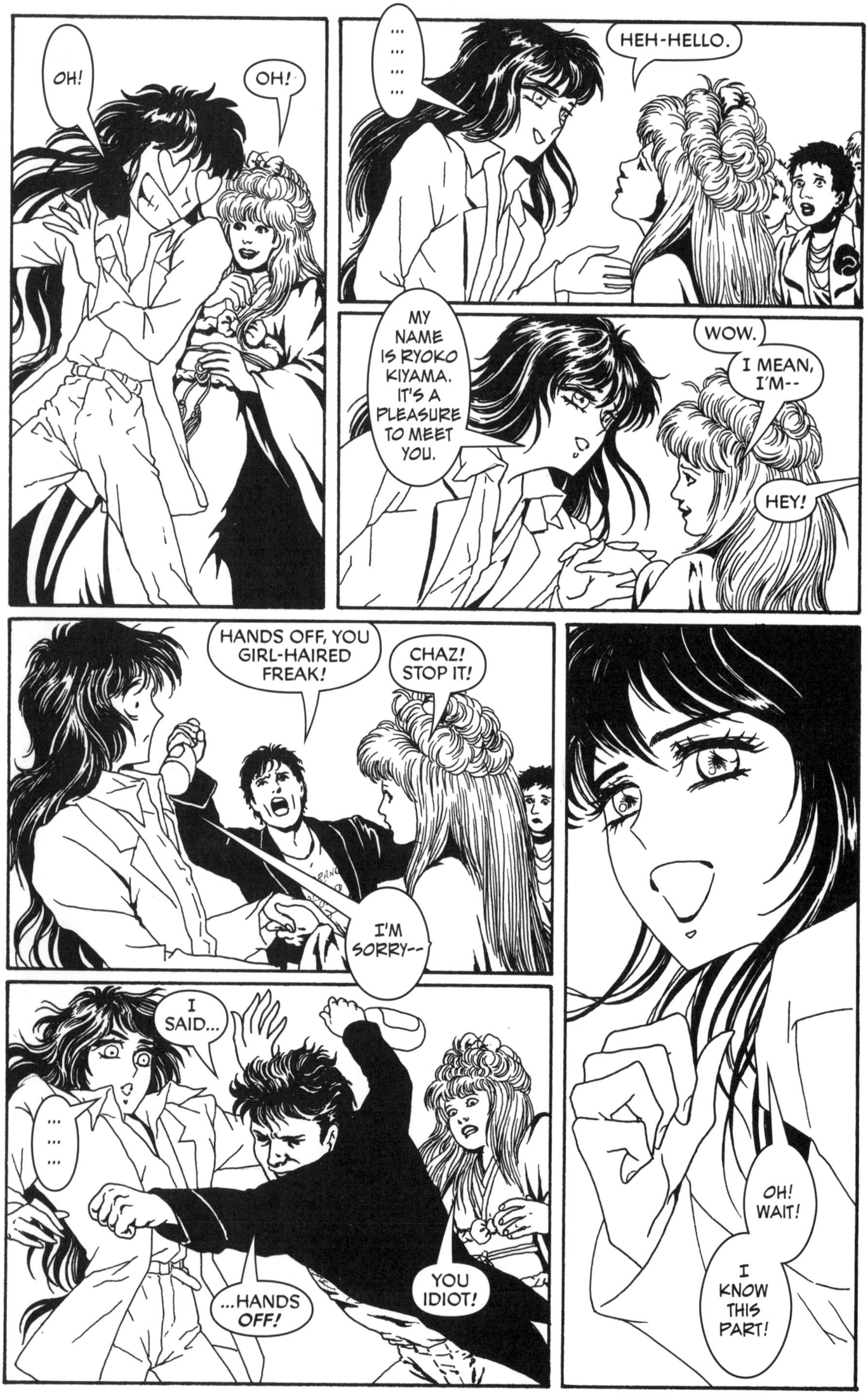
OH!
OH!
...
...
...
...
HEH-HELLO.
MY NAME IS RYOKO KIYAMA. IT'S A PLEASURE TO MEET YOU.
WOW.
I MEAN, I'M--
HEY!
HANDS OFF, YOU GIRL-HAIRED FREAK!
CHAZ! STOP IT!
I'M SORRY--
I SAID...
...
...
...
...HANDS *OFF!*
YOU IDIOT!
OH! WAIT!
I KNOW THIS PART!

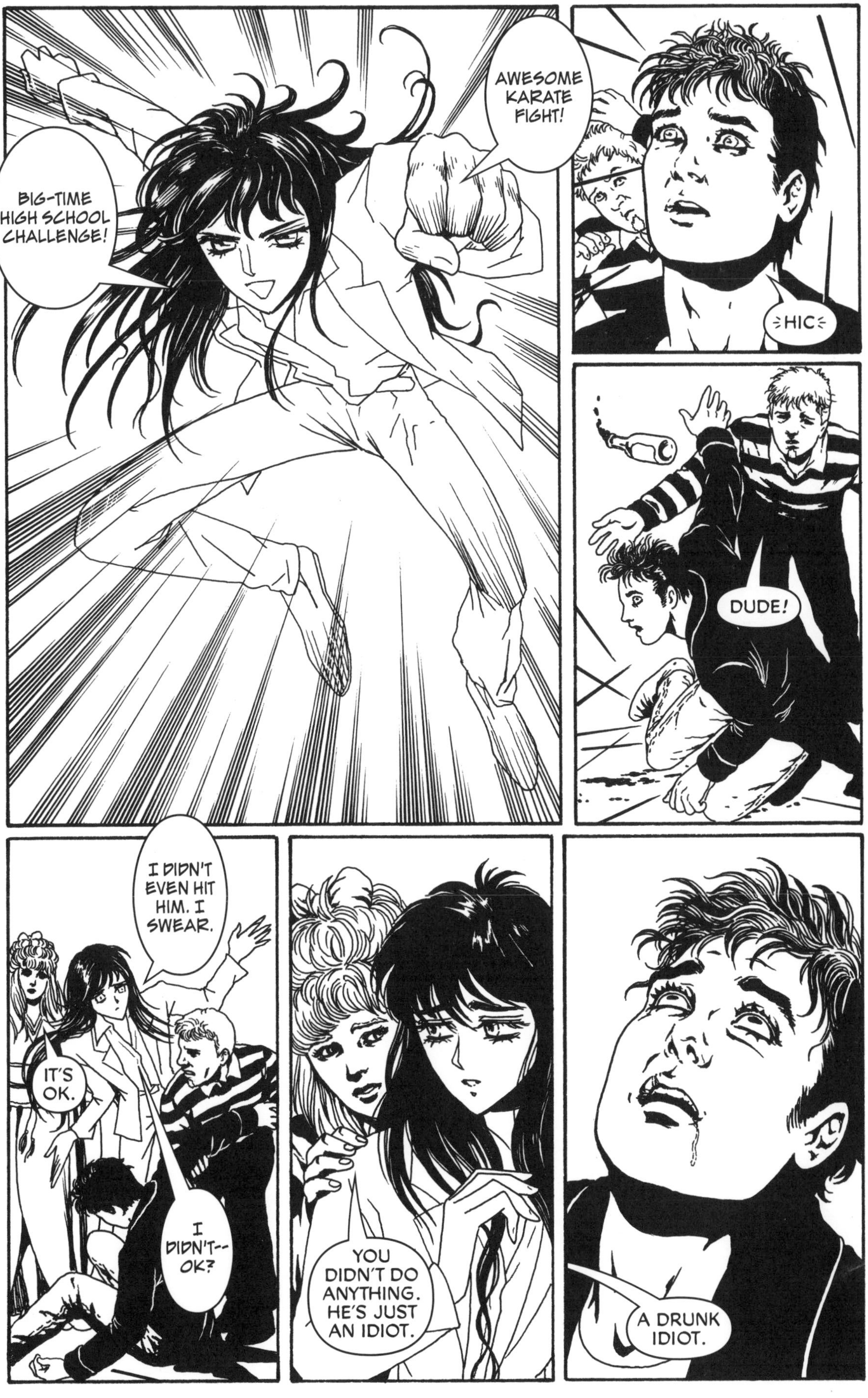

BIG-TIME HIGH SCHOOL CHALLENGE!
AWESOME KARATE FIGHT!
HIC
DUDE!
I DIDN'T EVEN HIT HIM. I SWEAR.
IT'S OK.
I DIDN'T-- OK?
YOU DIDN'T DO ANYTHING. HE'S JUST AN IDIOT.
A DRUNK IDIOT.

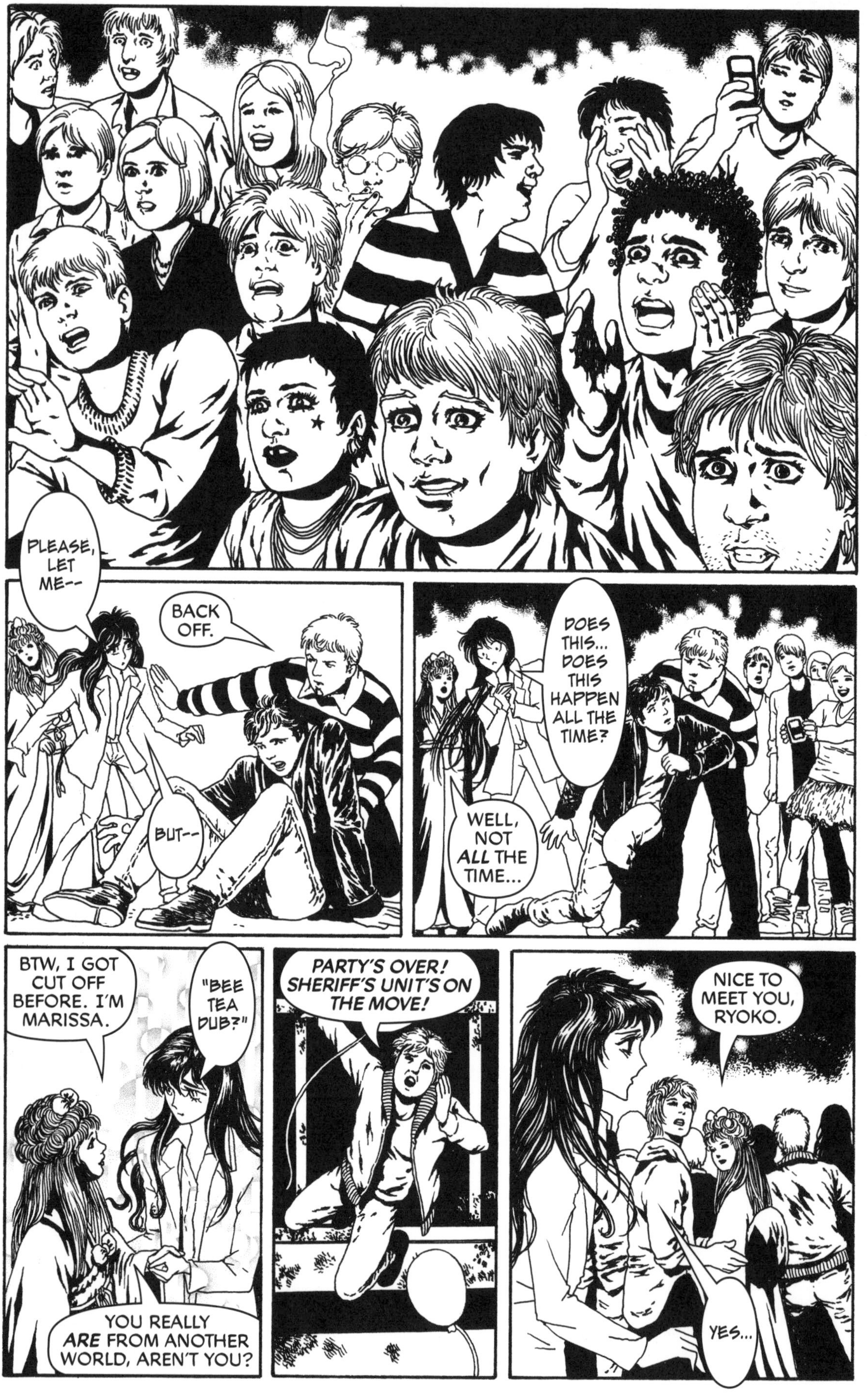
PLEASE, LET ME--
BACK OFF.
BUT--
DOES THIS... DOES THIS HAPPEN ALL THE TIME?
WELL, NOT ALL THE TIME...
BTW, I GOT CUT OFF BEFORE. I'M MARISSA.
"BEE TEA DUB?"
YOU REALLY ARE FROM ANOTHER WORLD, AREN'T YOU?
PARTY'S OVER! SHERIFF'S UNIT'S ON THE MOVE!
NICE TO MEET YOU, RYOKO.
YES...

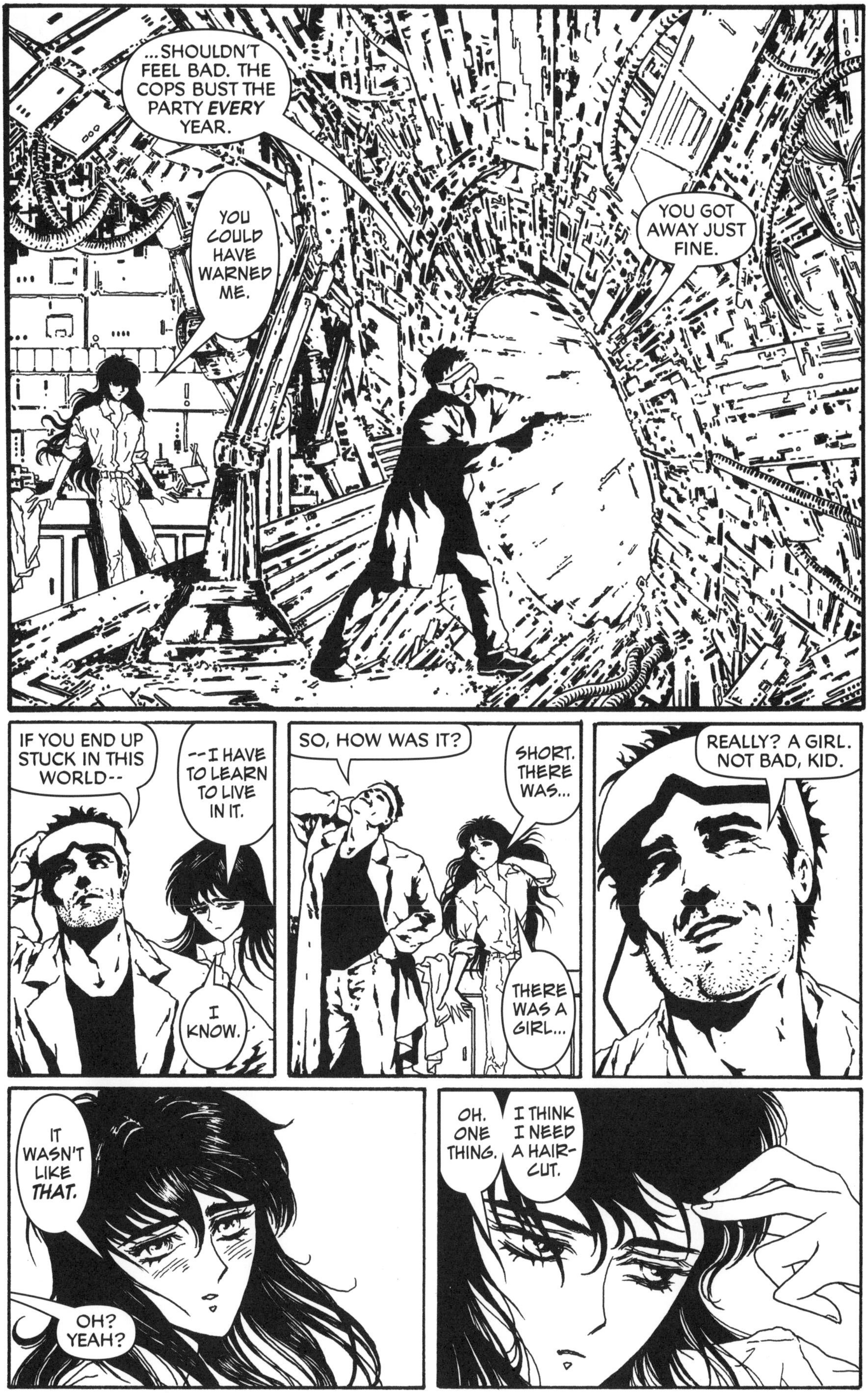
...SHOULDN'T FEEL BAD. THE COPS BUST THE PARTY *EVERY* YEAR.
YOU COULD HAVE WARNED ME.
YOU GOT AWAY JUST FINE.
IF YOU END UP STUCK IN THIS WORLD--
--I HAVE TO LEARN TO LIVE IN IT.
I KNOW.
SO, HOW WAS IT?
SHORT. THERE WAS...
THERE WAS A GIRL...
REALLY? A GIRL. NOT BAD, KID.
IT WASN'T LIKE *THAT.*
OH? YEAH?
OH. ONE THING.
I THINK I NEED A HAIR-CUT.

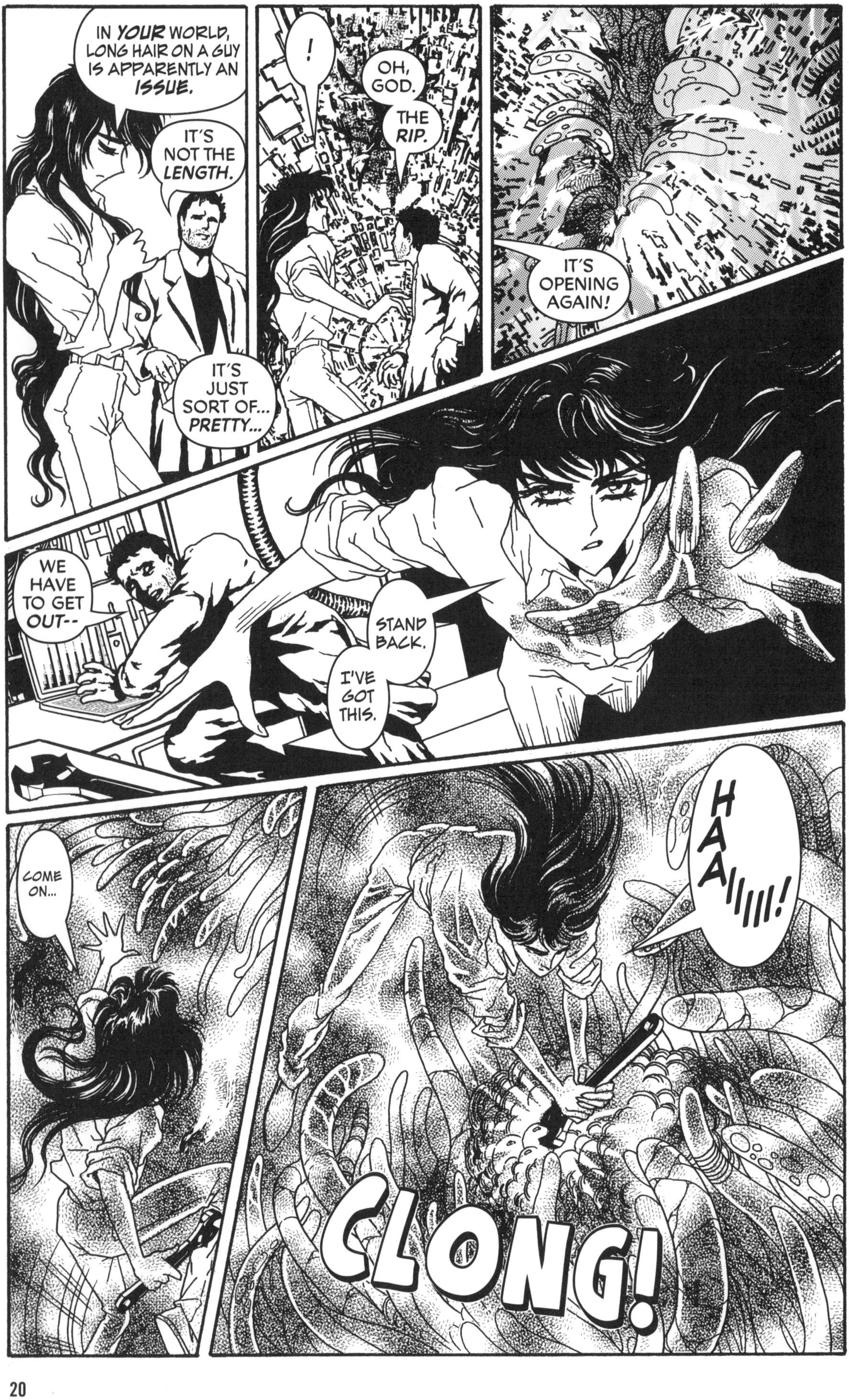
IN *YOUR* WORLD, LONG HAIR ON A GUY IS APPARENTLY AN *ISSUE.*
IT'S NOT THE *LENGTH.*
IT'S JUST SORT OF... *PRETTY...*
!
OH, GOD.
THE *RIP.*
IT'S OPENING AGAIN!
WE HAVE TO GET *OUT*--
STAND BACK.
I'VE GOT THIS.
COME ON...
HAAIIIII!
CLONG!

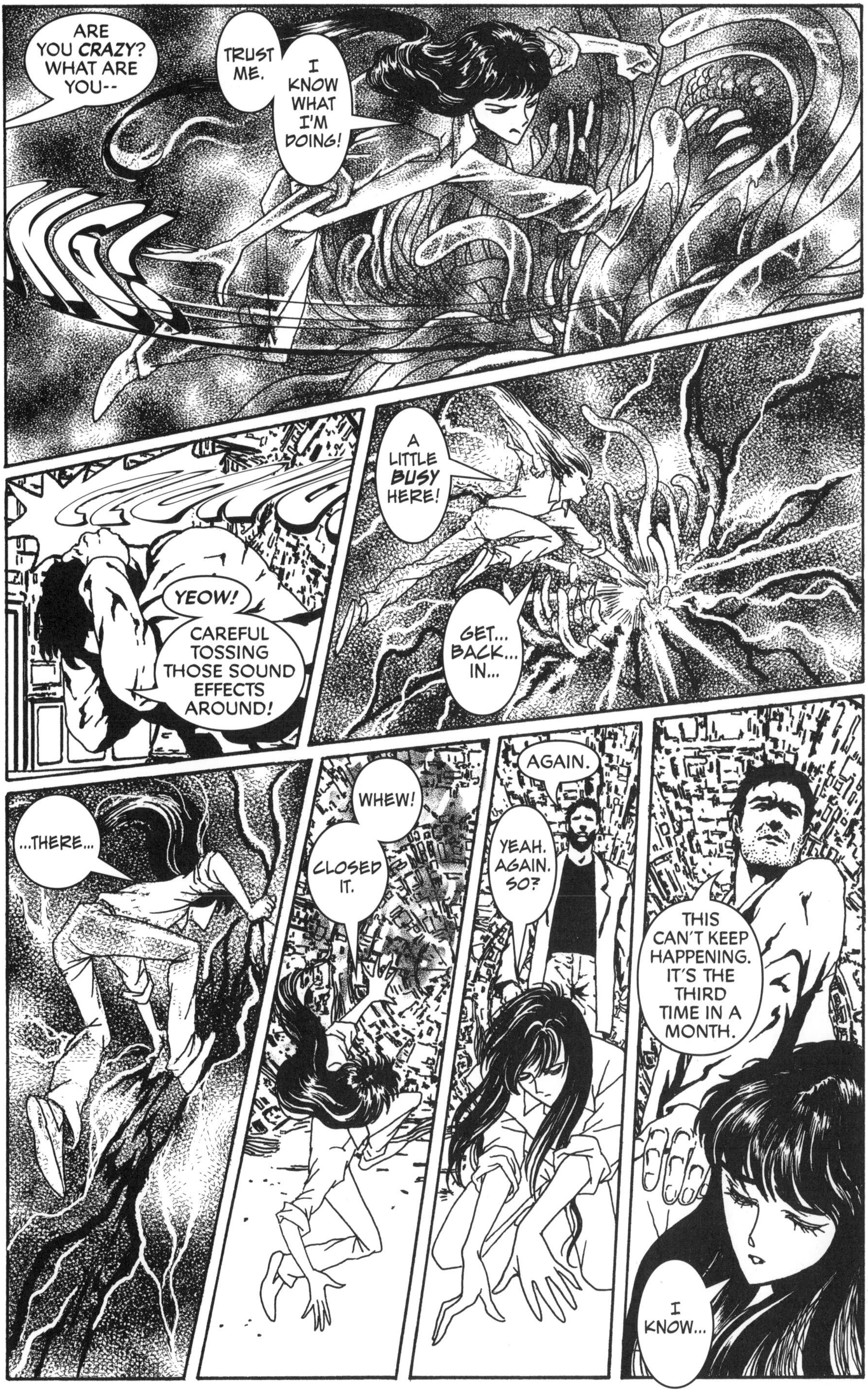
ARE YOU CRAZY? WHAT ARE YOU--
TRUST ME.
I KNOW WHAT I'M DOING!
YEOW!
CAREFUL TOSSING THOSE SOUND EFFECTS AROUND!
A LITTLE BUSY HERE!
GET... BACK... IN...
...THERE...
WHEW!
CLOSED IT.
AGAIN.
YEAH. AGAIN. SO?
THIS CAN'T KEEP HAPPENING. IT'S THE THIRD TIME IN A MONTH.
I KNOW...

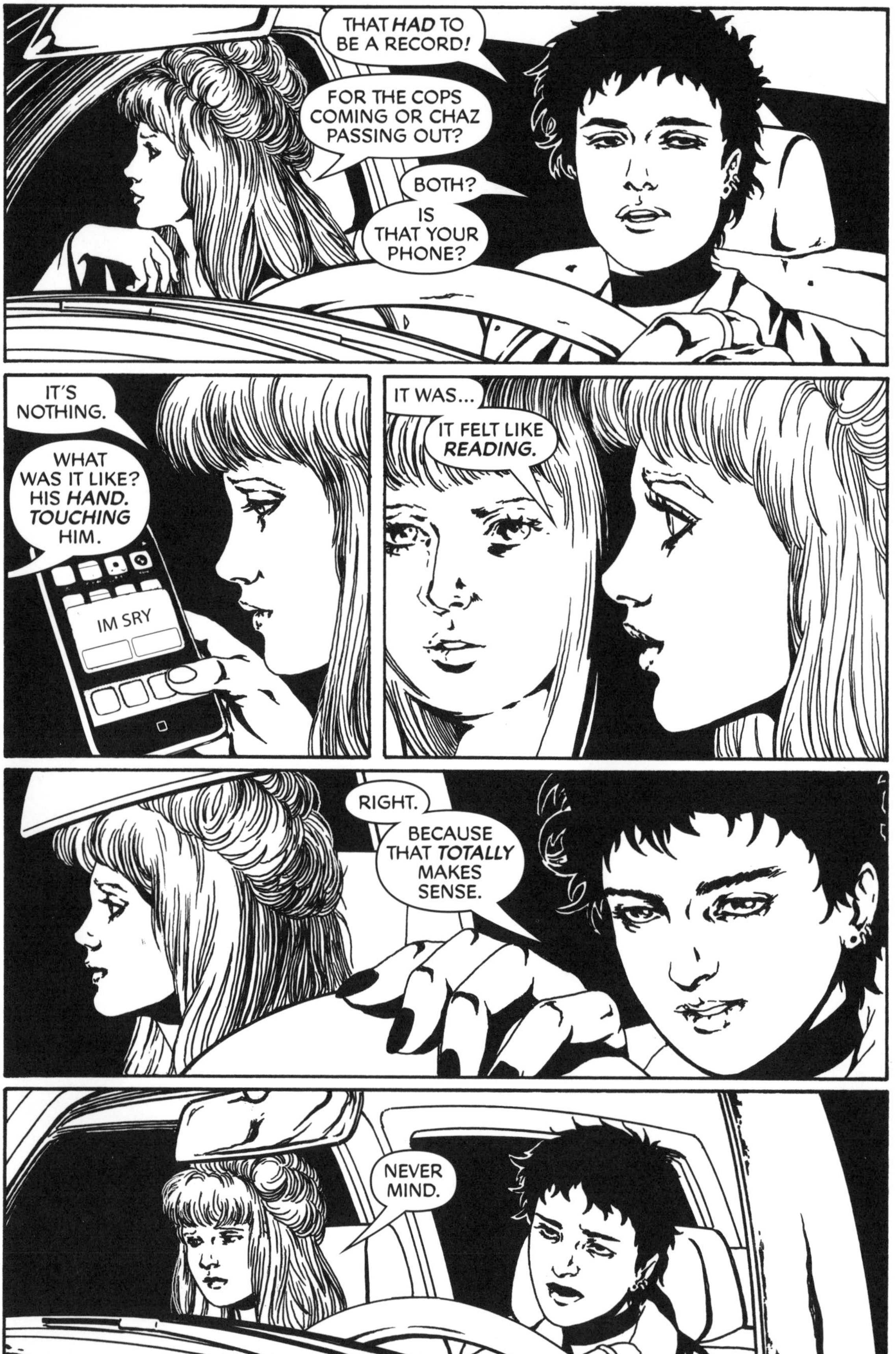
THAT *HAD* TO BE A RECORD!
FOR THE COPS COMING OR CHAZ PASSING OUT?
BOTH?
IS THAT YOUR PHONE?
IT'S NOTHING.
WHAT WAS IT LIKE? HIS *HAND*. *TOUCHING* HIM.
IM SRY
IT WAS...
IT FELT LIKE *READING*.
RIGHT.
BECAUSE THAT *TOTALLY* MAKES SENSE.
NEVER MIND.

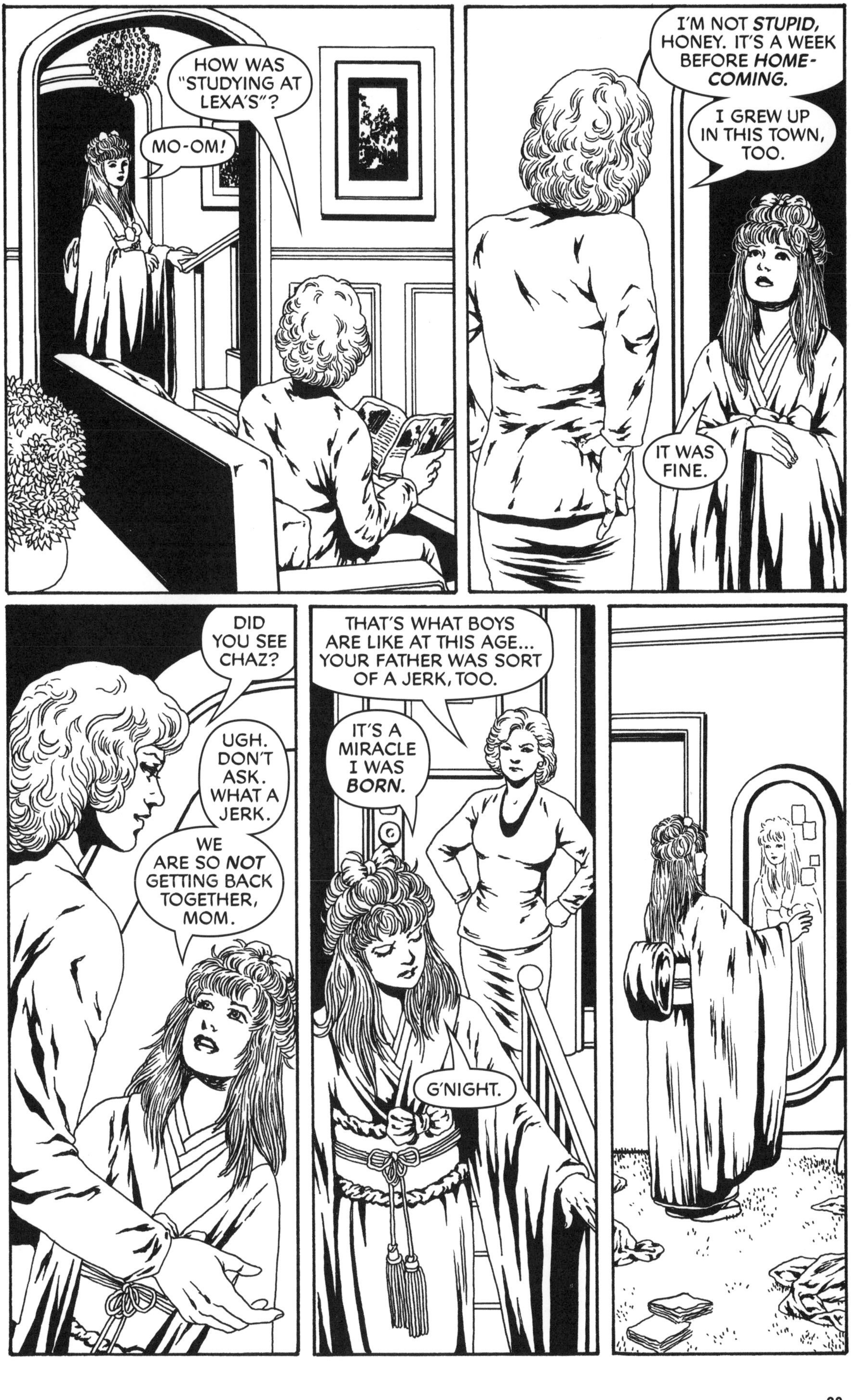
HOW WAS "STUDYING AT LEXA'S"?
MO-OM!
I'M NOT STUPID, HONEY. IT'S A WEEK BEFORE HOME-COMING.
I GREW UP IN THIS TOWN, TOO.
IT WAS FINE.
DID YOU SEE CHAZ?
UGH. DON'T ASK. WHAT A JERK.
WE ARE SO NOT GETTING BACK TOGETHER, MOM.
THAT'S WHAT BOYS ARE LIKE AT THIS AGE... YOUR FATHER WAS SORT OF A JERK, TOO.
IT'S A MIRACLE I WAS BORN.
G'NIGHT.

Dr. Louis Capeletti (left) with "The Boy From the Rip."

crossed over from another dimension that to our perceptions appears to be a two-dimensional rather than a three-dimensional space. Most bizarrely, this world seems to be nothing more than a version of Japanese comic books (or manga, as fans call them). The boy, Ryoko Kiyama, has no explanation for how or why The Rip opened, and thus far scientists are at a loss to explain the event. "It's the equivalent of the thermodynamic miracle," explained Capeletti. "As near as we can tell, this may very well be an extrascientific event."

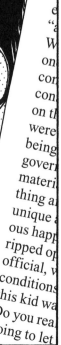

CHAPTER 3

PRINCIPAL AVERON: *I see PUNCHES, I start handing out EXPULSIONS.*

No excuses.

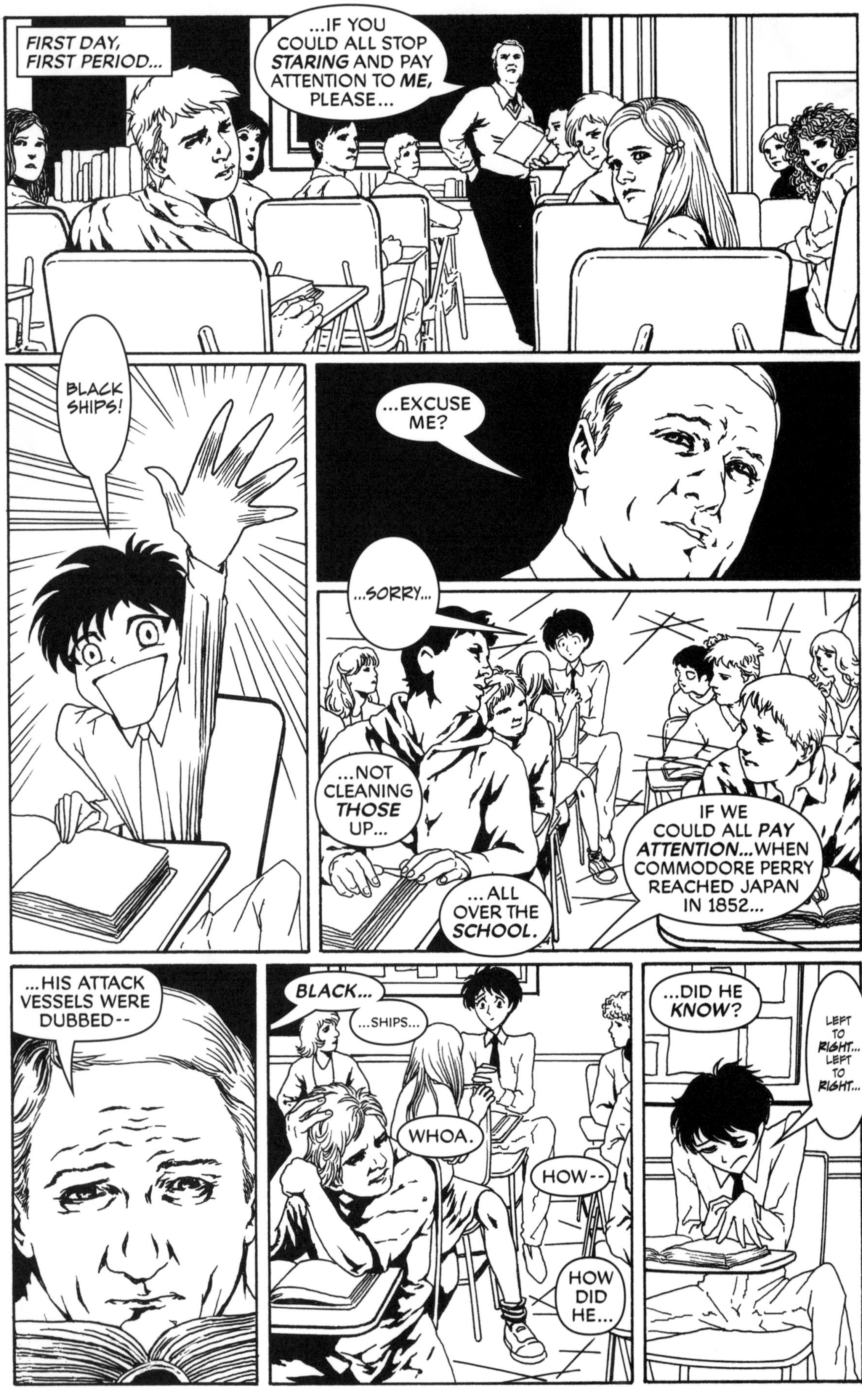
FIRST DAY, FIRST PERIOD...
...IF YOU COULD ALL STOP STARING AND PAY ATTENTION TO ME, PLEASE...
BLACK SHIPS!
...EXCUSE ME?
...SORRY...
...NOT CLEANING THOSE UP...
...ALL OVER THE SCHOOL.
IF WE COULD ALL PAY ATTENTION...WHEN COMMODORE PERRY REACHED JAPAN IN 1852...
...HIS ATTACK VESSELS WERE DUBBED--
BLACK...
...SHIPS...
WHOA.
HOW--
HOW DID HE...
...DID HE KNOW?
LEFT TO RIGHT... LEFT TO RIGHT...

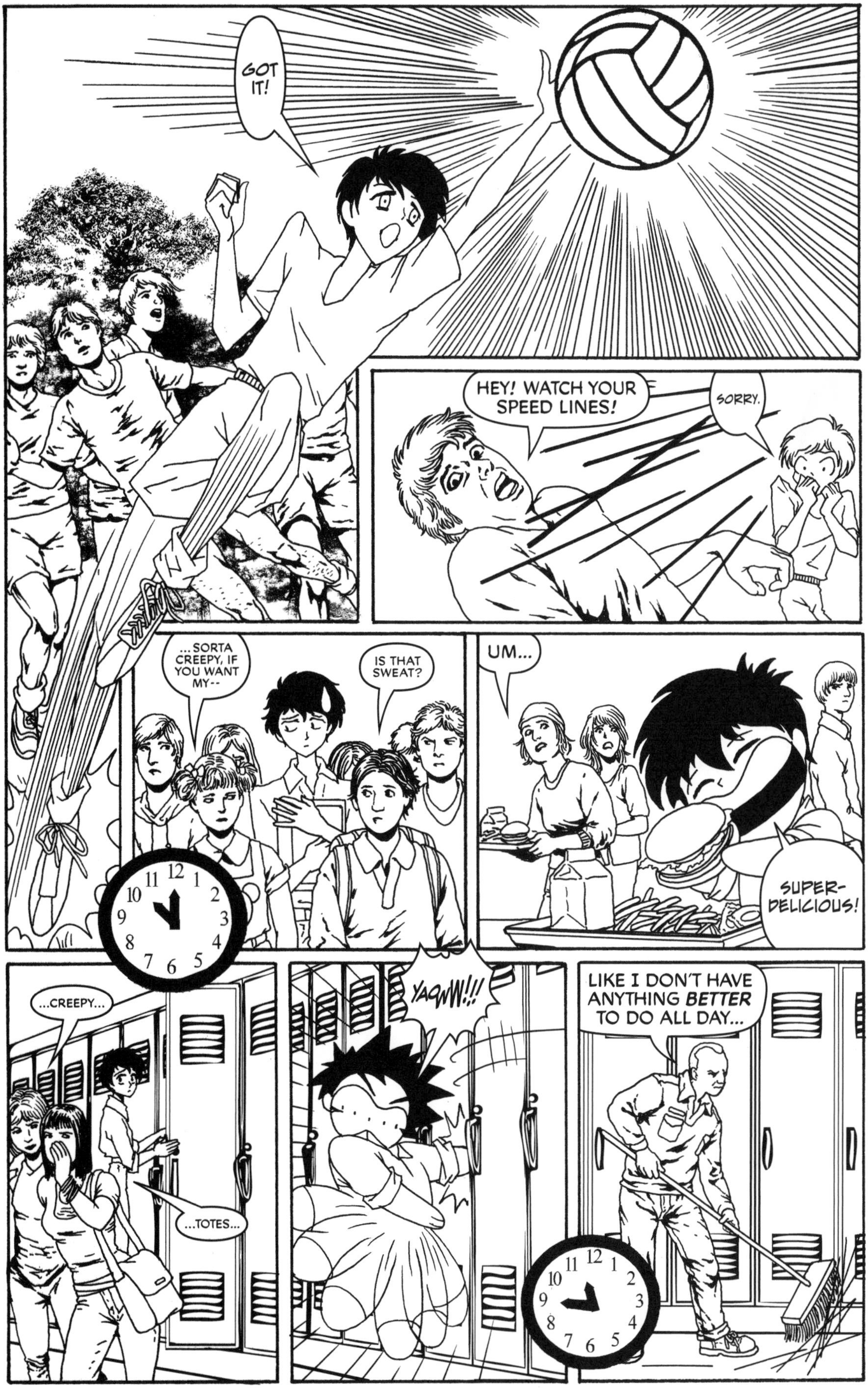
GOT IT!
HEY! WATCH YOUR SPEED LINES!
SORRY.
...SORTA CREEPY, IF YOU WANT MY--
IS THAT SWEAT?
UM...
SUPER-DELICIOUS!
...CREEPY...
...TOTES...
YAQWW!!!
LIKE I DON'T HAVE ANYTHING *BETTER* TO DO ALL DAY...

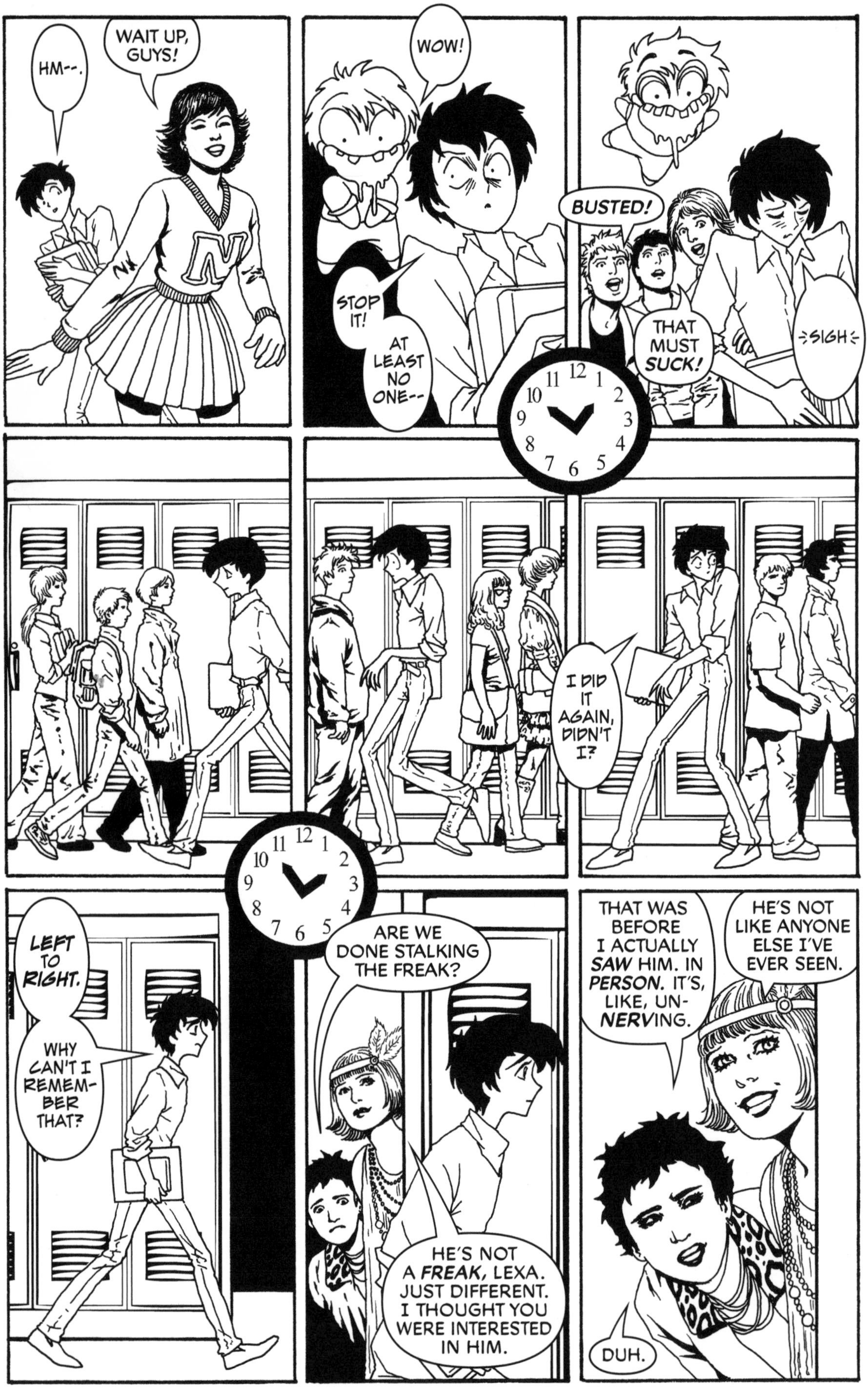
HM--.
WAIT UP, GUYS!
WOW!
STOP IT!
AT LEAST NO ONE--
BUSTED!
THAT MUST SUCK!
SIGH
I DID IT AGAIN, DIDN'T I?
LEFT TO RIGHT.
WHY CAN'T I REMEMBER THAT?
ARE WE DONE STALKING THE FREAK?
HE'S NOT A FREAK, LEXA. JUST DIFFERENT. I THOUGHT YOU WERE INTERESTED IN HIM.
THAT WAS BEFORE I ACTUALLY SAW HIM. IN PERSON. IT'S, LIKE, UNNERVING.
HE'S NOT LIKE ANYONE ELSE I'VE EVER SEEN.
DUH.

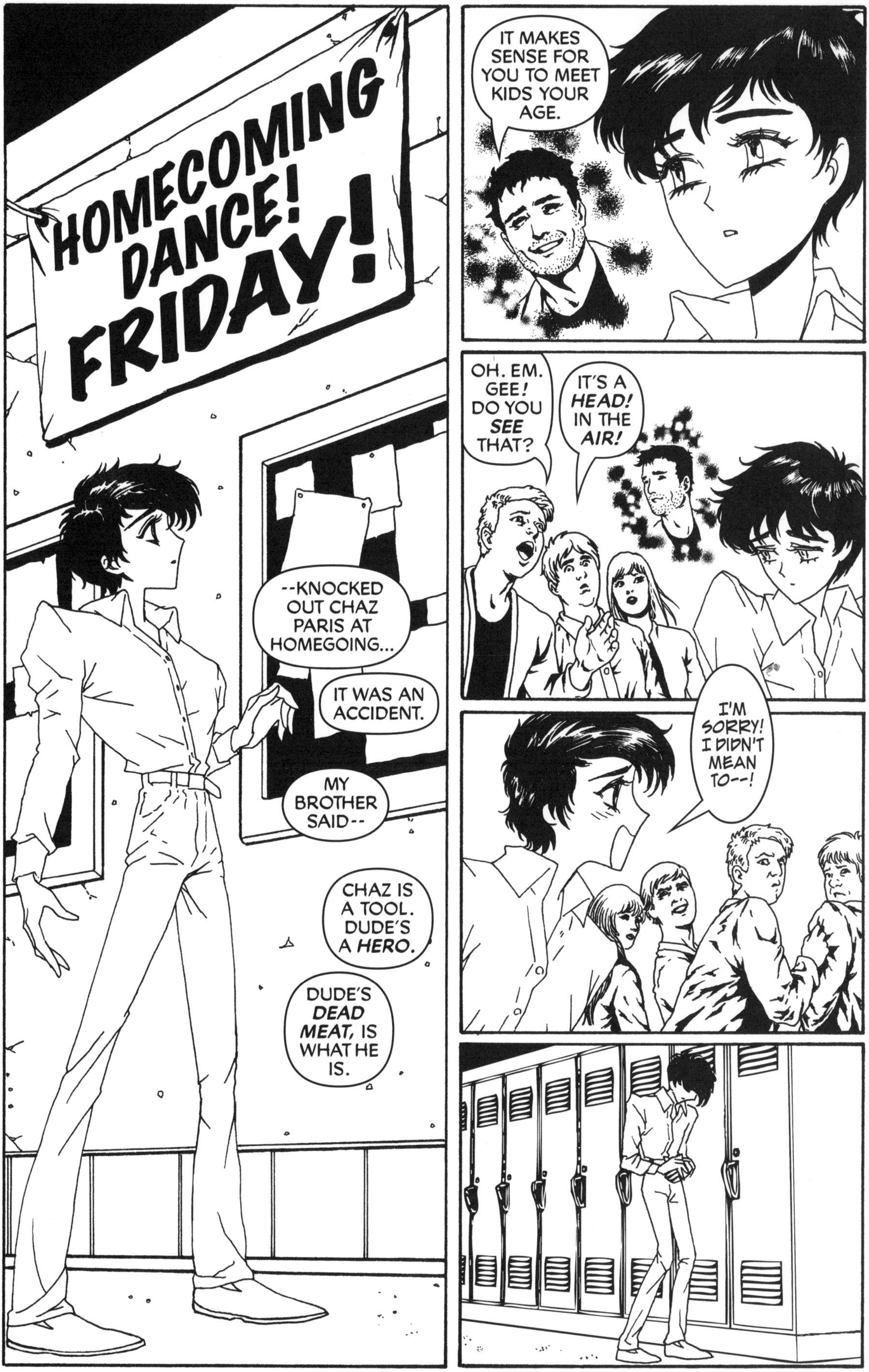
HOMECOMING DANCE! FRIDAY!
--KNOCKED OUT CHAZ PARIS AT HOMEGOING...
IT WAS AN ACCIDENT.
MY BROTHER SAID--
CHAZ IS A TOOL. DUDE'S A *HERO*.
DUDE'S *DEAD MEAT*, IS WHAT HE IS.
IT MAKES SENSE FOR YOU TO MEET KIDS YOUR AGE.
OH. EM. GEE! DO YOU *SEE* THAT?
IT'S A *HEAD!* IN THE *AIR!*
I'M SORRY! I DIDN'T MEAN TO--!

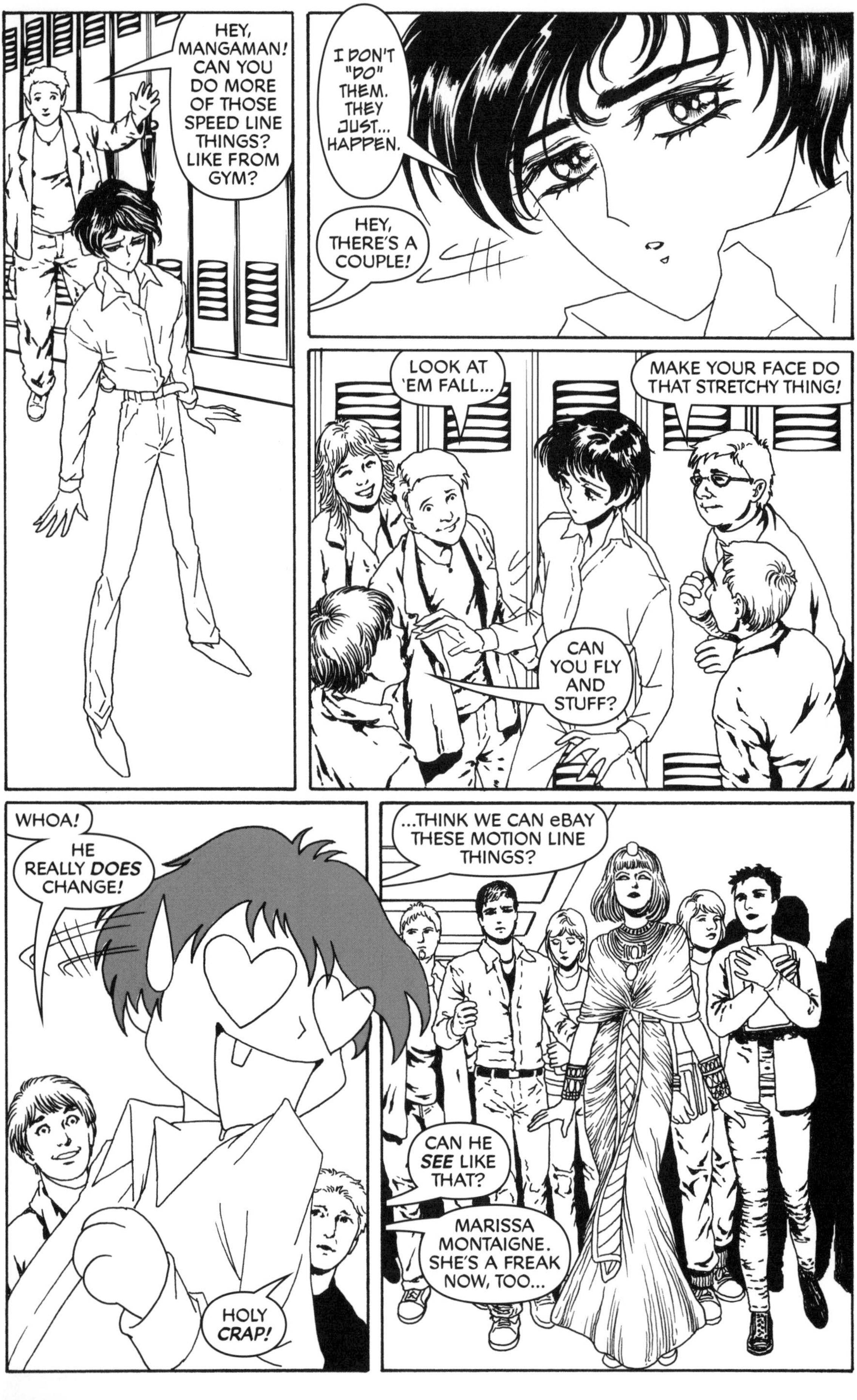
HEY, MANGAMAN! CAN YOU DO MORE OF THOSE SPEED LINE THINGS? LIKE FROM GYM?
I DON'T "DO" THEM. THEY JUST... HAPPEN.
HEY, THERE'S A COUPLE!
LOOK AT 'EM FALL...
MAKE YOUR FACE DO THAT STRETCHY THING!
CAN YOU FLY AND STUFF?
WHOA!
HE REALLY *DOES* CHANGE!
HOLY *CRAP!*
...THINK WE CAN eBAY THESE MOTION LINE THINGS?
CAN HE *SEE* LIKE THAT?
MARISSA MONTAIGNE. SHE'S A FREAK NOW, TOO...

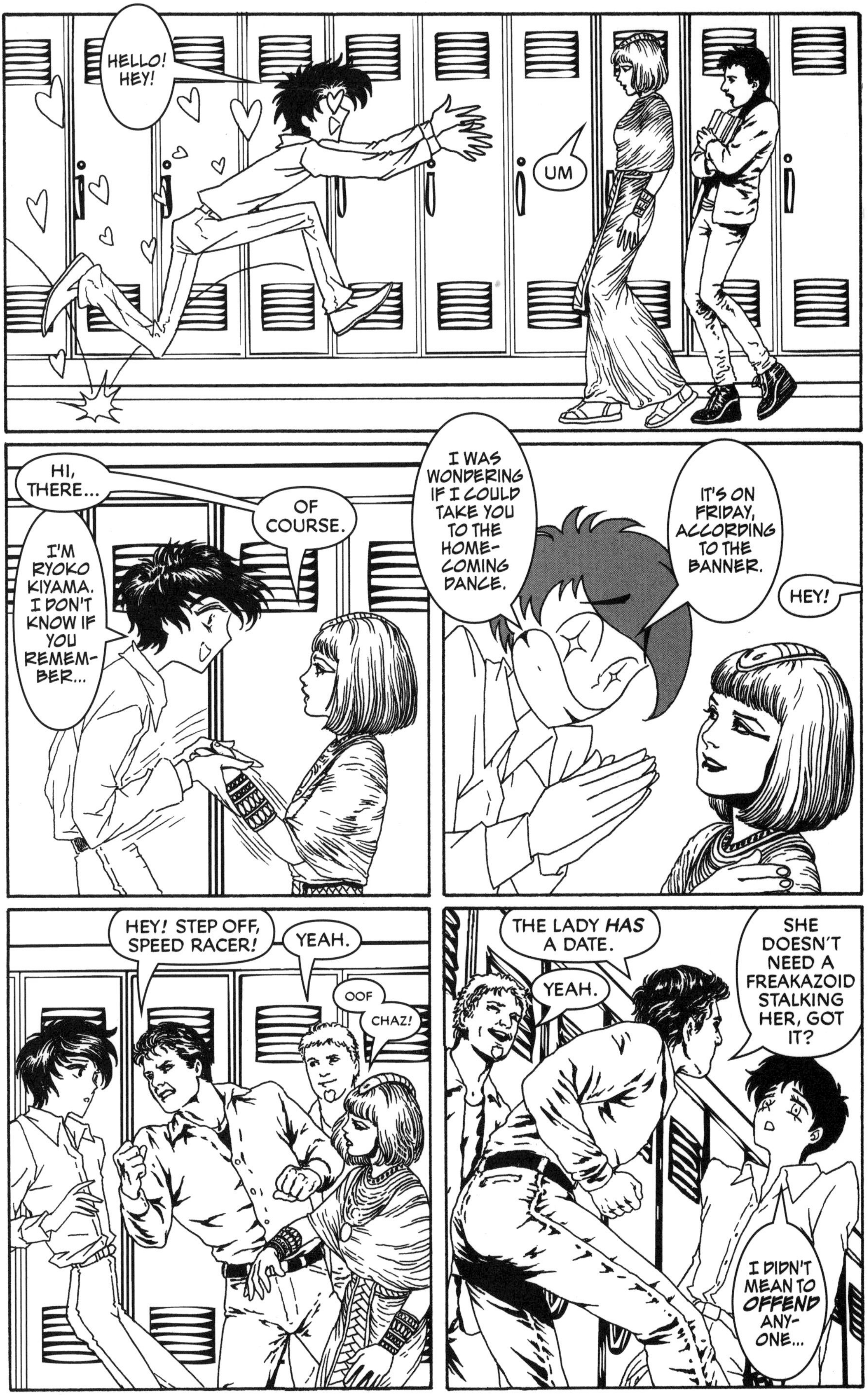
HELLO! HEY!
UM
HI, THERE...
I'M RYOKO KIYAMA. I DON'T KNOW IF YOU REMEMBER...
OF COURSE.
I WAS WONDERING IF I COULD TAKE YOU TO THE HOMECOMING DANCE.
IT'S ON FRIDAY, ACCORDING TO THE BANNER.
HEY!
HEY! STEP OFF, SPEED RACER!
YEAH.
OOF
CHAZ!
THE LADY HAS A DATE.
YEAH.
SHE DOESN'T NEED A FREAKAZOID STALKING HER, GOT IT?
I DIDN'T MEAN TO OFFEND ANYONE...

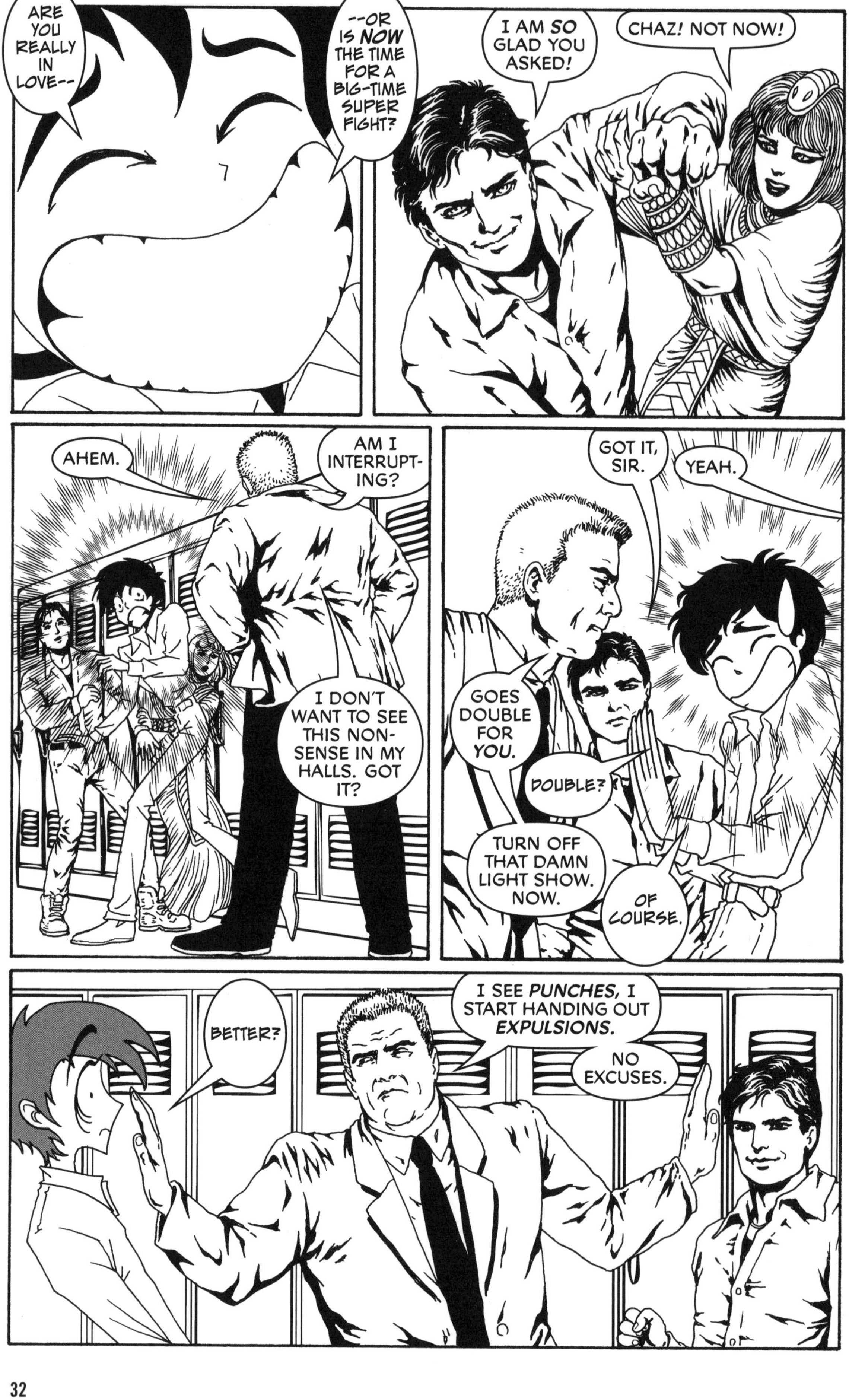
ARE YOU REALLY IN LOVE--
--OR IS NOW THE TIME FOR A BIG-TIME SUPER FIGHT?
I AM SO GLAD YOU ASKED!
CHAZ! NOT NOW!
AHEM.
AM I INTERRUPT-ING?
I DON'T WANT TO SEE THIS NON-SENSE IN MY HALLS. GOT IT?
GOT IT, SIR.
YEAH.
GOES DOUBLE FOR YOU.
DOUBLE?
TURN OFF THAT DAMN LIGHT SHOW. NOW.
OF COURSE.
BETTER?
I SEE PUNCHES, I START HANDING OUT EXPULSIONS.
NO EXCUSES.

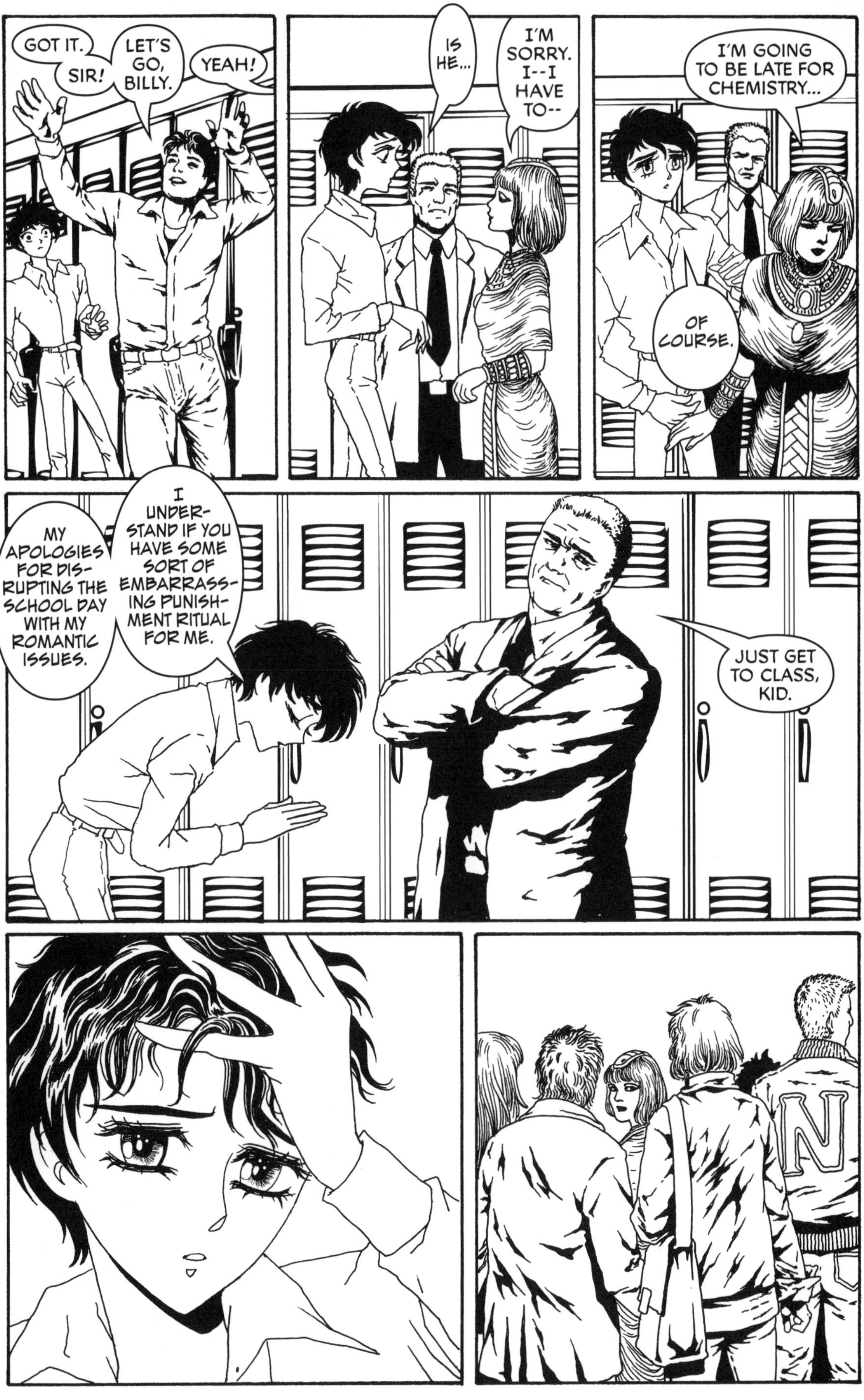
GOT IT.
SIR!
LET'S GO, BILLY.
YEAH!
IS HE...
I'M SORRY. I--I HAVE TO--
I'M GOING TO BE LATE FOR CHEMISTRY...
OF COURSE.
MY APOLOGIES FOR DISRUPTING THE SCHOOL DAY WITH MY ROMANTIC ISSUES.
I UNDERSTAND IF YOU HAVE SOME SORT OF EMBARRASSING PUNISHMENT RITUAL FOR ME.
JUST GET TO CLASS, KID.
N

CHAPTER 4

MARISSA: *Is that BLUSHING? It looks like LINES.*

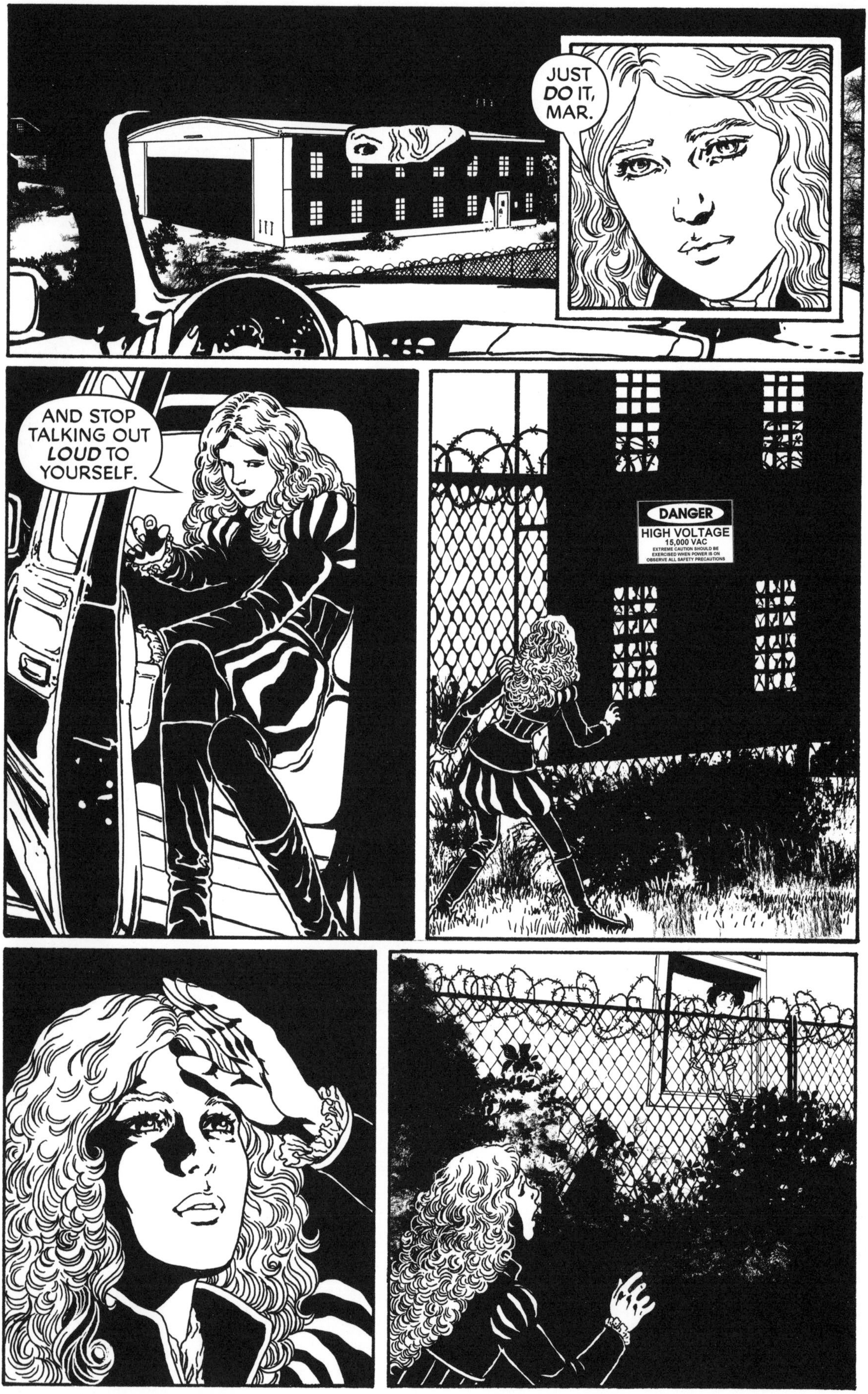
JUST *DO* IT, MAR.
AND STOP TALKING OUT *LOUD* TO YOURSELF.
DANGER
HIGH VOLTAGE
15,000 VAC
EXTREME CAUTION SHOULD BE EXERCISED WHEN POWER IS ON
OBSERVE ALL SAFETY PRECAUTIONS

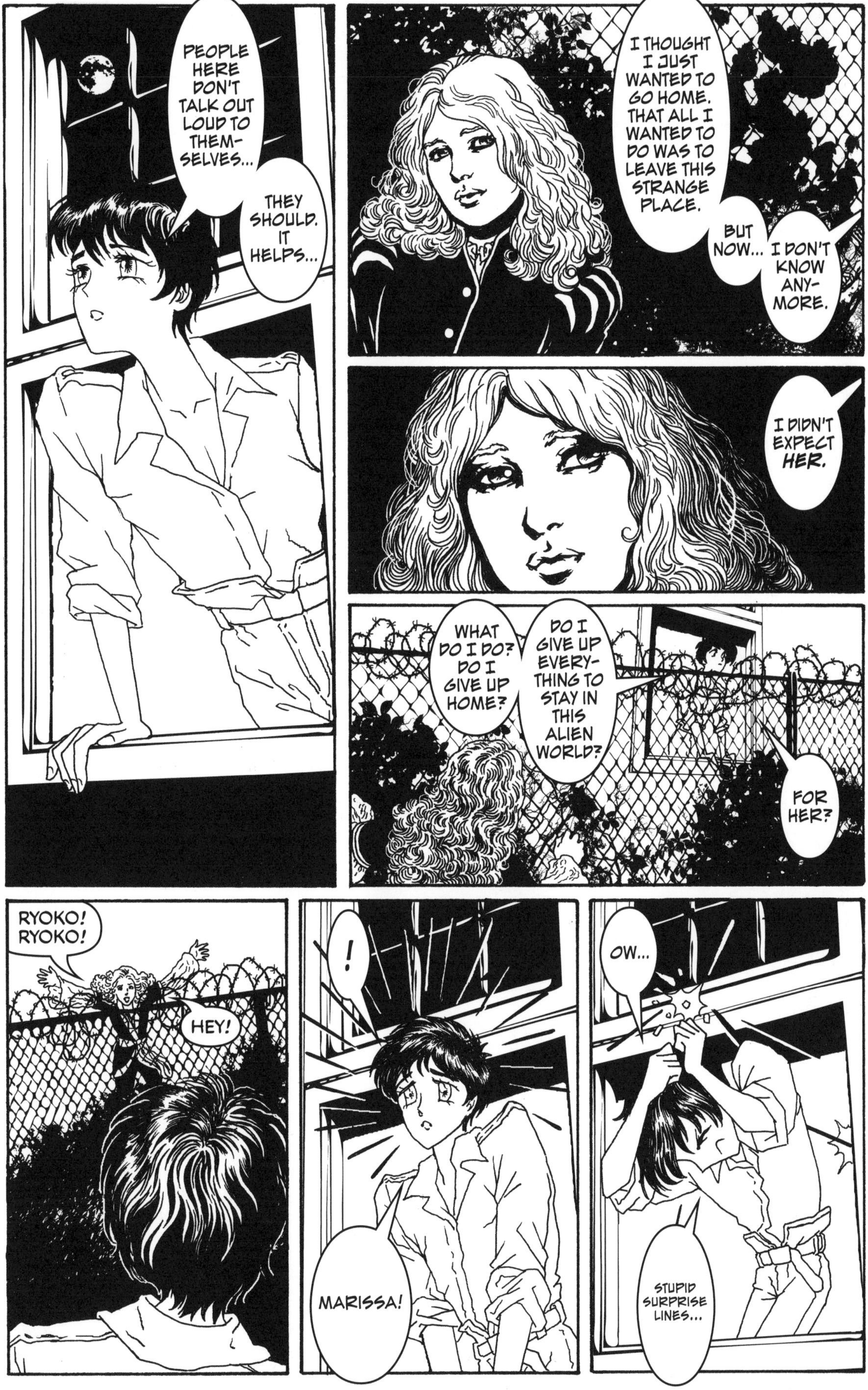
PEOPLE HERE DON'T TALK OUT LOUD TO THEM-SELVES...
THEY SHOULD. IT HELPS...
I THOUGHT I JUST WANTED TO GO HOME. THAT ALL I WANTED TO DO WAS TO LEAVE THIS STRANGE PLACE.
BUT NOW...
I DON'T KNOW ANY-MORE.
I DIDN'T EXPECT HER.
WHAT DO I DO? DO I GIVE UP HOME?
DO I GIVE UP EVERY-THING TO STAY IN THIS ALIEN WORLD?
FOR HER?
RYOKO! RYOKO!
HEY!
!
MARISSA!
OW...
STUPID SURPRISE LINES...

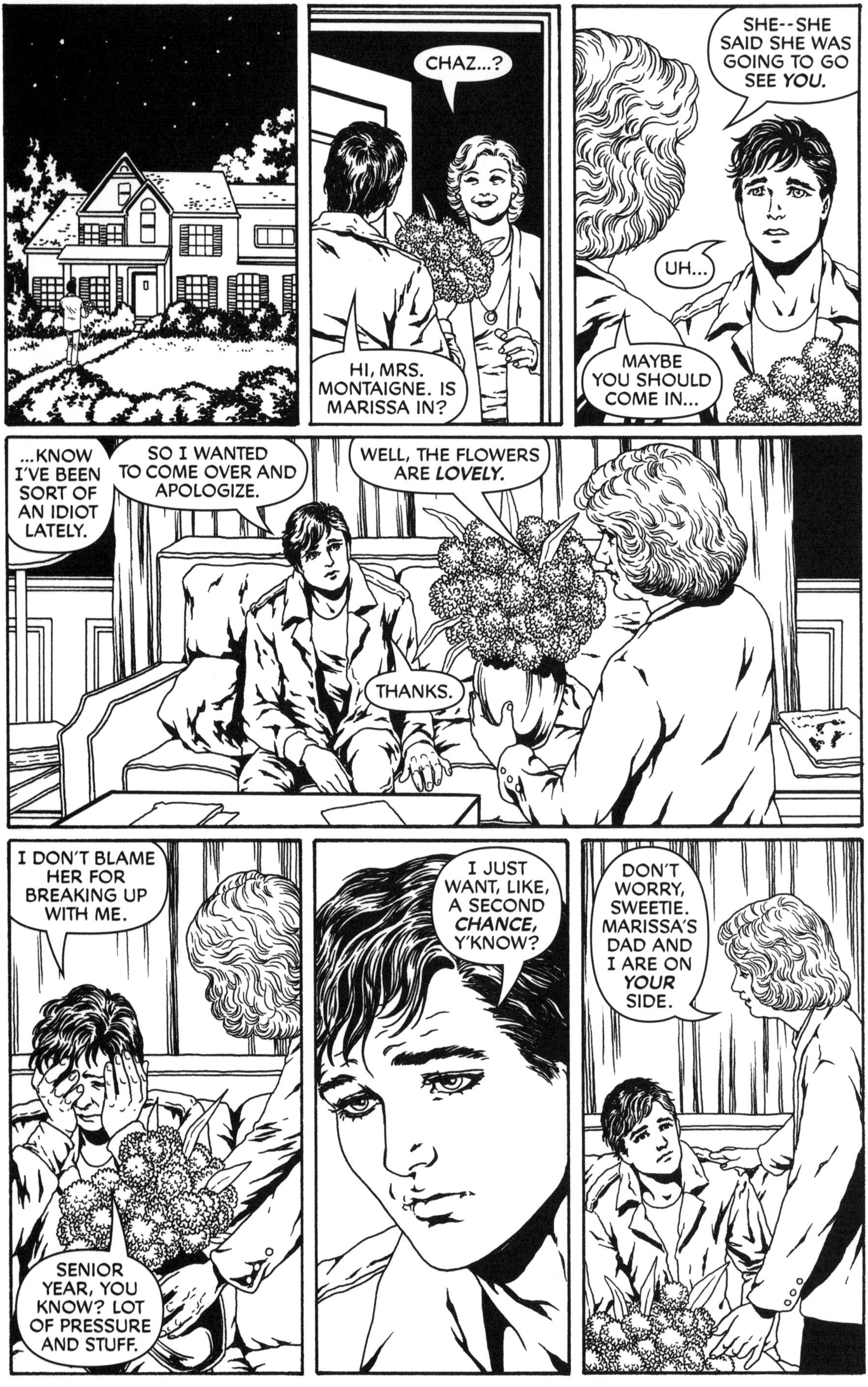
CHAZ...?
HI, MRS. MONTAIGNE. IS MARISSA IN?
SHE--SHE SAID SHE WAS GOING TO GO SEE *YOU.*
UH...
MAYBE YOU SHOULD COME IN...
...KNOW I'VE BEEN SORT OF AN IDIOT LATELY.
SO I WANTED TO COME OVER AND APOLOGIZE.
WELL, THE FLOWERS ARE *LOVELY.*
THANKS.
I DON'T BLAME HER FOR BREAKING UP WITH ME.
SENIOR YEAR, YOU KNOW? LOT OF PRESSURE AND STUFF.
I JUST WANT, LIKE, A SECOND *CHANCE,* Y'KNOW?
DON'T WORRY, SWEETIE. MARISSA'S DAD AND I ARE ON *YOUR* SIDE.

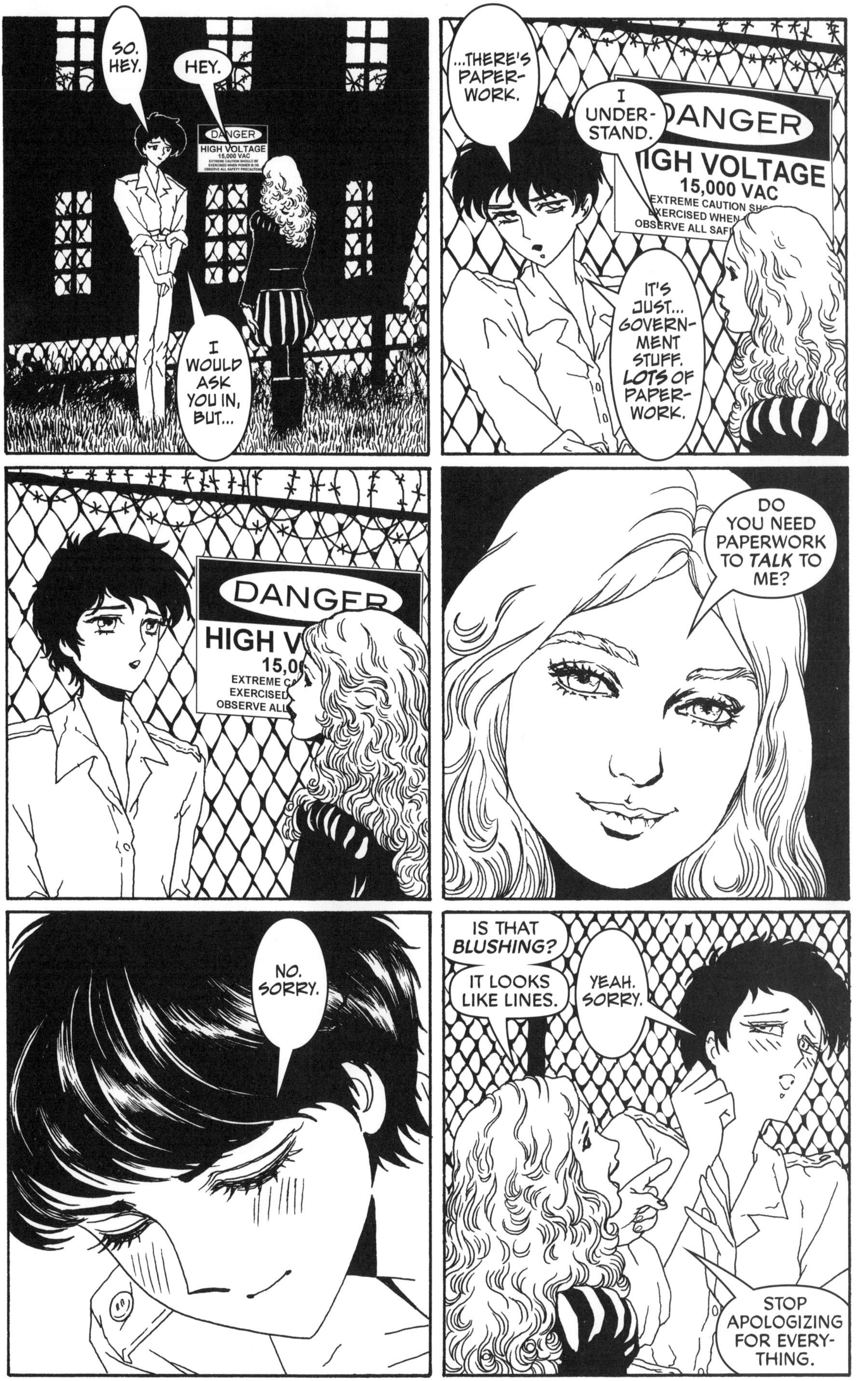
SO. HEY.
HEY.
DANGER
HIGH VOLTAGE
15,000 VAC
I WOULD ASK YOU IN, BUT...
...THERE'S PAPER-WORK.
I UNDER-STAND.
DANGER
HIGH VOLTAGE
15,000 VAC
IT'S JUST... GOVERN-MENT STUFF. *LOTS* OF PAPER-WORK.
DANGER
DO YOU NEED PAPERWORK TO *TALK* TO ME?
NO. SORRY.
IS THAT *BLUSHING?*
IT LOOKS LIKE LINES.
YEAH. SORRY.
STOP APOLOGIZING FOR EVERY-THING.

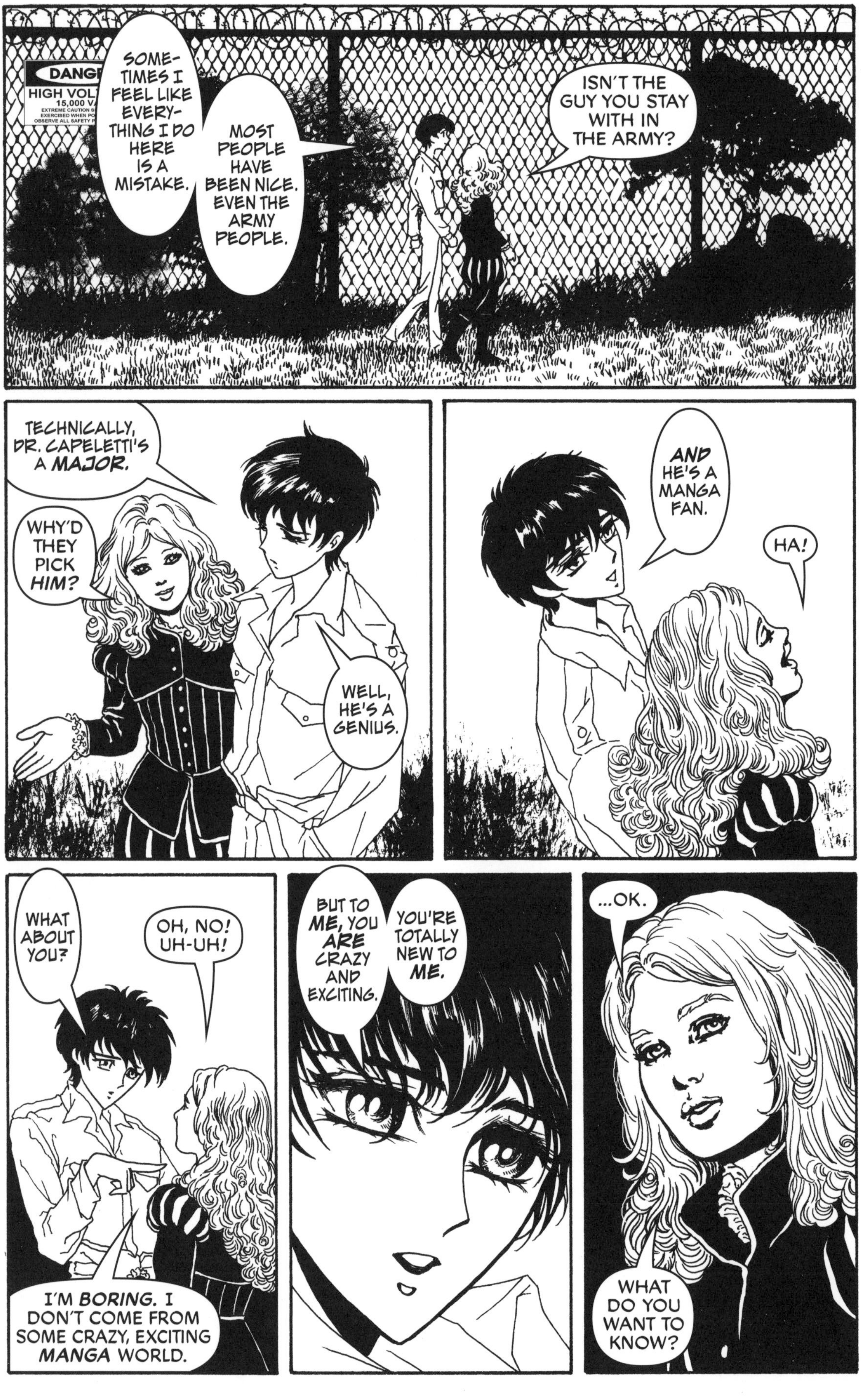
DANGER
HIGH VOLTAGE
15,000 V
SOMETIMES I FEEL LIKE EVERYTHING I DO HERE IS A MISTAKE.
MOST PEOPLE HAVE BEEN NICE. EVEN THE ARMY PEOPLE.
ISN'T THE GUY YOU STAY WITH IN THE ARMY?
TECHNICALLY, DR. CAPELETTI'S A MAJOR.
WHY'D THEY PICK HIM?
WELL, HE'S A GENIUS.
AND HE'S A MANGA FAN.
HA!
WHAT ABOUT YOU?
OH, NO! UH-UH!
I'M BORING. I DON'T COME FROM SOME CRAZY, EXCITING MANGA WORLD.
BUT TO ME, YOU ARE CRAZY AND EXCITING.
YOU'RE TOTALLY NEW TO ME.
...OK.
WHAT DO YOU WANT TO KNOW?

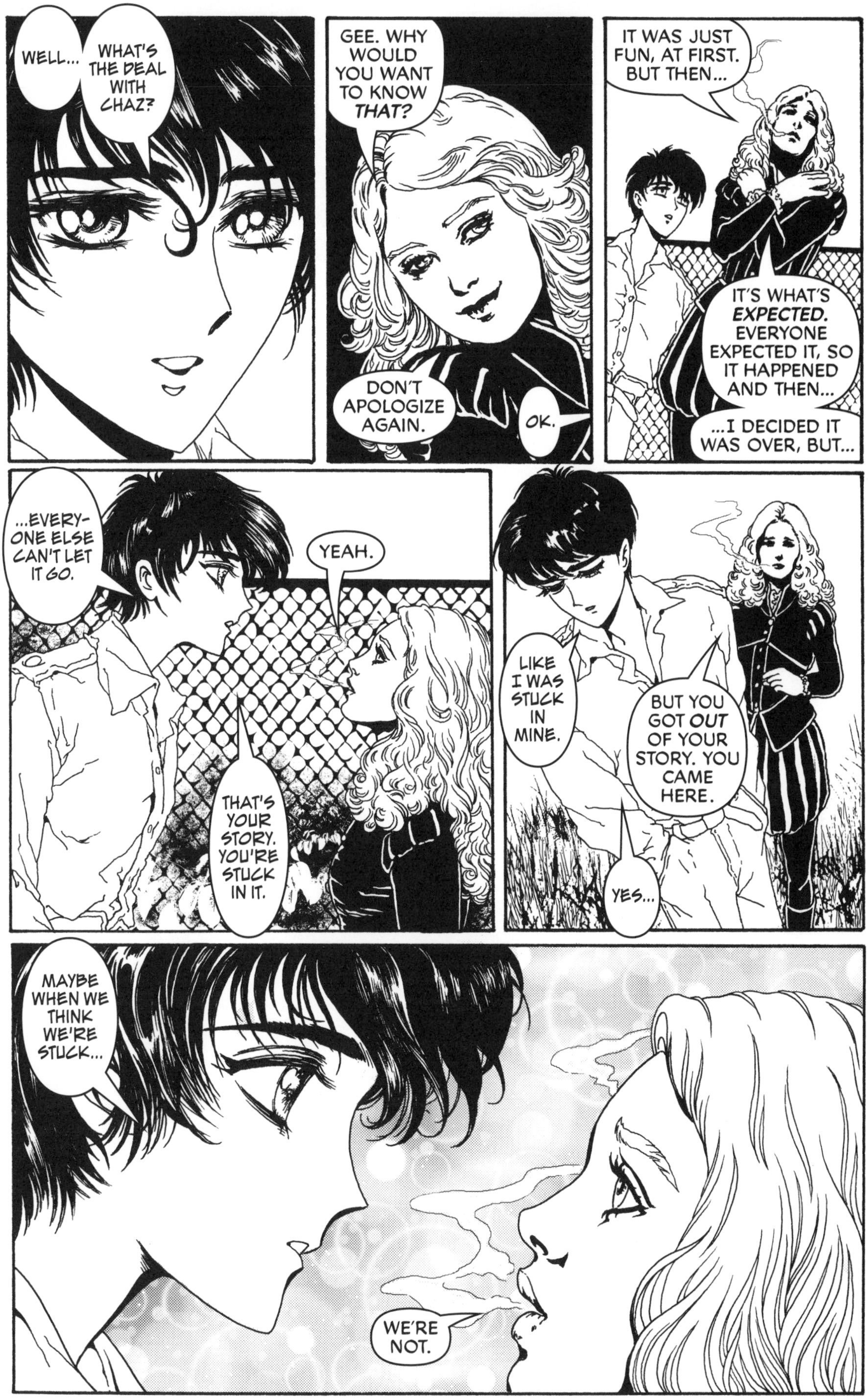
WELL...
WHAT'S THE DEAL WITH CHAZ?
GEE. WHY WOULD YOU WANT TO KNOW *THAT?*
DON'T APOLOGIZE AGAIN.
OK.
IT WAS JUST FUN, AT FIRST. BUT THEN...
IT'S WHAT'S *EXPECTED.* EVERYONE EXPECTED IT, SO IT HAPPENED AND THEN...
...I DECIDED IT WAS OVER, BUT...
...EVERY-ONE ELSE CAN'T LET IT GO.
YEAH.
THAT'S YOUR STORY. YOU'RE STUCK IN IT.
LIKE I WAS STUCK IN MINE.
BUT YOU GOT *OUT* OF YOUR STORY. YOU CAME HERE.
YES...
MAYBE WHEN WE THINK WE'RE STUCK...
WE'RE NOT.

CHAPTER 5

CAPELETTI: *Ryoko! Get down!*

They've broken through again!

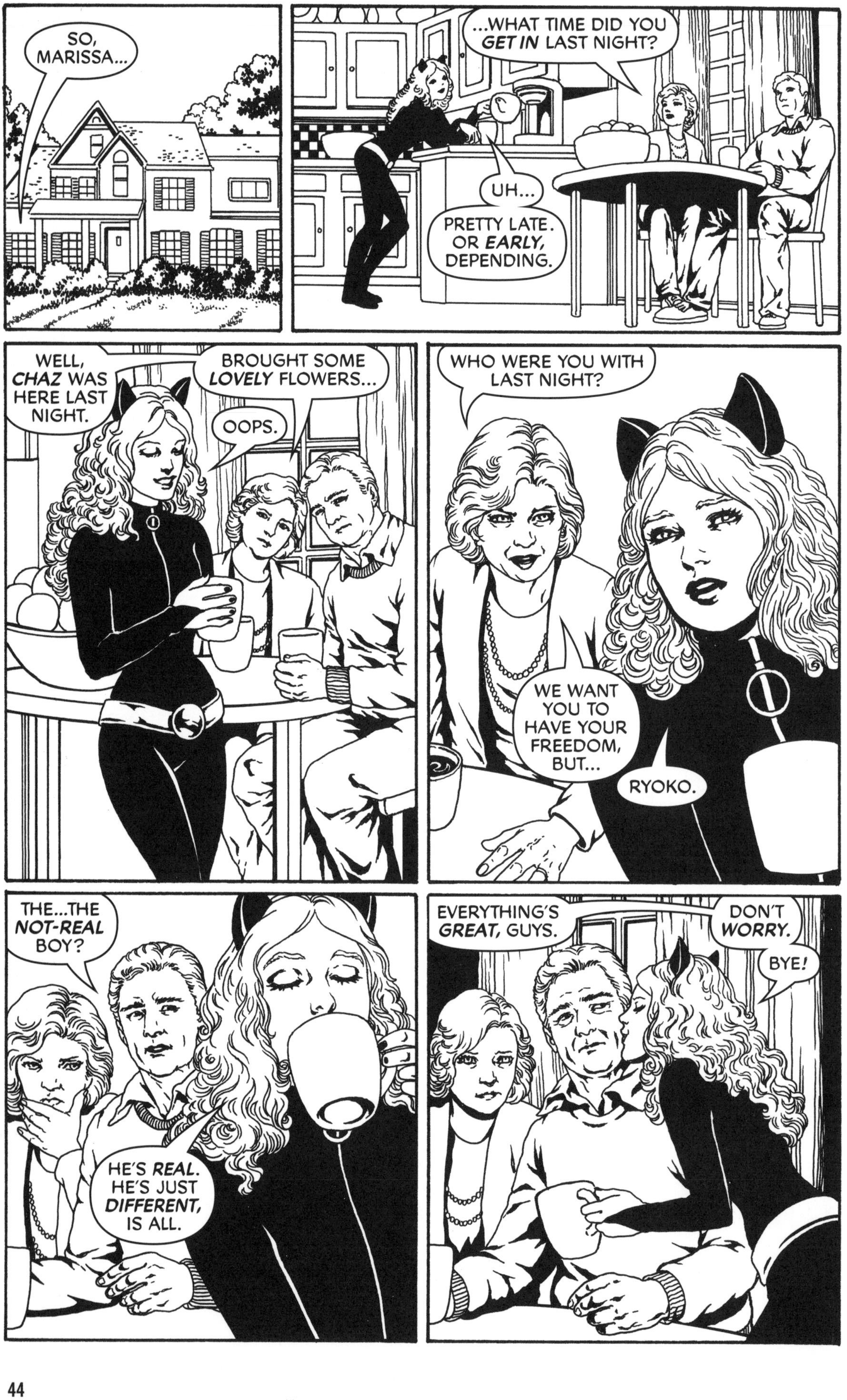
SO, MARISSA...
...WHAT TIME DID YOU *GET IN* LAST NIGHT?
UH...
PRETTY LATE. OR *EARLY,* DEPENDING.
WELL, *CHAZ* WAS HERE LAST NIGHT.
BROUGHT SOME *LOVELY* FLOWERS...
OOPS.
WHO WERE YOU WITH LAST NIGHT?
WE WANT YOU TO HAVE YOUR FREEDOM, BUT...
RYOKO.
THE...THE *NOT-REAL* BOY?
HE'S *REAL.* HE'S JUST *DIFFERENT,* IS ALL.
EVERYTHING'S *GREAT,* GUYS.
DON'T *WORRY.*
BYE!

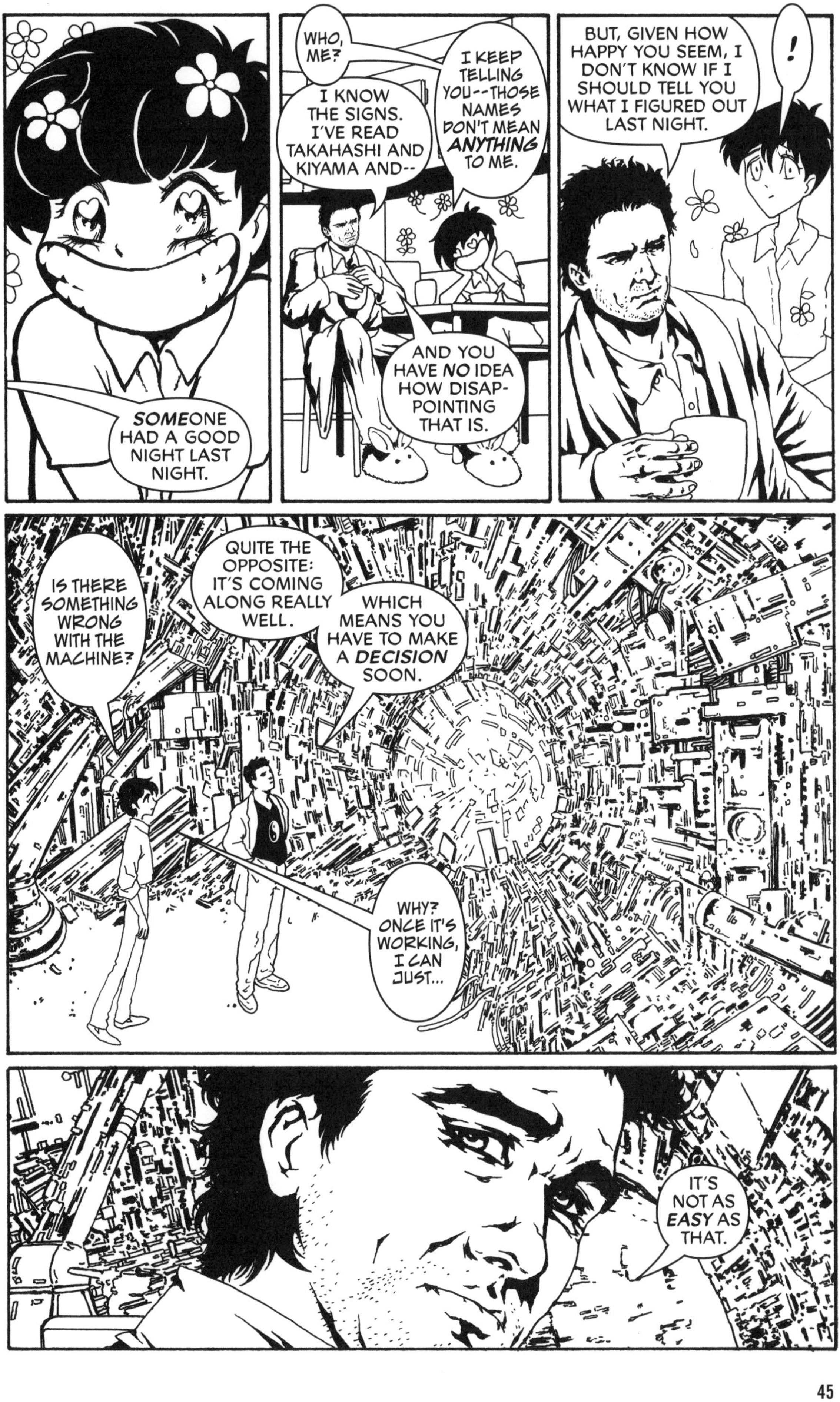
SOMEONE HAD A GOOD NIGHT LAST NIGHT.
WHO, ME?
I KNOW THE SIGNS. I'VE READ TAKAHASHI AND KIYAMA AND--
I KEEP TELLING YOU--THOSE NAMES DON'T MEAN ANYTHING TO ME.
AND YOU HAVE NO IDEA HOW DISAP-POINTING THAT IS.
BUT, GIVEN HOW HAPPY YOU SEEM, I DON'T KNOW IF I SHOULD TELL YOU WHAT I FIGURED OUT LAST NIGHT.
!
IS THERE SOMETHING WRONG WITH THE MACHINE?
QUITE THE OPPOSITE: IT'S COMING ALONG REALLY WELL.
WHICH MEANS YOU HAVE TO MAKE A DECISION SOON.
WHY? ONCE IT'S WORKING, I CAN JUST...
IT'S NOT AS EASY AS THAT.

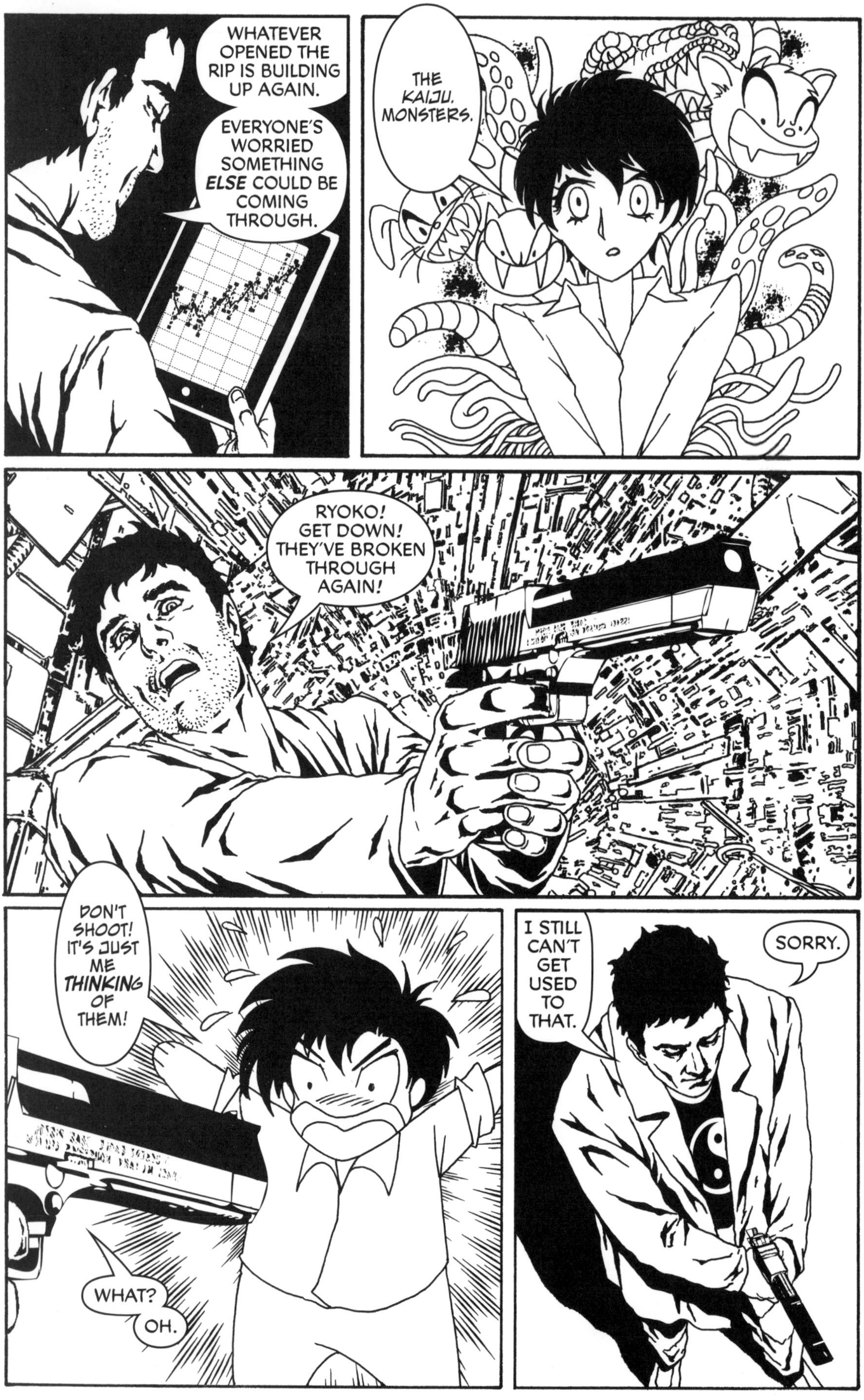
WHATEVER OPENED THE RIP IS BUILDING UP AGAIN.
EVERYONE'S WORRIED SOMETHING *ELSE* COULD BE COMING THROUGH.
THE *KAIJU.* MONSTERS.
RYOKO! GET DOWN! THEY'VE BROKEN THROUGH AGAIN!
DON'T SHOOT! IT'S JUST ME *THINKING* OF THEM!
WHAT? OH.
I STILL CAN'T GET USED TO THAT.
SORRY.

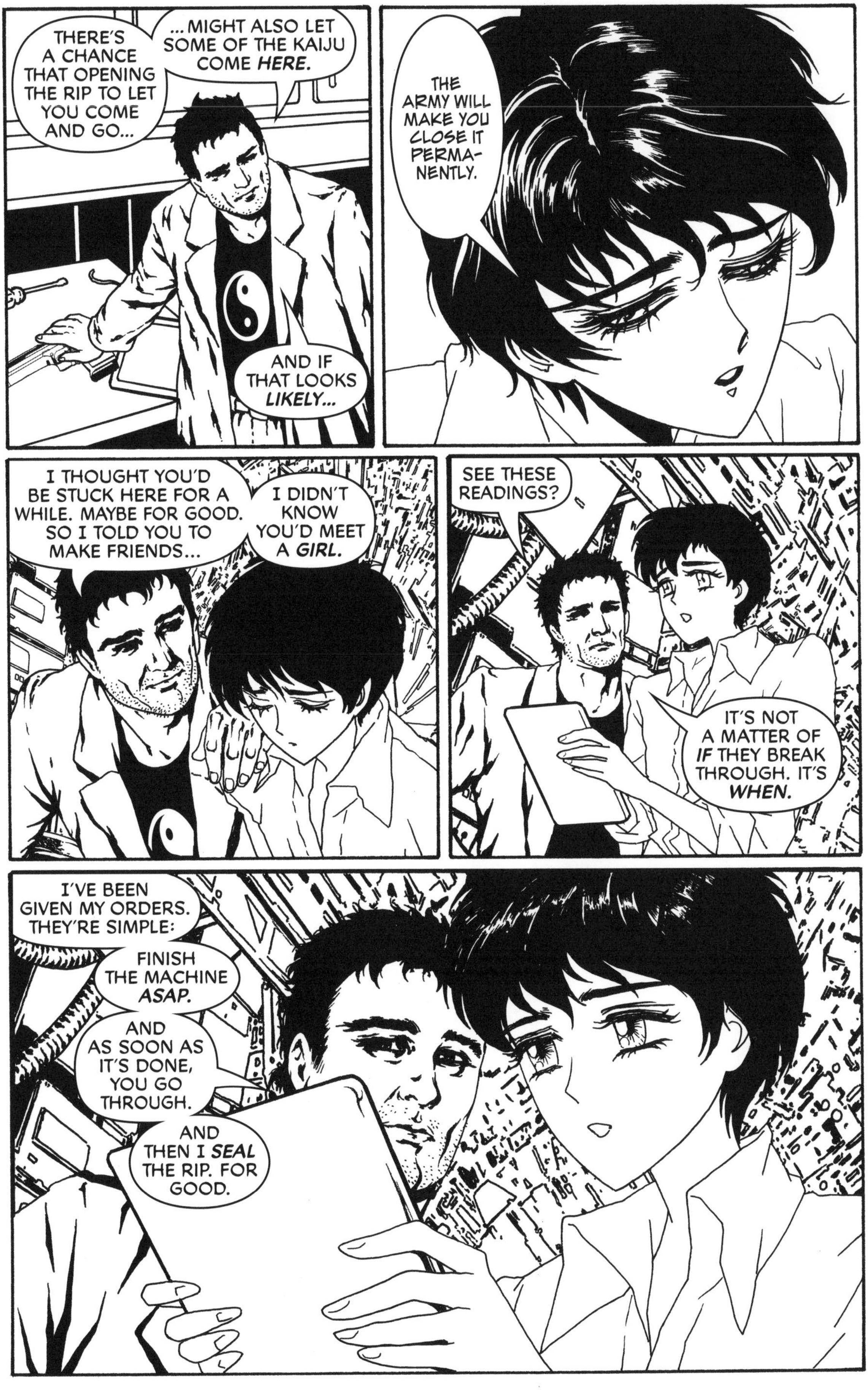
THERE'S A CHANCE THAT OPENING THE RIP TO LET YOU COME AND GO...
...MIGHT ALSO LET SOME OF THE KAIJU COME *HERE.*
AND IF THAT LOOKS *LIKELY...*
THE ARMY WILL MAKE YOU CLOSE IT PERMA-NENTLY.
I THOUGHT YOU'D BE STUCK HERE FOR A WHILE. MAYBE FOR GOOD. SO I TOLD YOU TO MAKE FRIENDS...
I DIDN'T KNOW YOU'D MEET A *GIRL.*
SEE THESE READINGS?
IT'S NOT A MATTER OF *IF* THEY BREAK THROUGH. IT'S *WHEN.*
I'VE BEEN GIVEN MY ORDERS. THEY'RE SIMPLE:
FINISH THE MACHINE *ASAP.*
AND AS SOON AS IT'S DONE, YOU GO THROUGH.
AND THEN I *SEAL* THE RIP. FOR GOOD.

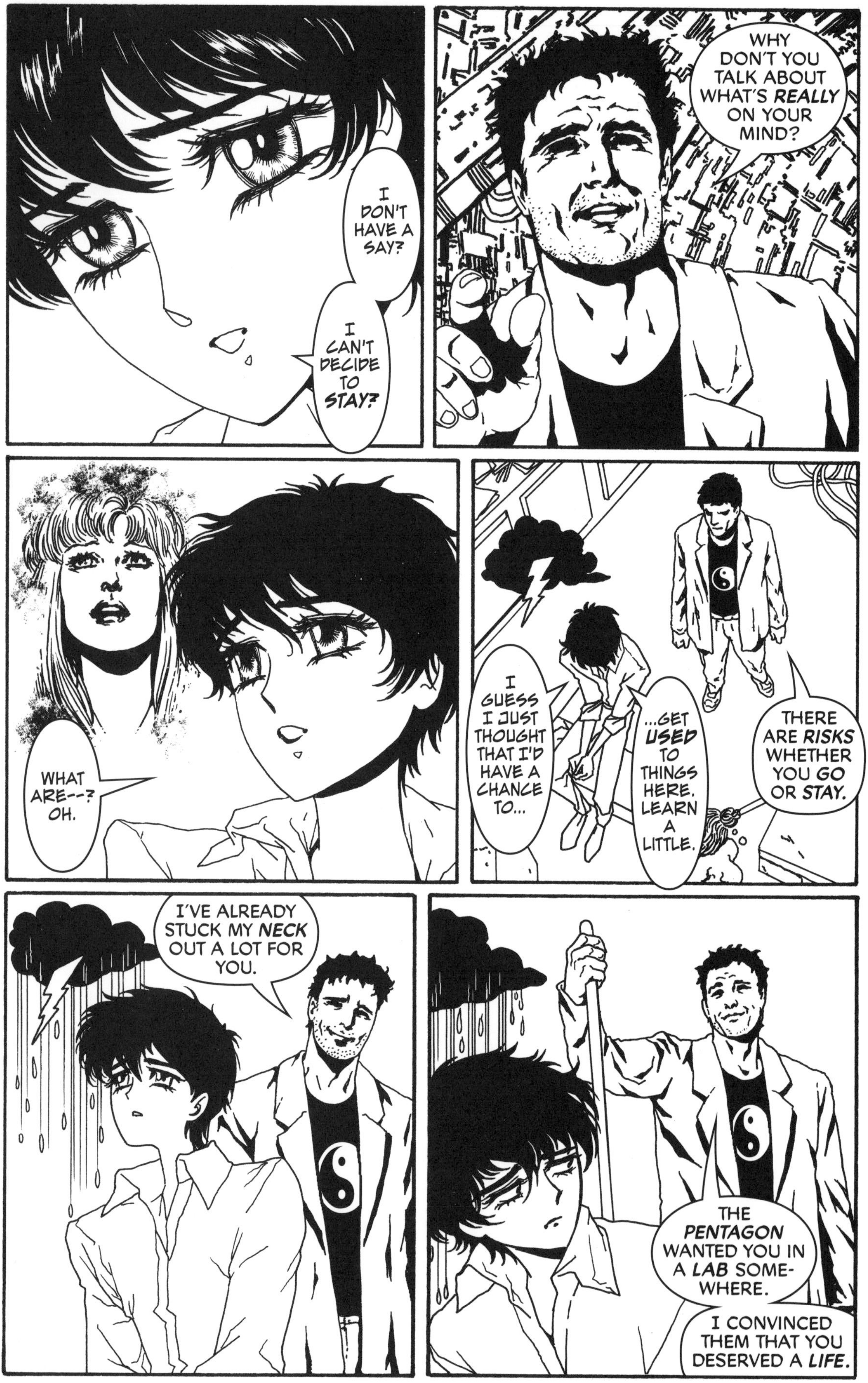
I DON'T HAVE A SAY?
I CAN'T DECIDE TO STAY?
WHY DON'T YOU TALK ABOUT WHAT'S REALLY ON YOUR MIND?
WHAT ARE--? OH.
I GUESS I JUST THOUGHT THAT I'D HAVE A CHANCE TO...
...GET USED TO THINGS HERE. LEARN A LITTLE.
THERE ARE RISKS WHETHER YOU GO OR STAY.
I'VE ALREADY STUCK MY NECK OUT A LOT FOR YOU.
THE PENTAGON WANTED YOU IN A LAB SOME-WHERE.
I CONVINCED THEM THAT YOU DESERVED A LIFE.

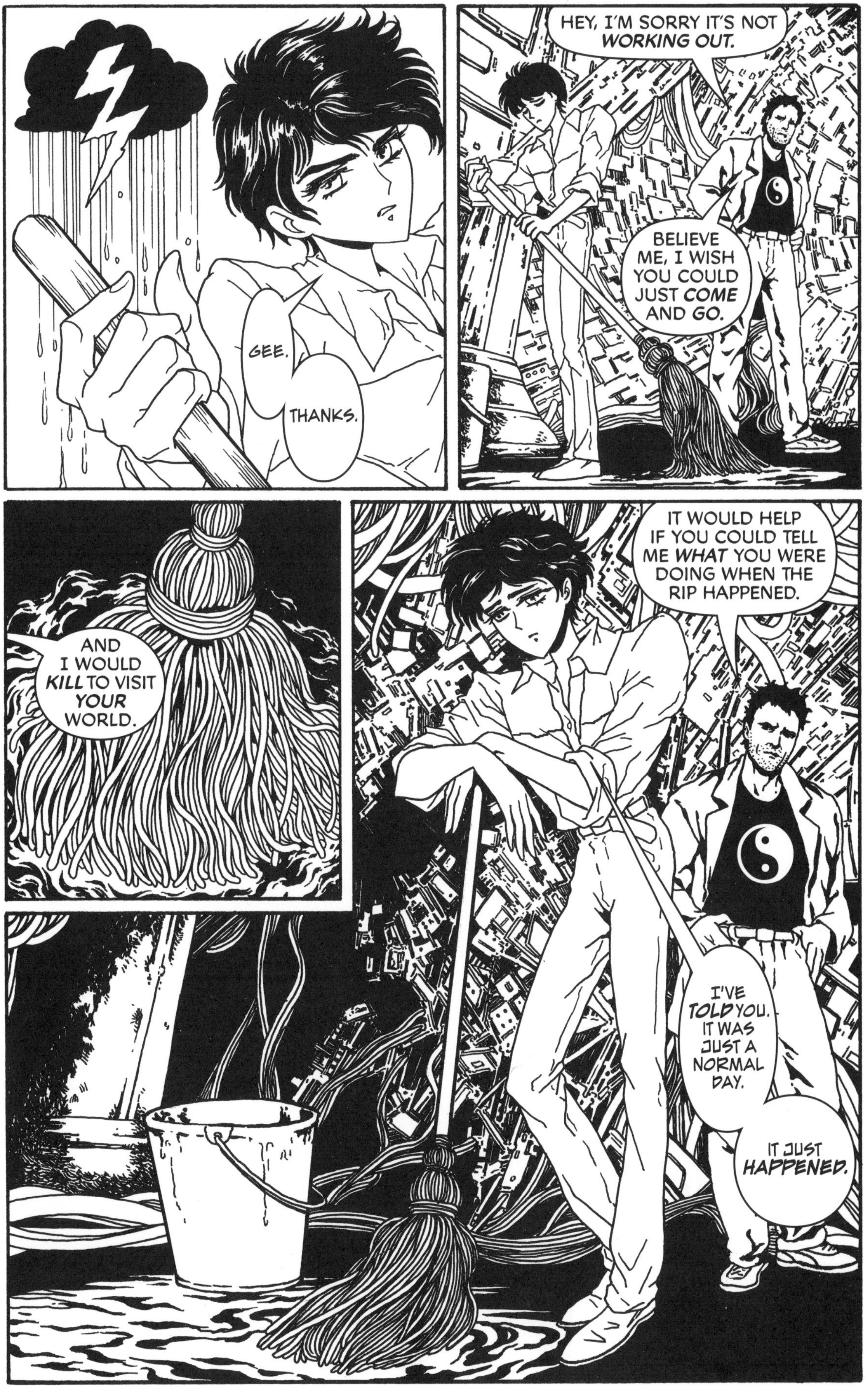
GEE.
THANKS.
HEY, I'M SORRY IT'S NOT *WORKING OUT.*
BELIEVE ME, I WISH YOU COULD JUST *COME* AND *GO.*
AND I WOULD *KILL* TO VISIT *YOUR* WORLD.
IT WOULD HELP IF YOU COULD TELL ME *WHAT* YOU WERE DOING WHEN THE RIP HAPPENED.
I'VE *TOLD* YOU. IT WAS JUST A NORMAL DAY.
IT JUST *HAPPENED.*

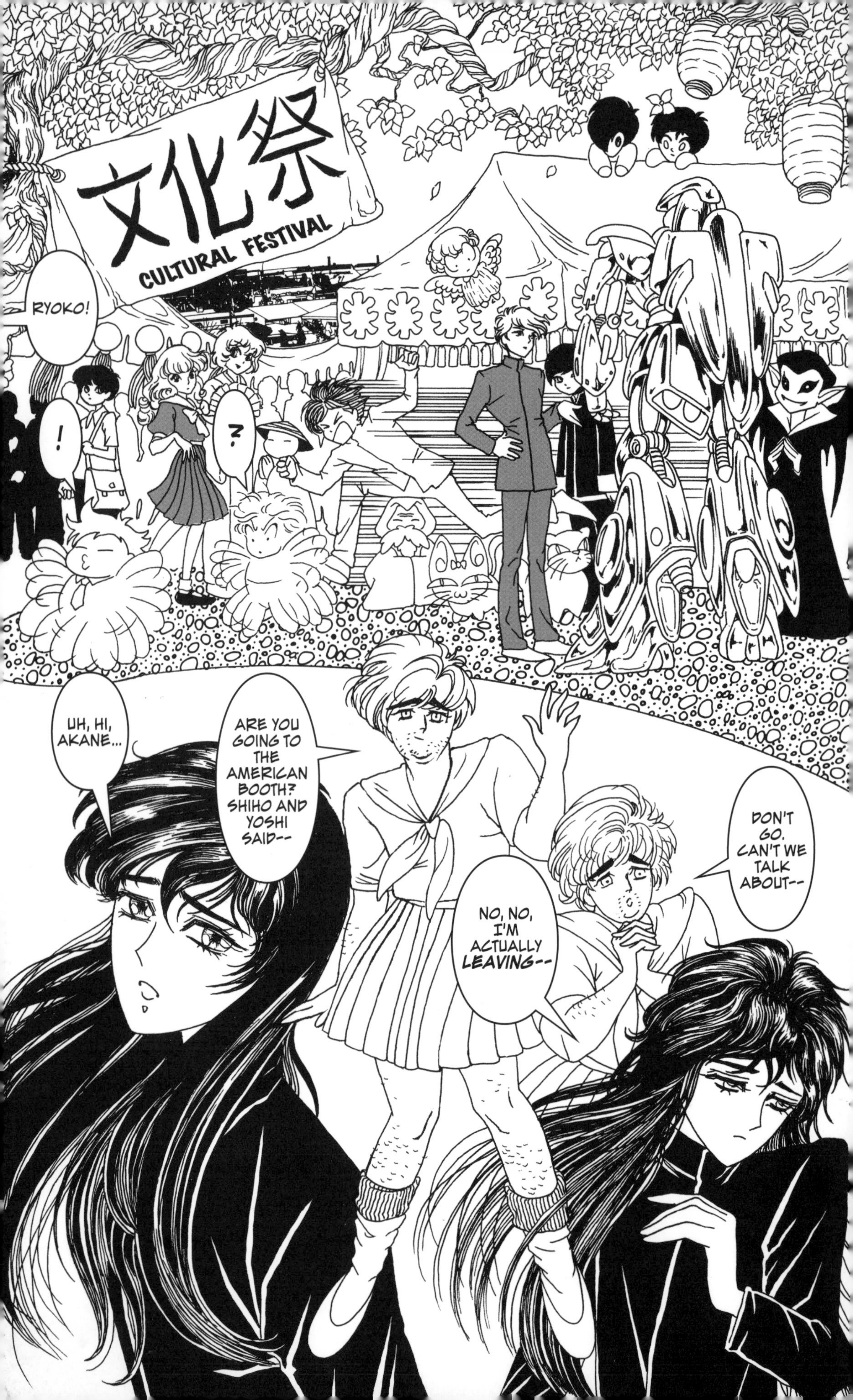
文化祭
CULTURAL FESTIVAL
RYOKO!
!
?
UH, HI, AKANE...
ARE YOU GOING TO THE AMERICAN BOOTH? SHIHO AND YOSHI SAID--
NO, NO, I'M ACTUALLY **LEAVING**--
DON'T GO. CAN'T WE TALK ABOUT--

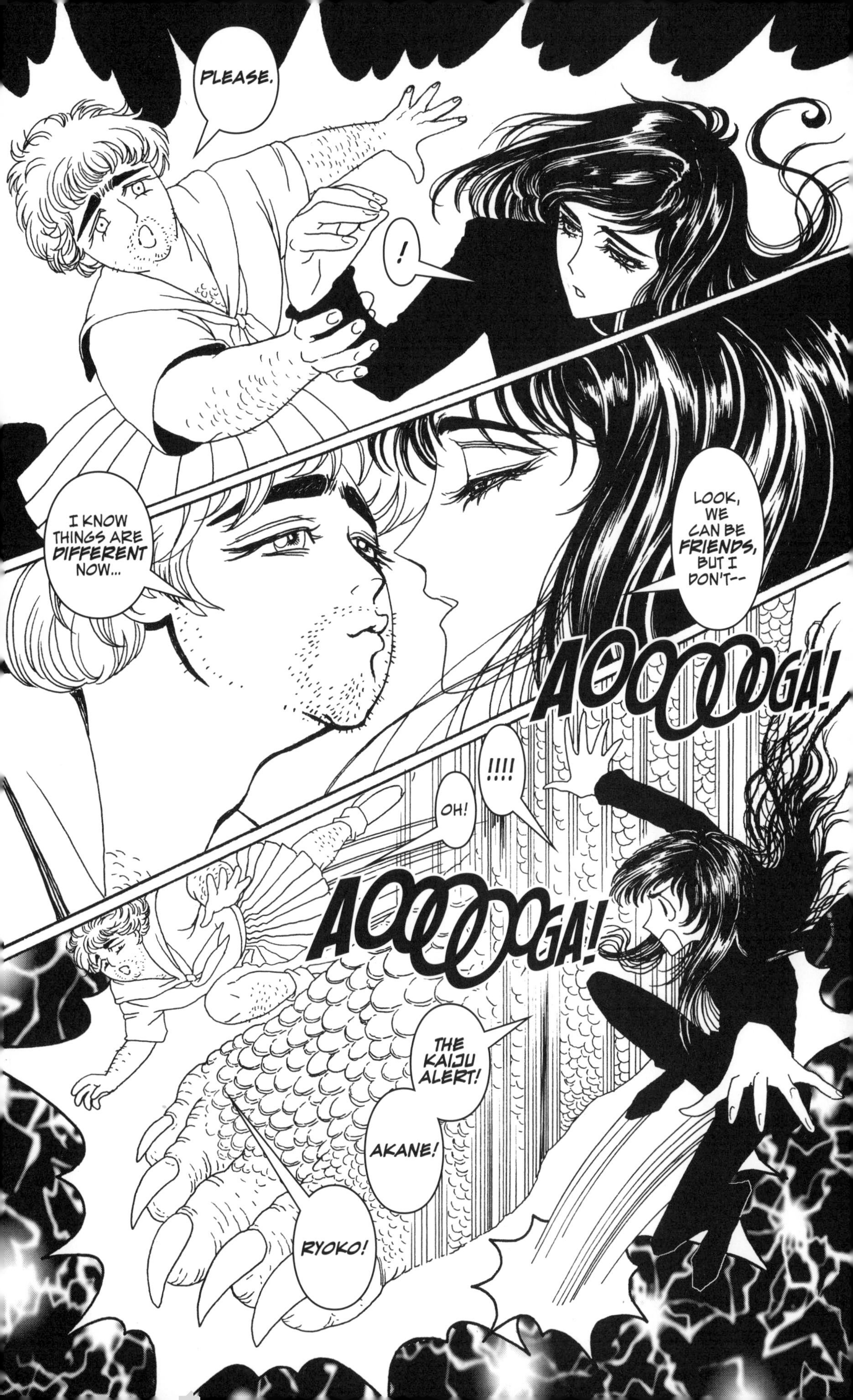
PLEASE.
!
I KNOW THINGS ARE DIFFERENT NOW...
LOOK, WE CAN BE FRIENDS, BUT I DON'T--
AOOOOOGA!
OH!
!!!!
AOOOOGA!
THE KAIJU ALERT!
AKANE!
RYOKO!

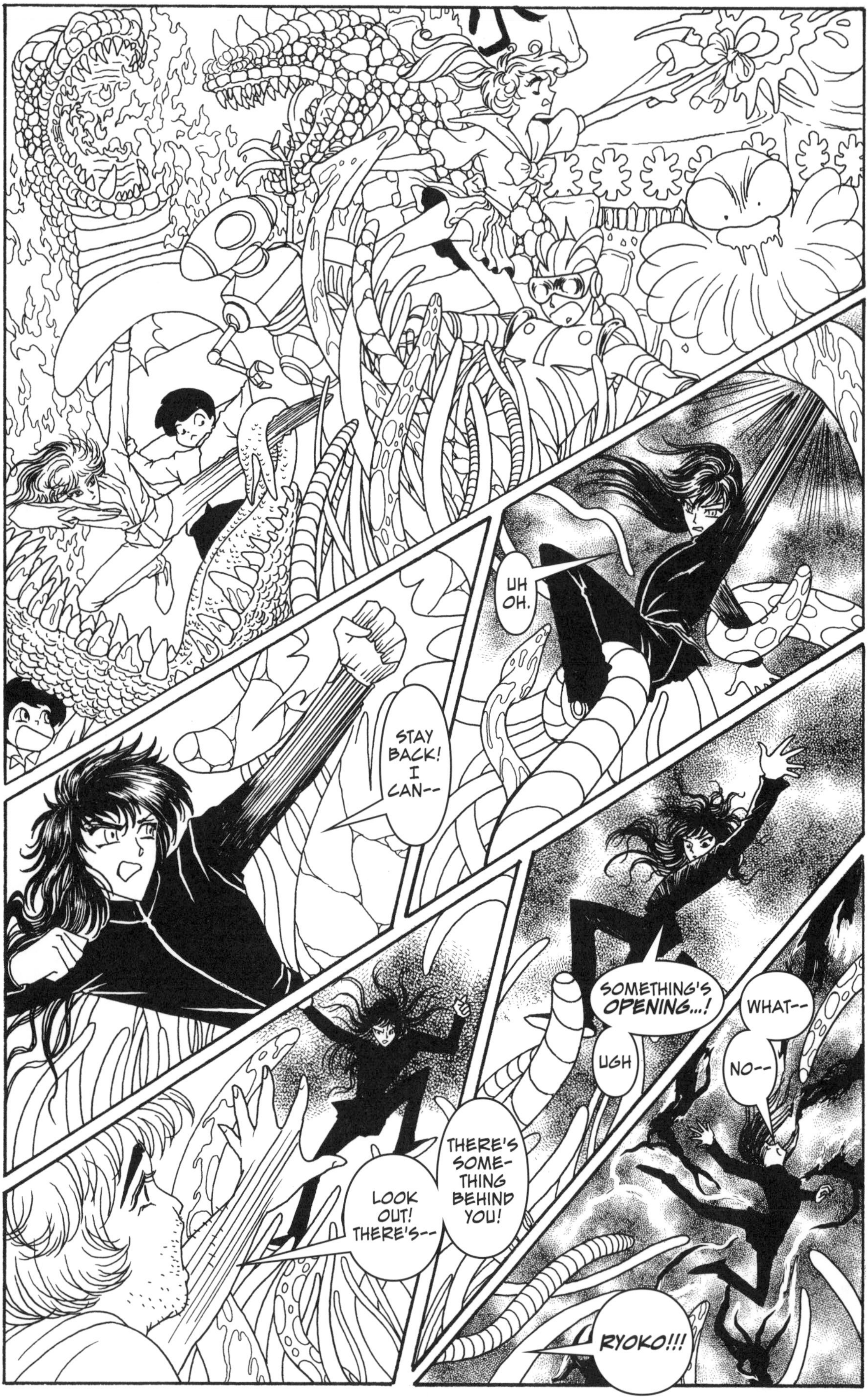
STAY BACK! I CAN--
UH OH.
LOOK OUT! THERE'S--
THERE'S SOMETHING BEHIND YOU!
SOMETHING'S **OPENING**...!
UGH
WHAT--
NO--
RYOKO!!!

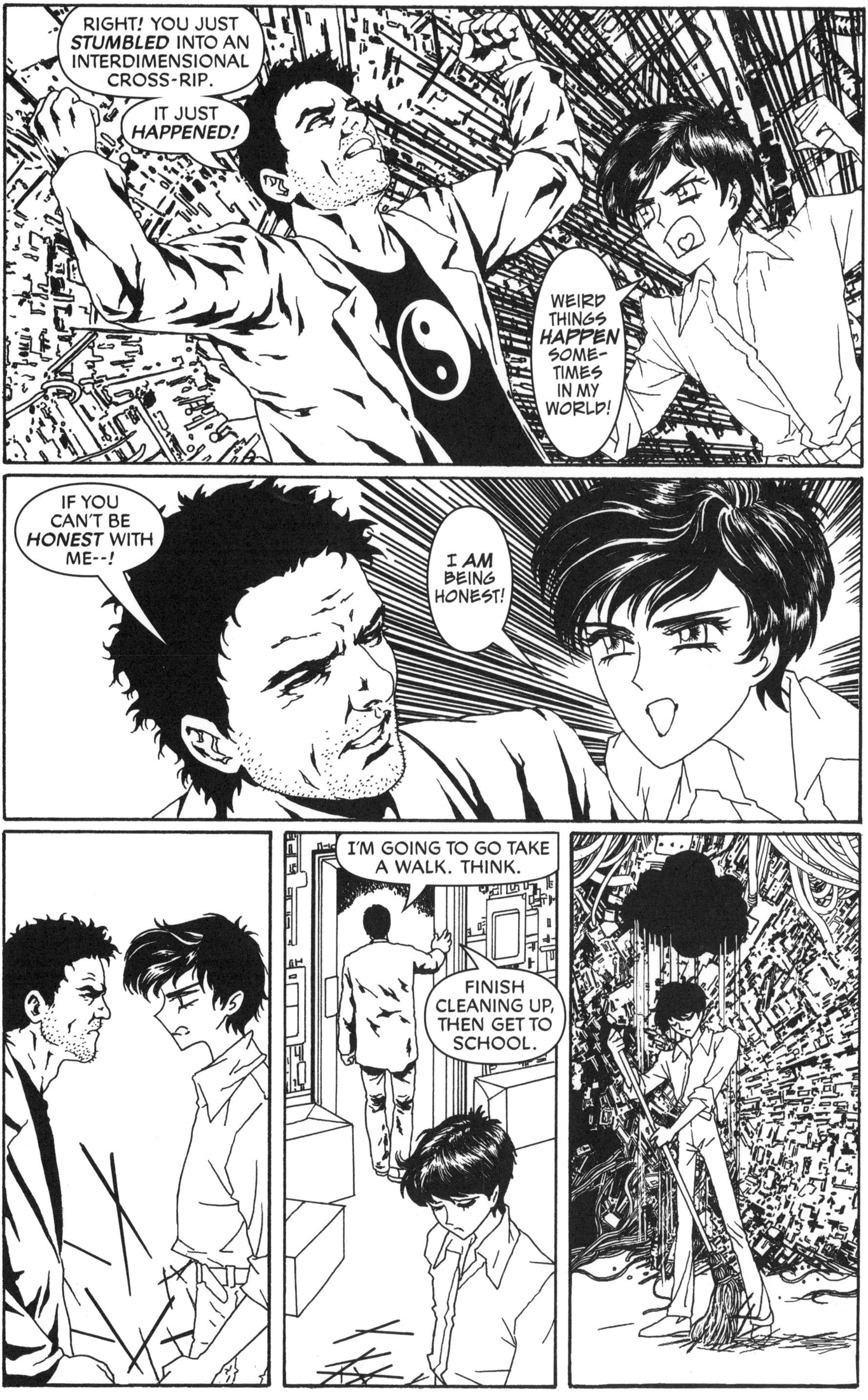
RIGHT! YOU JUST STUMBLED INTO AN INTERDIMENSIONAL CROSS-RIP.
IT JUST HAPPENED!
WEIRD THINGS HAPPEN SOME-TIMES IN MY WORLD!
IF YOU CAN'T BE HONEST WITH ME--!
I AM BEING HONEST!
I'M GOING TO GO TAKE A WALK. THINK.
FINISH CLEANING UP, THEN GET TO SCHOOL.

CHAPTER 6

MARISSA: *Oh my God! Oh my GOD!*

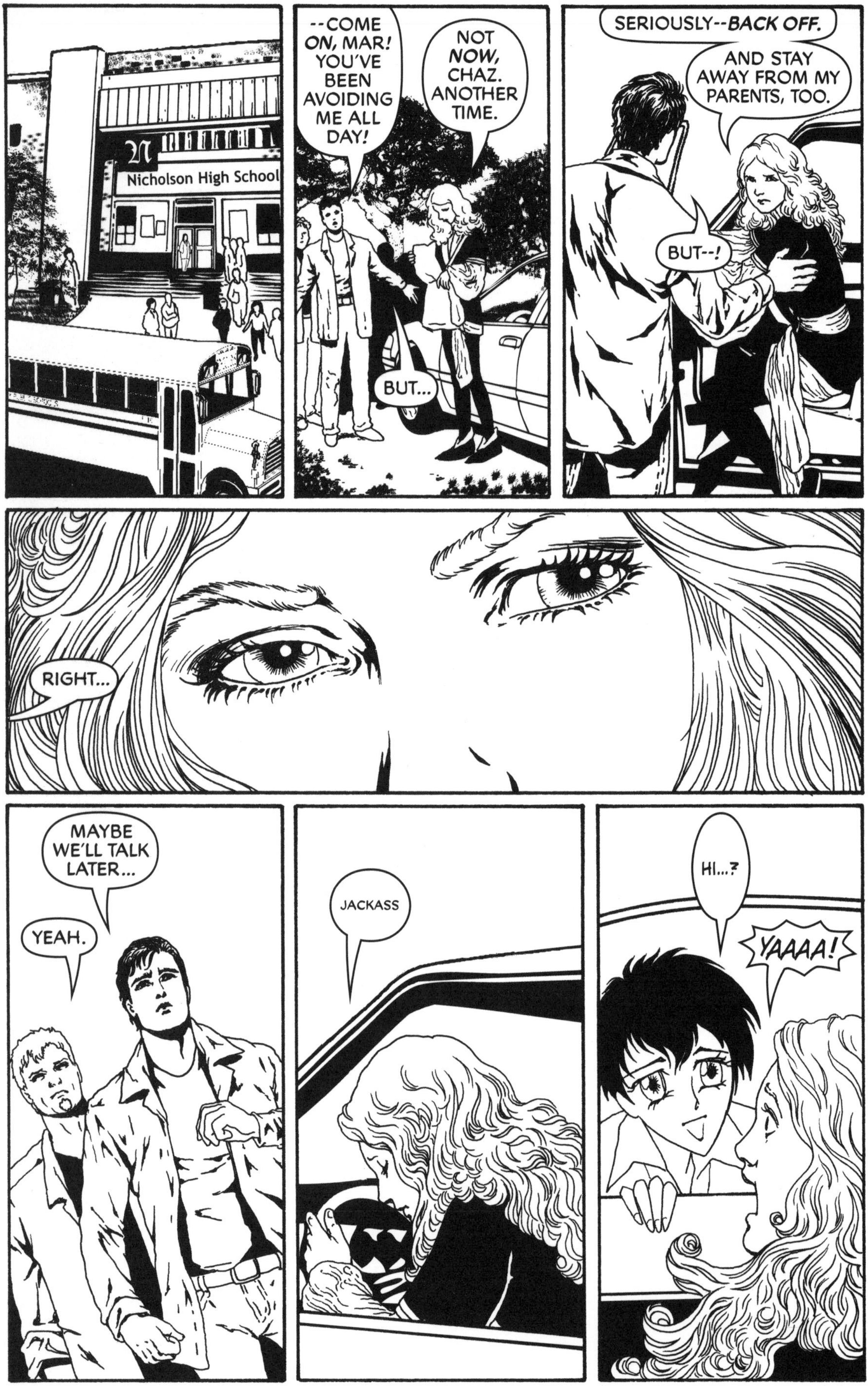
Nicholson High School
--COME ON, MAR! YOU'VE BEEN AVOIDING ME ALL DAY!
NOT NOW, CHAZ. ANOTHER TIME.
BUT...
SERIOUSLY--BACK OFF.
AND STAY AWAY FROM MY PARENTS, TOO.
BUT--!
RIGHT...
MAYBE WE'LL TALK LATER...
YEAH.
JACKASS
HI...?
YAAAA!

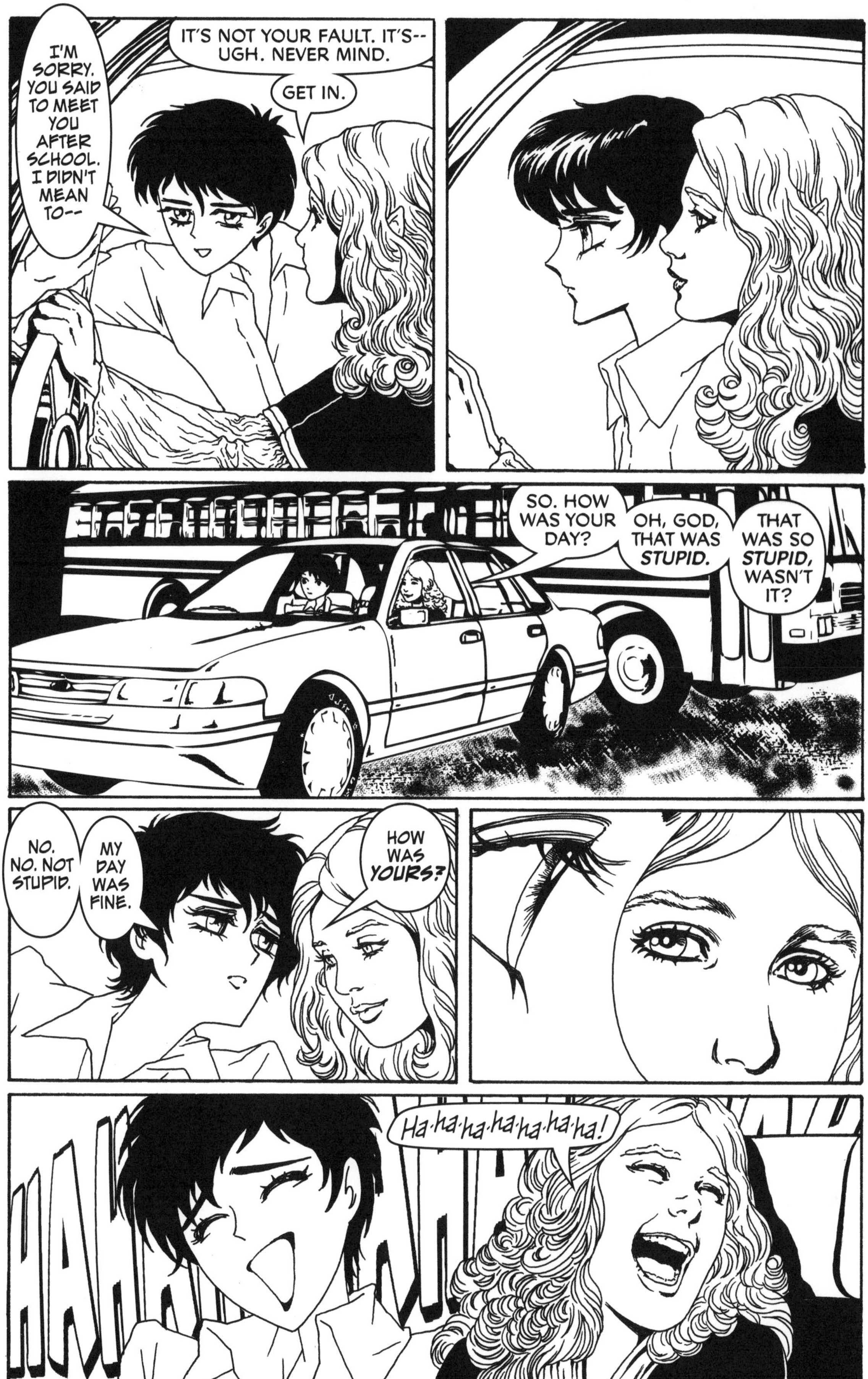
I'M SORRY. YOU SAID TO MEET YOU AFTER SCHOOL. I DIDN'T MEAN TO--
IT'S NOT YOUR FAULT. IT'S-- UGH. NEVER MIND.
GET IN.
SO. HOW WAS YOUR DAY?
OH, GOD, THAT WAS *STUPID.*
THAT WAS SO *STUPID,* WASN'T IT?
NO. NO. NOT STUPID.
MY DAY WAS FINE.
HOW WAS *YOURS?*
Ha-ha-ha-ha-ha-ha-ha!
HAHA

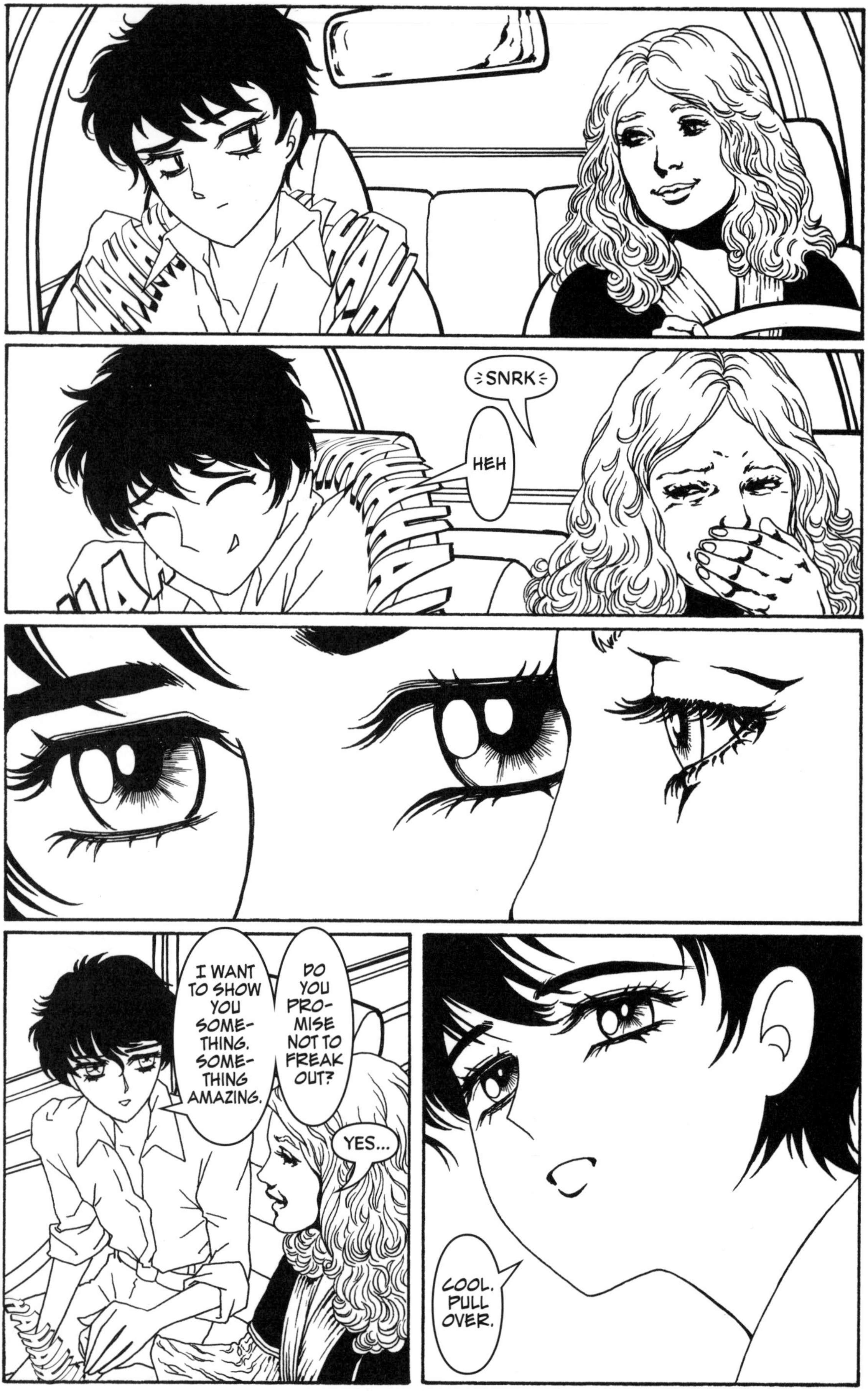
SNRK
HEH
I WANT TO SHOW YOU SOME-THING. SOME-THING AMAZING.
DO YOU PRO-MISE NOT TO FREAK OUT?
YES...
COOL. PULL OVER.

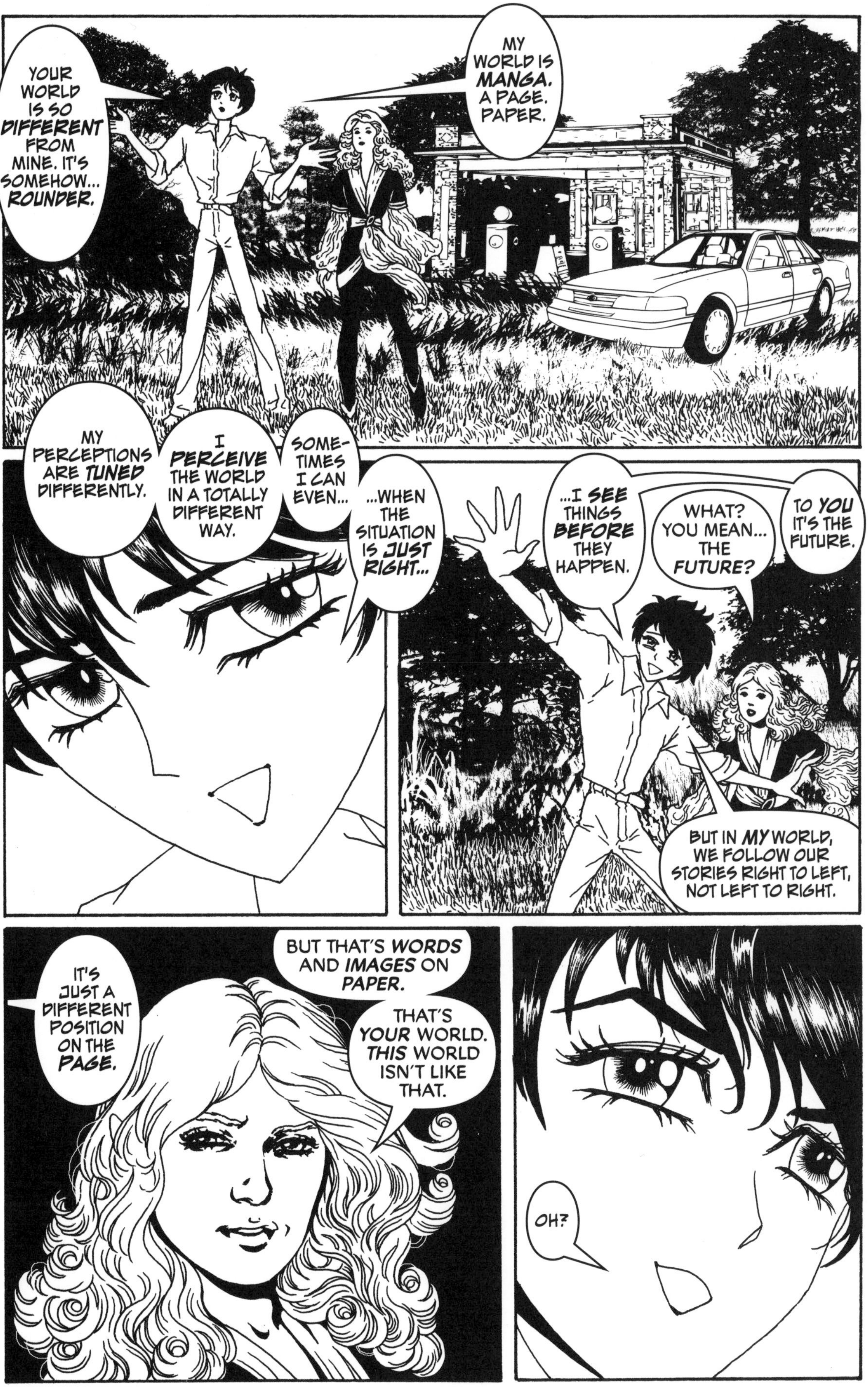
YOUR WORLD IS SO DIFFERENT FROM MINE. IT'S SOMEHOW... ROUNDER.
MY WORLD IS MANGA. A PAGE. PAPER.
MY PERCEPTIONS ARE TUNED DIFFERENTLY.
I PERCEIVE THE WORLD IN A TOTALLY DIFFERENT WAY.
SOME-TIMES I CAN EVEN...
...WHEN THE SITUATION IS JUST RIGHT...
...I SEE THINGS BEFORE THEY HAPPEN.
WHAT? YOU MEAN... THE FUTURE?
TO YOU IT'S THE FUTURE.
BUT IN MY WORLD, WE FOLLOW OUR STORIES RIGHT TO LEFT, NOT LEFT TO RIGHT.
IT'S JUST A DIFFERENT POSITION ON THE PAGE.
BUT THAT'S WORDS AND IMAGES ON PAPER.
THAT'S YOUR WORLD. THIS WORLD ISN'T LIKE THAT.
OH?

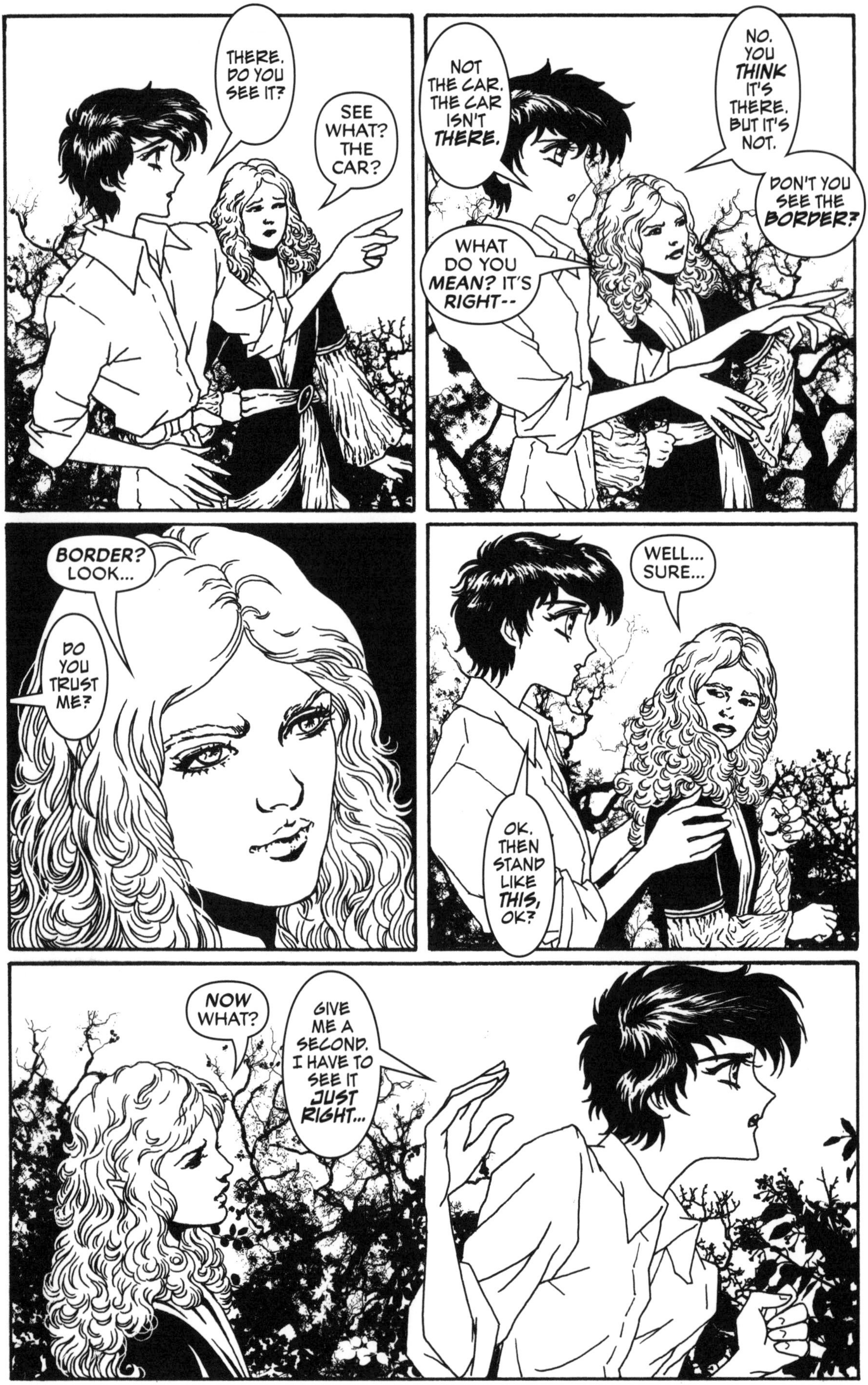
THERE. DO YOU SEE IT?
SEE WHAT? THE CAR?
NOT THE CAR. THE CAR ISN'T *THERE.*
WHAT DO YOU *MEAN?* IT'S *RIGHT--*
NO. YOU *THINK* IT'S THERE. BUT IT'S NOT.
DON'T YOU SEE THE *BORDER?*
BORDER? LOOK...
DO YOU TRUST ME?
WELL... SURE...
OK. THEN STAND LIKE *THIS,* OK?
NOW WHAT?
GIVE ME A SECOND. I HAVE TO SEE IT *JUST RIGHT...*

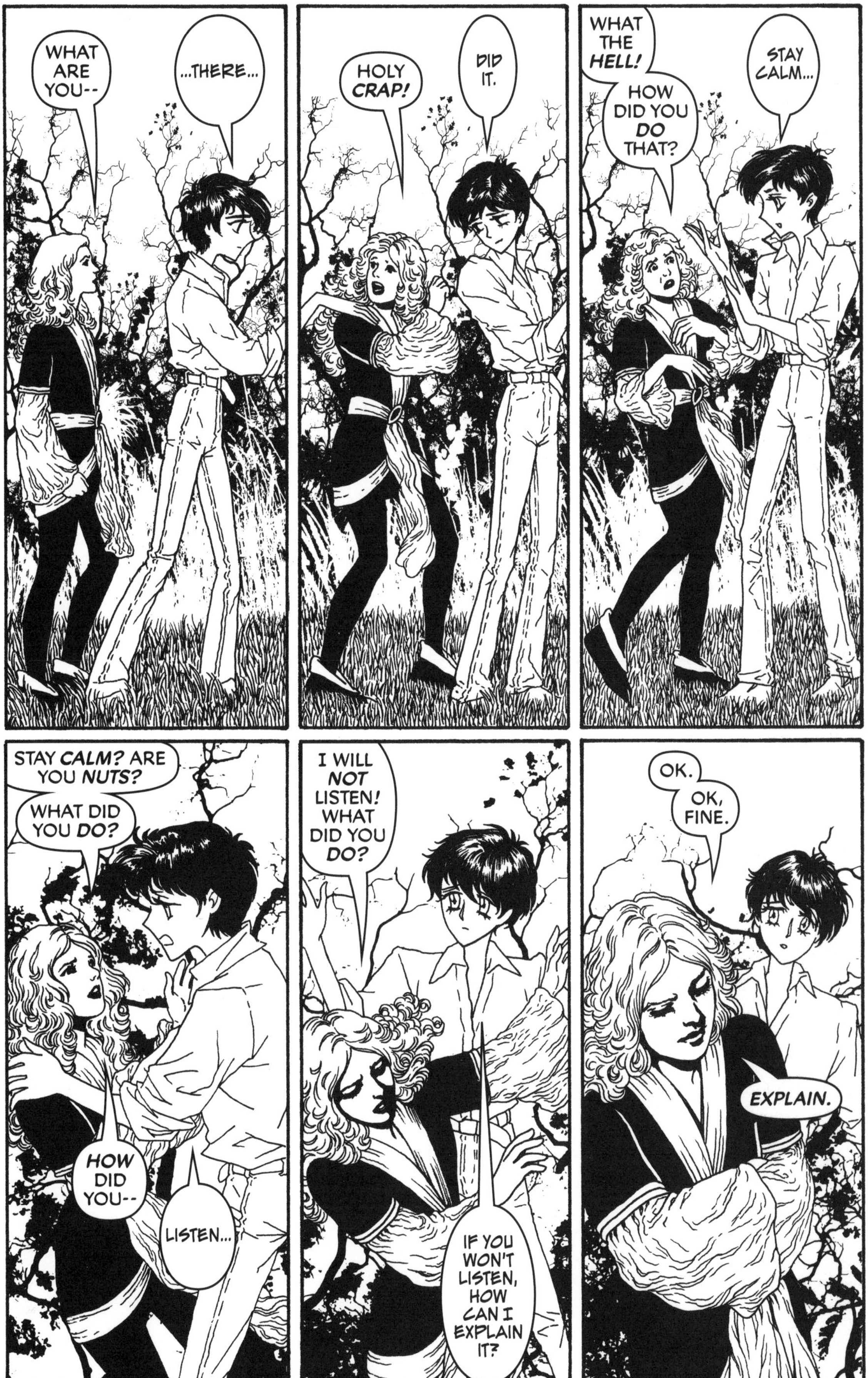
WHAT ARE YOU--
...THERE...
HOLY *CRAP!*
DID IT.
WHAT THE *HELL!*
HOW DID YOU *DO* THAT?
STAY CALM...
STAY *CALM?* ARE YOU *NUTS?*
WHAT DID YOU *DO?*
HOW DID YOU--
LISTEN...
I WILL *NOT* LISTEN! WHAT DID YOU *DO?*
IF YOU WON'T LISTEN, HOW CAN I EXPLAIN IT?
OK.
OK, FINE.
EXPLAIN.

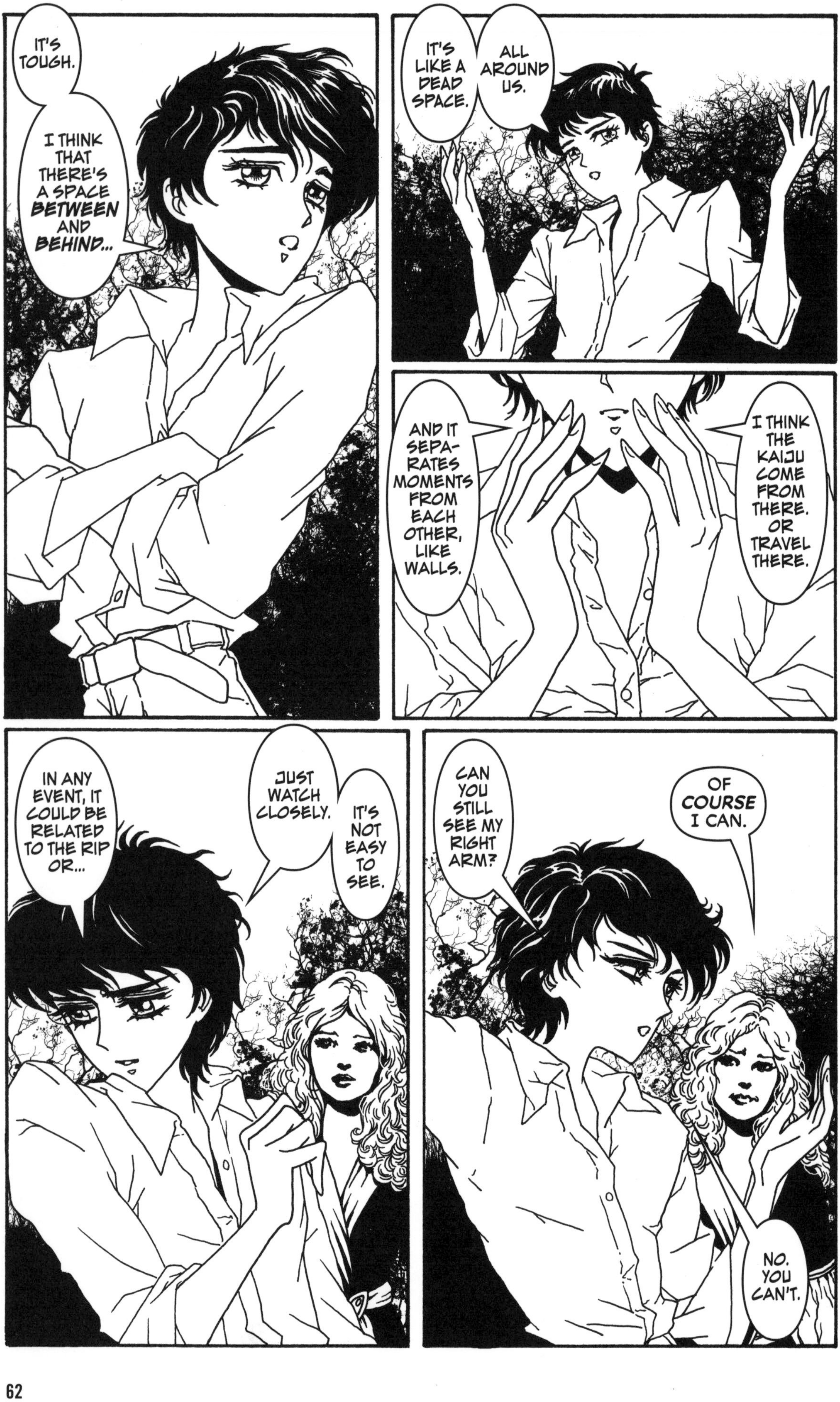
IT'S TOUGH.
I THINK THAT THERE'S A SPACE **BETWEEN** AND **BEHIND**...
IT'S LIKE A DEAD SPACE.
ALL AROUND US.
AND IT SEPA-RATES MOMENTS FROM EACH OTHER, LIKE WALLS.
I THINK THE KAIJU COME FROM THERE. OR TRAVEL THERE.
IN ANY EVENT, IT COULD BE RELATED TO THE RIP OR...
JUST WATCH CLOSELY.
IT'S NOT EASY TO SEE.
CAN YOU STILL SEE MY RIGHT ARM?
OF **COURSE** I CAN.
NO. YOU CAN'T.

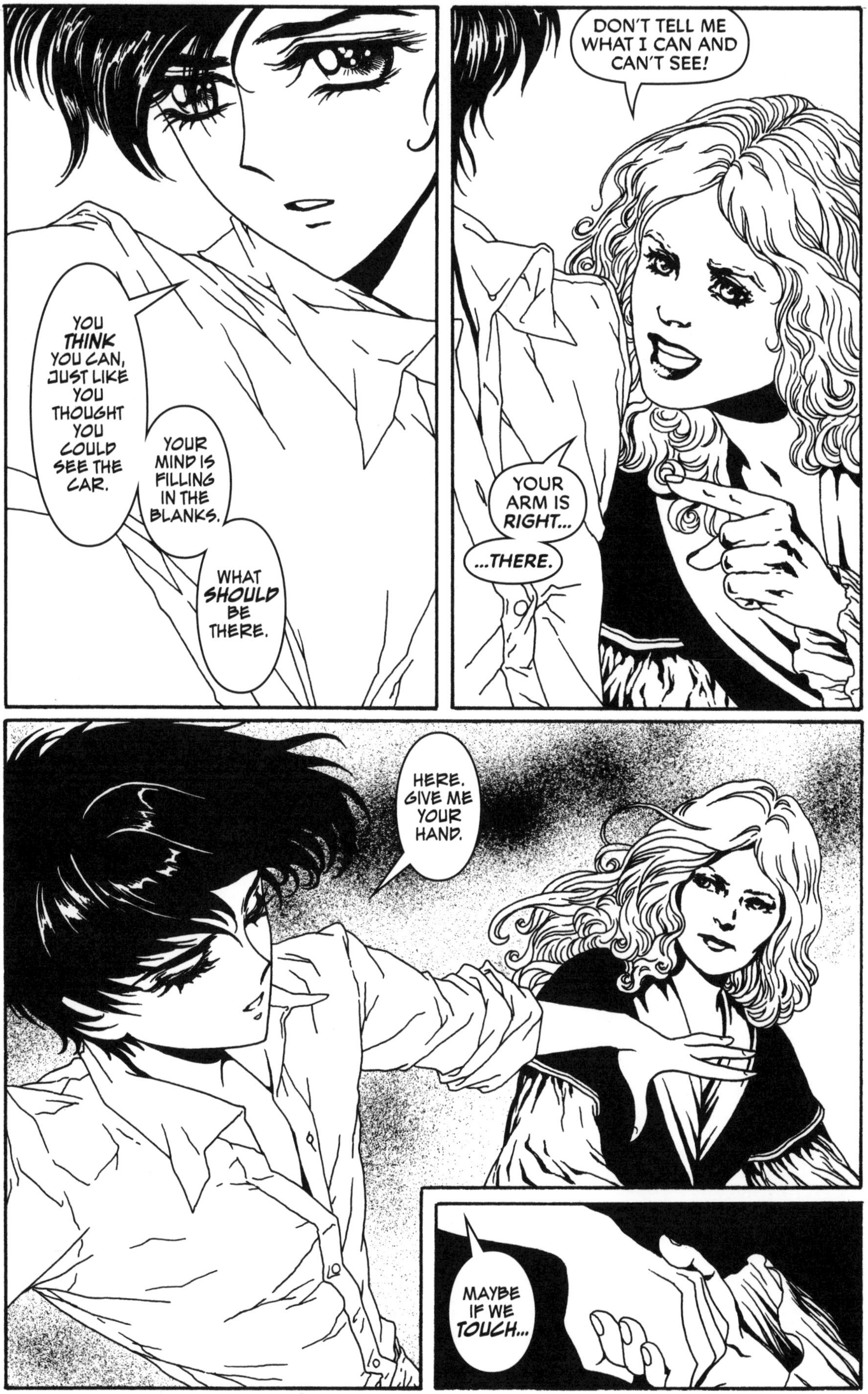
YOU *THINK* YOU CAN, JUST LIKE YOU THOUGHT YOU COULD SEE THE CAR.
YOUR MIND IS FILLING IN THE BLANKS.
WHAT *SHOULD* BE THERE.
DON'T TELL ME WHAT I CAN AND CAN'T SEE!
YOUR ARM IS *RIGHT*...
...*THERE.*
HERE. GIVE ME YOUR HAND.
MAYBE IF WE *TOUCH*...

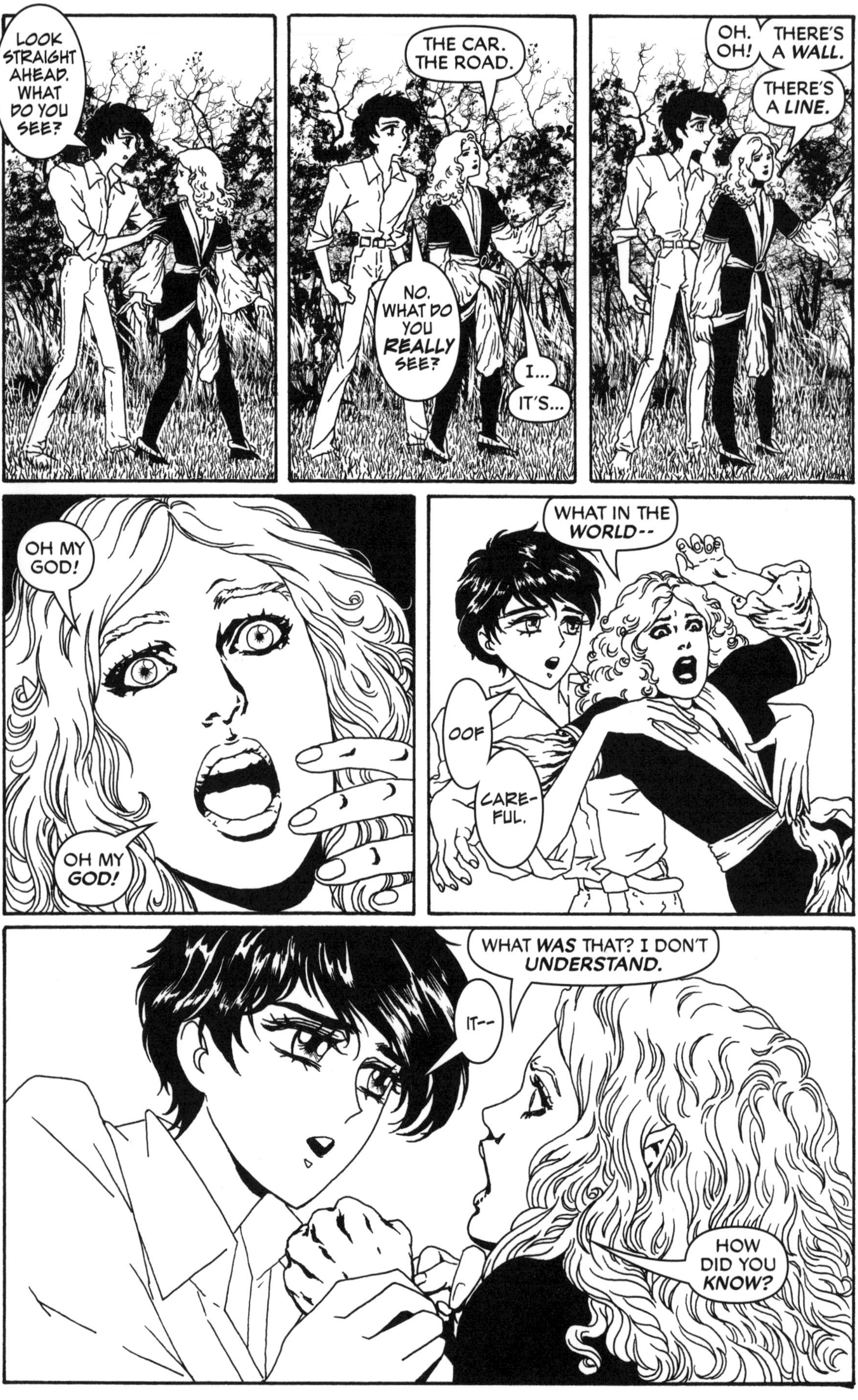
LOOK STRAIGHT AHEAD. WHAT DO YOU SEE?
THE CAR. THE ROAD.
NO. WHAT DO YOU *REALLY* SEE?
I...
IT'S...
OH. OH!
THERE'S A *WALL.*
THERE'S A *LINE.*
OH MY GOD!
OH MY *GOD!*
WHAT IN THE *WORLD--*
OOF
OOF
CAREFUL.
WHAT *WAS* THAT? I DON'T *UNDERSTAND.*
IT--
HOW DID YOU *KNOW?*

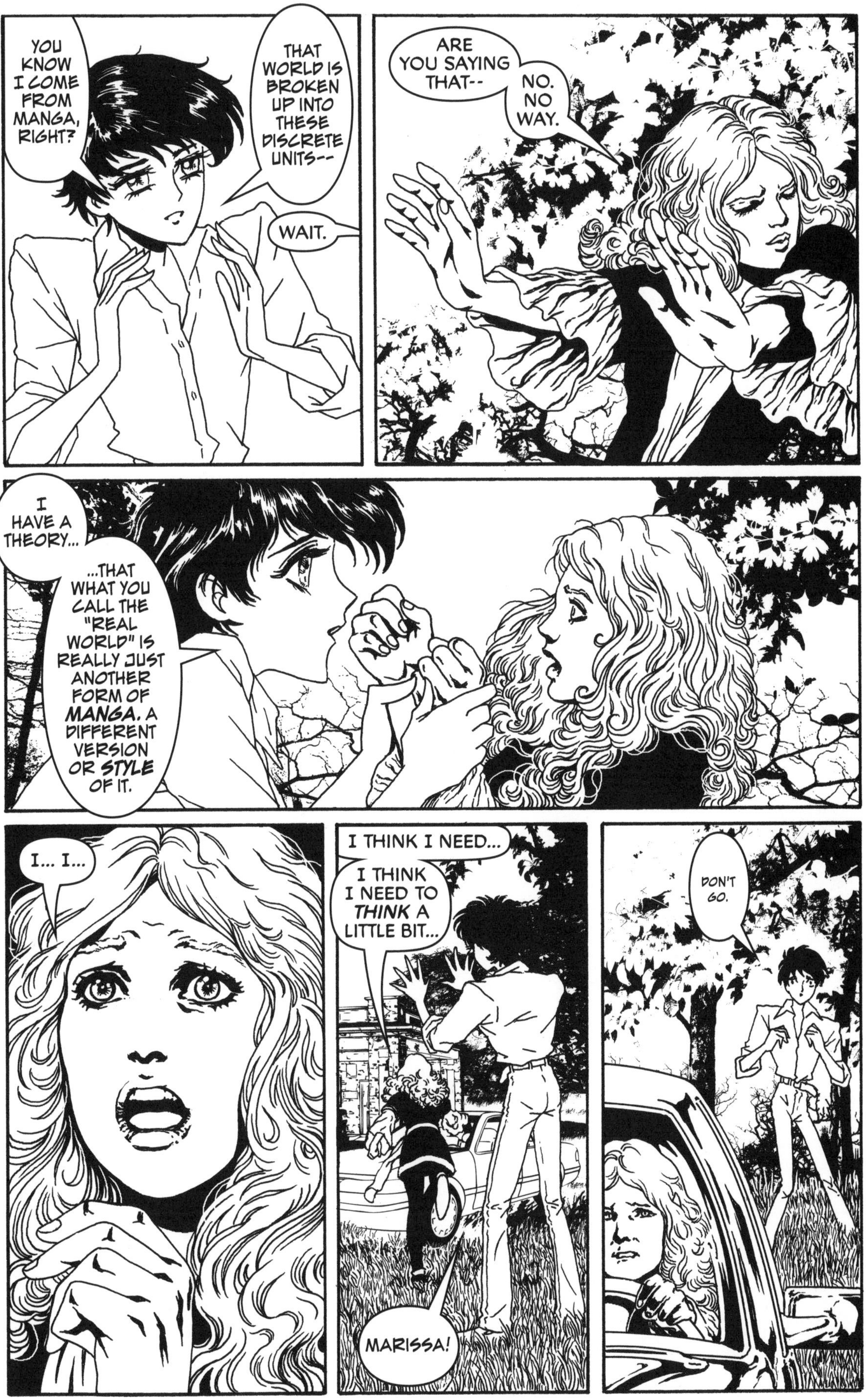
YOU KNOW I COME FROM MANGA, RIGHT?
THAT WORLD IS BROKEN UP INTO THESE DISCRETE UNITS--
WAIT.
ARE YOU SAYING THAT--
NO. NO WAY.
I HAVE A THEORY...
...THAT WHAT YOU CALL THE "REAL WORLD" IS REALLY JUST ANOTHER FORM OF **MANGA.** A DIFFERENT VERSION OR **STYLE** OF IT.
I... I...
I THINK I NEED...
I THINK I NEED TO *THINK* A LITTLE BIT...
MARISSA!
DON'T GO.

CHAPTER 7

MARISSA: *You've taught me a lot already.*

Show me how to slow down.

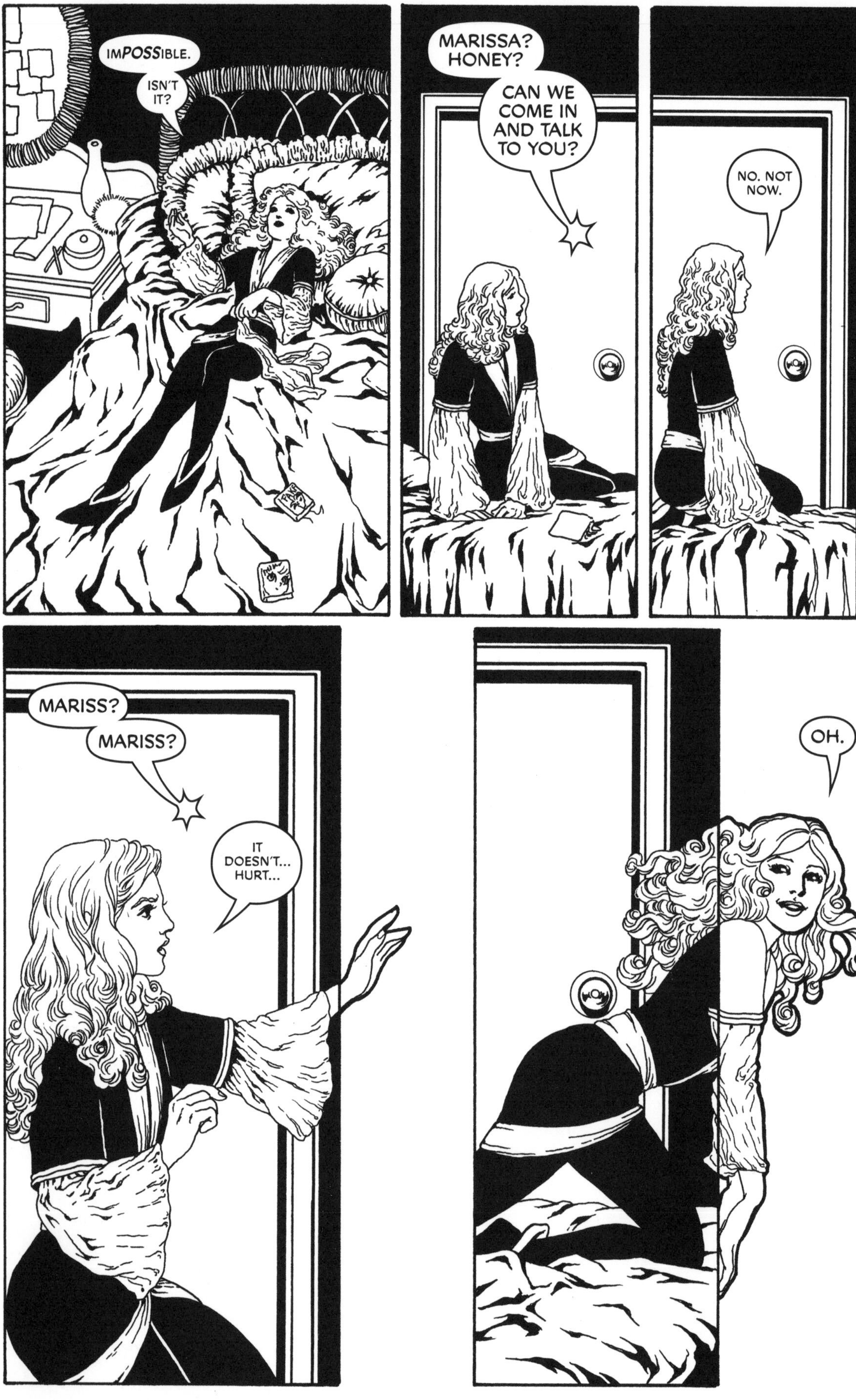

imPOSSible.
ISN'T IT?
MARISSA? HONEY?
CAN WE COME IN AND TALK TO YOU?
NO. NOT NOW.
MARISS?
MARISS?
IT DOESN'T... HURT...
OH.

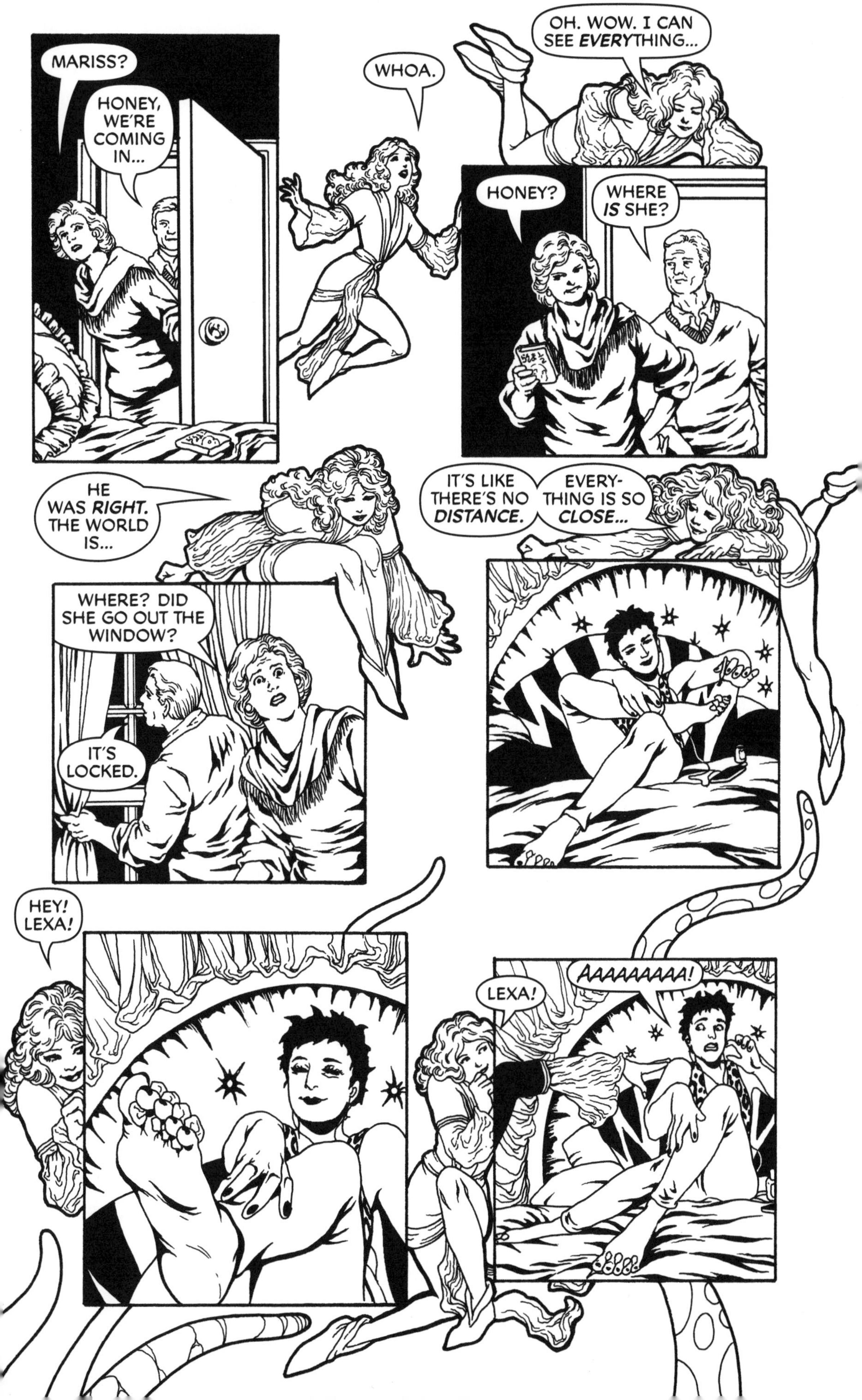
MARISS?
HONEY, WE'RE COMING IN...
WHOA.
OH. WOW. I CAN SEE *EVERY*THING...
HONEY?
WHERE *IS* SHE?
HE WAS *RIGHT*. THE WORLD IS...
WHERE? DID SHE GO OUT THE WINDOW?
IT'S LOCKED.
IT'S LIKE THERE'S NO *DISTANCE*.
EVERY-THING IS SO *CLOSE*...
HEY! LEXA!
LEXA!
AAAAAAAAA!

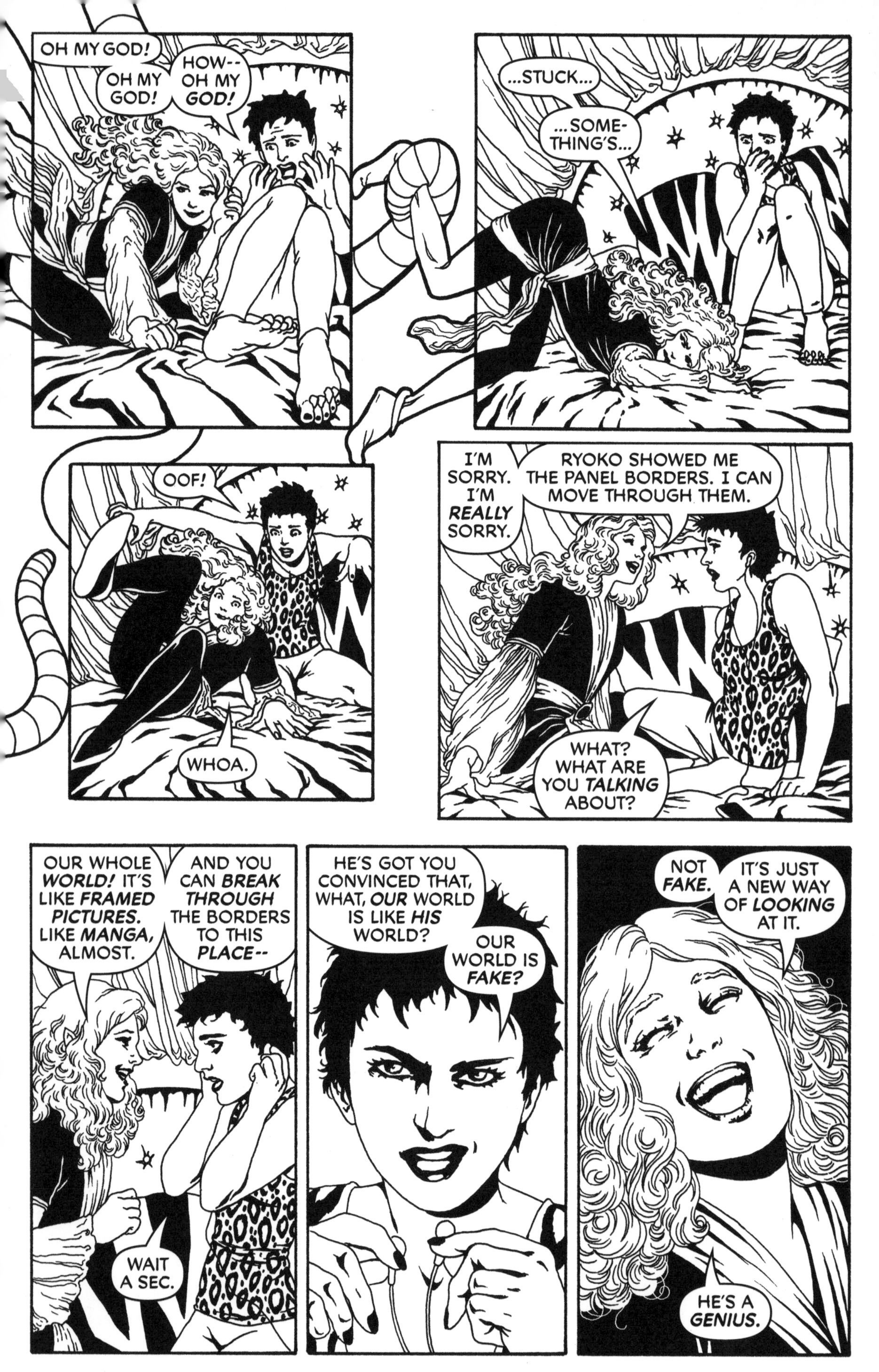
OH MY GOD!
OH MY GOD!
HOW-- OH MY GOD!
...STUCK...
...SOME-THING'S...
OOF!
WHOA.
I'M SORRY. I'M REALLY SORRY.
RYOKO SHOWED ME THE PANEL BORDERS. I CAN MOVE THROUGH THEM.
WHAT? WHAT ARE YOU TALKING ABOUT?
OUR WHOLE WORLD! IT'S LIKE FRAMED PICTURES. LIKE MANGA, ALMOST.
AND YOU CAN BREAK THROUGH THE BORDERS TO THIS PLACE--
WAIT A SEC.
HE'S GOT YOU CONVINCED THAT, WHAT, OUR WORLD IS LIKE HIS WORLD?
OUR WORLD IS FAKE?
NOT FAKE.
IT'S JUST A NEW WAY OF LOOKING AT IT.
HE'S A GENIUS.

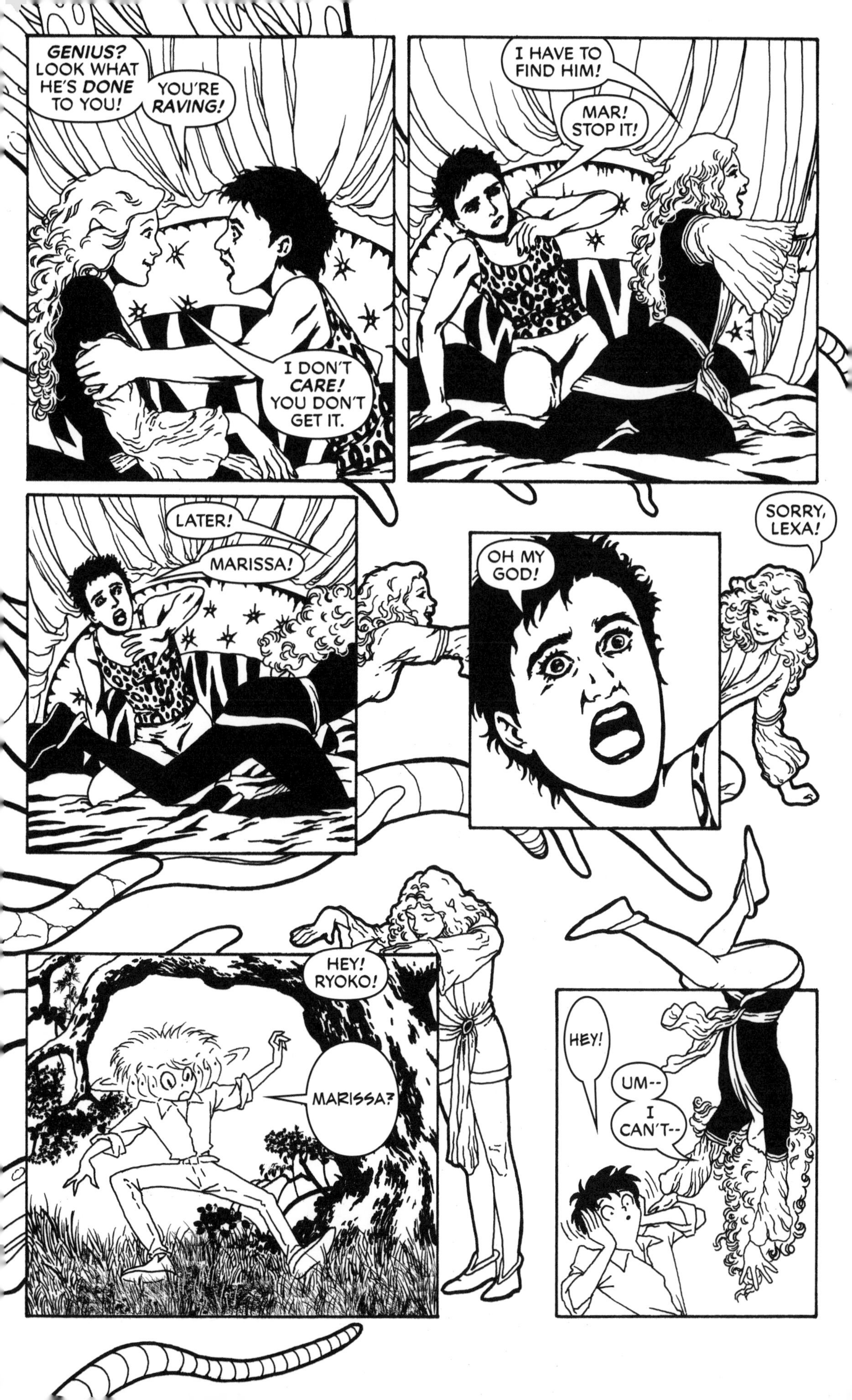
GENIUS? LOOK WHAT HE'S DONE TO YOU!
YOU'RE RAVING!
I DON'T CARE! YOU DON'T GET IT.
I HAVE TO FIND HIM!
MAR! STOP IT!
LATER!
MARISSA!
OH MY GOD!
SORRY, LEXA!
HEY! RYOKO!
MARISSA?
HEY!
UM--
I CAN'T--

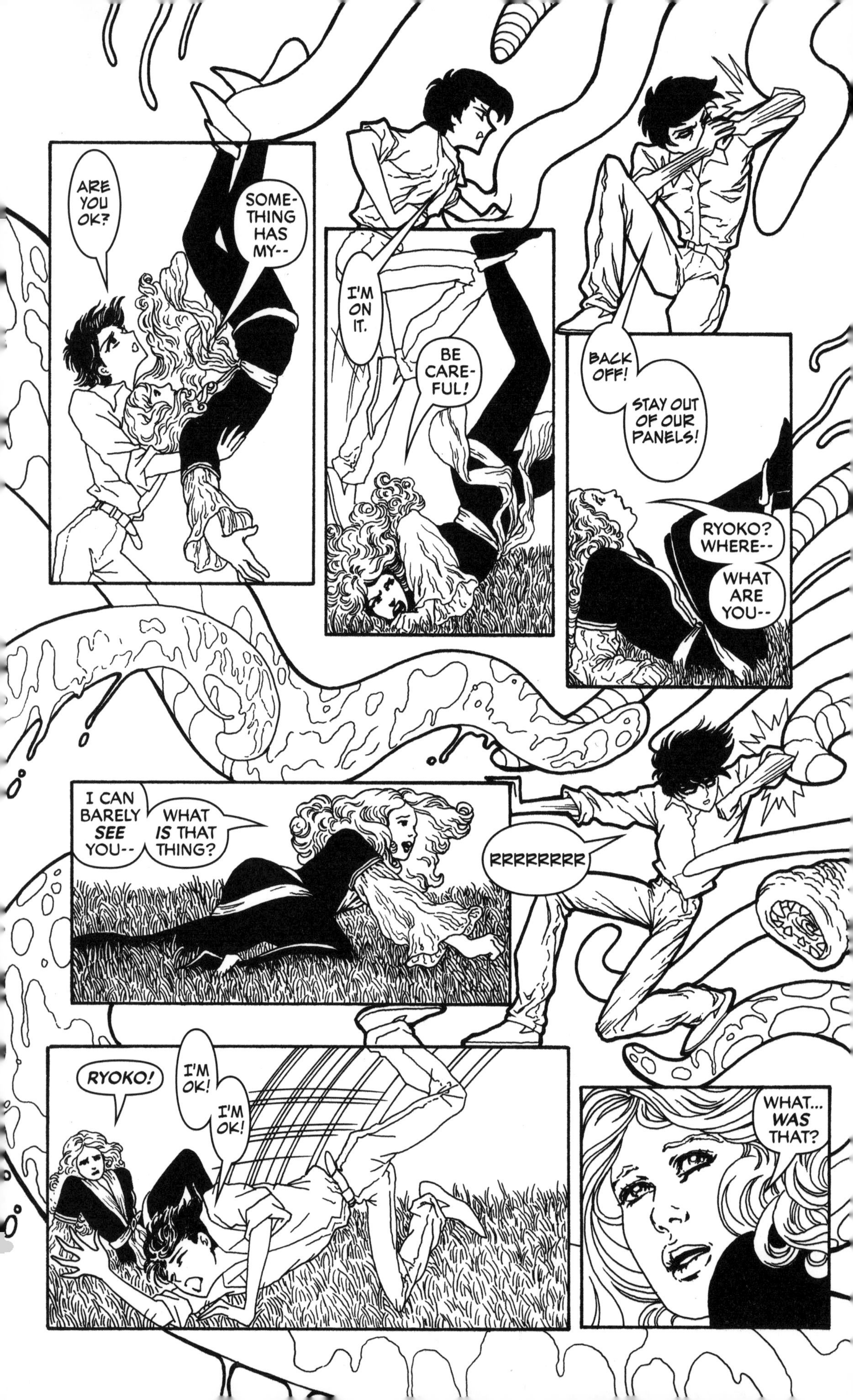
ARE YOU OK?
SOME-THING HAS MY--
I'M ON IT.
BE CARE-FUL!
BACK OFF!
STAY OUT OF OUR PANELS!
RYOKO? WHERE--
WHAT ARE YOU--
I CAN BARELY *SEE* YOU--
WHAT *IS* THAT THING?
RRRRRRRR
RYOKO!
I'M OK!
I'M OK!
WHAT... *WAS* THAT?

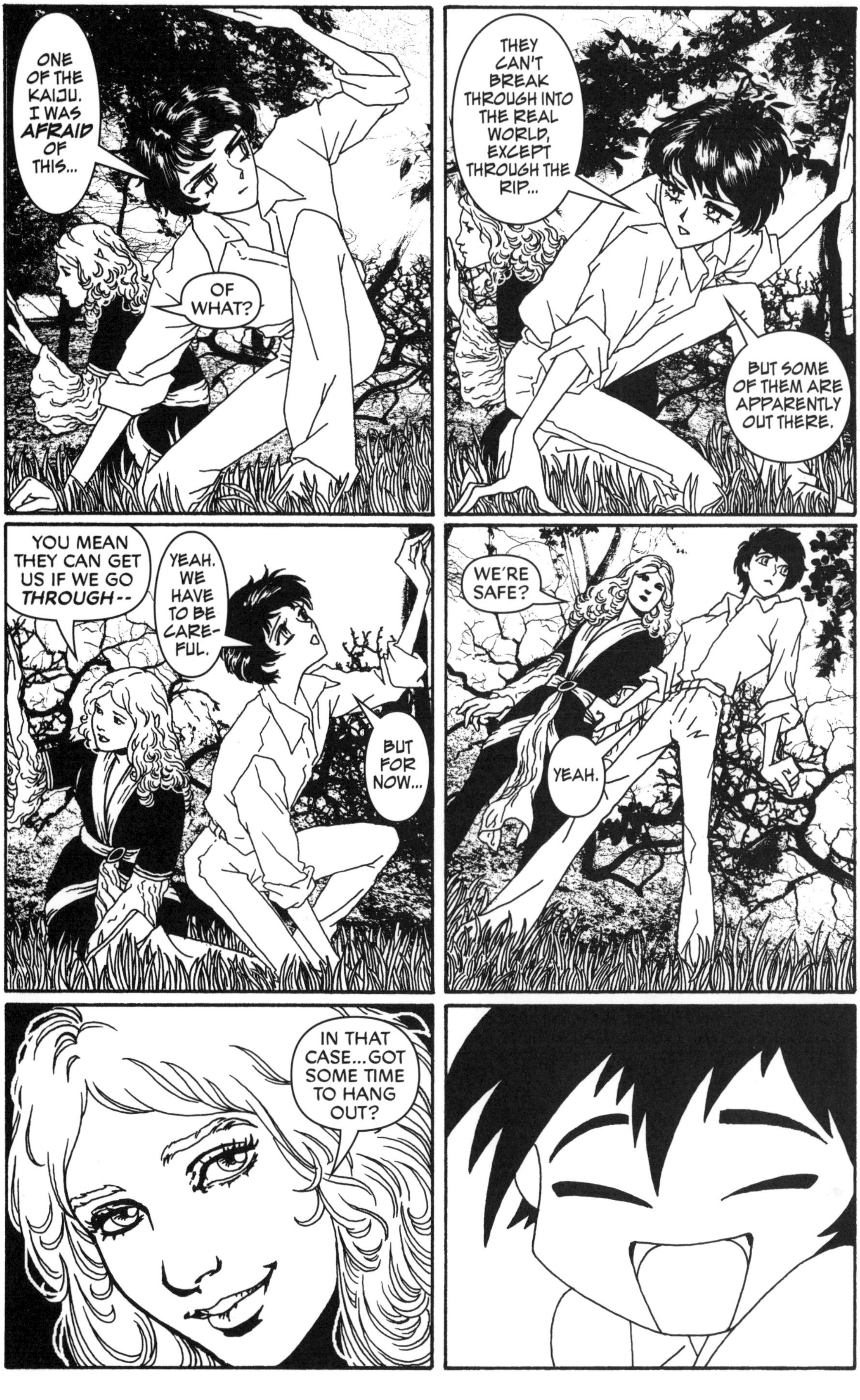
ONE OF THE KAIJU. I WAS *AFRAID* OF THIS...
OF WHAT?
THEY CAN'T BREAK THROUGH INTO THE REAL WORLD, EXCEPT THROUGH THE RIP...
BUT SOME OF THEM ARE APPARENTLY OUT THERE.
YOU MEAN THEY CAN GET US IF WE GO *THROUGH*--
YEAH. WE HAVE TO BE CARE-FUL.
BUT FOR NOW...
WE'RE SAFE?
YEAH.
IN THAT CASE...GOT SOME TIME TO HANG OUT?

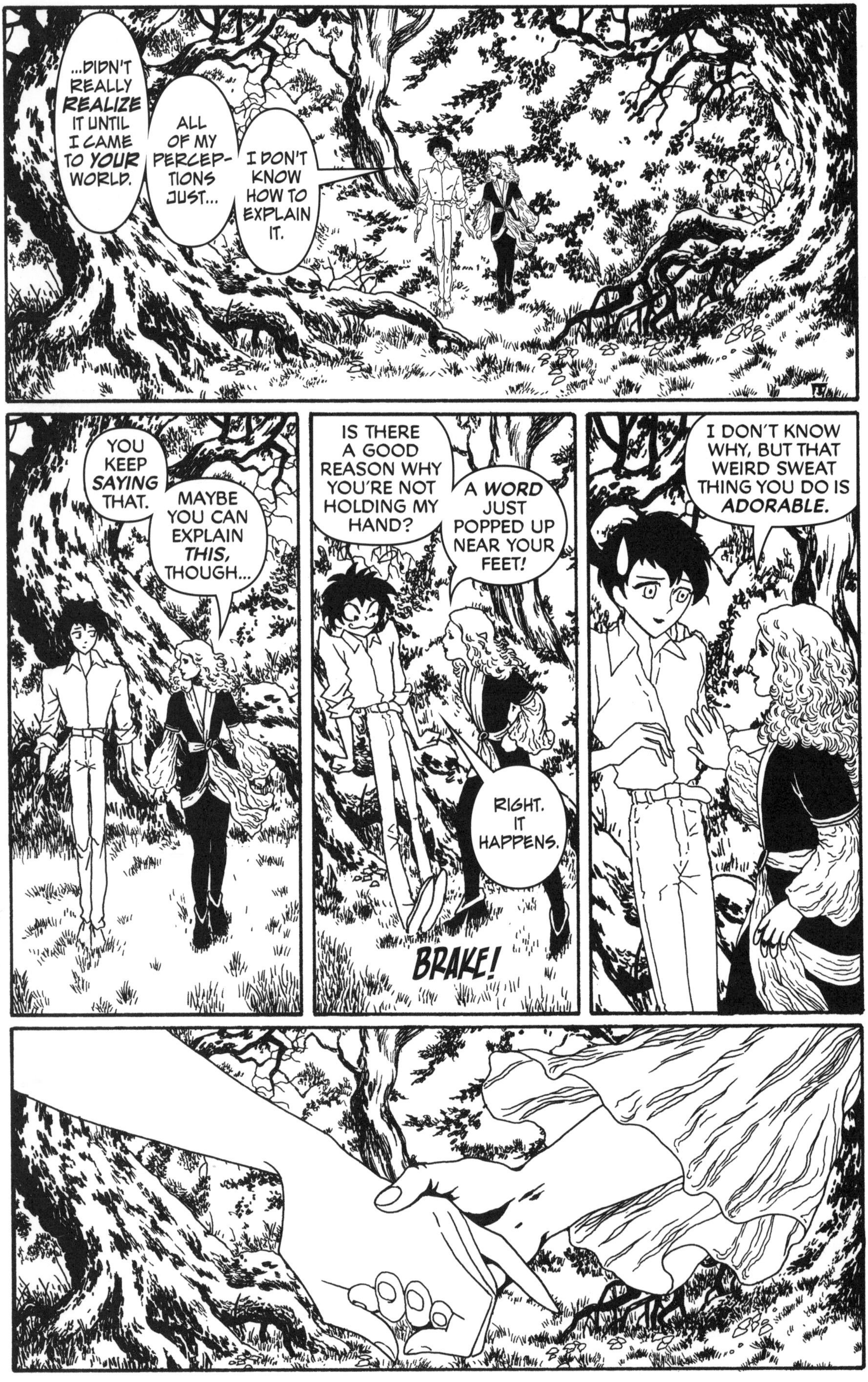
...DIDN'T REALLY **REALIZE** IT UNTIL I CAME TO **YOUR** WORLD.
ALL OF MY PERCEPTIONS JUST...
I DON'T KNOW HOW TO EXPLAIN IT.
YOU KEEP ***SAYING*** THAT.
MAYBE YOU CAN EXPLAIN ***THIS,*** THOUGH...
IS THERE A GOOD REASON WHY YOU'RE NOT HOLDING MY HAND?
A ***WORD*** JUST POPPED UP NEAR YOUR FEET!
RIGHT. IT HAPPENS.
BRAKE!
I DON'T KNOW WHY, BUT THAT WEIRD SWEAT THING YOU DO IS ***ADORABLE.***

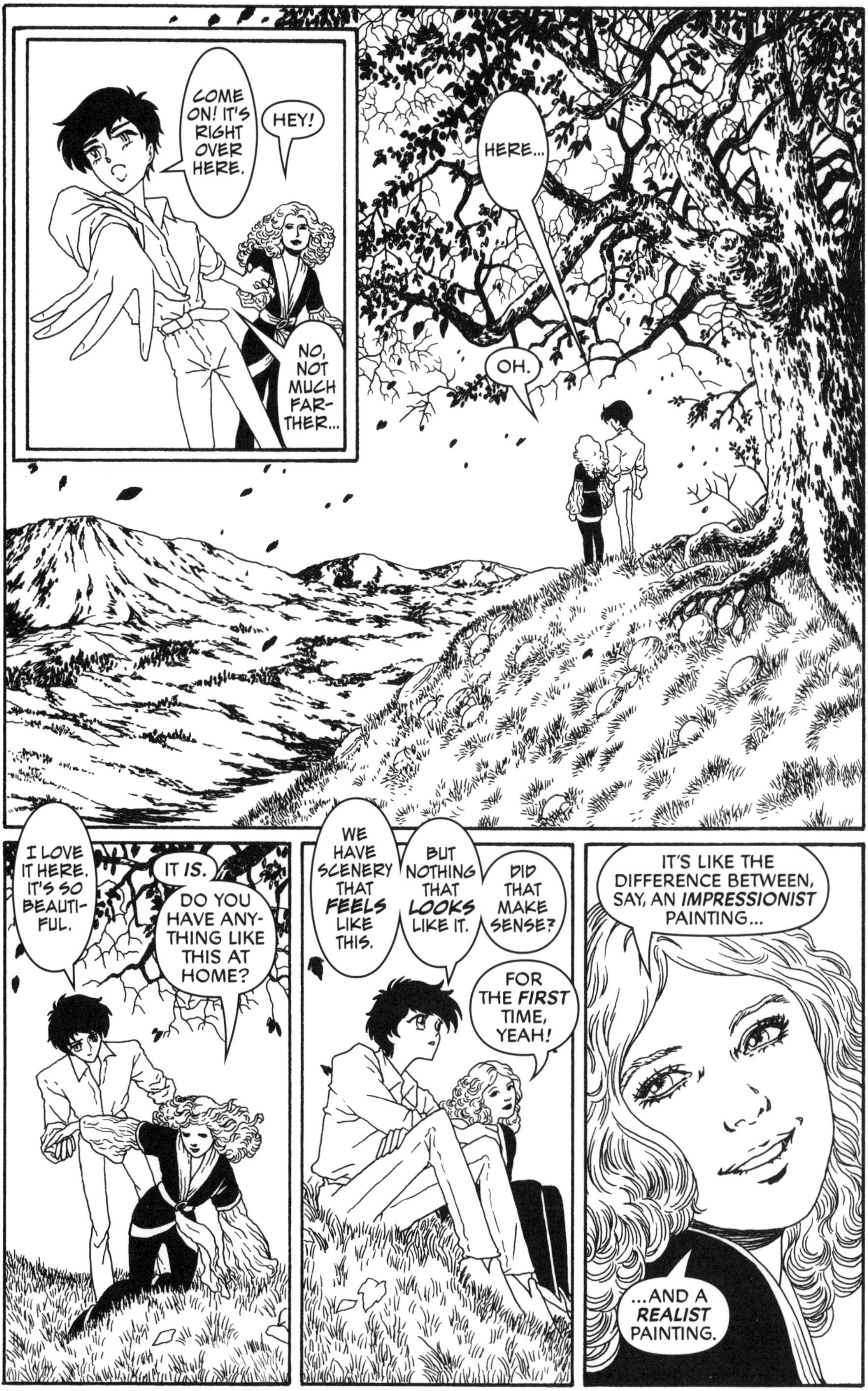
COME ON! IT'S RIGHT OVER HERE.
HEY!
NO, NOT MUCH FAR-THER...
HERE...
OH.
I LOVE IT HERE. IT'S SO BEAUTI-FUL.
IT *IS.*
DO YOU HAVE ANY-THING LIKE THIS AT HOME?
WE HAVE SCENERY THAT **FEELS** LIKE THIS.
BUT NOTHING THAT **LOOKS** LIKE IT.
DID THAT MAKE SENSE?
FOR THE *FIRST* TIME, YEAH!
IT'S LIKE THE DIFFERENCE BETWEEN, SAY, AN *IMPRESSIONIST* PAINTING...
...AND A ***REALIST*** PAINTING.

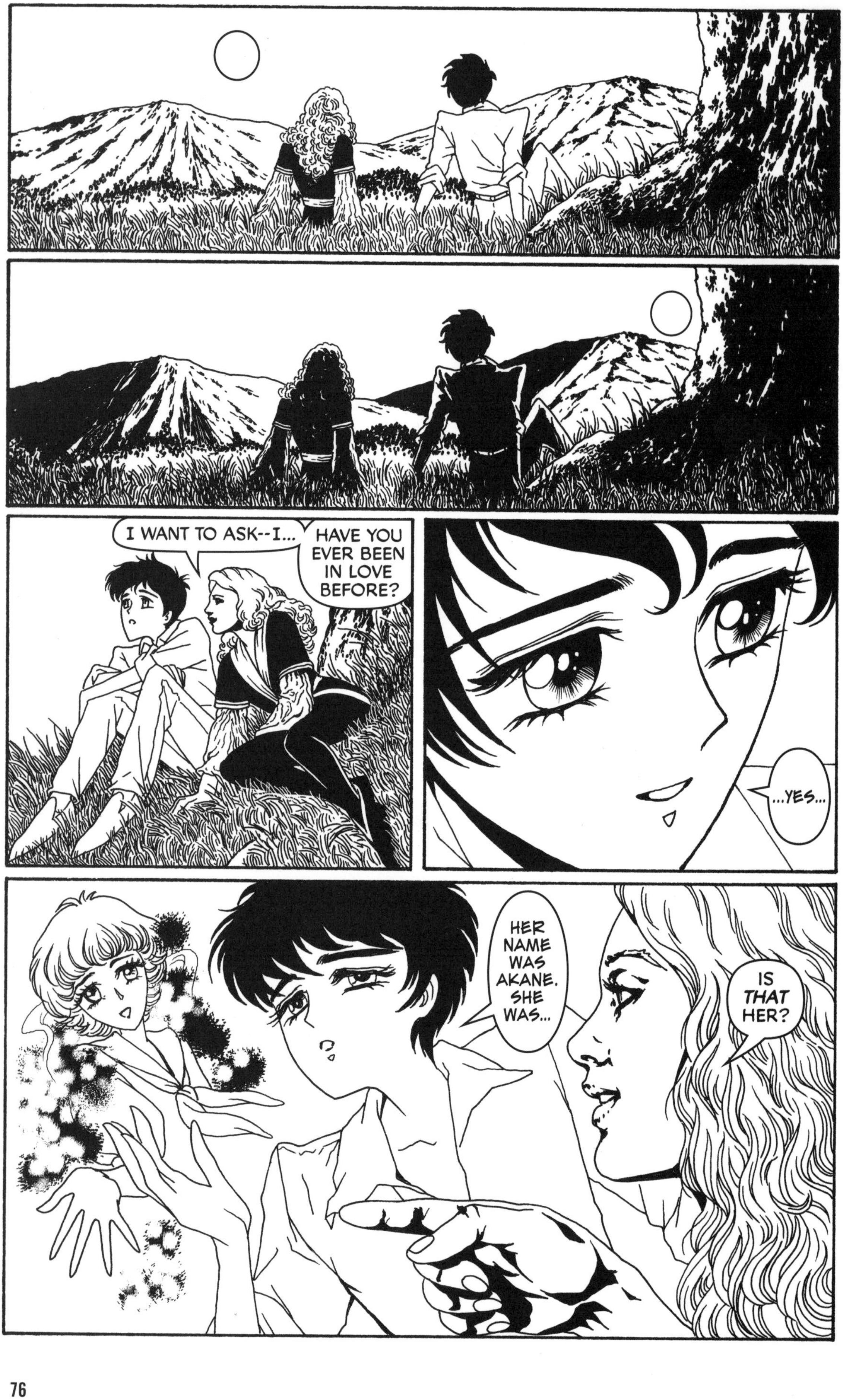
I WANT TO ASK--I...
HAVE YOU EVER BEEN IN LOVE BEFORE?
...YES...
HER NAME WAS AKANE. SHE WAS...
IS *THAT* HER?

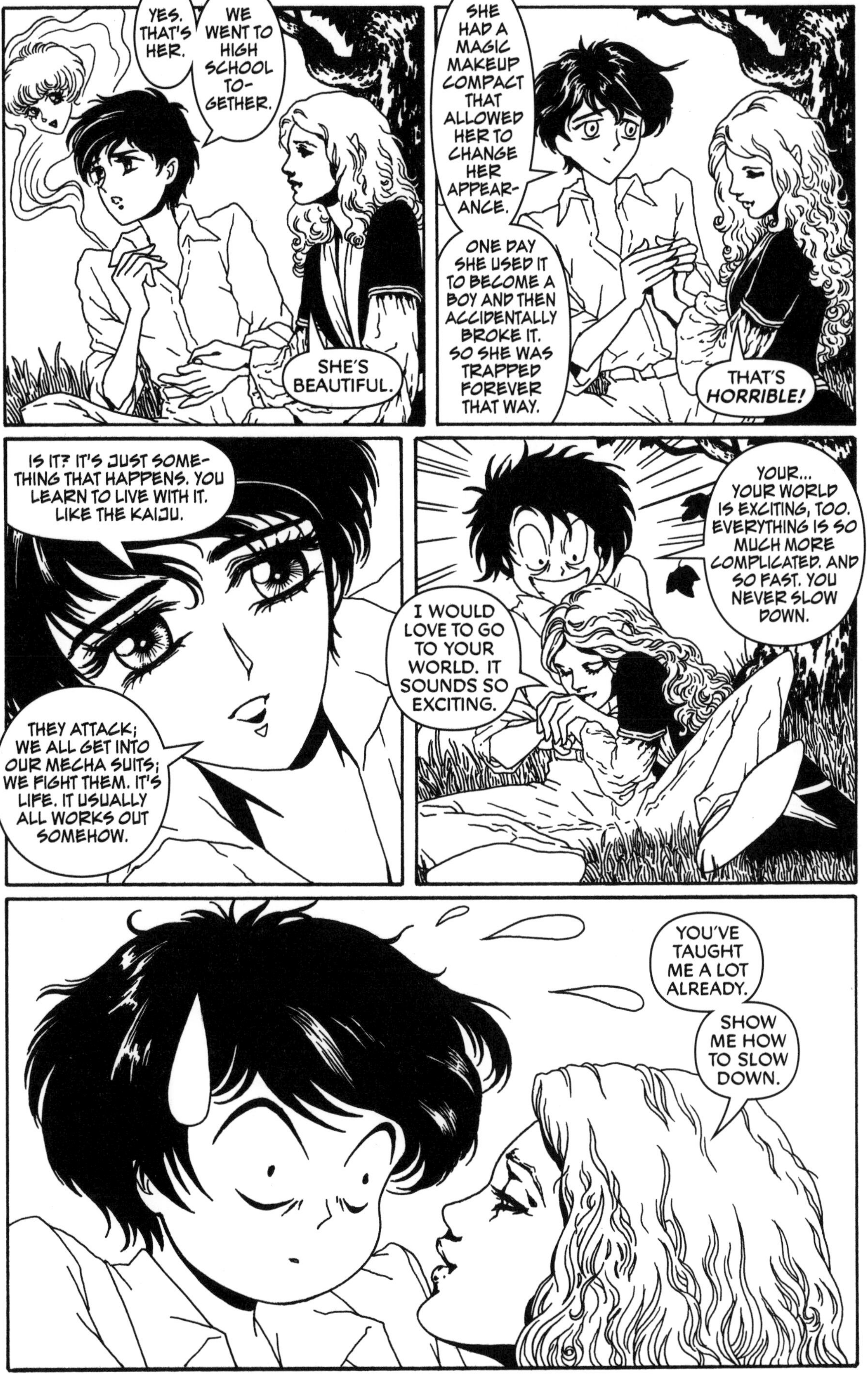
YES. THAT'S HER.
WE WENT TO HIGH SCHOOL TO-GETHER.
SHE'S BEAUTIFUL.
SHE HAD A MAGIC MAKEUP COMPACT THAT ALLOWED HER TO CHANGE HER APPEAR-ANCE.
ONE DAY SHE USED IT TO BECOME A BOY AND THEN ACCIDENTALLY BROKE IT. SO SHE WAS TRAPPED FOREVER THAT WAY.
THAT'S *HORRIBLE!*
IS IT? IT'S JUST SOME-THING THAT HAPPENS. YOU LEARN TO LIVE WITH IT. LIKE THE KAIJU.
THEY ATTACK; WE ALL GET INTO OUR MECHA SUITS; WE FIGHT THEM. IT'S LIFE. IT USUALLY ALL WORKS OUT SOMEHOW.
I WOULD LOVE TO GO TO YOUR WORLD. IT SOUNDS SO EXCITING.
YOUR... YOUR WORLD IS EXCITING, TOO. EVERYTHING IS SO MUCH MORE COMPLICATED. AND SO FAST. YOU NEVER SLOW DOWN.
YOU'VE TAUGHT ME A LOT ALREADY.
SHOW ME HOW TO SLOW DOWN.

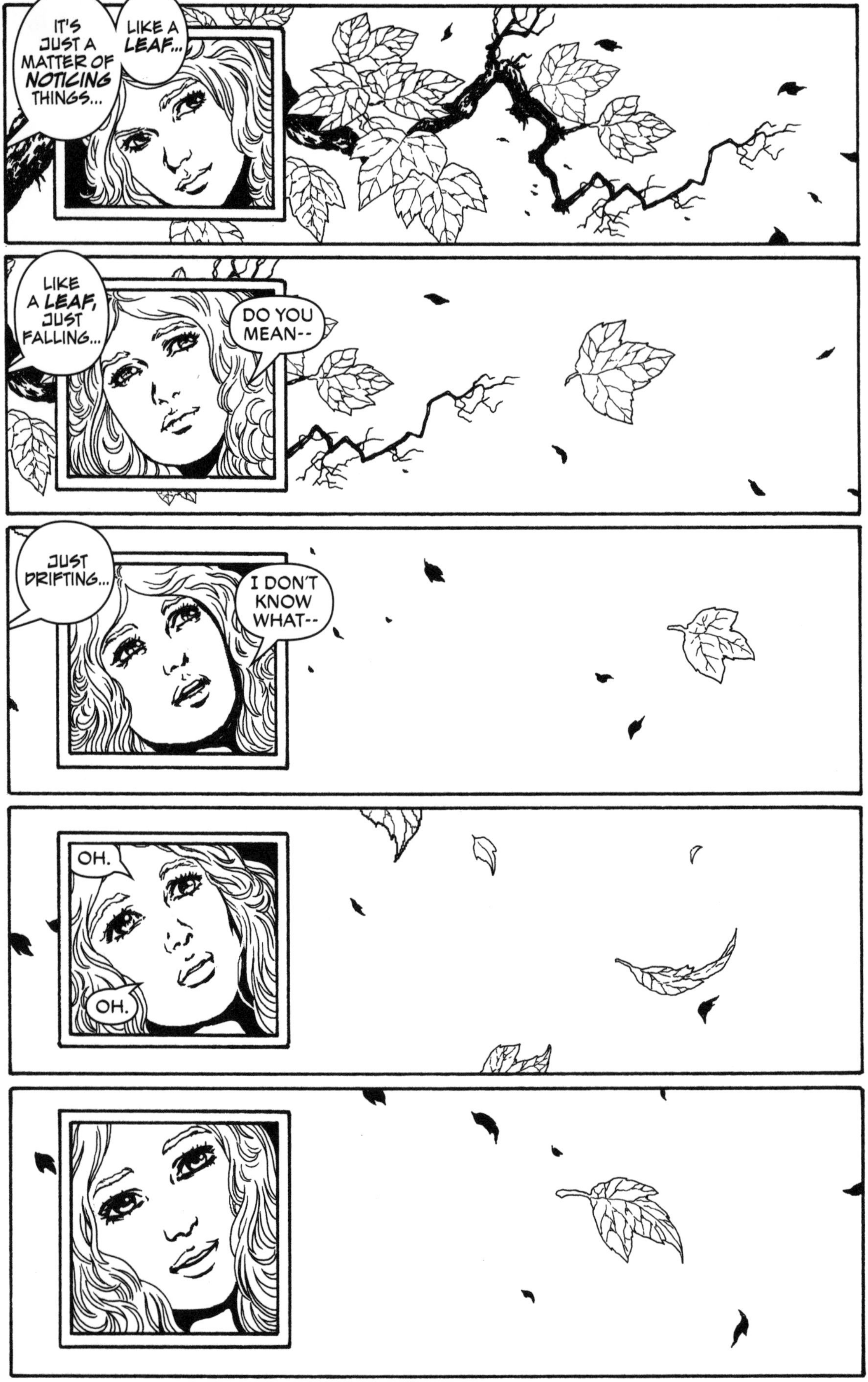

IT'S JUST A MATTER OF NOTICING THINGS...
LIKE A LEAF...
LIKE A LEAF, JUST FALLING...
DO YOU MEAN--
JUST DRIFTING...
I DON'T KNOW WHAT--
OH.
OH.

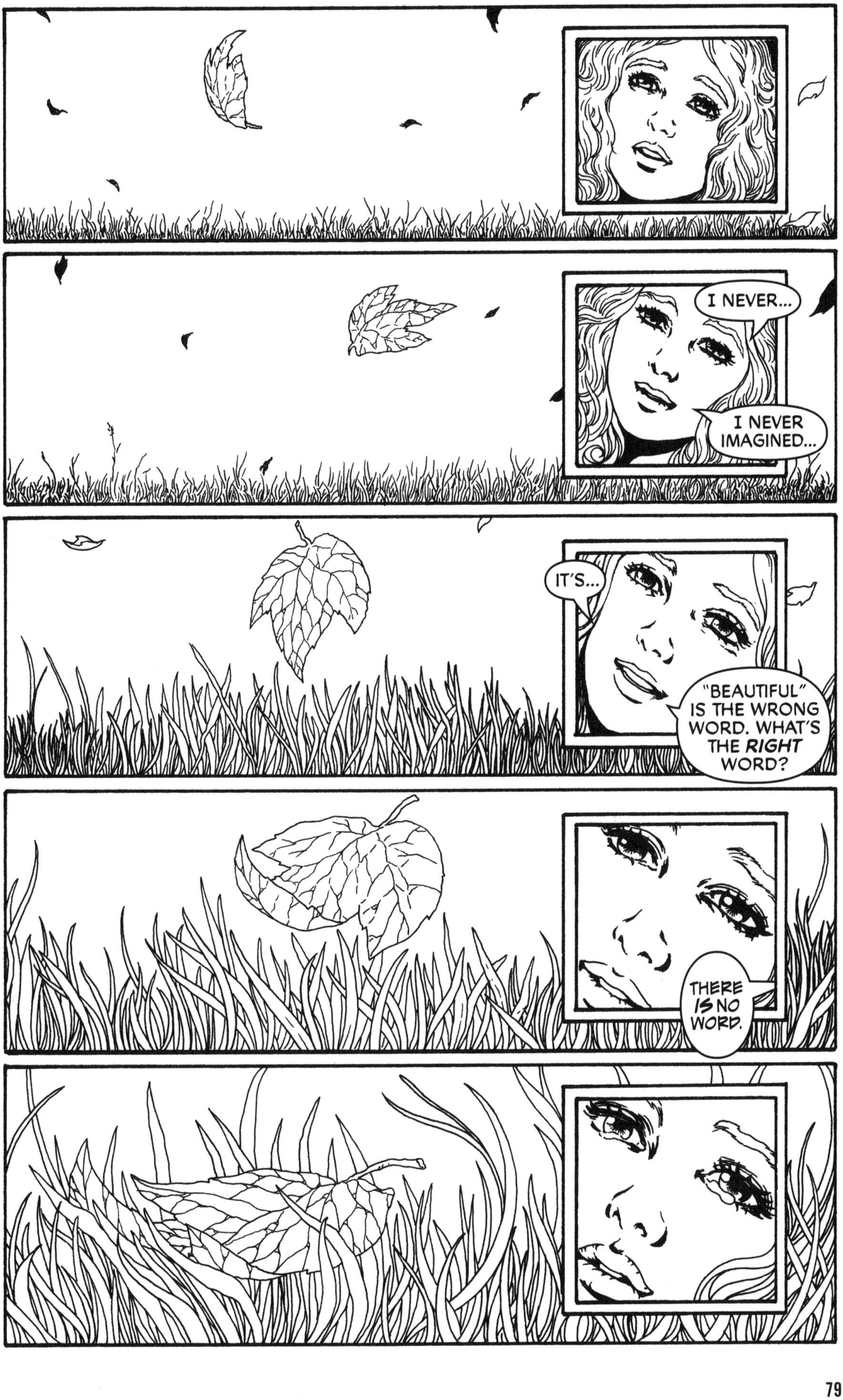
I NEVER...
I NEVER IMAGINED...
IT'S...
"BEAUTIFUL" IS THE WRONG WORD. WHAT'S THE *RIGHT* WORD?
THERE *IS* NO WORD.

CHAPTER 8

RYOKO: *MAYBE. Do we have to talk about THAT...*

MARISSA: *Don't ... Don't go all STORMY...*

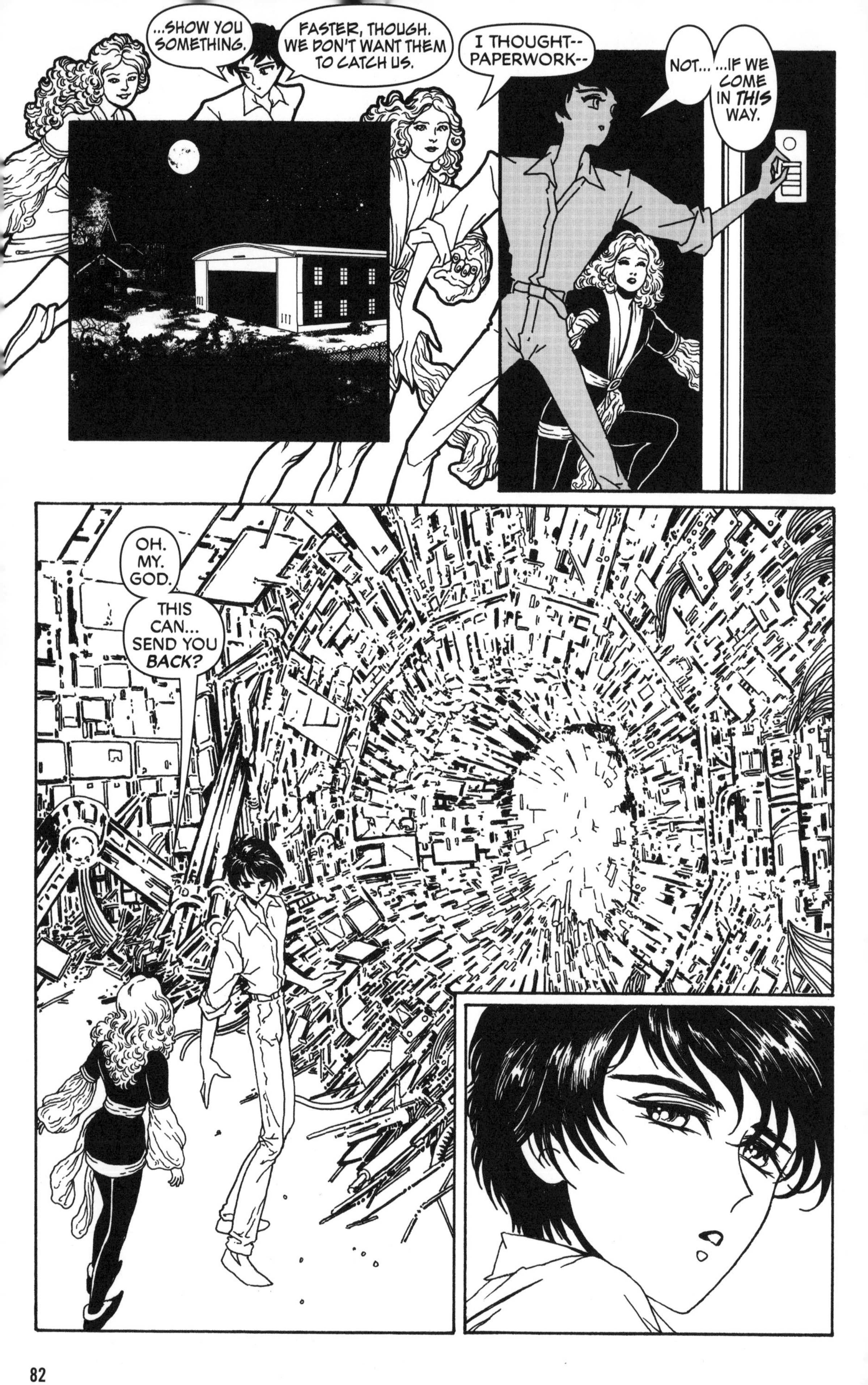
...SHOW YOU SOMETHING.
FASTER, THOUGH. WE DON'T WANT THEM TO CATCH US.
I THOUGHT-- PAPERWORK--
NOT...
...IF WE COME IN *THIS* WAY.
OH. MY. GOD.
THIS CAN... SEND YOU *BACK?*

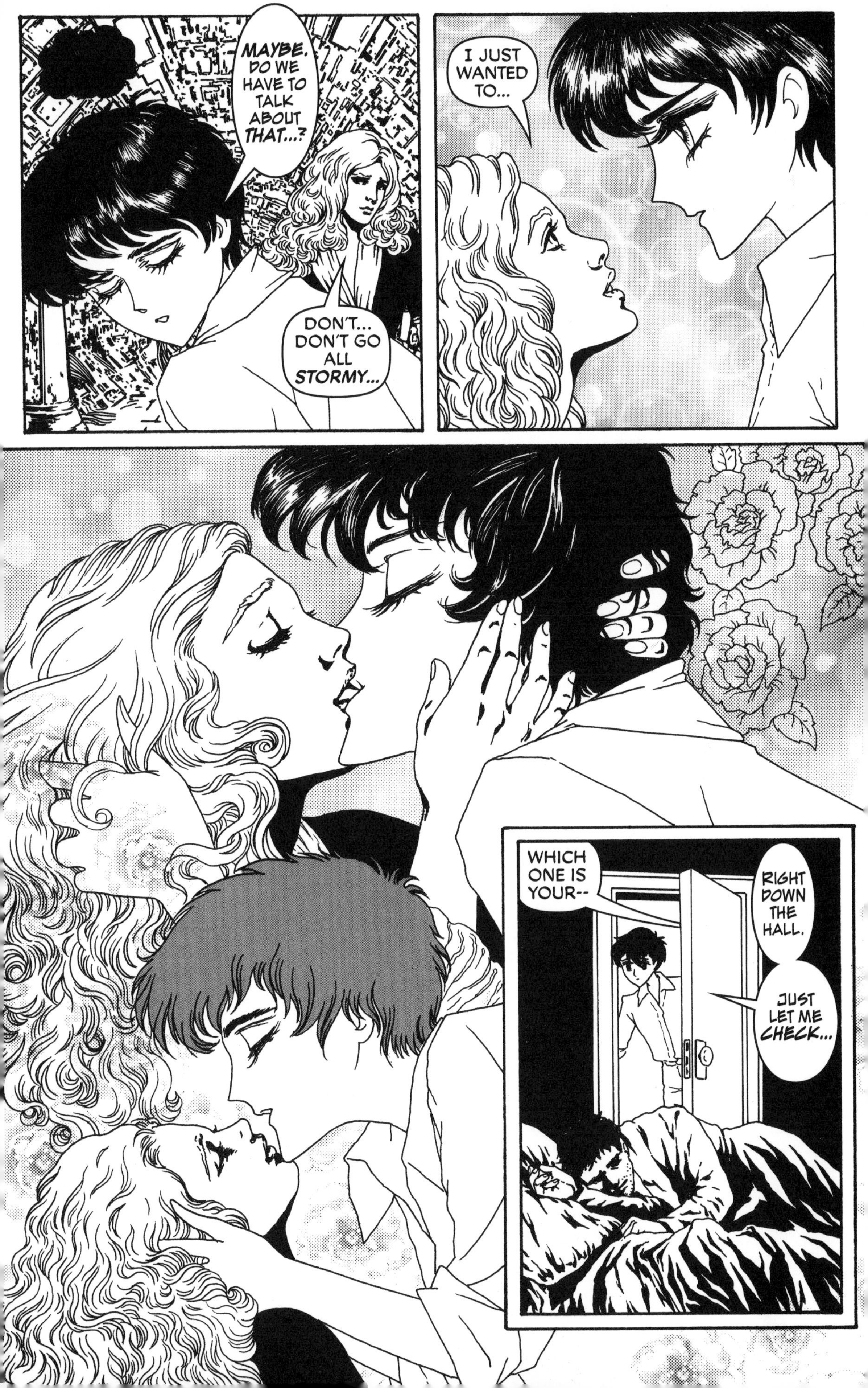
MAYBE. DO WE HAVE TO TALK ABOUT THAT...?
DON'T... DON'T GO ALL STORMY...
I JUST WANTED TO...
WHICH ONE IS YOUR--
RIGHT DOWN THE HALL.
JUST LET ME CHECK...

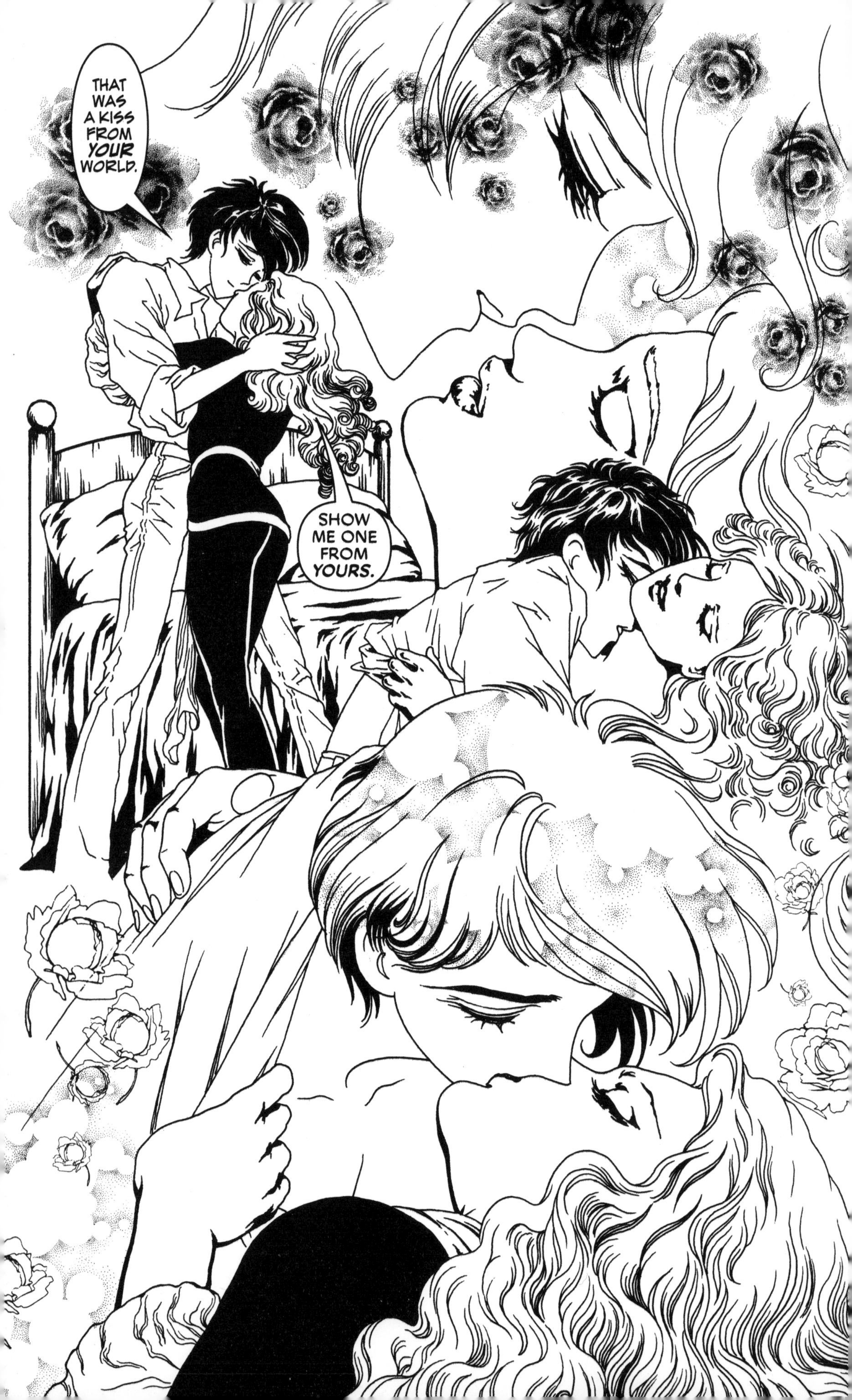
THAT WAS A KISS FROM YOUR WORLD.
SHOW ME ONE FROM YOURS.

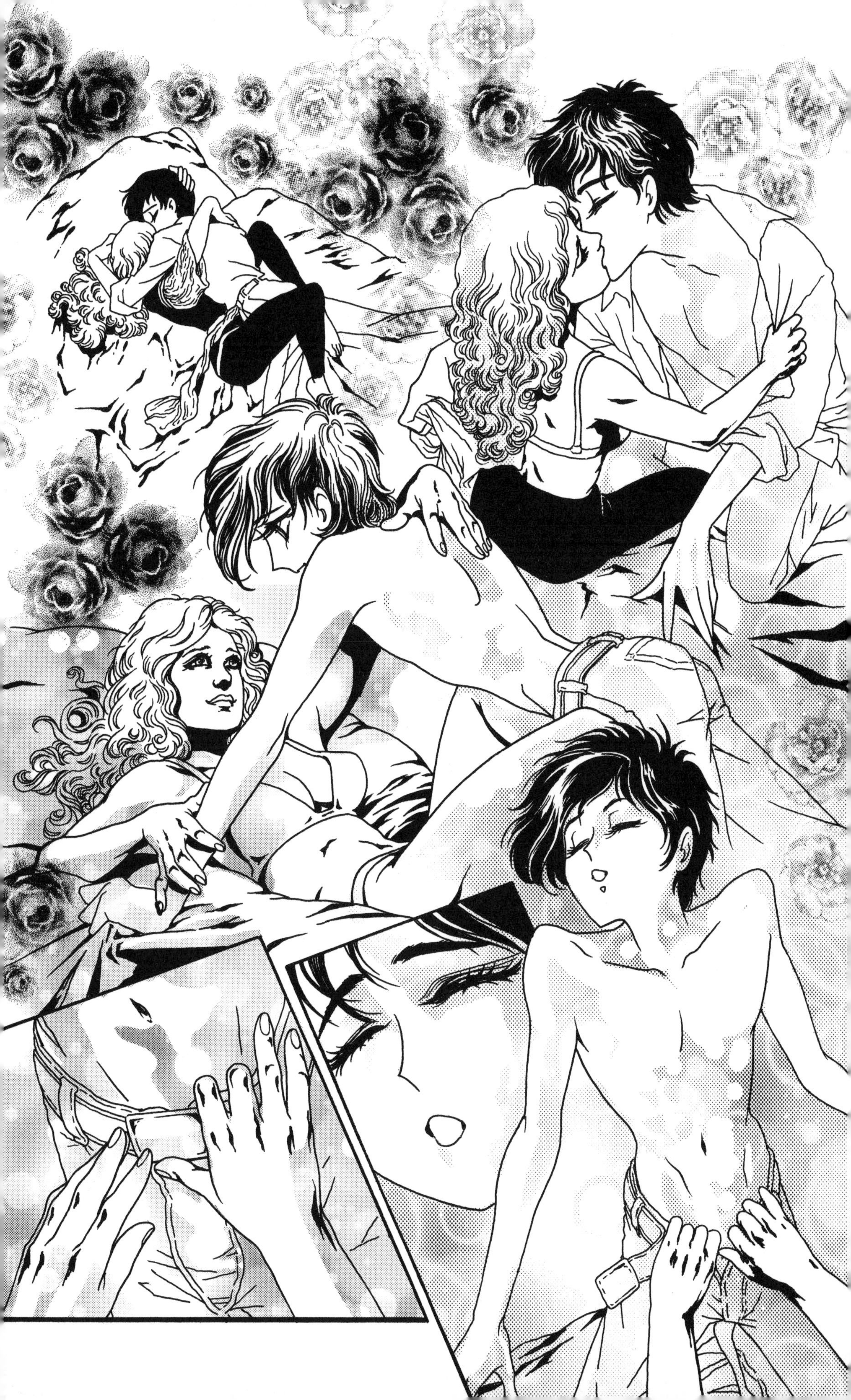

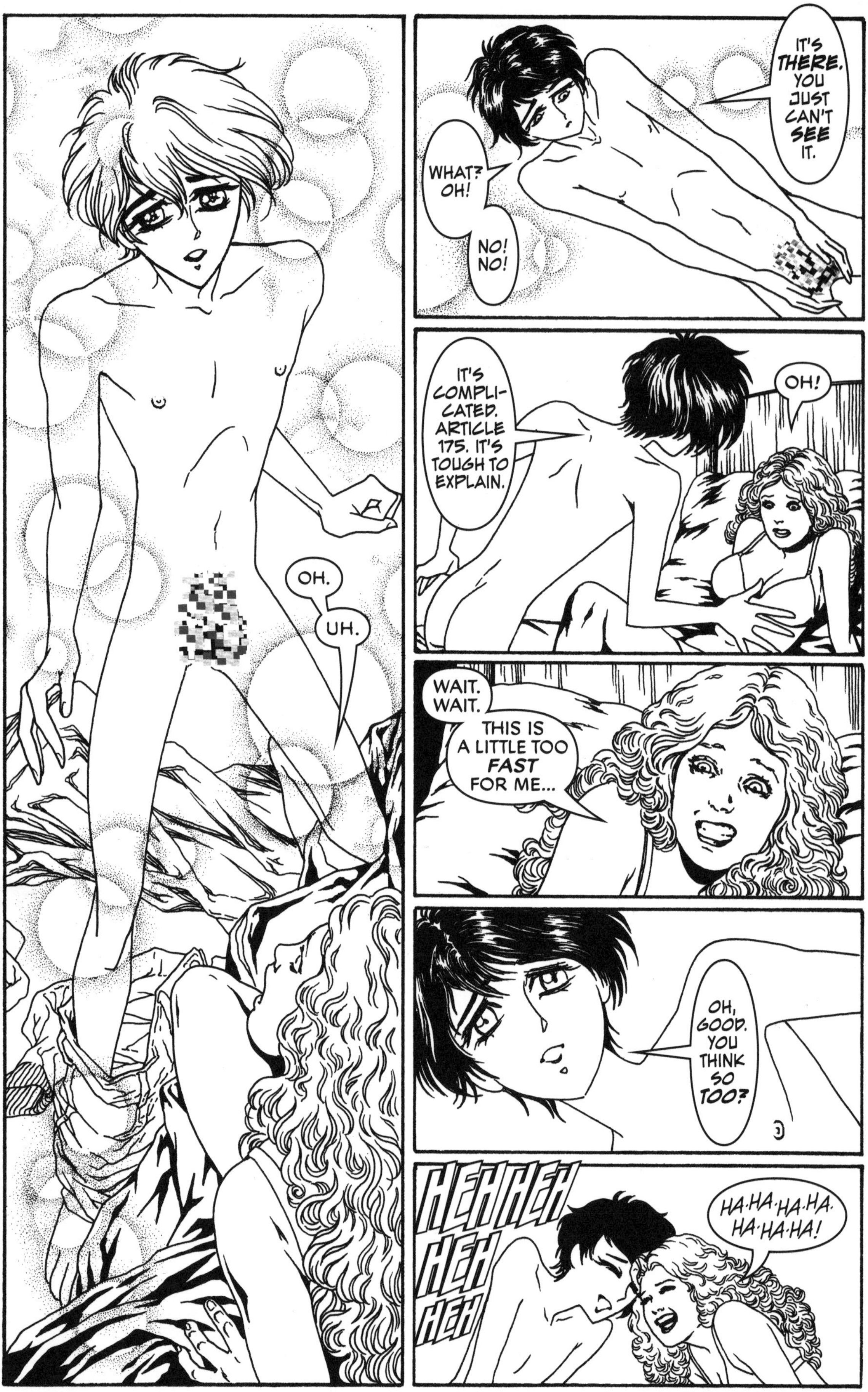
OH.
UH.
IT'S THERE. YOU JUST CAN'T SEE IT.
WHAT? OH!
NO! NO!
IT'S COMPLICATED. ARTICLE 175. IT'S TOUGH TO EXPLAIN.
OH!
WAIT. WAIT.
THIS IS A LITTLE TOO FAST FOR ME...
OH, GOOD. YOU THINK SO TOO?
HEH HEH HEH HEH HEH
HA·HA·HA·HA. HA·HA·HA!

CHAPTER 9

CHAZ: *You're not explaining ANYTHING.*
Especially not to Marissa. Keep away from her.
RYOKO: *So it's FINALLY the part*
where we fight over the girl!

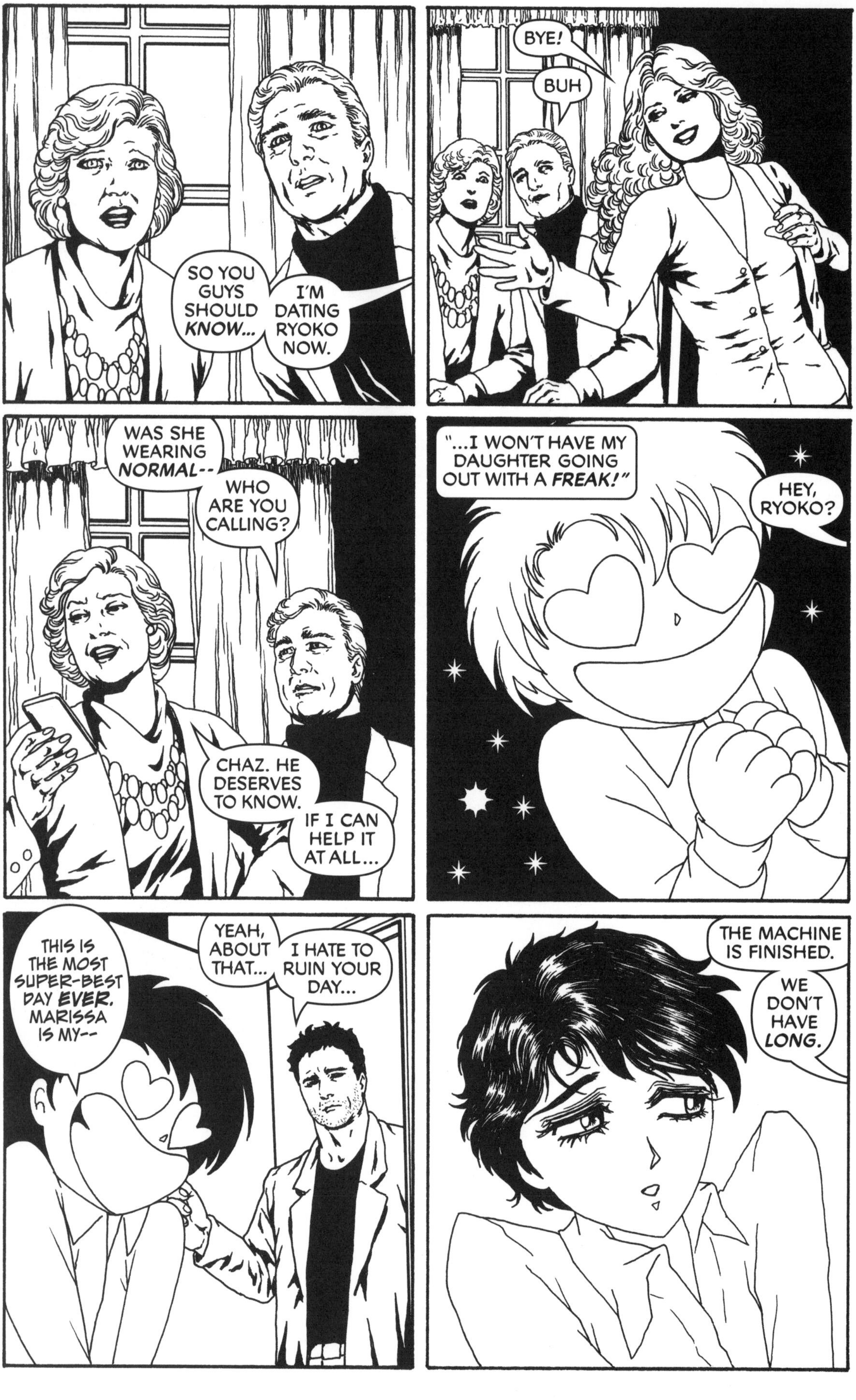
SO YOU GUYS SHOULD KNOW...
I'M DATING RYOKO NOW.
BYE!
BUH
WAS SHE WEARING NORMAL--
WHO ARE YOU CALLING?
CHAZ. HE DESERVES TO KNOW.
IF I CAN HELP IT AT ALL...
"...I WON'T HAVE MY DAUGHTER GOING OUT WITH A FREAK!"
HEY, RYOKO?
THIS IS THE MOST SUPER-BEST DAY EVER. MARISSA IS MY--
YEAH, ABOUT THAT...
I HATE TO RUIN YOUR DAY...
THE MACHINE IS FINISHED.
WE DON'T HAVE LONG.

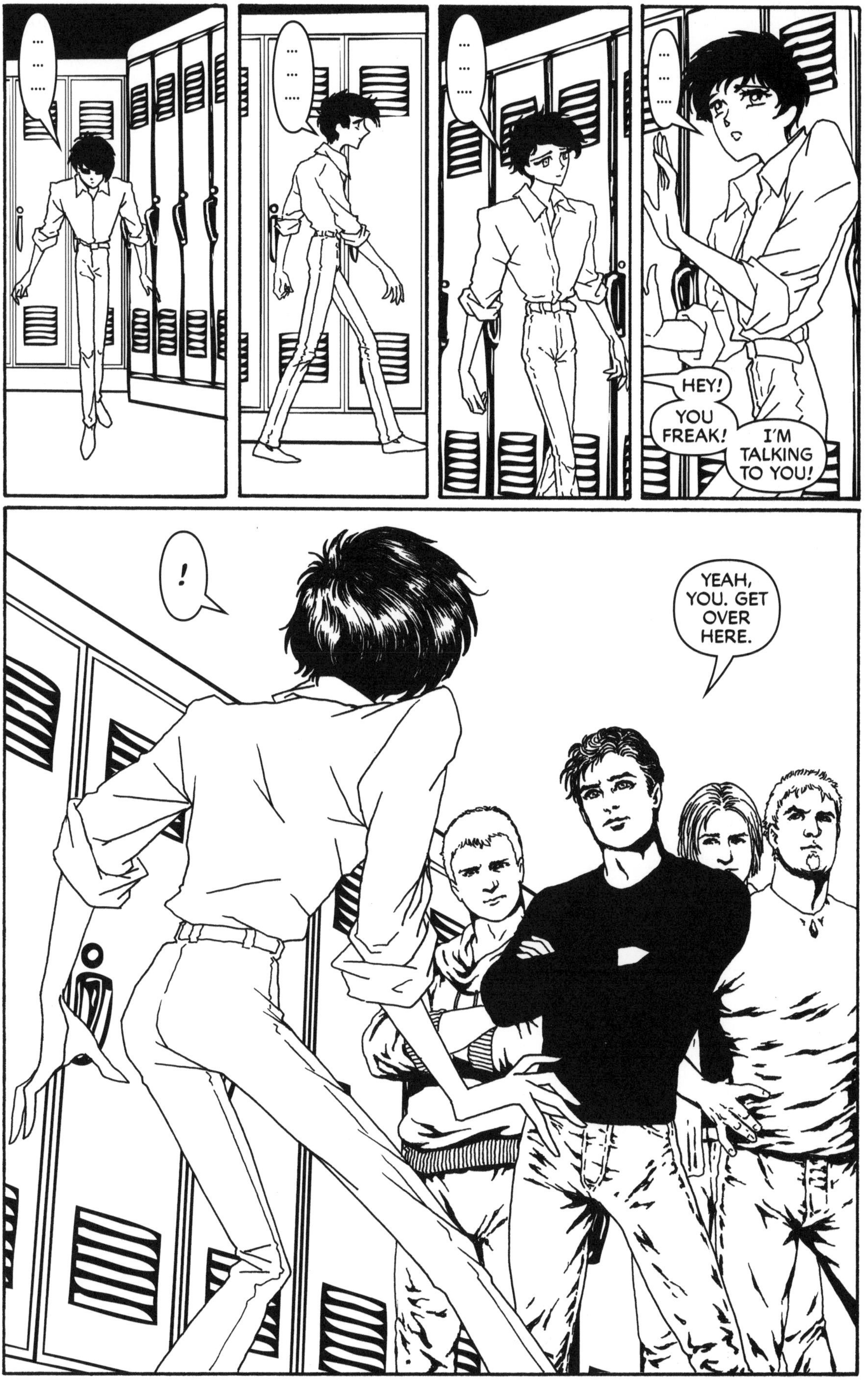
...
...
....
...
...
....
...
...
....
...
...
....
HEY!
YOU FREAK!
I'M TALKING TO YOU!
!
YEAH, YOU. GET OVER HERE.

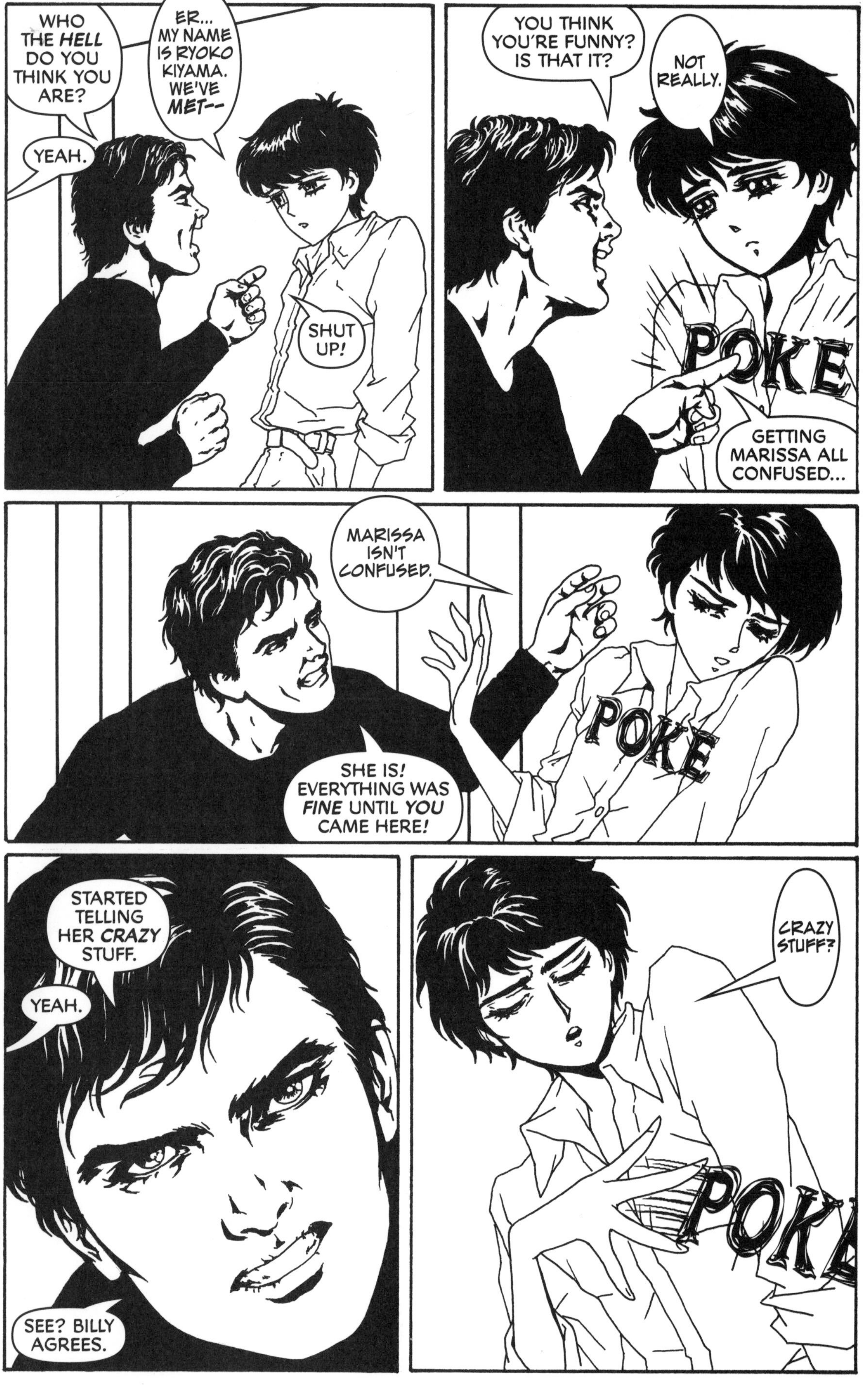
WHO THE HELL DO YOU THINK YOU ARE?
ER... MY NAME IS RYOKO KIYAMA. WE'VE MET--
YEAH.
SHUT UP!
YOU THINK YOU'RE FUNNY? IS THAT IT?
NOT REALLY.
POKE
GETTING MARISSA ALL CONFUSED...
MARISSA ISN'T CONFUSED.
POKE
SHE IS! EVERYTHING WAS FINE UNTIL YOU CAME HERE!
STARTED TELLING HER CRAZY STUFF.
YEAH.
SEE? BILLY AGREES.
CRAZY STUFF?
POKE

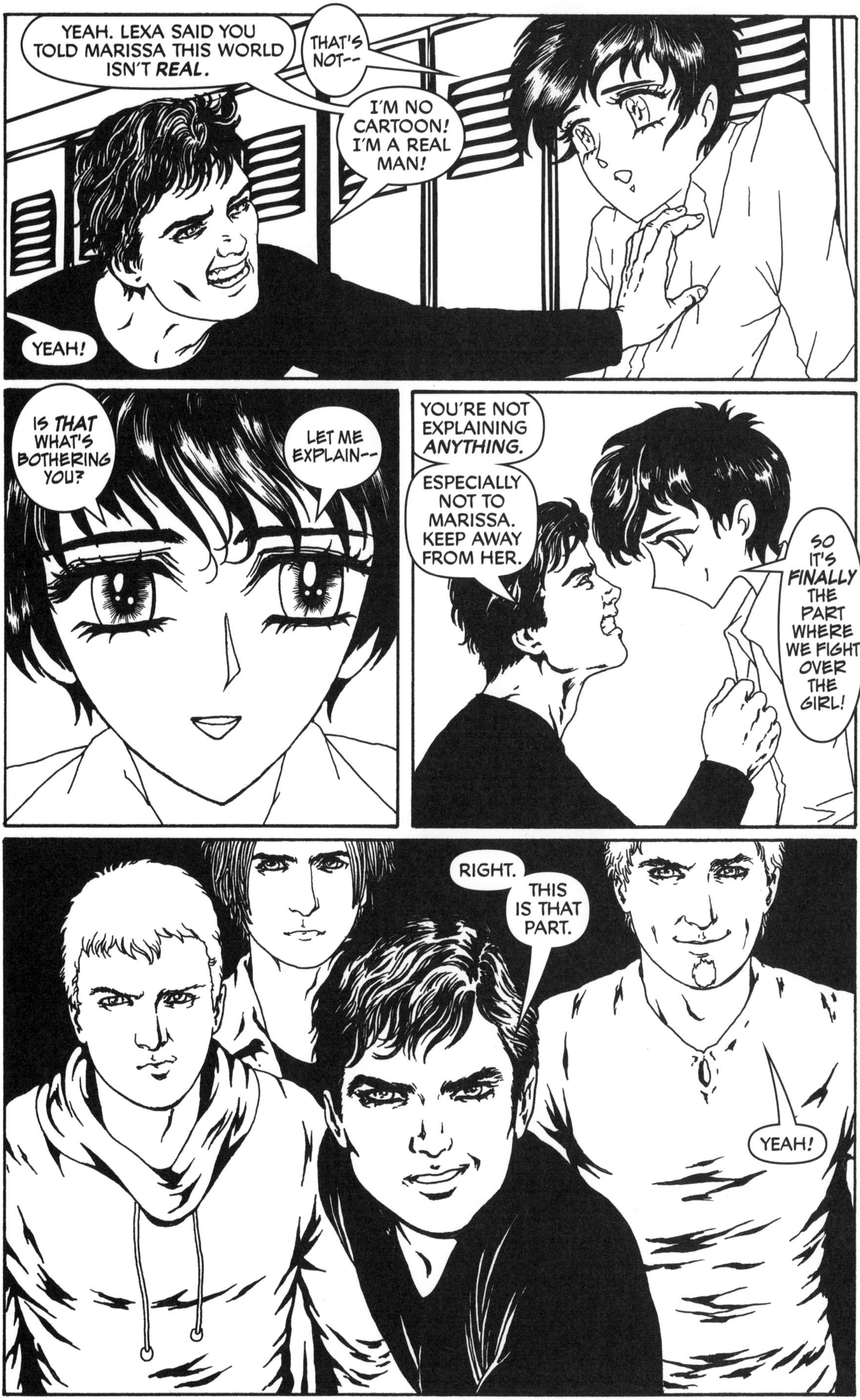
YEAH. LEXA SAID YOU TOLD MARISSA THIS WORLD ISN'T *REAL*.
THAT'S NOT--
I'M NO CARTOON! I'M A REAL MAN!
YEAH!
IS *THAT* WHAT'S BOTHERING YOU?
LET ME EXPLAIN--
YOU'RE NOT EXPLAINING *ANYTHING*.
ESPECIALLY NOT TO MARISSA. KEEP AWAY FROM HER.
SO IT'S *FINALLY* THE PART WHERE WE FIGHT OVER THE GIRL!
RIGHT.
THIS IS THAT PART.
YEAH!

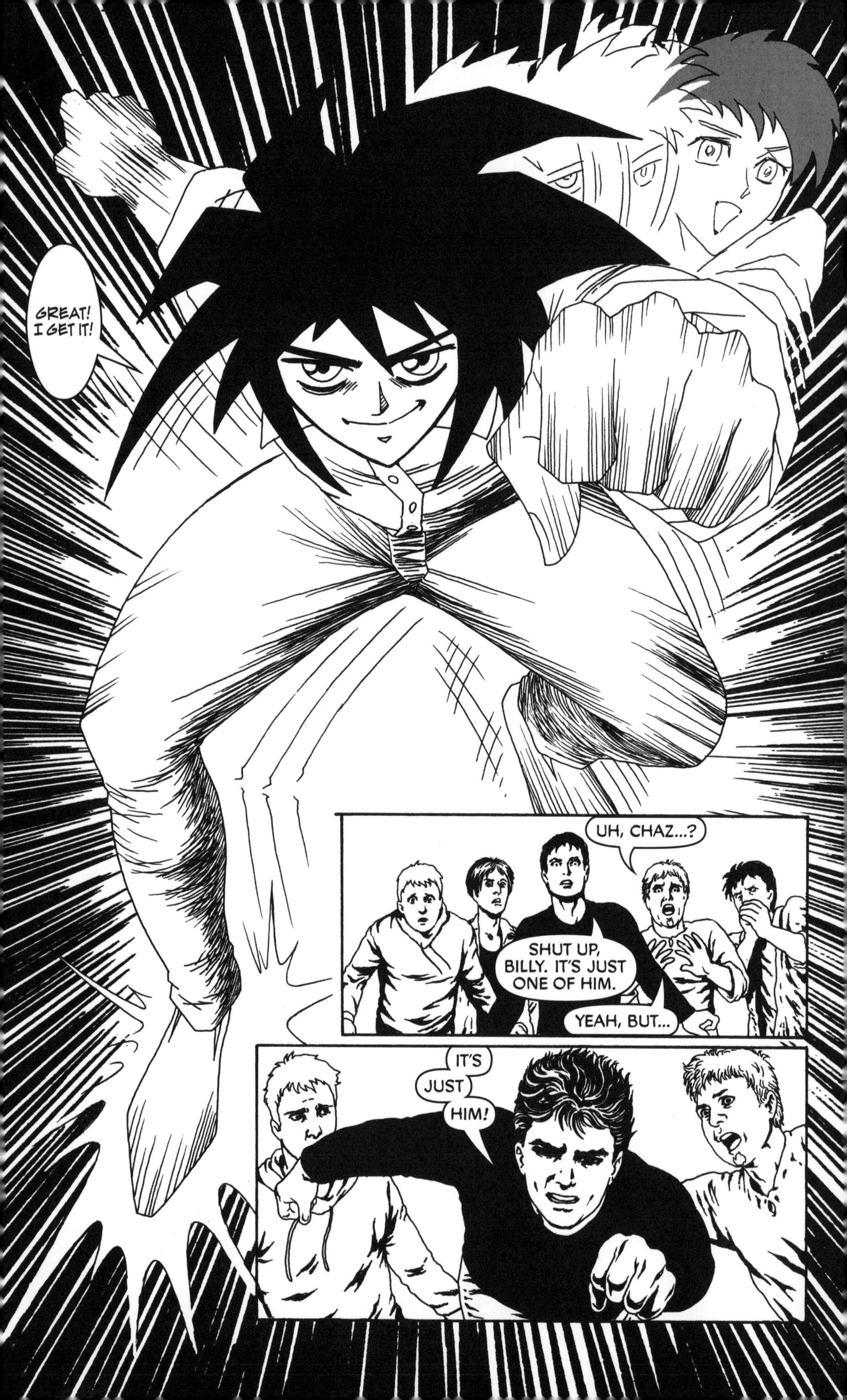
GREAT! I GET IT!
UH, CHAZ...?
SHUT UP, BILLY. IT'S JUST ONE OF HIM.
YEAH, BUT...
IT'S JUST HIM!

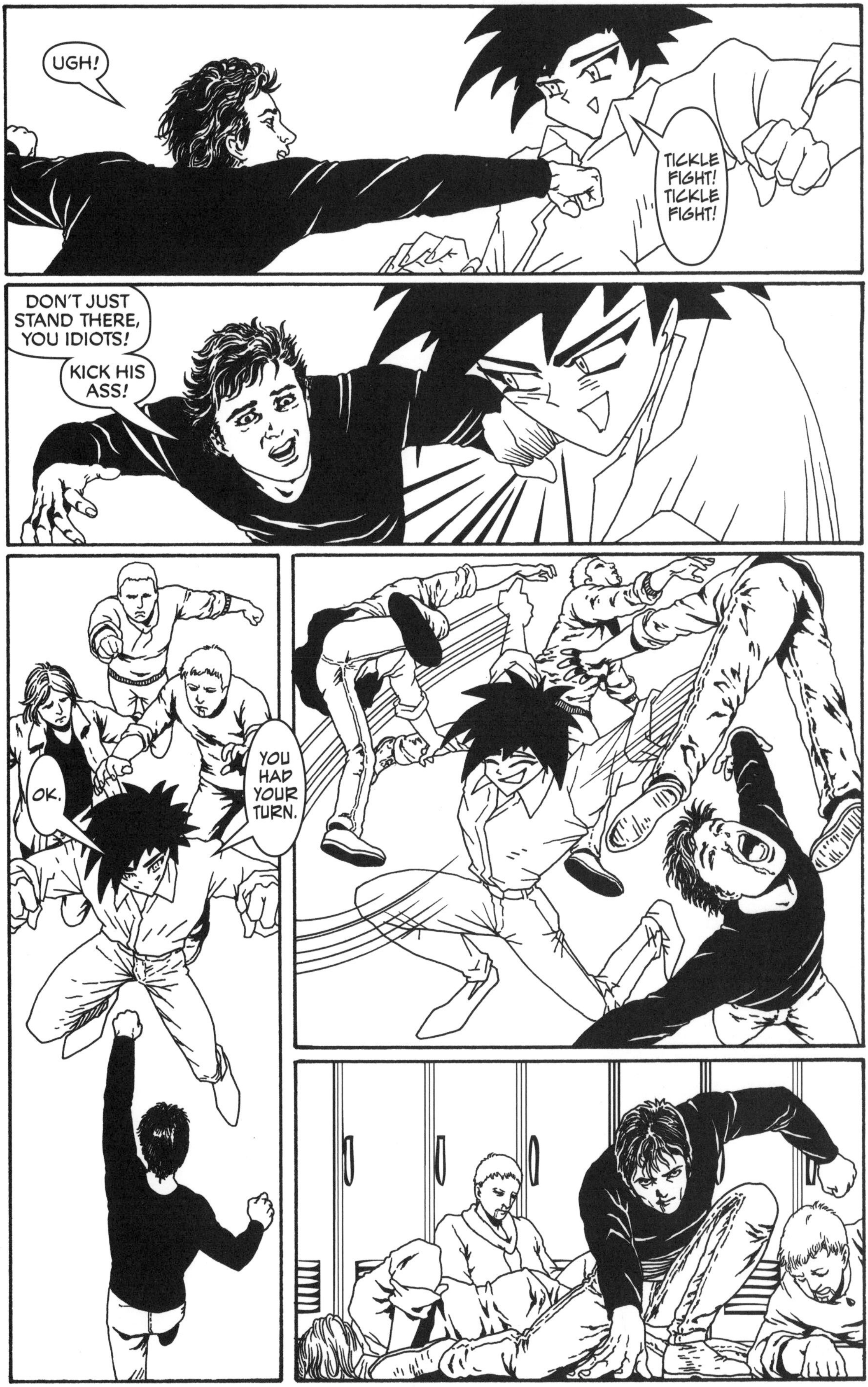
UGH!
TICKLE FIGHT! TICKLE FIGHT!
DON'T JUST STAND THERE, YOU IDIOTS!
KICK HIS ASS!
OK.
YOU HAD YOUR TURN.

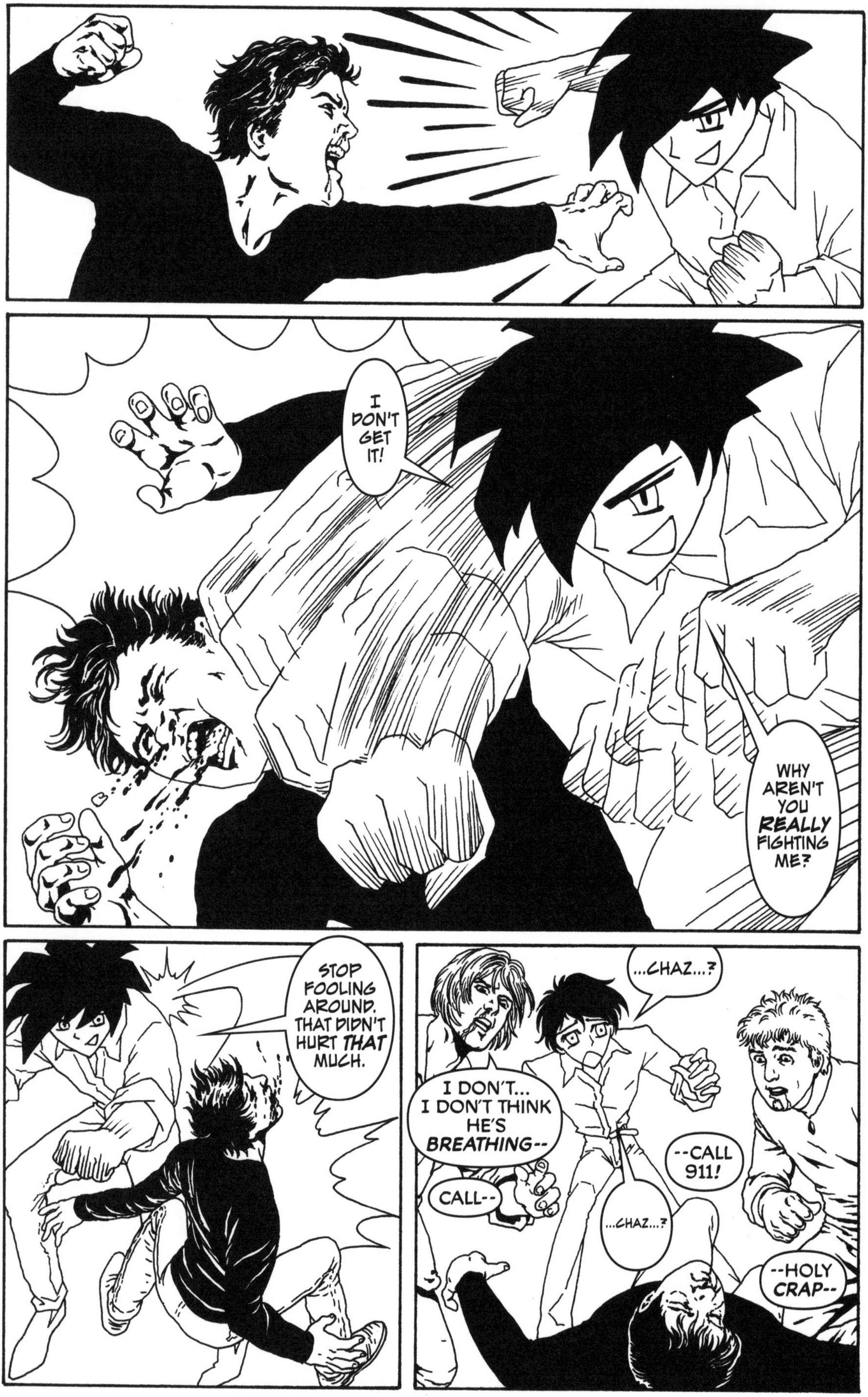
I DON'T GET IT!
WHY AREN'T YOU REALLY FIGHTING ME?
STOP FOOLING AROUND. THAT DIDN'T HURT THAT MUCH.
...CHAZ...?
I DON'T... I DON'T THINK HE'S BREATHING--
--CALL 911!
CALL--
...CHAZ...?
--HOLY CRAP--

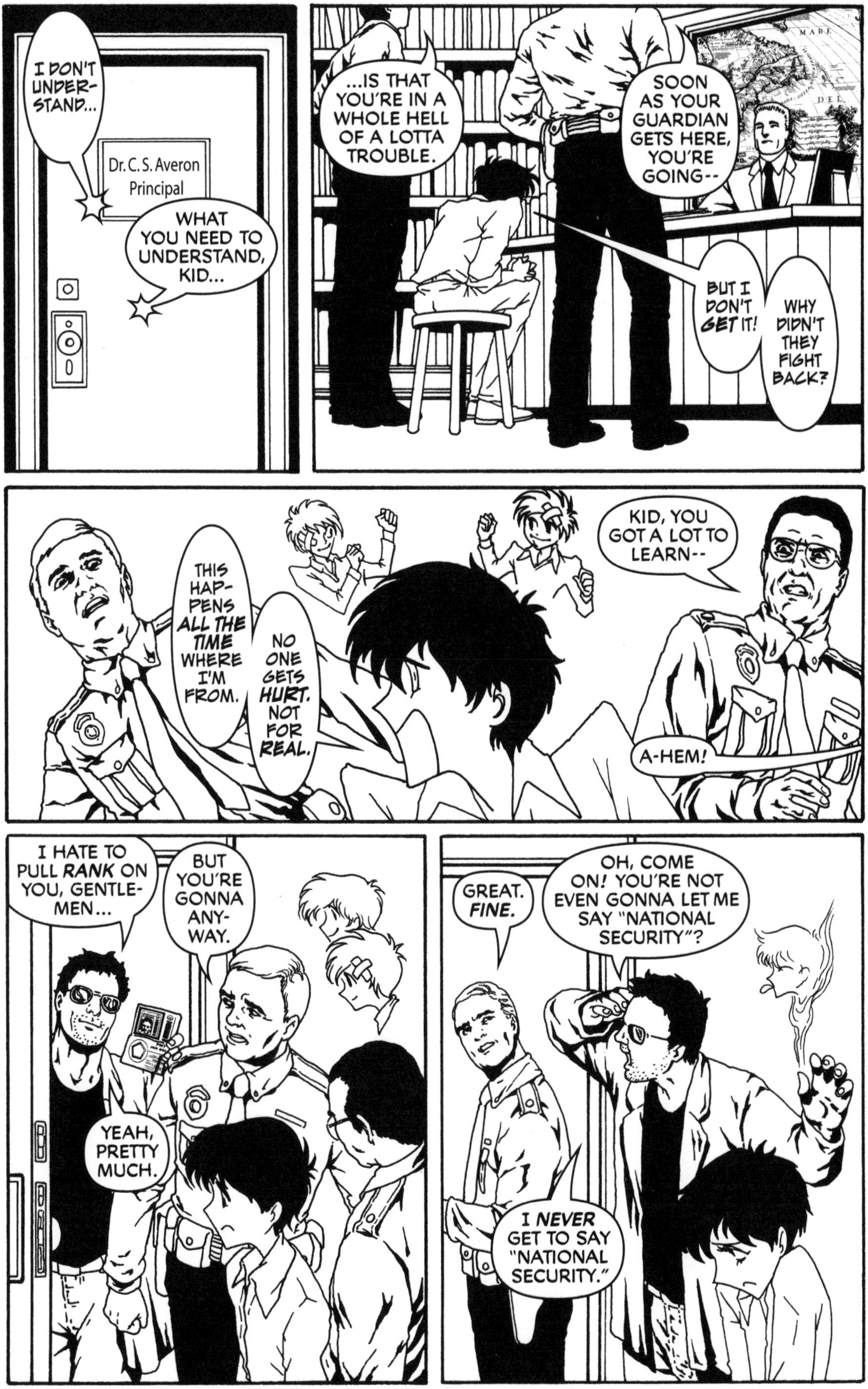
I DON'T UNDERSTAND...
Dr. C. S. Averon
Principal
WHAT YOU NEED TO UNDERSTAND, KID...
...IS THAT YOU'RE IN A WHOLE HELL OF A LOTTA TROUBLE.
SOON AS YOUR GUARDIAN GETS HERE, YOU'RE GOING--
BUT I DON'T GET IT!
WHY DIDN'T THEY FIGHT BACK?
THIS HAPPENS ALL THE TIME WHERE I'M FROM.
NO ONE GETS HURT. NOT FOR REAL.
KID, YOU GOT A LOT TO LEARN--
A-HEM!
I HATE TO PULL RANK ON YOU, GENTLEMEN...
BUT YOU'RE GONNA ANYWAY.
YEAH, PRETTY MUCH.
GREAT. FINE.
OH, COME ON! YOU'RE NOT EVEN GONNA LET ME SAY "NATIONAL SECURITY"?
I NEVER GET TO SAY "NATIONAL SECURITY."

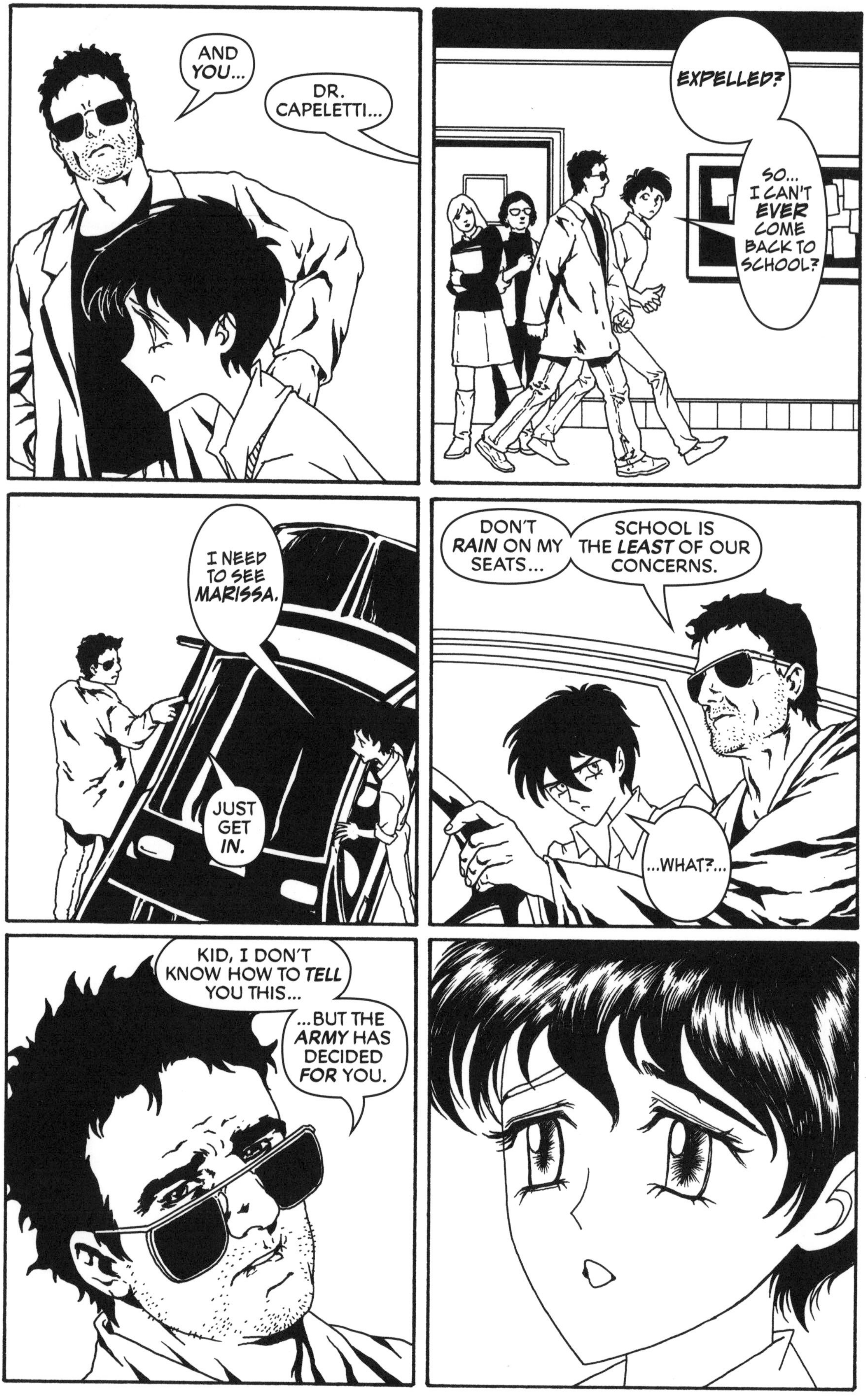
AND YOU...
DR. CAPELETTI...
EXPELLED?
SO... I CAN'T EVER COME BACK TO SCHOOL?
I NEED TO SEE MARISSA.
JUST GET IN.
DON'T RAIN ON MY SEATS...
SCHOOL IS THE LEAST OF OUR CONCERNS.
...WHAT?...
KID, I DON'T KNOW HOW TO TELL YOU THIS...
...BUT THE ARMY HAS DECIDED FOR YOU.

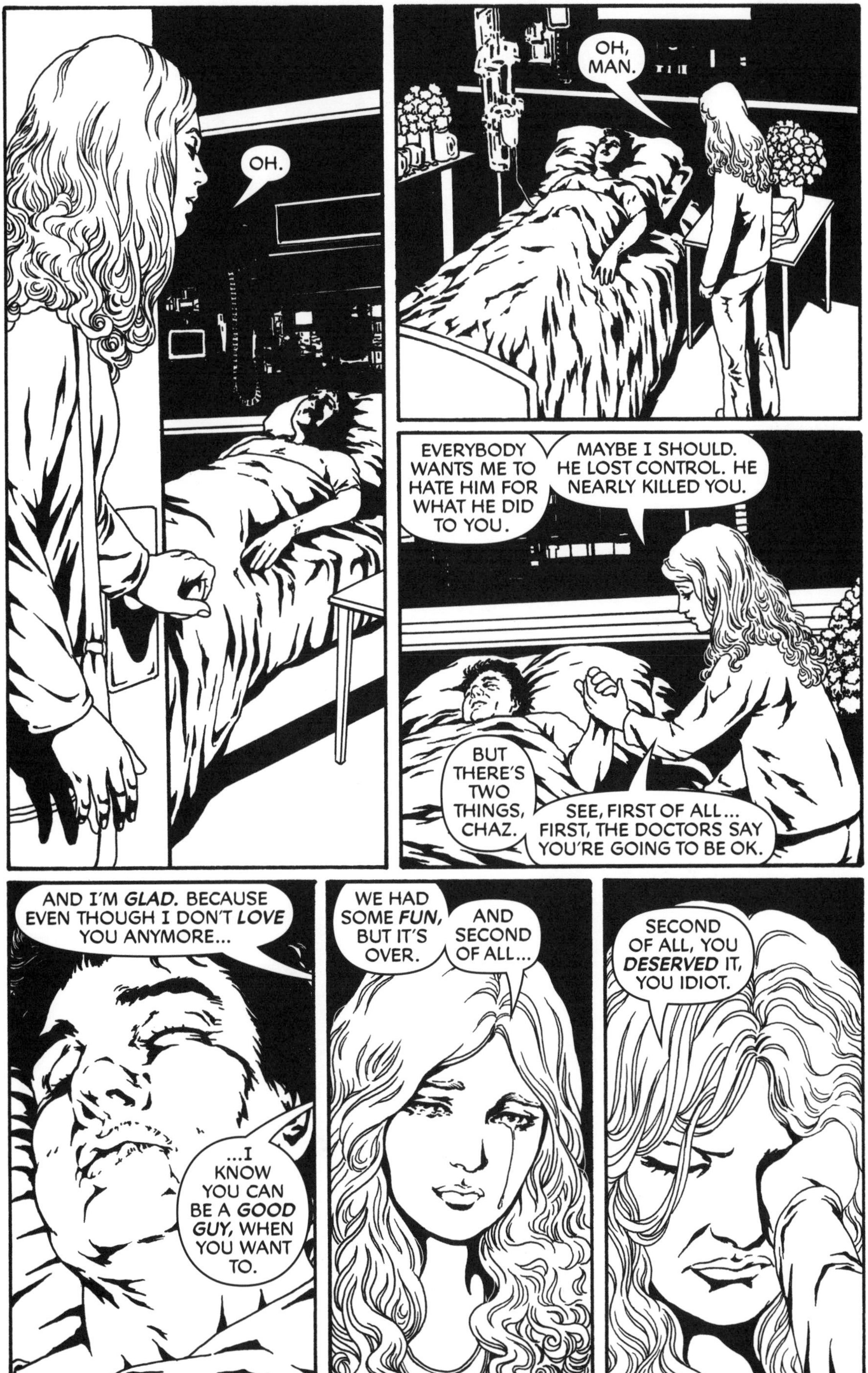
OH.
OH, MAN.
EVERYBODY WANTS ME TO HATE HIM FOR WHAT HE DID TO YOU.
MAYBE I SHOULD. HE LOST CONTROL. HE NEARLY KILLED YOU.
BUT THERE'S TWO THINGS, CHAZ.
SEE, FIRST OF ALL... FIRST, THE DOCTORS SAY YOU'RE GOING TO BE OK.
AND I'M *GLAD.* BECAUSE EVEN THOUGH I DON'T *LOVE* YOU ANYMORE...
...I KNOW YOU CAN BE A *GOOD GUY,* WHEN YOU WANT TO.
WE HAD SOME *FUN,* BUT IT'S OVER.
AND SECOND OF ALL...
SECOND OF ALL, YOU *DESERVED* IT, YOU IDIOT.

CHAPTER 10

RYOKO: *I'm sorry, too.*

CAPELETTI: *Huh?*

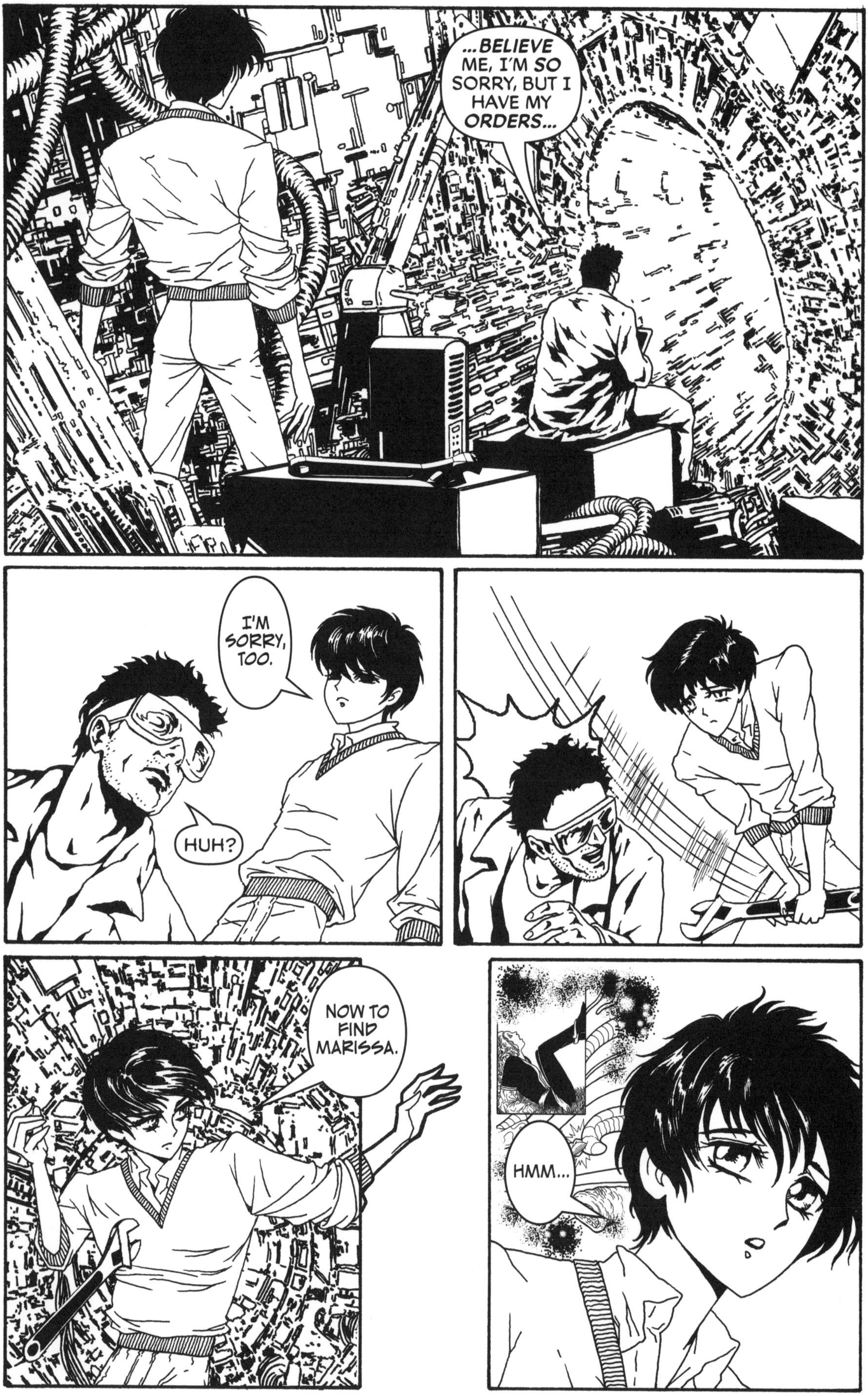
...BELIEVE ME, I'M SO SORRY, BUT I HAVE MY ORDERS...
I'M SORRY, TOO.
HUH?
NOW TO FIND MARISSA.
HMM...

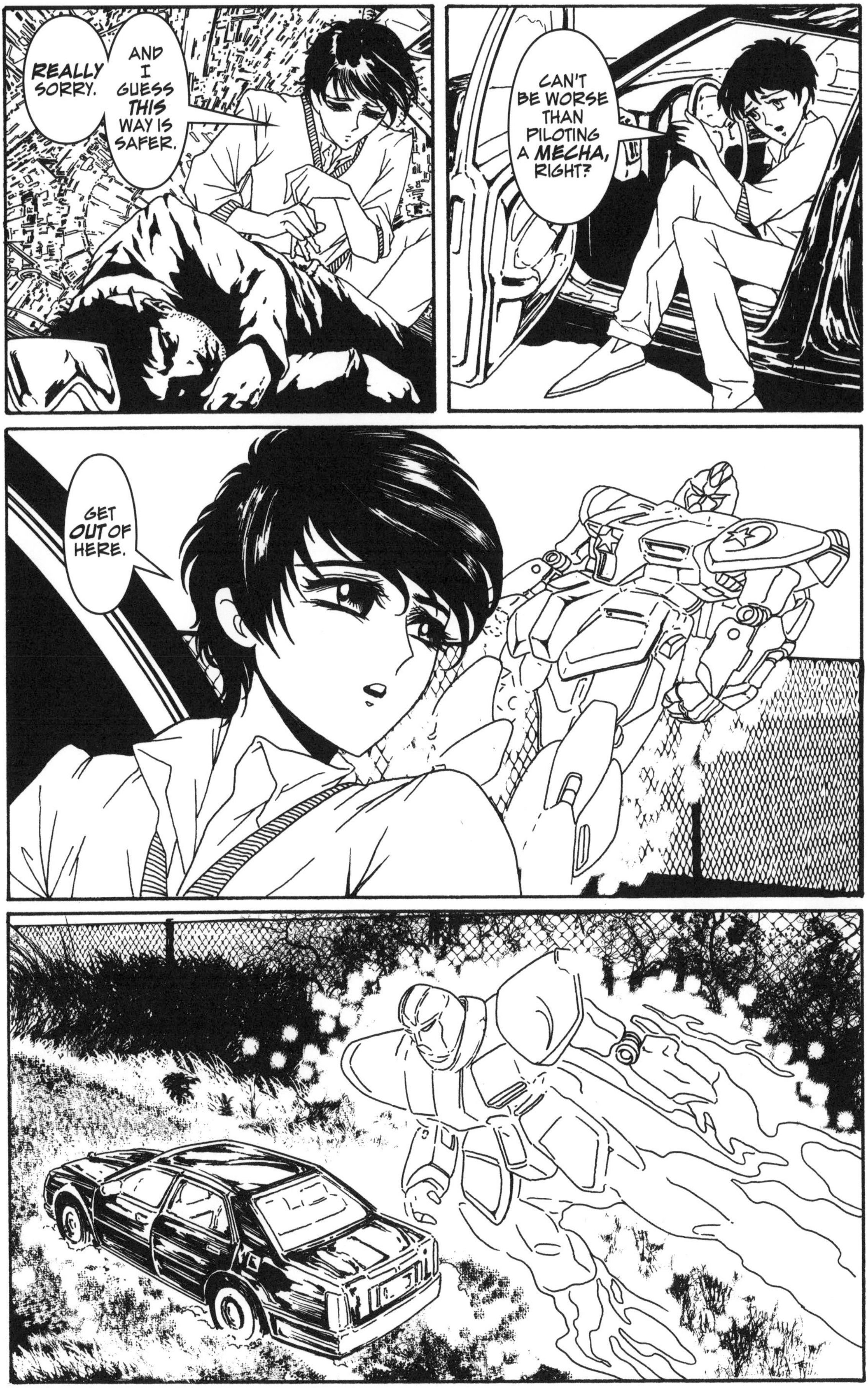
REALLY SORRY.
AND I GUESS THIS WAY IS SAFER.
CAN'T BE WORSE THAN PILOTING A MECHA, RIGHT?
GET OUT OF HERE.

CHAPTER 11

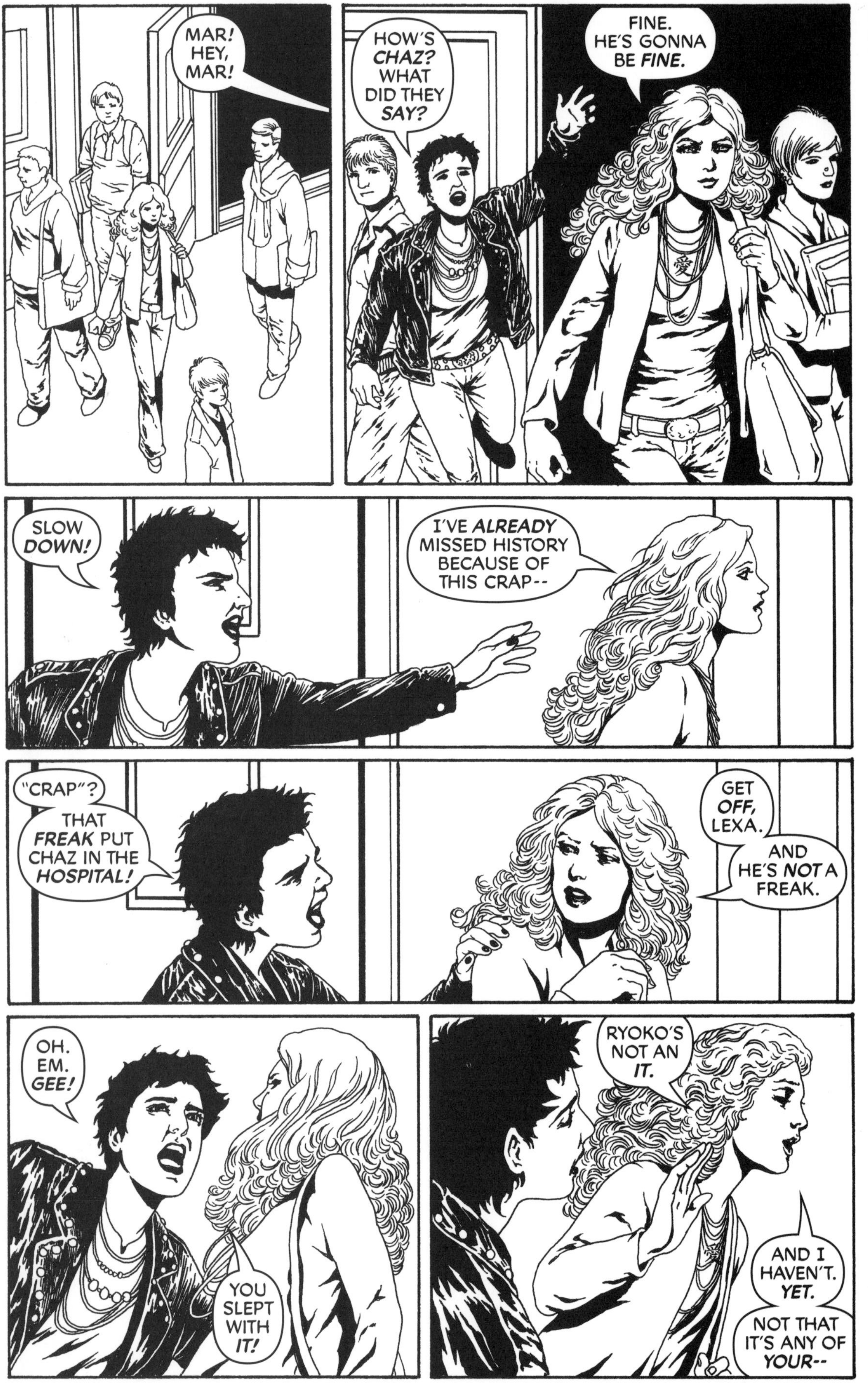
MAR! HEY, MAR!
HOW'S CHAZ? WHAT DID THEY SAY?
FINE. HE'S GONNA BE FINE.
SLOW DOWN!
I'VE ALREADY MISSED HISTORY BECAUSE OF THIS CRAP--
"CRAP"?
THAT FREAK PUT CHAZ IN THE HOSPITAL!
GET OFF, LEXA.
AND HE'S NOT A FREAK.
OH. EM. GEE!
YOU SLEPT WITH IT!
RYOKO'S NOT AN IT.
AND I HAVEN'T. YET.
NOT THAT IT'S ANY OF YOUR--

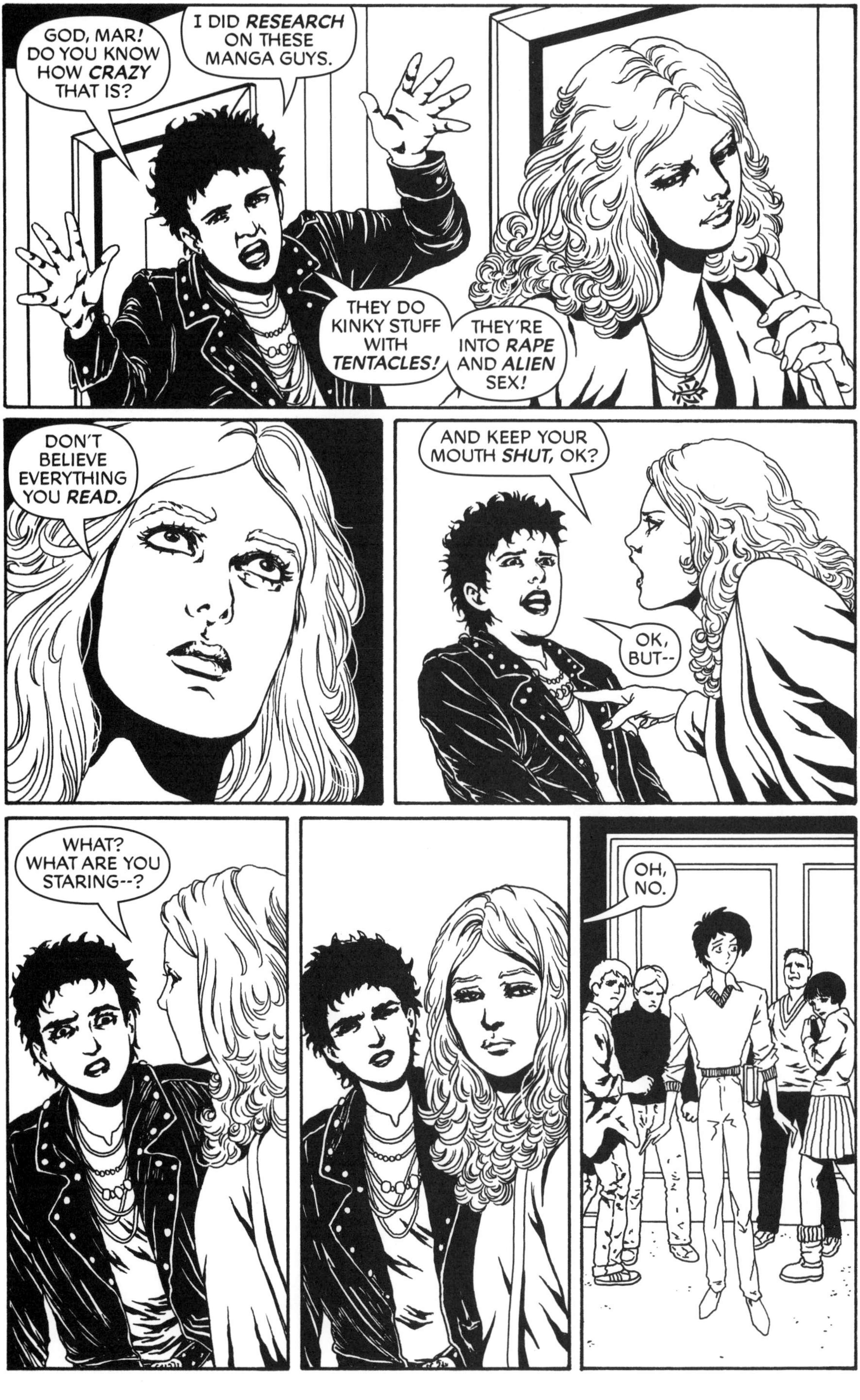
GOD, MAR! DO YOU KNOW HOW *CRAZY* THAT IS?
I DID *RESEARCH* ON THESE MANGA GUYS.
THEY DO KINKY STUFF WITH *TENTACLES!*
THEY'RE INTO *RAPE* AND *ALIEN* SEX!
DON'T BELIEVE EVERYTHING YOU *READ.*
AND KEEP YOUR MOUTH *SHUT,* OK?
OK, BUT--
WHAT? WHAT ARE YOU STARING--?
OH, NO.

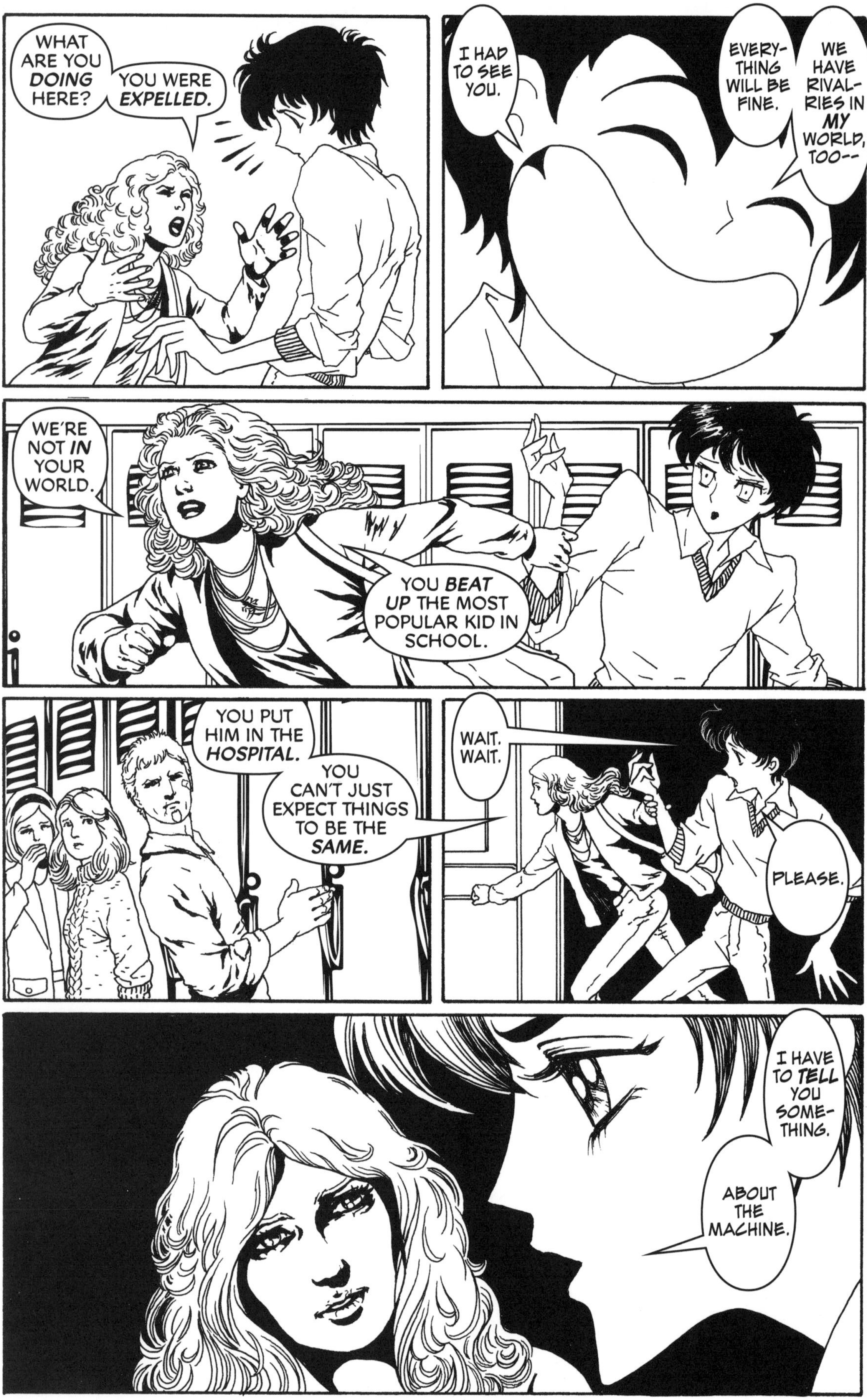
WHAT ARE YOU DOING HERE?
YOU WERE EXPELLED.
I HAD TO SEE YOU.
EVERY-THING WILL BE FINE.
WE HAVE RIVAL-RIES IN MY WORLD, TOO--
WE'RE NOT IN YOUR WORLD.
YOU BEAT UP THE MOST POPULAR KID IN SCHOOL.
YOU PUT HIM IN THE HOSPITAL.
YOU CAN'T JUST EXPECT THINGS TO BE THE SAME.
WAIT. WAIT.
PLEASE.
I HAVE TO TELL YOU SOME-THING.
ABOUT THE MACHINE.

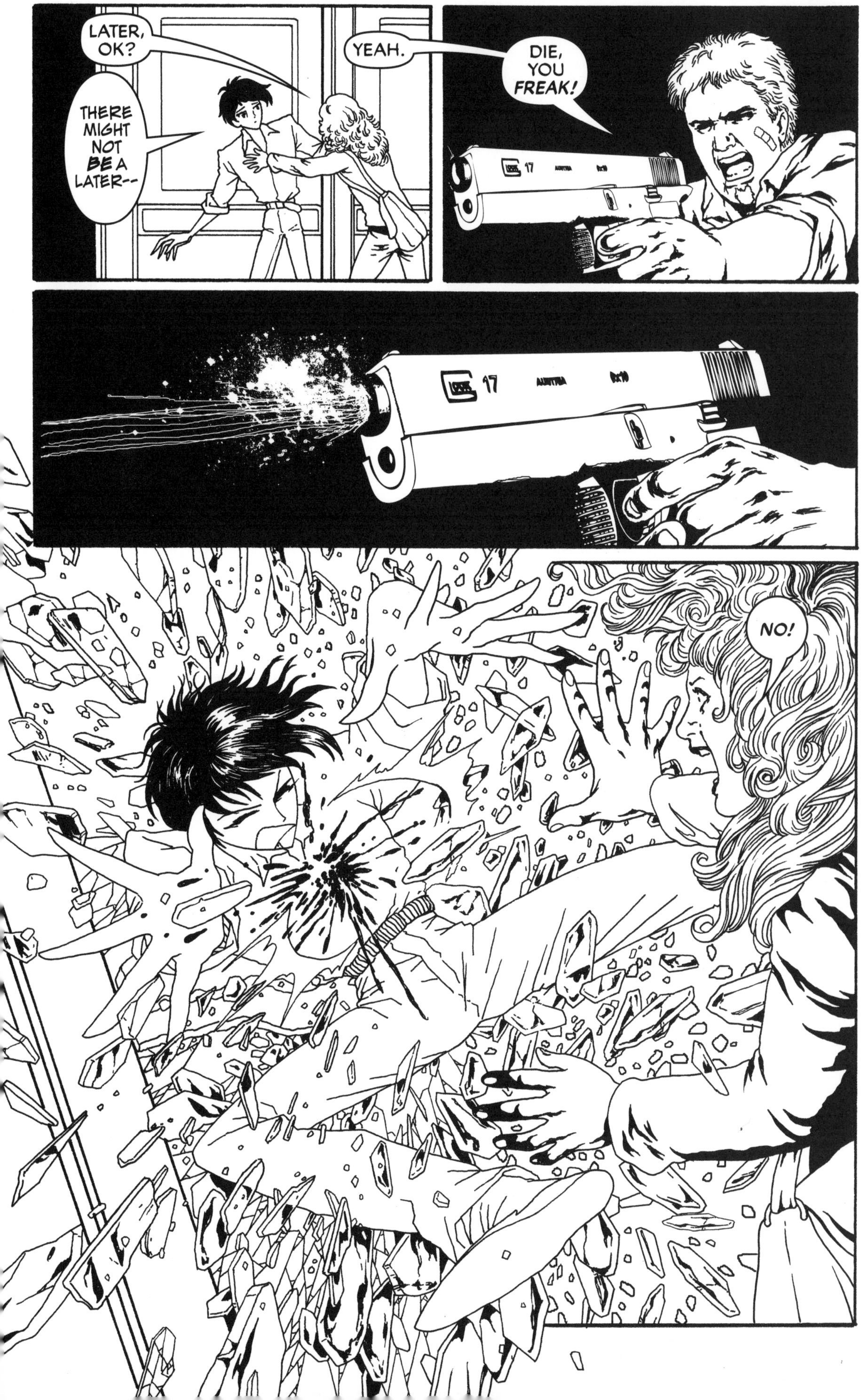
LATER, OK?
THERE MIGHT NOT BE A LATER--
YEAH.
DIE, YOU FREAK!
NO!

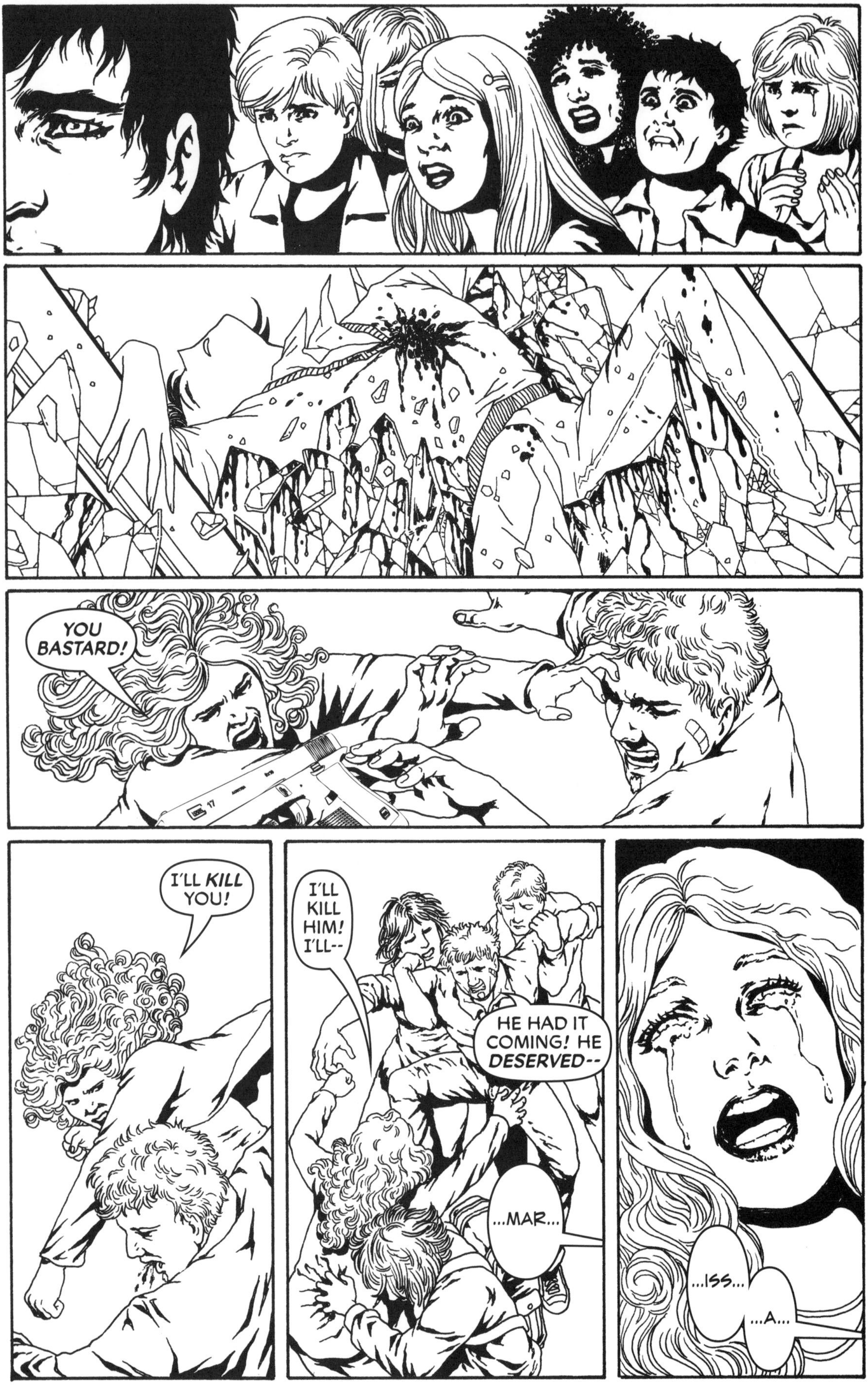
YOU BASTARD!
I'LL KILL YOU!
I'LL KILL HIM! I'LL--
HE HAD IT COMING! HE DESERVED--
...MAR...
...ISS...
...A...

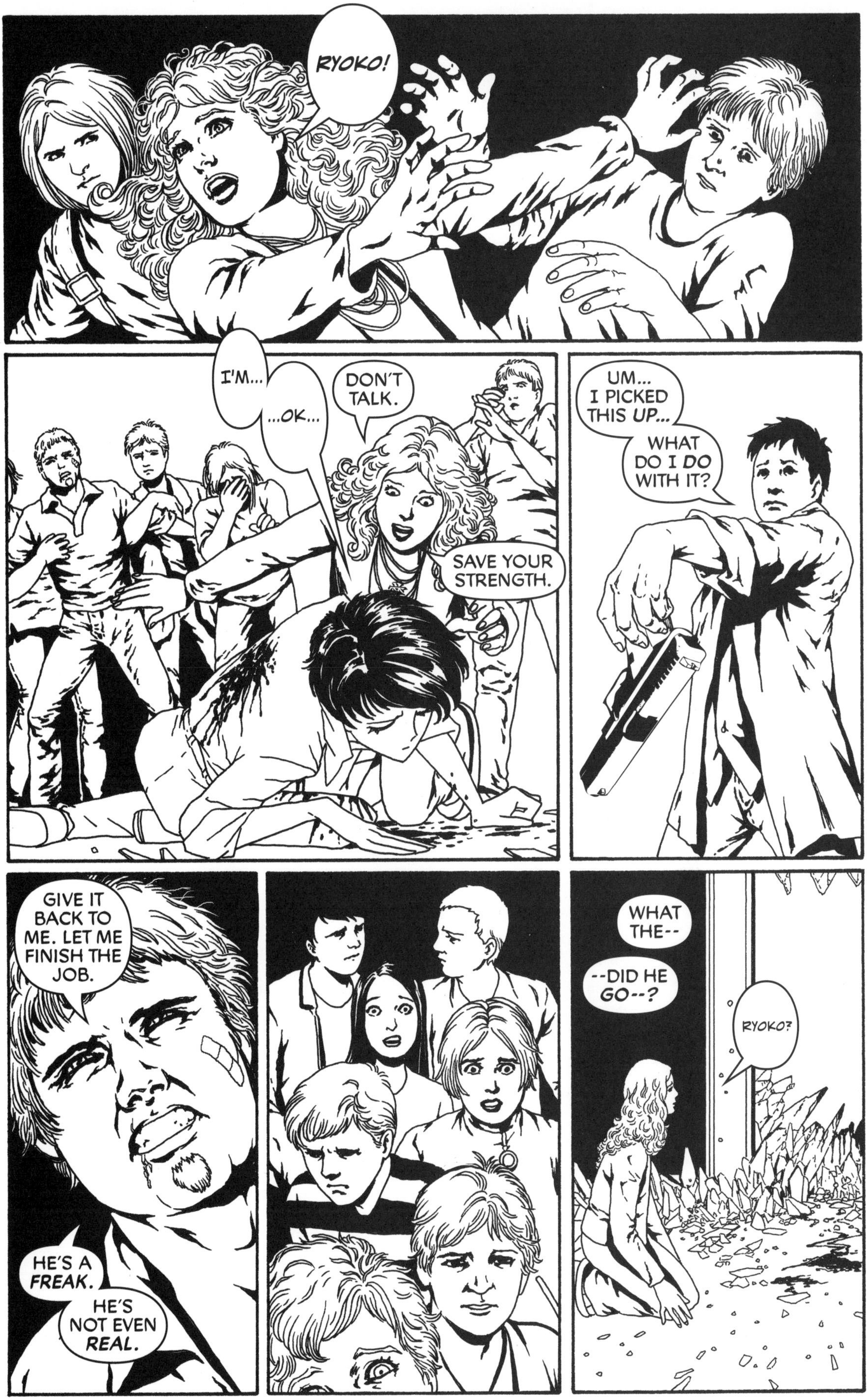
RYOKO!
I'M...
...OK...
DON'T TALK.
SAVE YOUR STRENGTH.
UM... I PICKED THIS *UP*...
WHAT DO I *DO* WITH IT?
GIVE IT BACK TO ME. LET ME FINISH THE JOB.
HE'S A *FREAK*.
HE'S NOT EVEN *REAL*.
WHAT THE--
--DID HE *GO*--?
RYOKO?

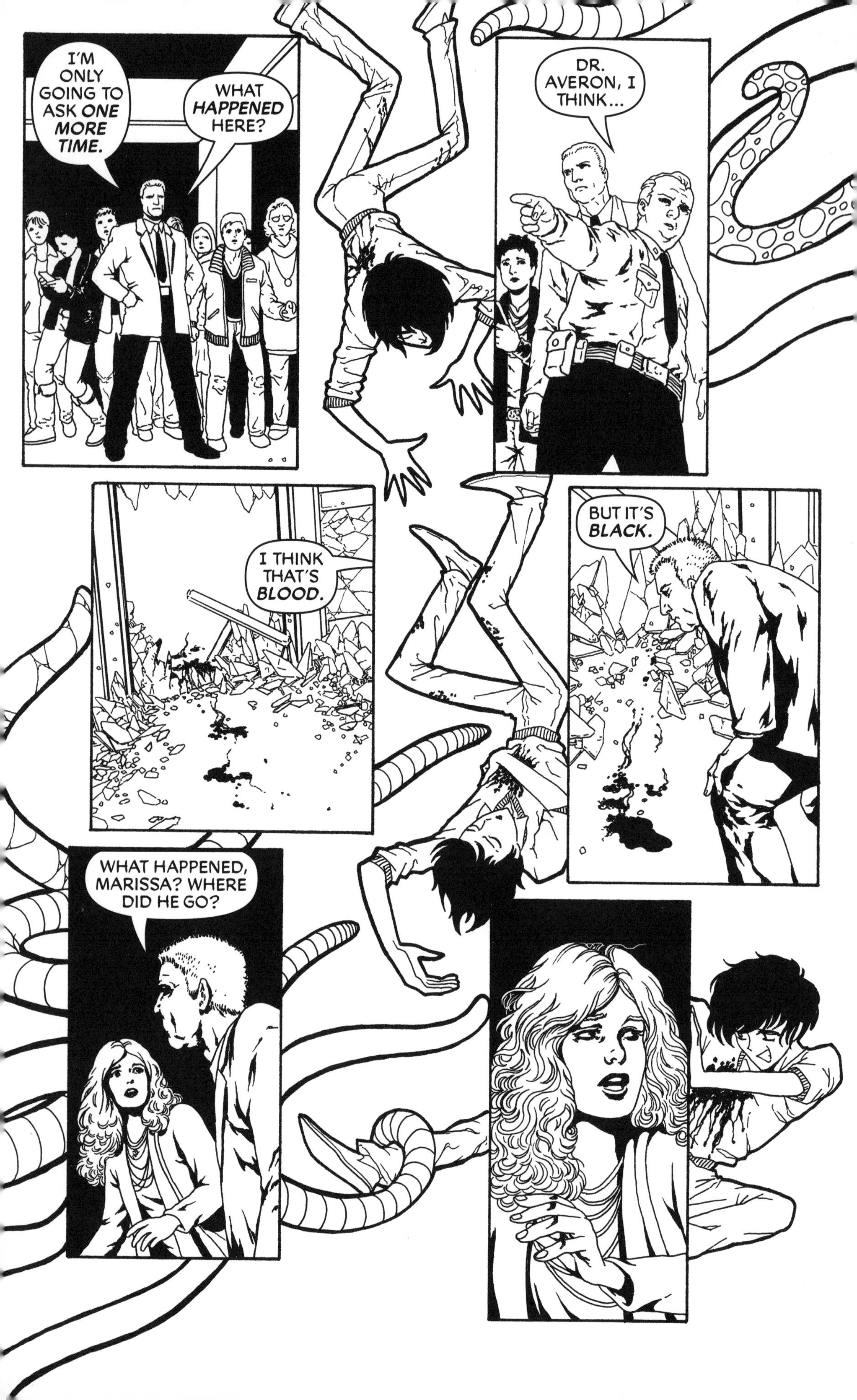
I'M ONLY GOING TO ASK ONE MORE TIME.
WHAT HAPPENED HERE?
DR. AVERON, I THINK...
I THINK THAT'S BLOOD.
BUT IT'S BLACK.
WHAT HAPPENED, MARISSA? WHERE DID HE GO?

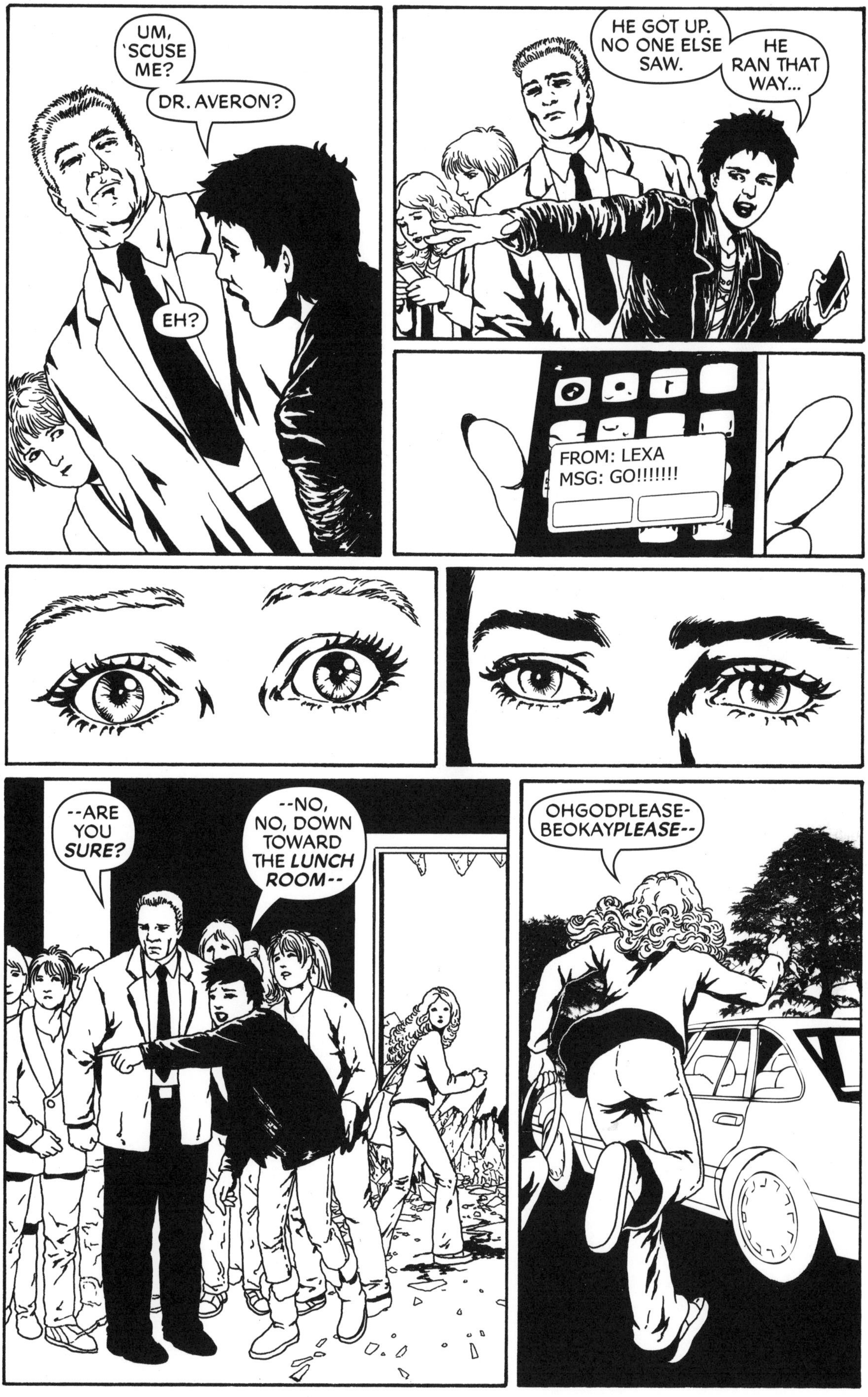
UM, 'SCUSE ME?
DR. AVERON?
EH?
HE GOT UP. NO ONE ELSE SAW.
HE RAN THAT WAY...
FROM: LEXA
MSG: GO!!!!!!!
--ARE YOU *SURE?*
--NO, NO, DOWN TOWARD THE *LUNCH ROOM*--
OHGODPLEASE-BEOKAY*PLEASE*--

CHAPTER 12

MARISSA: *Not for nothing.*

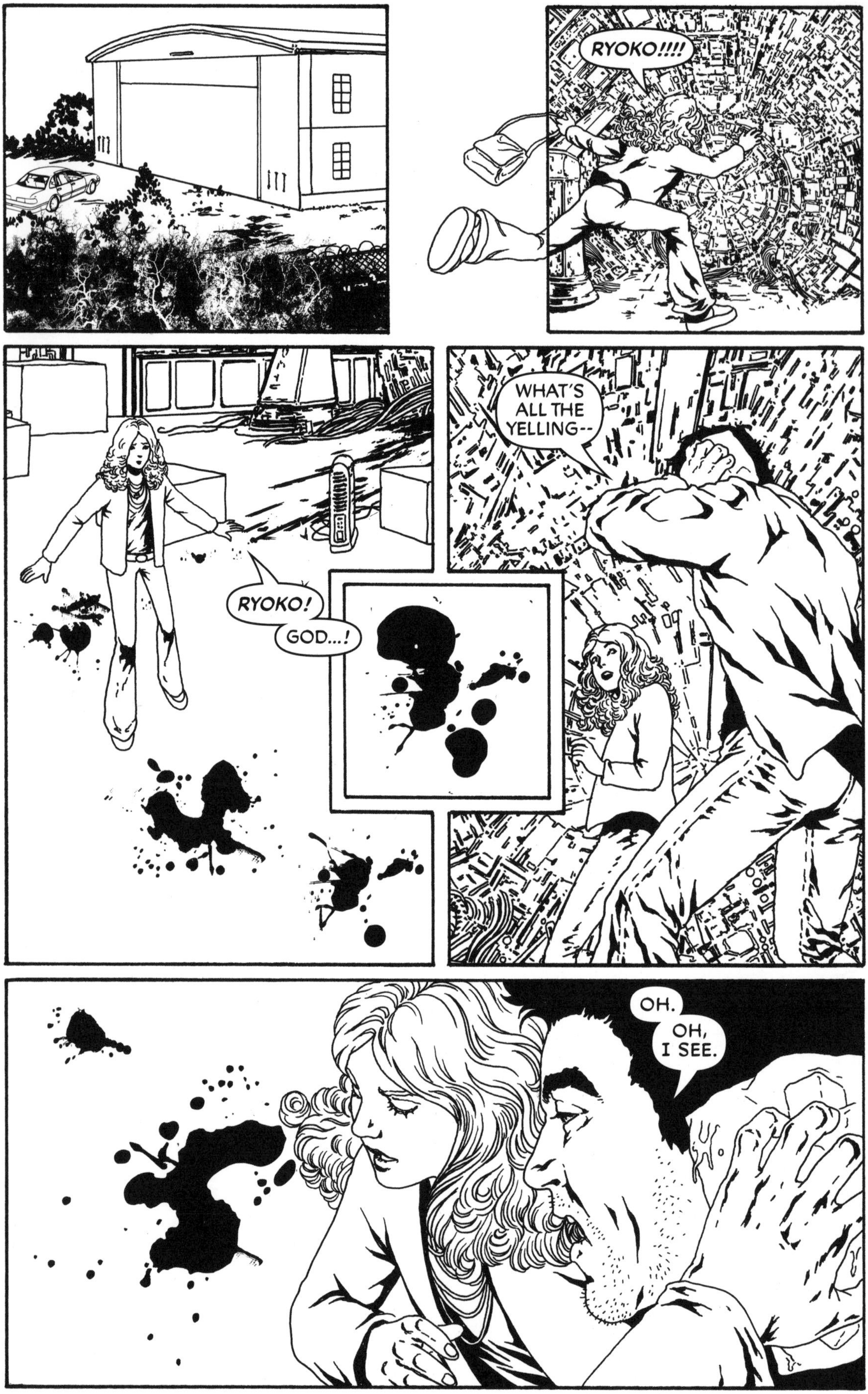
RYOKO!!!!
RYOKO!
GOD...!
WHAT'S ALL THE YELLING--
OH.
OH, I SEE.

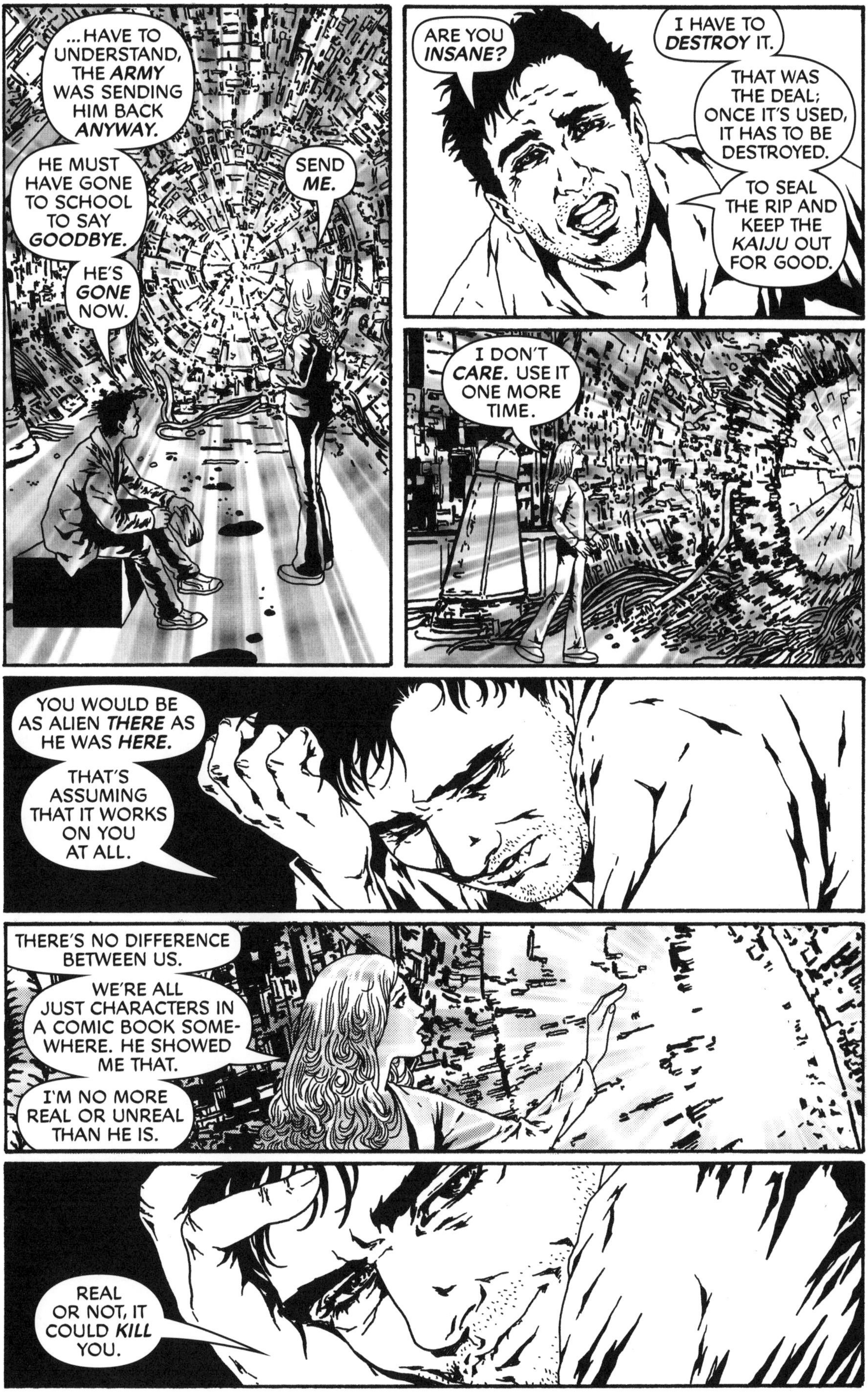
...HAVE TO UNDERSTAND, THE *ARMY* WAS SENDING HIM BACK *ANYWAY.*
HE MUST HAVE GONE TO SCHOOL TO SAY *GOODBYE.*
HE'S *GONE* NOW.
SEND *ME.*
ARE YOU *INSANE?*
I HAVE TO *DESTROY* IT.
THAT WAS THE DEAL; ONCE IT'S USED, IT HAS TO BE DESTROYED.
TO SEAL THE RIP AND KEEP THE *KAIJU* OUT FOR GOOD.
I DON'T *CARE.* USE IT ONE MORE TIME.
YOU WOULD BE AS ALIEN *THERE* AS HE WAS *HERE.*
THAT'S ASSUMING THAT IT WORKS ON YOU AT ALL.
THERE'S NO DIFFERENCE BETWEEN US.
WE'RE ALL JUST CHARACTERS IN A COMIC BOOK SOME-WHERE. HE SHOWED ME THAT.
I'M NO MORE REAL OR UNREAL THAN HE IS.
REAL OR NOT, IT COULD *KILL* YOU.

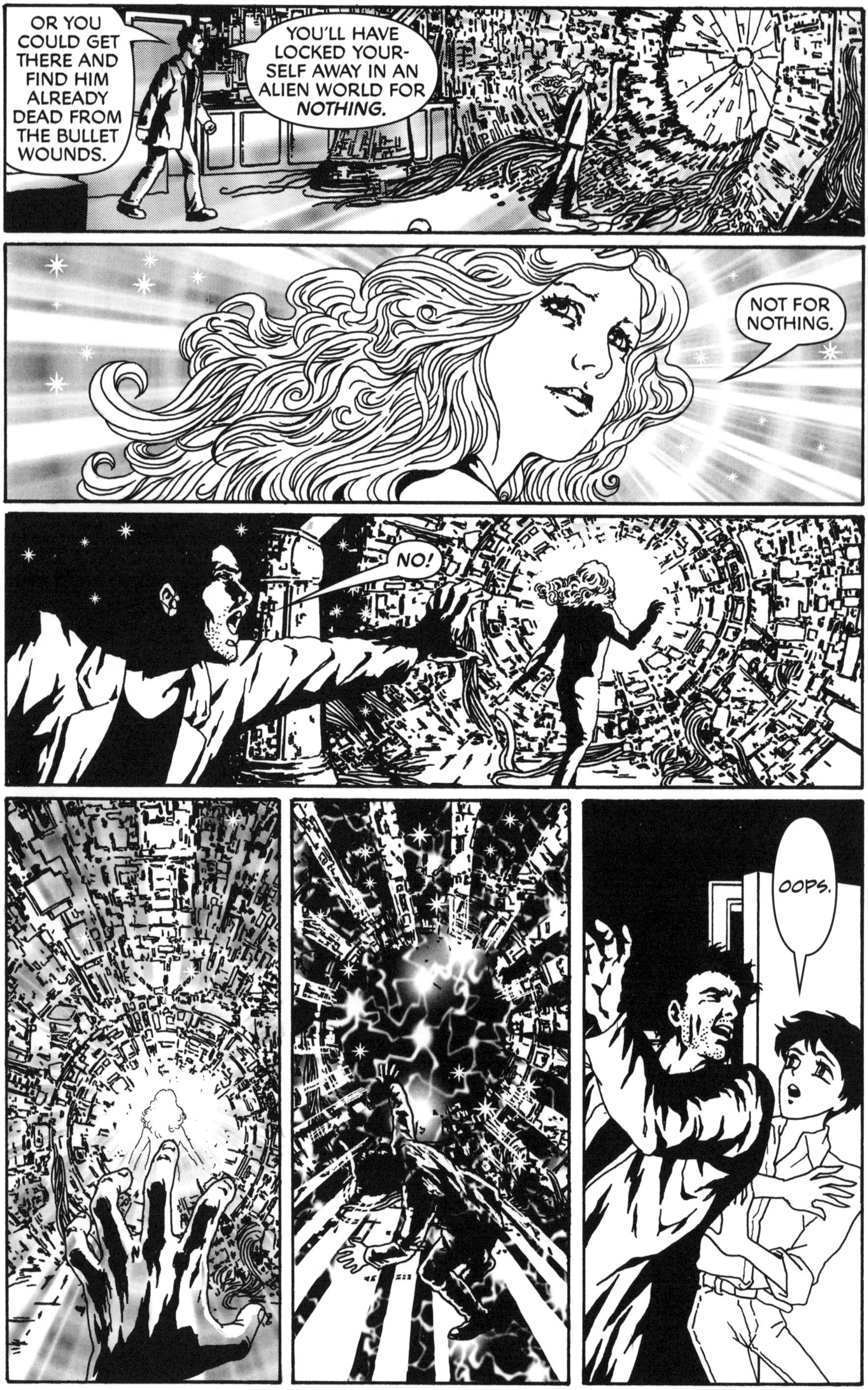
OR YOU COULD GET THERE AND FIND HIM ALREADY DEAD FROM THE BULLET WOUNDS.
YOU'LL HAVE LOCKED YOUR-SELF AWAY IN AN ALIEN WORLD FOR *NOTHING.*
NOT FOR NOTHING.
NO!
OOPS.

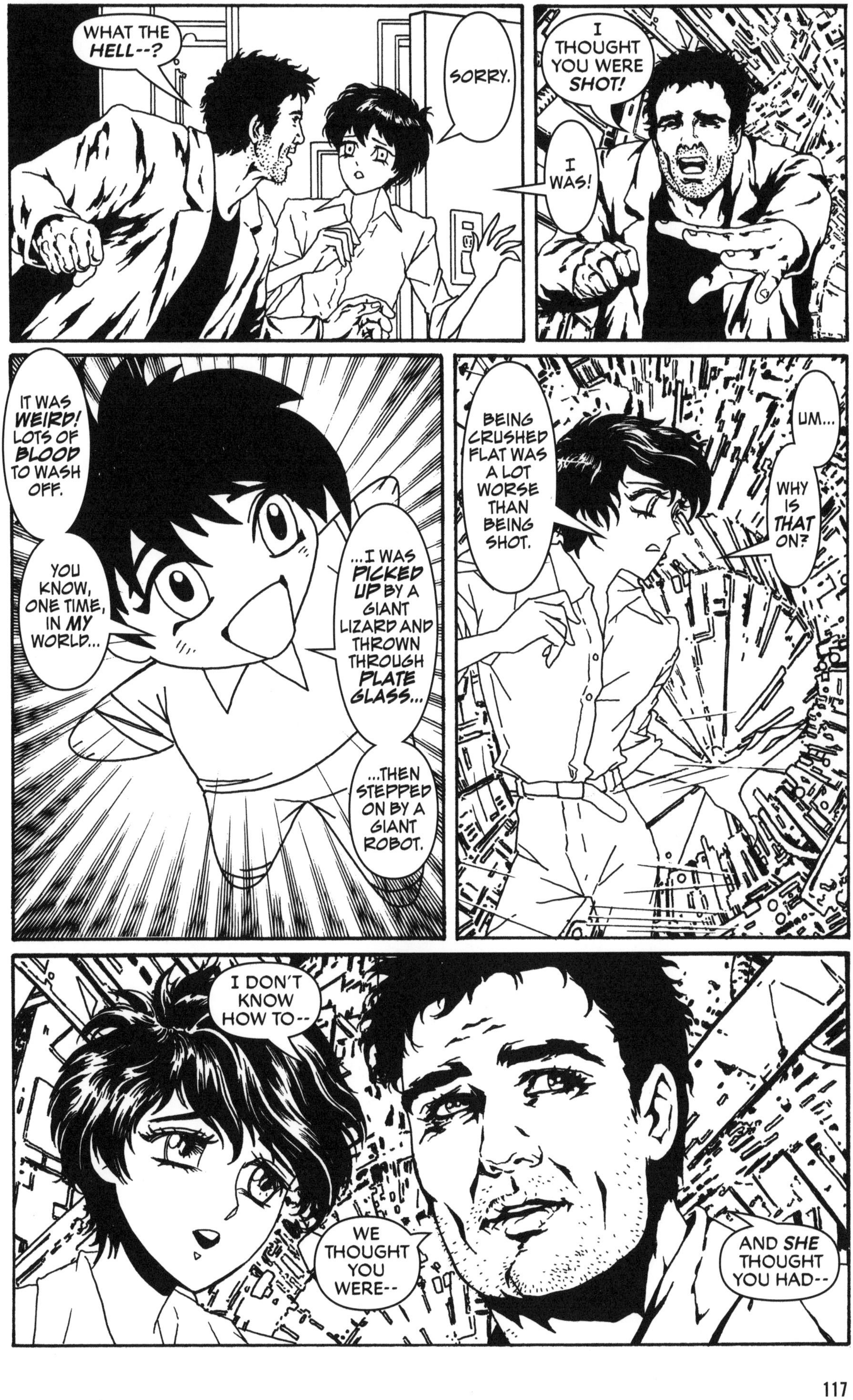
WHAT THE HELL--?
SORRY.
I THOUGHT YOU WERE SHOT!
I WAS!
IT WAS WEIRD! LOTS OF BLOOD TO WASH OFF.
YOU KNOW, ONE TIME, IN MY WORLD...
...I WAS PICKED UP BY A GIANT LIZARD AND THROWN THROUGH PLATE GLASS...
...THEN STEPPED ON BY A GIANT ROBOT.
BEING CRUSHED FLAT WAS A LOT WORSE THAN BEING SHOT.
UM...
WHY IS THAT ON?
I DON'T KNOW HOW TO--
WE THOUGHT YOU WERE--
AND SHE THOUGHT YOU HAD--

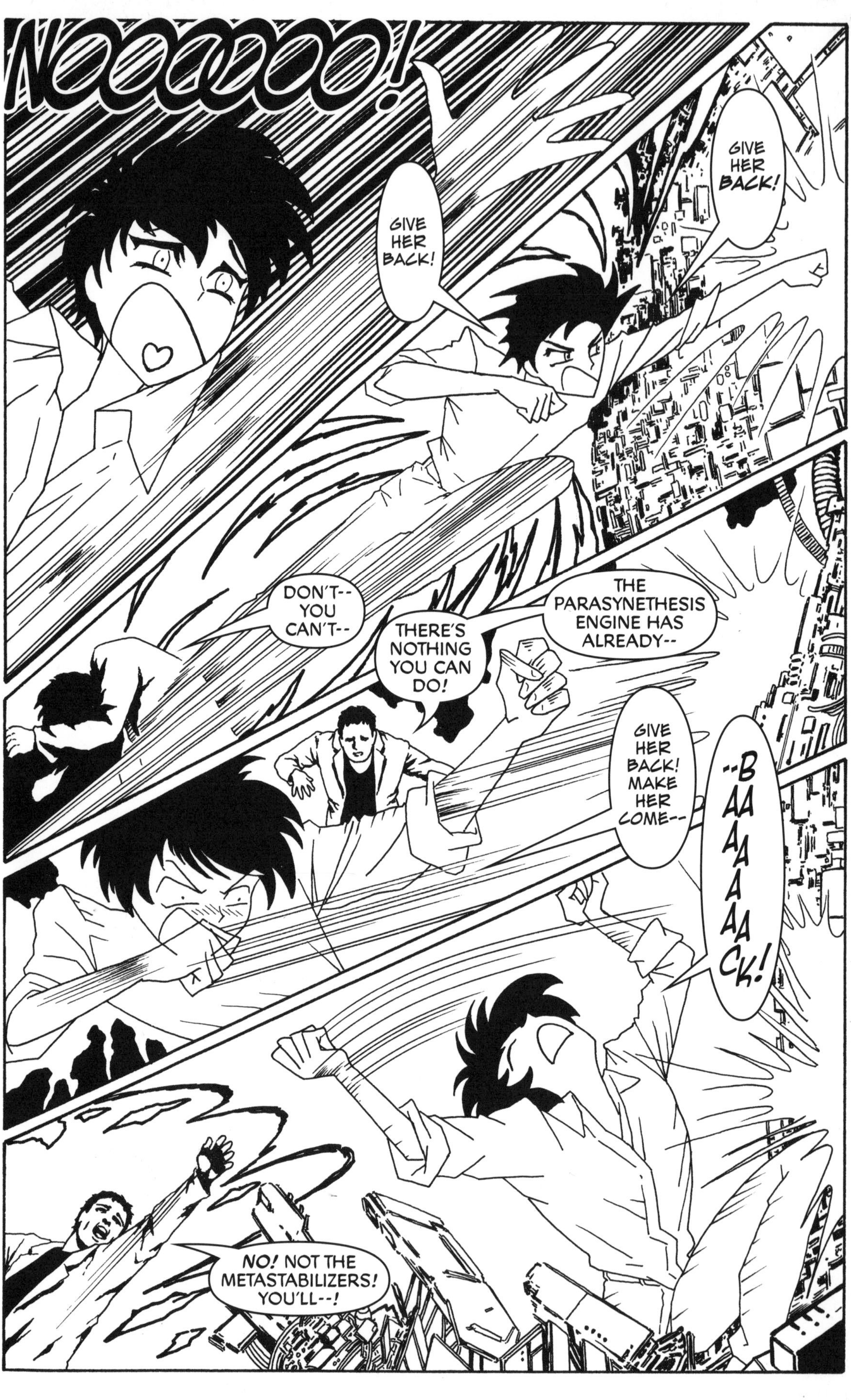
NOOOOOOO!
GIVE HER BACK!
GIVE HER BACK!
DON'T-- YOU CAN'T--
THERE'S NOTHING YOU CAN DO!
THE PARASYNETHESIS ENGINE HAS ALREADY--
GIVE HER BACK! MAKE HER COME--
--BAAAAAAACK!
NO! NOT THE METASTABILIZERS! YOU'LL--!

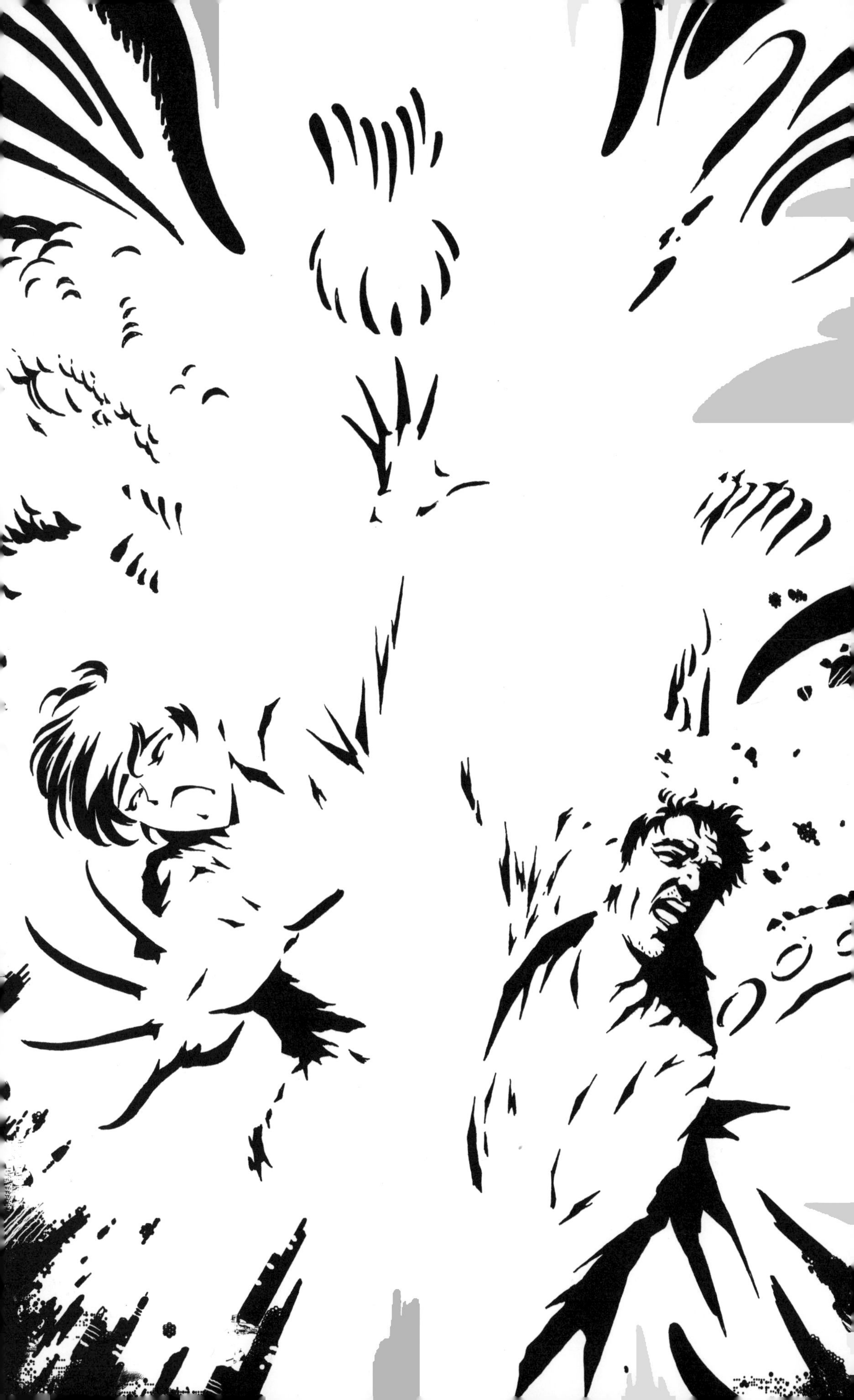

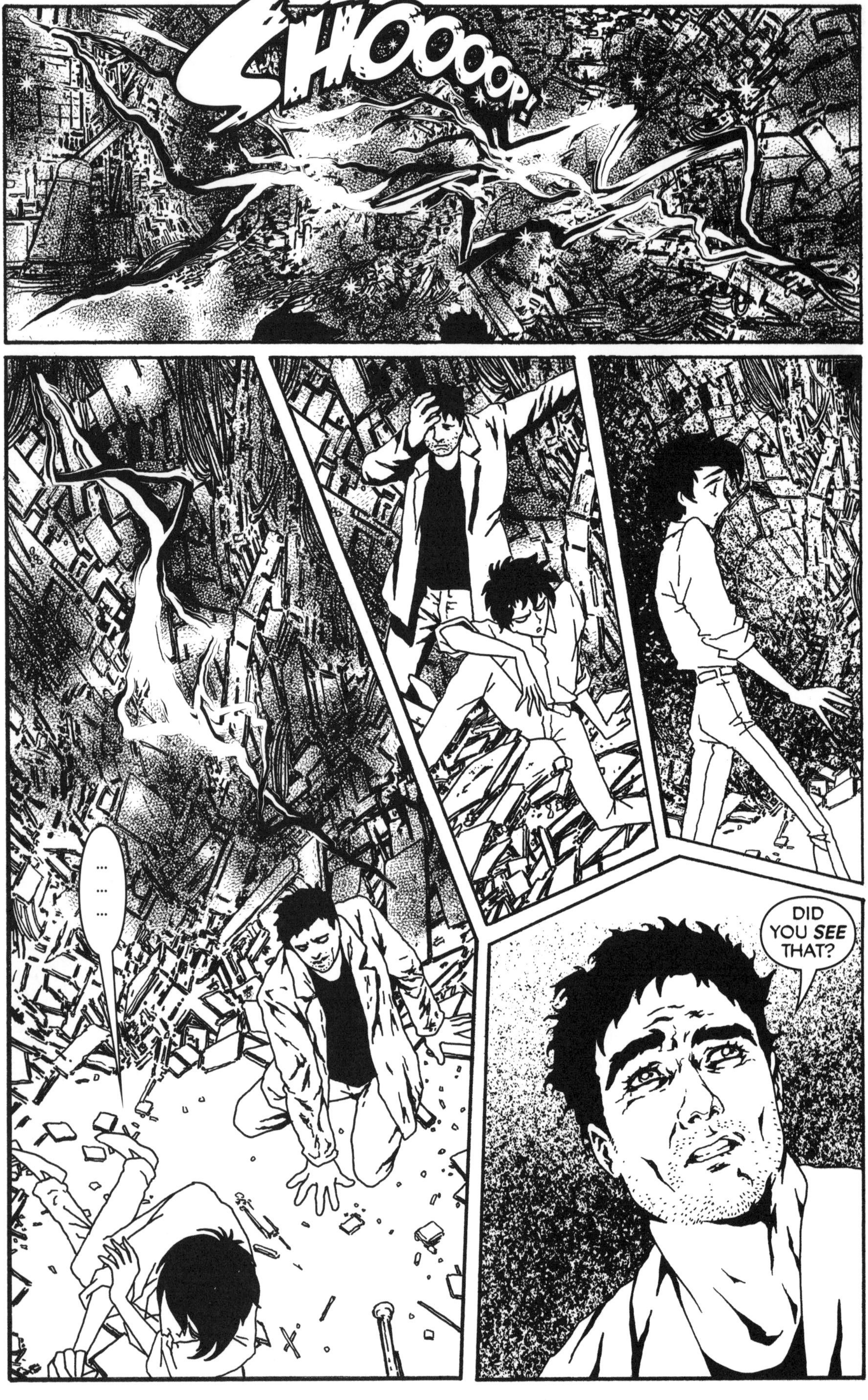
SHOOOOP!
... ...
DID YOU SEE THAT?

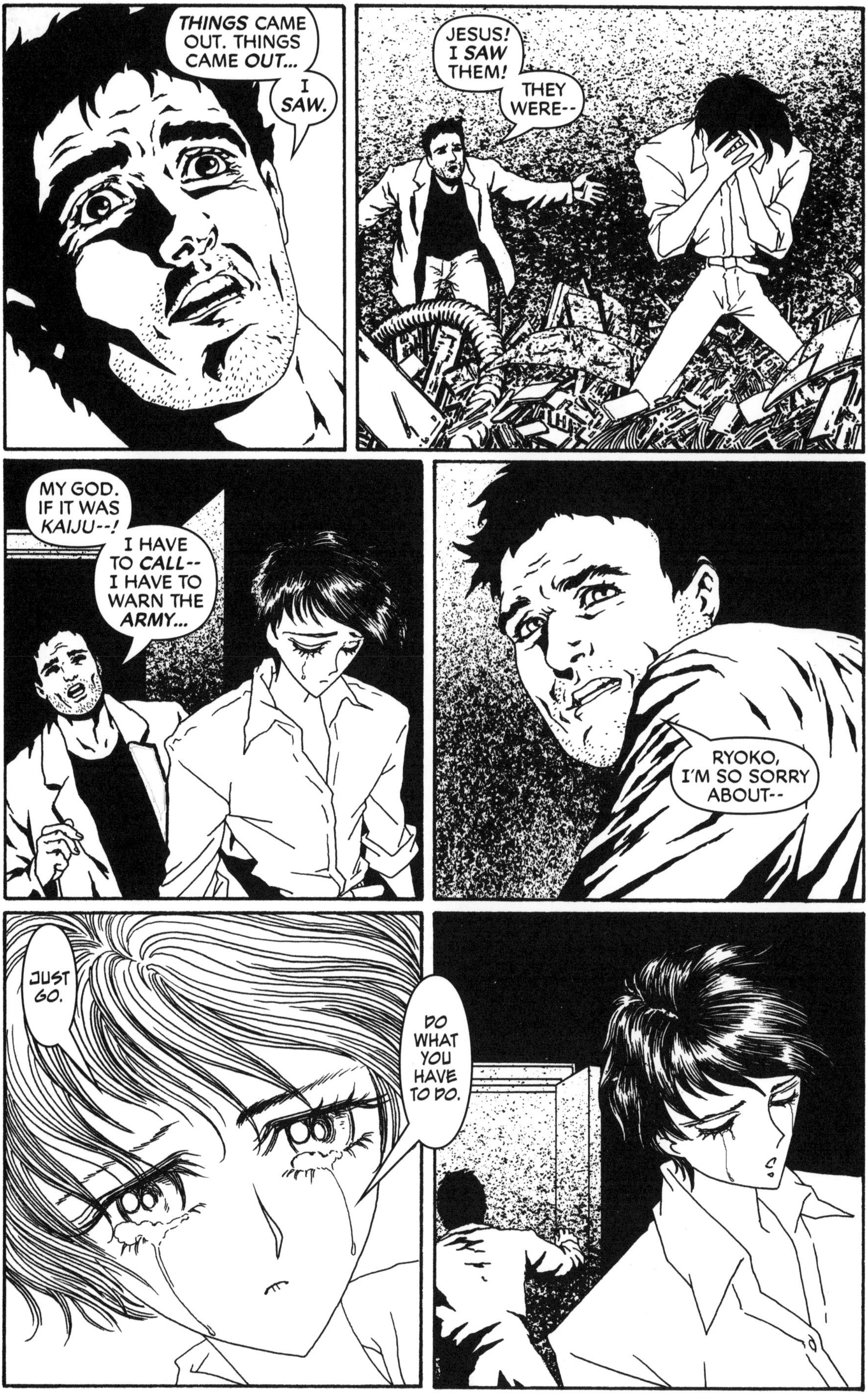

THINGS CAME OUT. THINGS CAME OUT...
I SAW.
JESUS! I SAW THEM!
THEY WERE--
MY GOD. IF IT WAS KAIJU--!
I HAVE TO CALL-- I HAVE TO WARN THE ARMY...
RYOKO, I'M SO SORRY ABOUT--
JUST GO.
DO WHAT YOU HAVE TO DO.

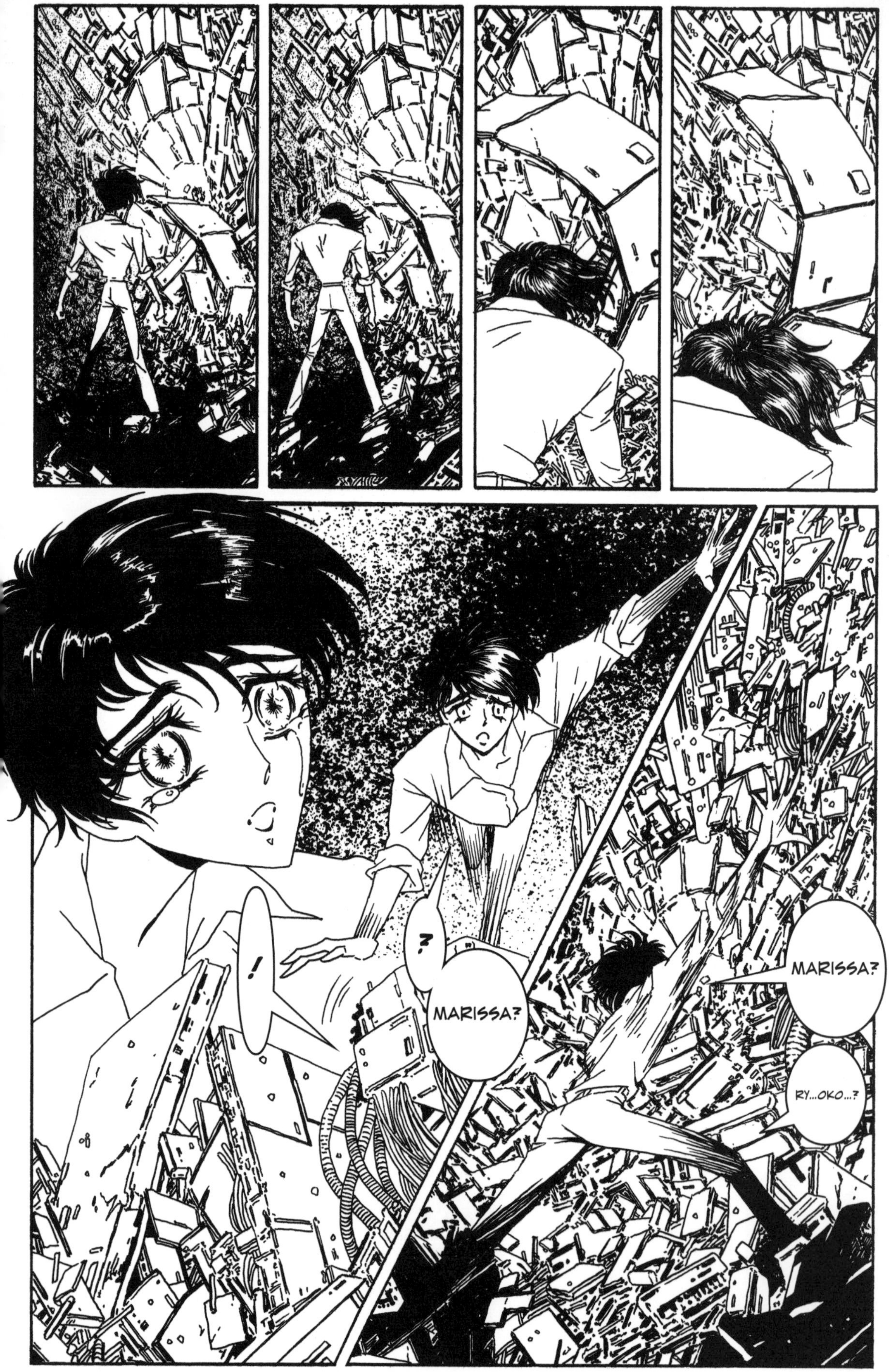
!
?
MARISSA?
MARISSA?
RY...OKO...?

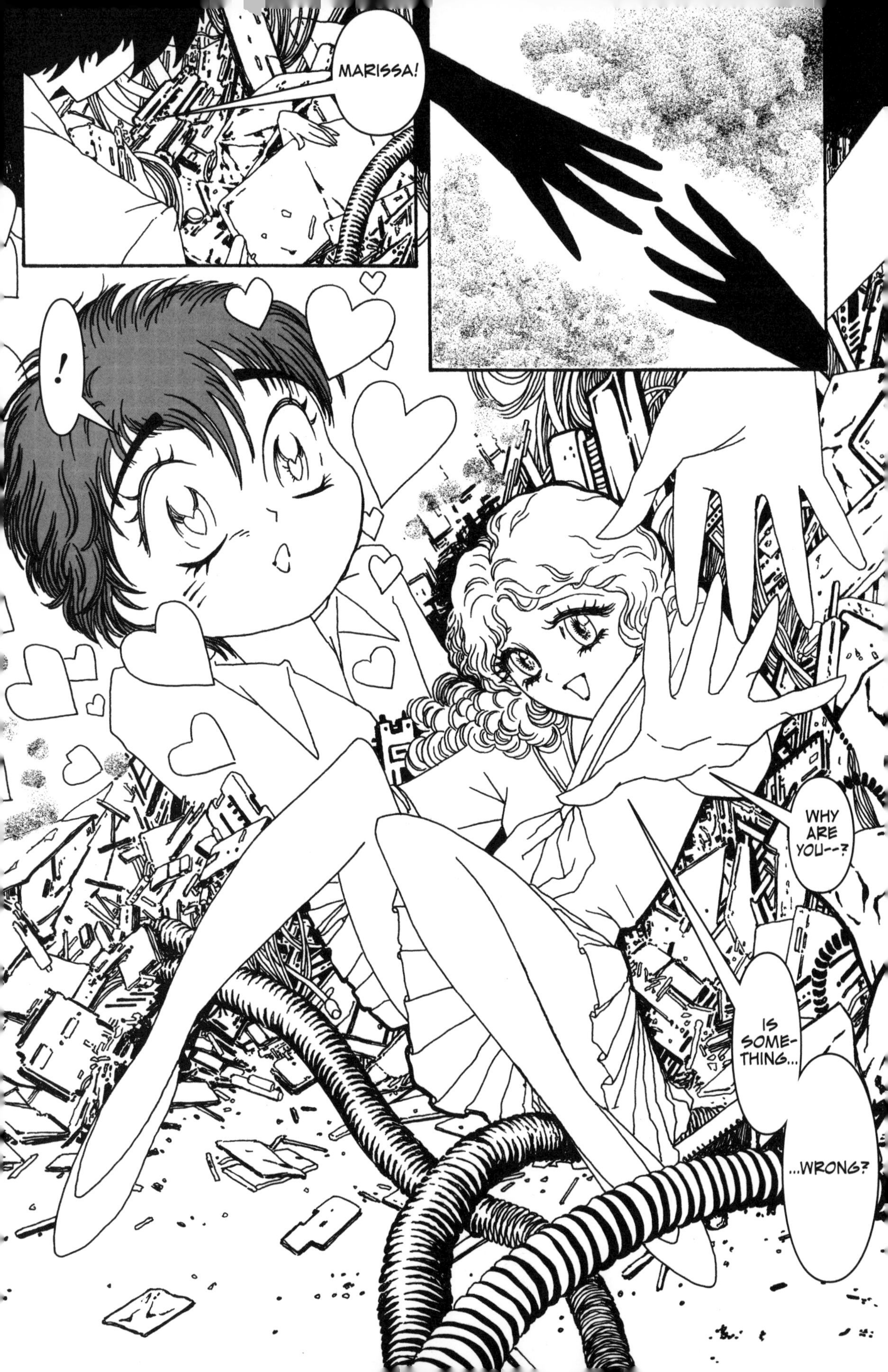
MARISSA!
!
WHY ARE YOU--?
IS SOMETHING...
...WRONG?

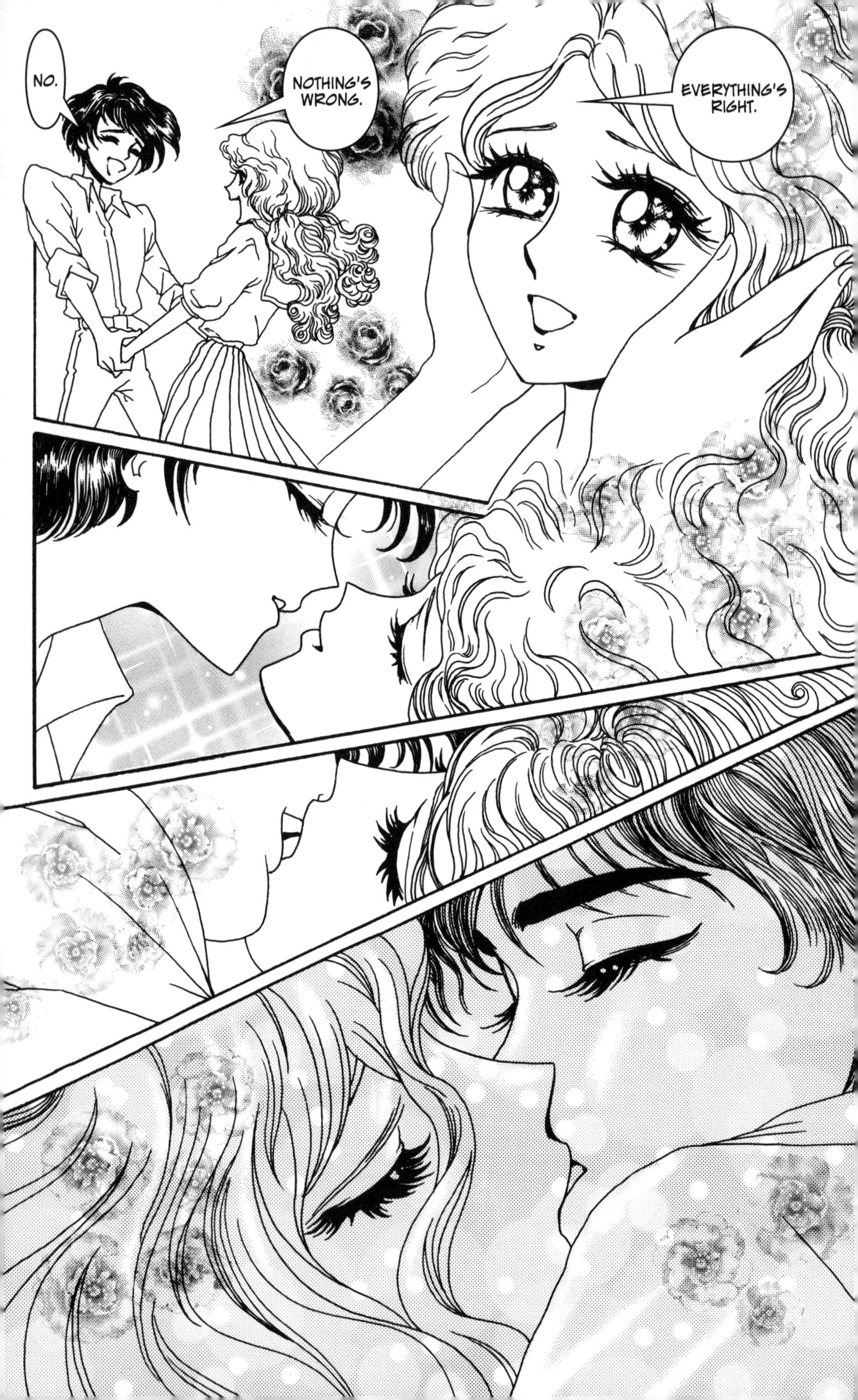
NO.
NOTHING'S WRONG.
EVERYTHING'S RIGHT.

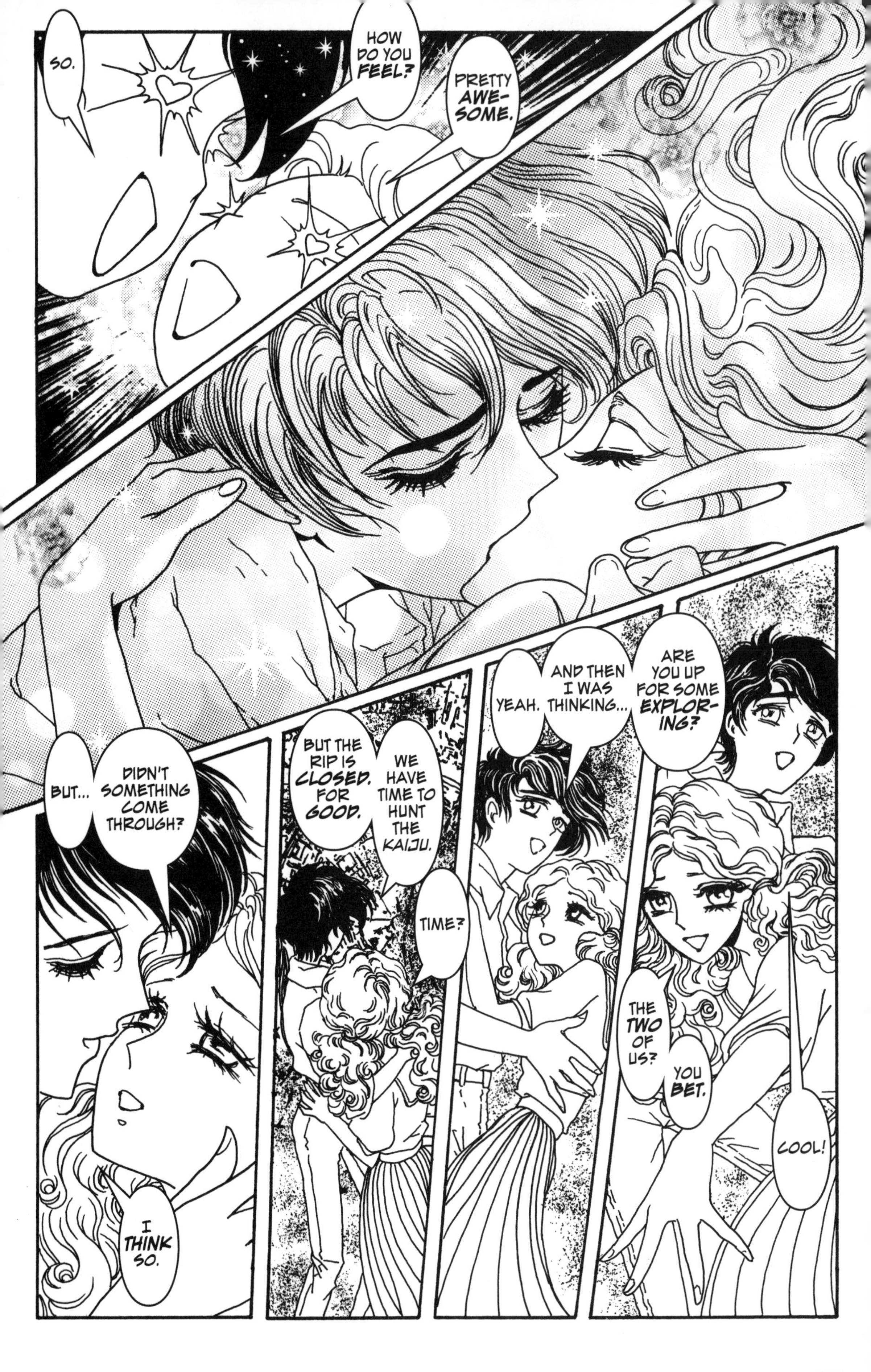
SO.
HOW DO YOU FEEL?
PRETTY AWESOME.
BUT...
DIDN'T SOMETHING COME THROUGH?
I THINK SO.
BUT THE RIP IS CLOSED. FOR GOOD.
WE HAVE TIME TO HUNT THE KAIJU.
TIME?
YEAH.
AND THEN I WAS THINKING...
ARE YOU UP FOR SOME EXPLORING?
THE TWO OF US?
YOU BET.
COOL!

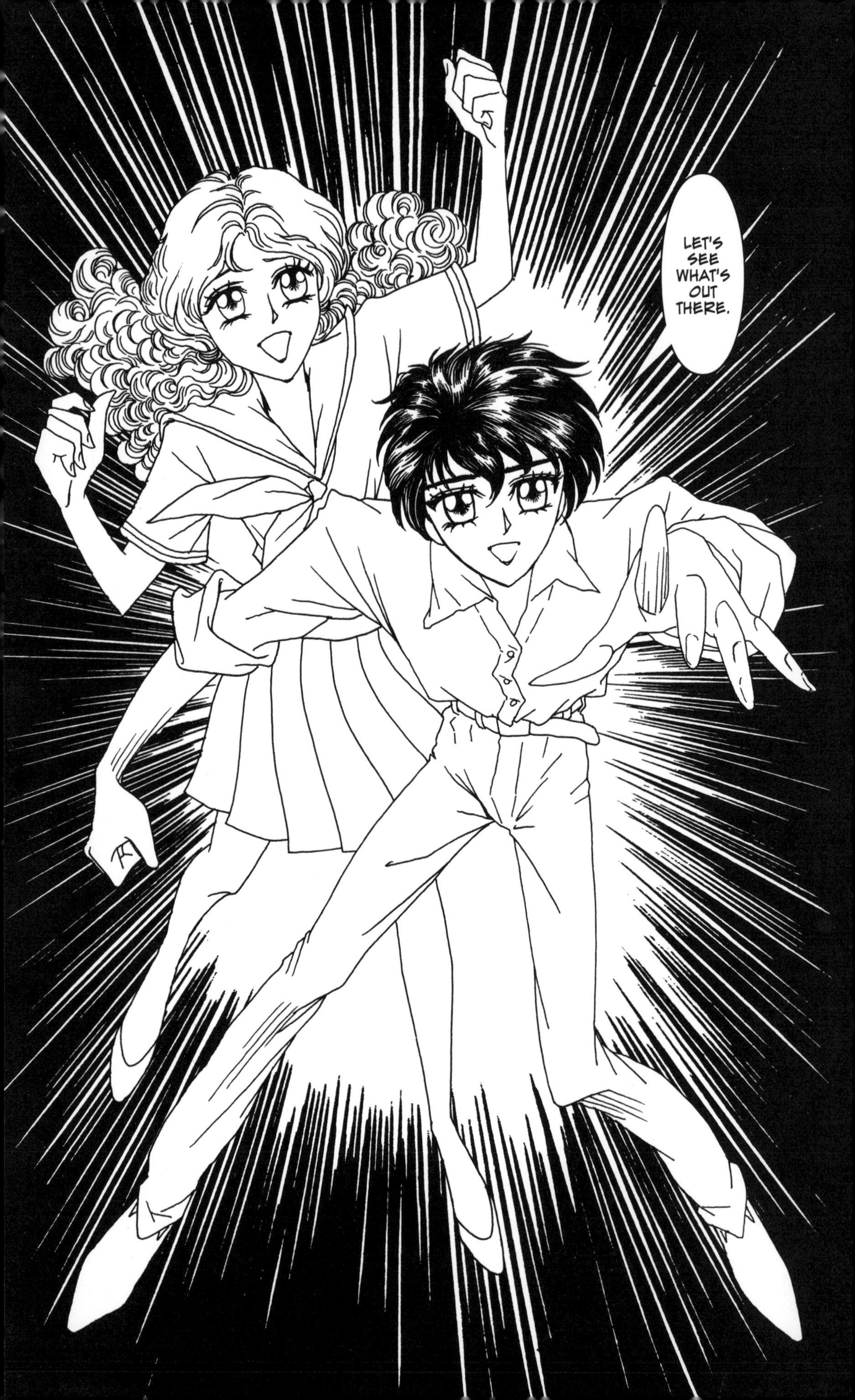
LET'S SEE WHAT'S OUT THERE.